THE DUKE OF HELL'S POCKET WATCH

D H ROSENBERG

Prepare to journey with Gomory

D H Rosenberg

Copyright © 2020 D H ROSENBERG

All rights reserved

The characters and events portrayed in this book are fictitious. Any similarity to real persons, living or dead, is coincidental and not intended by the author.

No part of this book may be reproduced, or stored in a retrieval system, or transmitted in any form or by any means, electronic, mechanical, photocopying, recording, or otherwise, without express written permission of the publisher.

ISBN-13: 979-8642873557

CONTENTS

Title Page	1
Copyright	2
ONE	11
TWO	20
THREE	35
FOUR	47
FIVE	60
SIX	70
SEVEN	99
EIGHT	111
NINE	135
TEN	147
ELEVEN	168
TWELVE	195
THIRTEEN	217
FOURTEEN	233
FIFTEEN	250
SIXTEEN	264
SEVENTEEN	280
EIGHTEEN	293

NINETEEN

THE DUKE OF HELL'S POCKET WATCH

A dark journey across time and humanity

Gomory: A Duke of Hell

Gremory (aka Gamory, Gemory, or Gomory) is a strong Duke of Hell who governs twenty-six legions of demons. He tells and knows of all things past, present and future, about hidden treasures, and procures the love of women, young and old, but especially maidens.

He is depicted as appearing in the form of a beautiful woman with the crown of a duchess tied around his waist, and riding a camel.

Conrad of Marburgh: A man of God
Conrad of Marburgh

Conrad, after receiving a commission from the Archbishop of Mainz also set to work seeking out heresy in both Thuringia and Hesse, and quickly gained a reputation for being unreasonable and unjust. According to most accounts, Conrad accepted almost any accusation as truth, and regarded suspects as guilty until proven innocent. Those accused of being heretics were quickly sought out by Conrad's mobs, and told to repent or else be burnt at the stake. Those accused of heresy were also encouraged to denounce others, with the implication that their own lives might be spared if they did so. Conrad included commoners, nobles and priests in his inquisition: Heinrich Minnike, Provist of Goslar, was one of Conrad's first targets, and was burnt at the stake. In 1227 Pope Gregory XI commissioned Conrad to eliminate heresy throughout the whole of Germany, granting him permission to ignore standard church procedure for the investigation of heresy. According to many sources, news that Conrad was to pass through an area almost invariably caused widespread panic.

* * *

Conrad pulled the cowl of his papal ordained cloak over his head, before relaxing his belt to ease the tightness of the harsh fabric chaffing against his whiplashed waist. Striding with determined rhythm, he passed through the doorway of an old flour mill recently acquisitioned by the Pope as another resource to eradicate heretics. On entering a dark inner chamber, he held back his next footstep to look up at what was suspended above his hooded head.

He smiled at the man above him, his thin lips stretched to their full extent, assuming the same grey pallor as his sunken cheeks. Tracing his thumb over the red-jewelled snake's eyes from the left to right, he sensed a thrill of awe as he watched the casing open to reveal the rings of time that passed the recently tortured hours and days with their turning. Pausing from the distraction of the Devil's timepiece, he craned his head upwards to check his prisoner was secured in the manner he desired. Through the flickering flames of heavily fuelled and smoking torches mounted on each wall, he saw with latent excitement the arms of his next subject were stretched out horizontally, held fast by manacle and chains. Looking down the naked form of his victim, he observed his legs were held in a vertical attitude by the weight of an open topped barrel fastened by iron rings to his ankles. The similar pose his captive held to an image of Christ's crucifixion in the Pope's private chambers, provoked arousal to course through his withered loins, whetting his appetite for the forthcoming torment to follow. He took a step back and called up to his victim.

"Count Gemory, demon and Duke of Satan. On this day of our Lord, twelve hundred and twenty eight, I, Conrad of Marburg, appointee of Pope Gregory the Ninth, do assume the right as Chief Inquisitor, to extract a confession from your tormented soul. I have in my possession your artefact of evil, your demonic keeper of time. If you confess your sins and admit you are a demon of Satan, a Duke of Hades, I will order your release from the chains of torture and administer the purification of your wretched soul. If you do not confess to me *now*, the butt hanging from your feet will be filled with water until your limbs are torn sinew by sinew from your wretched body."

From his position above the black robed inquisitor, Count Gemory looked down and replied with firm authority. "By *puri-*

fication of my wretched soul, I assume you mean burning my wretched body while blood flows through my veins and air fills my lungs. I fear not the stake or its fires. My flesh may be consumed, but my presence will not whither by your evil fetishes for self-gratification at watching others suffer. You know not whom or what you are dealing with, Conrad of Marburg. No fires of Hell can purify my soul, no dismemberment of my body will break my will and there is no such time as *now*."

"You talk with the forked tongue of the Devil. I will give orders for your foul mouth to be silenced by red-hot irons before the sun sets tonight. Your time has come, Count Gemory. Confess your sins now."

"You forget that I said there is no such time as now. As soon as the present has passed it becomes the past. The present that is yet to come is the future and in the nature of all things, the past, present and future are one and the same. I see the future that comes for you, five years from now, all of your pasts, presents and futures will merge into nothingness and oblivion. I on the other hand, who live in the past, present and future, will never cease to inhabit the portents of time."

Conrad felt the previously surging excitement of impending torture engorging his bodily parts draining away as rapidly as a manhood satiated by a string of whores. He shouted out orders for the water butt to be filled and walked away. Two hours later a messenger arrived at his rooms.

The messenger spoke impassively. "It is done, his arms have torn from their sockets and he is down."

"Is he – still living?"

"He is. They poured molten lead into the holes left in his shoulders to stop him from bleeding to his death."

"Is he conscious?"

"He is. Surprisingly he seems relaxed."

Conrad turned around and stroked his chin with his hand. "Maybe he needs a little more stimulation. Burn out his tongue with red-hot irons and then take him out to the stake. When he is made ready, I will come to watch him burn."

As the messenger departed, Conrad opened the case of the silver timepiece on his desk. "You may be the work of Satan, but you are the most beautiful and marvellous thing I have ever seen," he said aloud, gazing at the keeper of time acquired from the condemned man. He waited until the movement of the outer ring indicated the passing of five minutes, before making his way to the open yard where the condemned were burned on the stake.

It took over twenty minutes for Count Gemory to surrender his essence to the floundering flames seeping insipidly from the dampened branches spread out below him. Conrad stood mesmerised, his face creased with future lines of aging, as hand-sized blisters yellowed, before scorching through ochre to burnt umber on the writhing torso of the dying heretic. Satisfied another soul had been purified, he returned to his rooms.

When he opened the door to his quarters, a sulphurous aroma tore into his nose, making his eyes water and bile reflux into his mouth. He rushed to find the source of the obnoxious stench. His feet rooted to the floor when he saw what lay on his desk. In the exact spot he'd left Gemory's timepiece, there was now a black and smouldering circular shell that crumbled into charred flakes before his eyes.

Five years later, on his way home and accompanied by a Franciscan monk, he was assassinated.

ONE

"So how does His Majesty feel about making his living by tossing burgers?" Sonya shouted from the other side of the hot and humid kitchen.

"It's a job fit for a King," Henry replied, thinking two thoughts at once. *Why does everyone take the piss out of my name? Maybe that's why I've ended up working here for a few quid an hour after spending three years gaining my honour's degree.*

"Six Big M's and a double cheeseburger with extra mayo," Shaun shouted from the service counter.

"You're supposed to send the orders through your computer terminal," Henry shouted back over Sonya's clanging from the other side of the kitchen. He then threw eight semi-frozen meat patties onto the searing open griddle.

"It's frozen again. I'll be glad when this shift's over, only ten minutes until we close," Shaun called back over the sound of sizzling burgers.

"I think my shoulders frozen too, I knackered it playing tennis last night," Sonya called out across the kitchen.

"I can't imagine you playing tennis," Henry shouted back, as he watched globules of fat dribbling from the burgers.

"I'm really good at it, but I overstretched when Jake lobed the ball over my head."

"Where do you play?" Henry asked as, he turned over one of

the burgers.

"On my Wii," Sonya replied.

Henry continued to turn over the rest of the burgers. *We'll spend the next hour cleaning down the kitchen making it ready for the breakfast shift who'll only mess it up again,* he thought, as he watched the round burgers shrivel into glistening oval shaped pats of fatty protein.

Just after six o'clock in the morning, Henry fumbled with his key, jiggling it in the lock of his fifteen year old, not so hot hatchback. He was relieved he wouldn't have to return to work for two days but, besides catching up on sleep, he'd nothing planned for his only break this week. As he sunk into the addled memory foam of his tired car seat, he felt his phone buzz in his pocket. He checked to see who was calling him so early. *Mum, what does she want this time of the morning?*

He slipped his thumb over the green arrow glowing through his scratched phone screen and waited for her to speak.

"Henry, are you there?"

"Yes mum."

"Are you awake?"

"Yes mum, I've just finished work."

"Oh good, I want to tell you something."

He waited for her to continue – silence. "What did you want to tell me?"

"Do you remember great-uncle Roderick?"

"No. Do I have a great-uncle Roderick?"

"You did but he died a couple of weeks ago."

"Oh – is there going to be a funeral – do I have to go?"

"No, he's already been buried – it's just that he left you something."

"Money?"

"No, just something in a package that was delivered to me

yesterday. I've sent it to you by courier and it's being delivered sometime between ten and six today. You need to sign for it, so make sure you listen for your doorbell to ring."

"But mum I need to get some sleep. I've been working all night."

"You'll have to nap downstairs so you can hear your doorbell and catch him before he disappears. You know what those couriers are like; they wait ten seconds and then jump back in their white vans to the next job."

"Alright, I'll sleep downstairs. What's in the parcel?"

"I don't know, it was addressed to you by name so I didn't open it."

"Is it big?"

"No it's small?"

"Was great-uncle Roderick rich?"

"I don't think so; but he was a bit strange from what I can remember of him."

"I'll have to go now mum. I want to get home before the morning traffic builds up. Love you mum, bye."

Henry pushed the key into the ignition, closed his eyes and prayed to no one in particular that his car would start. Unusually, the engine burst into life on the first attempt, but stubbornly refused to restart after he stalled the car. He waited for a few minutes, turned the key again and sighed with relief as the one litre power house of his vehicle rumbled back into life. Through the morning and afternoon he dozed on his lumpy sofa, glancing occasionally at the offerings of daytime television, while contemplating how many people opted for suicide as an escape from the mundane entertainment provided for those who were unemployed or infirm. He switched over to the news channel, but found the pictures of the latest massacre by a group called Boko Haram too upsetting to watch. Just before six, the doorbell emitted a dying chime that fell through to a shaky buzz.

"Package for – Mr Henry King, pardon me for disturbing you, Your Majesty," laughed the courier, bowing slightly as he handed Henry a small box wrapped in brown paper and tied tightly with off-cream coloured string.

Henry winced, how many times had he heard that remark or something similar. "Thank you," he said politely, taking the parcel from the courier.

After signing a squiggle on the filthy screen of the courier's little black box, Henry carried the package to his kitchen, handling it as if it contained high-explosives that might detonate at any given moment. The only pair of scissors Henry owned was lurking under a mass of seldom used utensils in the last drawer he opened. Carefully, he snipped the tight string in two places, pulling it away from the parcel before tearing through the brown paper wrapping. Henry frowned and felt his lower lip fall as he read the label on top of the plain cardboard box. *Contents: 1 Polka dot teapot (Two cup). Fragile: handle with care.* With expectant disappointment, he pulled open the top flaps of the box. Lying on top of what was obviously a wad of cotton wool, he saw a creased and folded piece of paper. With his curiosity aroused, he took the sheet of paper out from the top of the box, something torn out of a spiral bound note pad, and unfolded it.

He read down the neatly scripted note and felt his frown grow as he tried to absorb the strange message.

Dear Henry,

I doubt you remember me. You were only about two years old when I last saw you. The object in this box came into my possession by chance when I was about the age you are now. There is more to this object than meets the eye. It has a means to choose its owner and as my time is drawing to a close, I know you are the rightful heir to this guardian of time. It is for you to decide what you will do with this gift I bestow on you, but do not act rashly, for time rules over all men. To reveal the wonders within, depress the left eye followed by the right. May your connections of passing time bring to you what I yearned for all my life. I have included a list so you can understand what the timepiece is telling you.

Yours Sincerely,

Roderick.

Henry paused, he dabbed the cotton wool in the box with his forefinger to see if he could feel what might be hidden in its labyrinth of fibres. A split second later, his impatience overpowered him and he pulled a large clump of the compressed packaging from the box. He slowly leant forward and peered down hoping his eyes would not meet the sight of a brightly coloured teapot, they didn't.

Cradled on a bed of fluffy cotton wool sat a silver circular object. Henry reached down and slipped his fingertips over the smooth edges of cool metal. Carefully, he removed the object from its protective tomb. He slowly turned it over and inwardly jerked as he focused on a pair of burning bright red eyes that seemed to pierce into him. They were the eyes of a delicately engraved snake, a snake coiled around a single letter G that covered the surface of a circular convex silver case. Through the moist skin of his hand, Henry thought he could detect a slow rhythmic pulse, like a slow almost indiscernible heartbeat. Was it his heartbeat?

He remembered Roderick's note and used his thumbs to depress the left and right eyes of the snake. He felt the front of the case move slightly. He eased opened the hinged case to reveal something strange. At first, he couldn't make sense of what he saw. There were nine concentric rings, each coated with a pearly sheen of slightly different hues. Each ring had several apertures cut into it, and through some of the small holes, he noticed there were strange symbols he did not recognise. He moved the object up to his ear and heard a faint but regular light ticking sound. He put the object down, guessing it must be some kind of watch. Tipping the box towards him, he pulled out the remainder of the cotton wool and found a second piece of paper.

The second sheet of paper had several columns of strange symbols written on it, alongside each symbol, Roderick had neatly written their meanings. The symbols in the first column related to the digits from 0 to 9, those in the second column the month and those in the third column signified the Sun, Moon, Venus, Mars and Jupiter. Henry looked down again at the object and picked it up. *What is it – some sort of pocket watch?* He checked the symbols in view and realised the outer ring displayed the minutes past the hour. The next ring showed the hour, the next the month, the next the year and the fiver inner ones appeared to show the positions of five celestial bodies. *How weird. I wonder if it's valuable.* "I bet you're really old. What stories could you tell me if you could talk?" Henry said aloud.

❋ ❋ ❋

A Christian village near the border of Chad and Nigeria: Present day.

Fourteen year old Yasuf tried to keep his eyes focussed on the end of the smoking barrel of his AK 47. The barrel was worn, so worn that he needed to pour oil down it after firing more than three clips of ammunition to prevent a round from jamming inside and destroying his weapon.

He had just released three magazines, each holding thirty rounds, into a group of old women and young boys who were now sprawled out on the ground in front of him. As the last vapour trails of hot oil dispersed in a gentle breeze, his eyes once again roamed over the torn bodies that were no more than ten paces away from him. He entered a state of abstract withdrawal as he watched a fat, black fly settle on the glistening pink froth spilling from the splintered skull bones of woman who was lying on top of a small boy. He swallowed the fluids rising up from his churning stomach as the unmistakable smell of intestinal waste overtook the noxious gases expelled by his gun.

He had fired his first rounds into the bellies of the prisoners, shutting his eyes when he saw their insides bursting out as their torsos were torn open by the twisting and toppling bullets. The next clip took a second to load, and he aimed for their heads, desperate to stop their screaming that cut through him like Akubar's machete had sliced through an old man's neck a few minutes earlier.

Two of the women and one boy continued to scream. One woman, who had half her face torn away by his shots, glared at him from her remaining eye so hatefully, the image remained with him for the remainder of his life. The third magazine would not clip in. He removed it three times before it finally snapped into place. He stepped forward to within three paces of the woman and put ten rounds into what was left of her head. Then he shot the other woman and the boy with the remaining rounds before stepping back to a comfortable distance from the massacred bodies.

He didn't see the arm come over his shoulder until it was across his chest. As he felt the arm clamp onto him, a stench that reminded him of an old male goat drifted up his nose. It was Akubar.

"Good shooting, Yasuf. I'm proud of you little man. This day you have proved yourself to me and God. Allah will reward you now and in heaven for what you have done," Akubar shouted in his ear as he shook him with his arm.

"How can killing people please God?"

"Yasuf, these people are enemies of Allah, they are the infidels and their teachings will prevent many good people from going to heaven."

"Don't – Christians believe in heaven too?"

"Their beliefs are false, their heaven is false – there is only one true God and that is Allah. You are now a soldier of Allah. Are you a man? Have your balls dropped? Has your cock grown? Let me see."

Yasuf felt Akubar's arm slide down his front. Before he could move, Akubar clamped his private parts with his hand. "What are you doing?" he cried in fear.

"I'm checking you're ready for your reward. Come with me, it's time for you to discover what it's like to be a real man."

Yasuf walked alongside Akubar as they made their way out of the village into the bush. A few minutes later, they entered a small clearing where a group of young girls sat on the ground. Around them were other members of Yasuf's new family, Boko Haram's soldiers holding up large machetes and knives as a warning to the frightened girls.

Akubar placed his hand on Yasuf's shoulder and looked briefly at each man. "This boy has proved himself to be one of us. He is now a man and I'm rewarding him with the first pick of a bride. As you all know, every martyr will be rewarded with a hundred virgins for every infidel they kill on this Earth. This young man has earned two thousand virgins today, so it's time he learns what to do with them. Yasuf, pick one of these girls to become your first wife. In fact – pick two. It's time for you to discover the joy of fresh and moist womanhood."

Yasuf looked at the terrified girls who were half hiding under grey blankets they'd been given to cover themselves. He found he was taken by the looks of a girl with large eyes who stared directly at him. Just behind her, another girl with an angular face was also staring at him. Her red rimmed eyes were filled with hatred, they reminded him of the way the woman with half a face had looked at him. "I'll take those two," he said, pointing at the two girls.

"I will ask the girls to pledge their allegiance to Allah. If they do, you must respect them as your wives, but if they don't, they are yours to treat as you wish."

Yasuf prayed that the angry girl would not pledge her allegiance to Allah, so he could release his anger on her hatred in the same way he'd seen the other men deal with infidel women. His wishes were granted and that night he gently penetrated the first girl, taking her as his new wife. An hour later, he forced himself on the second girl who refused to swear allegiance to Allah or him. Through the remainder of the night, he vented his anger and fear by repeatedly pleasuring himself in the body of his slave.

TWO

Bavarian Alps: 1436.

Hamczel tapped the hind quarters of the cow he escorted down the gentle slopes that led back to his village. For a moment, he became fascinated by the swirling dark smudges that buzzed excitedly around the encrusted remains of shit covering the rear of the beast in front of him. His thoughts were not buzzing like the hungry flies, but floating like wisps of clouds deforming as they were forced over the cruel peaks of the surrounding mountains. Was Crista thinking of him as she descended the pass? Would she arrive at the village before him? Was her mind in a constant churning turmoil like his?

This last summer he turned eighteen and was no longer a boy. The village elders gave him the responsibility of caring for their cows through the summer and he was pleased with how it had gone. This was the first year in many that not one cow had been taken by wolves.

In the spring, Crista arrived in his village. She lived in a village the other side of the mountain range, but her uncle arranged for her to spend the summer working as a milking maid because they were short of workers in his village. From the moment he saw her, he knew he was in love. Not only was she beautiful, but when she smiled at him, her eyes lit up and made his insides wobble.

From the first day, he'd noticed her throwing glances at him and he ached to talk to her. At first, he was too ashamed, felt too humble and lacked courage to open up a conversation with her, but by chance, they became acquainted when a cow she was milking became agitated and attacked her. He did not hesitate; he charged the animal and drove it away. From that day, their friendship had grown and two weeks ago, she accepted his offer of marriage. She returned to her village to inform her uncle of their plans and was due to return this evening. Even now, she would be skipping down the mountain path and tomorrow they would marry in the small chapel further down the valley.

A blast of cold air drove into Hamczel's back, reminding him that summer was all but over. It was late September and the warm barmy days were releasing their hold on the lower mountain slopes, giving way to the biting winds that carried frost, snow and long nights of darkness. He turned to look back up the mountain and froze in horror. A shadowy, almost black greyness was crawling over the peaks heralding an early snow storm on the upper slopes. He turned his thoughts to Crista, she would be well below the levels of the glacier by now; possibly she was already waiting for him.

As darkness enclosed the surrounding peaks, Hamczel paced back and forth outside his chalet, repeatedly casting his eyes to the path Crista should have descended from hours ago. *Where are you Crista, are you safe? Please be safe.* In his head, he pictured her long blond hair, oval face, soft pink cheeks and penetrating blue eyes. He watched her smile at him, displaying her perfect and dainty white teeth, gazed into her enticing eyes and listened to her gentle laughter.

A roar of cold air angrily tearing down the slopes altered the images in his mind. He saw her hair whipped like wild grasses in a winter storm, ripped back from her face to reveal blackened cheeks corrupted by frost's bite, her eyes cracked by shards of growing ice and her laughter torn into a crying scream of despair. He stampeded into his chalet, pulled on his thick fur jerkin, filled his oil lamp, lit it and headed to the path that led up to the slopes.

He lost track of time through the long night. As he climbed higher, the cutting wind drove into his face and deadened all feeling in his cheeks and lips. In the first pre-dawn light that smeared across the eastern sky, he made out the white wall of the glacier's fringes. In the dimness of blending greys, he picked out the darker blur of wooden steps they used to climb onto the top surface of the glacier. He stopped to fasten two pairs of leather straps over his boots; each strap having three metal nails hammered through the leather that would help him keep his grip on the icy sheet that formed the upper surface of the glacier. Slowly and carefully, he walked up the slippery slope and as the sun broke through a gap in the surrounding peaks, its rays picked out the form of someone sitting upright ahead of him. It was a girl, it was Crista.

She looked so beautiful, so peaceful, so still – too still. Her eyes were open – they did not blink – they glistened without tears in the early sun. Her face was at peace – white – unblemished – virginally intact. He called to her as he approached – then touched her hardened cold beauty – stroked her stone cheeks – caressed her rigid lips with his frozen fingertips. He would carry her back down the mountain – wait for her to warm – come back to life.

He gripped her under the arms so he could lift her, but she remained static, unmoving, restrained and held by the grip of the cruel ice. Respectfully, he lifted her skirt and jumped back in shock. Her left foot was booted, but her right foot was naked and embedded in the ice.

Through the transparency of the bubble filled ice he made out the trails of her veins, the nails of her toes and the despair of her prison. He guessed at what might have happened.

Sometimes a stone would break from the mountain and slide down the glacier until it came to rest. During the day, the sun warmed the stone until it sunk through the ice, leaving a small pool of freezing water. Undisturbed, the pool would remain liquid until it was touched, then it would freeze solid in an instant. If Crista stepped into one of these pools by accident her foot may have become trapped.

Had she tried to pull it out and lost her boot in doing so? It didn't matter now, she was dead; he knew that. He would go back to the village and find someone to help him bring her down from the mountain, put her to rest in the ground so he could lay flowers on her grave. He stood up and looked down into the valley, feeling the warmth from his tears stimulating his numb cheeks.

The sun had climbed higher into the sky, pouring out its midmorning warmth when Hamczel returned alone, so alone, to the village that had been his home since his parents died in the plague outbreak fifteen years ago. He had been too young to remember them and his memories of his mother and father were a creation from the stories Barak told him.

Barak was also orphaned, adopted by the village when he was a boy many years ago. Hamczel felt warmness towards him, despite his great size and slowness of body and mind.

Whenever he needed comfort, help or someone to hear his worries, Barak always stopped what he was doing and listened. Now he needed Barak, he needed him to understand his grief and to help him bring Crista down from the mountain. He broke the morning peace by shouting, "Barak, where are you? Barak you must help me, something terrible has happened."

His cries echoed through the valleys, bouncing from slope to slope until it melted away like a snow flake clinging onto a man's warm and red cheek.

"I'm here, in the log shed, splitting timbers. What is the matter little man? What is so terrible to make you cry out like that?" a reply echoed from the other side of the small habitation.

Hamczel ran past a row of wooden chalets that made up half of the village's houses. "Barak, I need your help, something dreadful has happened to Crista," he shouted out before he reached the woodshed.

Barak set down the long and heavy axe he was using to split open a tree trunk riddled with knots. "What's the matter little man?" he said, taking a step away from the half split trunk.

"It's Crista, she's trapped on the glacier and I need your help to fetch her back down."

"Trapped, how do you mean trapped?"

"It's so awful. Her foot is frozen into the ice. Barak, she's dead, frozen solid. What am I going to do? Why did this have to happen?" Hamczel cried out, staggering towards Barak.

Barak stepped forward and wrapped his huge arms around Hamczel's shoulders. "Are you sure she's dead, she may be sleeping?"

"She's dead. I know she's dead. I felt her with my hands. She's as cold and hard as the mountain rocks. Why did this have to happen to me – to her? I loved her with all my heart but I never had time to show her how I loved her. It's so unfair, if only I could turn back time, I would climb up onto the glacier and meet her before she…"

"Hamczel, what is done cannot be undone. There is nothing any of us can do to change what's happened. We must set our minds to bringing her back to rest in peace. How far up the glacier is she?"

"Not far, it's only a short way after you climb up the steps that lead onto the top of the glacier."

"We need to bring her down as quickly as possible, before the wolves find her."

"No, don't even mention that. I couldn't bear to lose her that way. We must go now and rescue her from those scavengers. I've seen what they do to dead or injured animals."

Although Barak appeared to be slow because of his massive frame, his mind was sharp and worked quickly. He knew he must keep Hamczel busy for the next few hours, or if possible, the next few days. "Hamczel, I will take a small sledge so we can bring her down easily. You said her foot was trapped in the ice, I'll need an axe to free her."

Hamczel pulled back out of Barak's arms and screamed, "You're not going to chop off her foot. I won't let you."

"No little man. The axe is for cutting away the ice to release her. We'll need food. Go and pack some food in a bag so we have some supplies. You know I can't work for long without eating," he joked, in an attempt to calm Hamczel. "Then go to widow Bruen and tell her I will give her two piles of logs in exchange for a couple of her best cheeses and a large loaf of bread. You'd better grab a large jug of beer while you're at it, the sky is clear today and the sun is still strong."

While Hamczel followed the instructions, Barak pulled a small light-weight sled onto his back and fastened it in place with several lengths of twine. He glanced around the disarray of the woodshed and spotted the small axe he sought. He lifted a large leather bag off a hook and checked his pair of leather straps embed with nails for walking on the icy glacier was at the bottom of his bag. Satisfied that with the addition of cheese, bread, and beer, he had everything he needed. He stepped out into the bright morning sun and yelled for Hamczel to join him.

It was a couple hours after the sun reached its highest point in the sky that they reached the ice wall marking the point of advancement of the glacier down the valley. Over the past ten years it had consistently crept down the valley. Each winter seemed colder and longer than the previous one, causing some of the villagers to say that soon the glacier would descend to consume their village. Barak levered the heavy bag from his shoulder and removed the stone jug of beer. "Hamczel, take a large swig, it isn't good for the body to lose water without replacing it. I need to fasten my ice straps onto my boots and you must do the same."

As Hamczel fastened the straps around his boots, he heard a strange warbling noise. He looked up to see Barak, with his arm crooked, balancing the large jug so that its neck was in his mouth. Barak noticed Hamczel was staring at him and lowered the jug. "I'm just lightening the load I have to carry. Do you want another swig before we climb up onto the glacier?"

Hamczel was about to reply when they heard a long drawn out howl. Both men froze, thinking the same thought. *The wolves are here.*

"Come on, let's get onto the glacier. If they catch our scent they'll run away," Barak said, lowering the jug into his bag.

Hamczel knew that wolves seldom attacked people, but if they found a dead or badly injured person on the slopes, they would tear apart their body and eat them within minutes. "Please don't let them find her, not now we're so close," he cried out, following Barak up the ladder.

A few minutes after they climbed onto the icy surface of the glacier, they spotted the first signs of wolf prints. Hamczel shielded his eyes with his hand from the glaring sun and looked ahead. Through the glare reflecting from the white surface, he thought he saw a dark streak smeared across the ice. "Barak, can you see those stains on the ice, what do you think they are?"

"I see them but I'm not sure what they are," Barak replied, certain he did know what was marking the ice.

Hamczel pushed forward, forcing his legs into longer strides. He saw something lying across the clean white ice ahead. At first it looked like piece of wet brown rope, measuring about twice the length of a man's height. As he drew closer, Hamczel's memory stirred.

He recalled the first time he'd seen the remains of a calf taken by wolves. Nearly every part of the animal was gone except for a large part of its head and a long trailing length of its intestine that the wolves rejected. He stopped to inspect the dark pink snake on the ice. Was that a glistening worm corrupting the purity of the sinless ice? He gently dabbed the soft yielding length of gut – the previously hidden insides of a living creature – the rejected offal of something torn apart by the wolf pack. "No." he cried. "Crista, are you there? Please still be there."

He felt Barak's heavy hand grab his shoulder, but broke away and ran further up the slope. He ran to the dark stain ahead of him. There was nothing left to see other than the discolouration of the ice, a blemish on the innocent purity of frozen water, strawberry spoils resembling the seeping discharge of a menstruating woman adorned in white.

He vomited, spewing his rancid turmoil over the remains of Crista's life blood that had dribbled from the jaws of ravenous scavengers. He stood up, staggered to the epicentre of the red scar and stared at the image of a red eye centred with a white pupil. It took a moment for him to realise he was looking at the top of Crista's severed foot, an oval of raw flesh wrapped around young white bone, the top of a foot still frozen into the ice. He dropped to his knees and began scrapping at the ice with his fingers, gouging at it with his chewed nails, striking it with his clenched fist and releasing gulping whoops of misery.

Barak gripped Hamczel's shoulders with his huge hands. "Stand up. It's better if we leave now. There's nothing more we can do for her," Barak said, pulling Hamczel up onto his feet.

"No, I cannot leave her here, I must take what is left back down with me," Hamczel cried out.

"Do you mean her foot?" Barak asked.

"Yes. Break the ice around it with your axe. I will dig a grave for her and lay her foot to rest," Hamczel blurted, as he began to cry and weep.

Barak fumbled in his bag for the axe. "Stand back little man. I will try to break up the ice around it."

"Barak, be careful not to damage her foot. Break the ice for me and I will ease it out with my bare hands."

Barak stood with his legs astride and started to chop at the ice. He carefully aimed the axe so that it struck a foot's length from the eye in the ice, working until he'd shattered the glass-like crystal in a full circle around the dismembered foot. As he stopped to look at the progress of his task, Hamczel began clawing at the fractured shards of ice, casting pieces down the slope.

For almost an hour, he dug feverishly with his bare fingers until Crista's foot was nearly free from its clawing prison. In frustration, he twisted at the foot until it tore away from the clinging ice. Holding up her foot in his blue hand, Hamczel noticed how her white skin contrasted with his blackened fingers. Only when he turned it in front of him, did he notice the little toe was missing – torn off and still buried in the cracked ice. "Her toe is gone, I must find her toe," Hamczel screamed, plunging his hands into the shattered hole.

By now his fingers were numb with the cold and could feel little. Time and time again he removed pieces of ice hoping they were Crista's missing toe. Only after another hour, did he remove a small pale pink toe, so perfectly preserved it looked as if it were part of a living person. Hamczel began to shake and Barak forced him to stand up. "It's time to go, little man. The air is cooling as fast as a stone dislodged from the mountain falls, and you've had your hands in the ice far too long. Come, let's get you down and sat by a warm fire before you are consumed by the cold."

Hamczel placed the toe in his pocket while Barak wrapped the foot in a cloth that had previously covered one of the cheeses. They began walking down the slope when Hamczel spotted something on the smooth icy surface. "What's that? What is it?"

"I'm not sure, wait here, I'll take a look," Barak replied, looking at a small object a few strides to their right.

Barak felt his stomach churning as he approached the object. The sun was now low in the sky and its rays picked out a neat row of small white teeth pointing skyward from a short length of bone. As he moved closer to the object, he realised it was part of a lower jaw bone, a discarded fragment of Crista that one of the wolves had dropped after finding it too hard to crush into smaller fragments.

"What is it?" Hamczel shouted.

"It's another part of Crista. I'll put it in my bag and show you when we return to the village.

"What part?"

"Hamczel, I'm so sorry. It's a piece of bone with some of her teeth in it."

"How many teeth are there?"

"I think there are five. They are the small ones at the front of her bottom jaw," Barak replied, unsure if he should be telling Hamczel what he'd found.

"They will always remind me of her smile, don't lose them Barak." Hamczel squealed.

"Don't worry, I'll keep them safe for you little man."

The following morning, Hamczel could not move from his bed. When they returned last night, Barak made him sit near an open fire for hours, telling him every few minutes to move a little closer to the dancing flames. He'd warmed up quickly, but his fingers burned as blood began to flow through them.

It was only later he realised the little finger on his right hand remained numb no matter how much he rubbed it. Now, as he tried to rise from his bed, his body refused to move. Every part of him ached and his face burned with a fever. He coughed and felt tightness in his chest as stabbing pains ripped under his ribs. He tried to turn onto his side, but his lungs seared with agonising spasms that forced him to remain still. He heard the flimsy wooden door to his chalet creak as it was thrust open. A large dark shape hovered over him.

"You look terrible," Barak's voice boomed out from the fuzzy cloud Hamczel could see looming over him.

"I feel terrible, what's happening to me?"

"Your body became chilled. Don't worry you'll be up and about in a couple of days. I want to look at your hands, little man."

"Why?"

"You had your fingers in the ice for too long, they may be damaged."

"They feel alright now, it's my chest that hurts," Hamczel replied, checking his fingers by touching each in turn. *That's strange I can't feel my little finger.*

Hamczel felt Barak lifting his hands from the under the bed covers. He felt reassurance as the man's thick fingers played over his, stroking each finger in turn. Barak said, "Can you feel that?"

"Feel what?"

"That."

Hamczel felt nothing. "What are you doing?"

"I'm digging my fingernail into your little finger, can you feel it?"

"I don't think so. That finger still feels numb from the cold."

"I'm going to fetch Peta to have a look at it."

A few minutes later, Barak returned with one of the village elders. Hamczel closed his eyes and tried to picture Crista's beautiful smile as the elder twisted and pulled on each of his fingers. He heard Barak and Peta discuss something from the other side of his room. Barak came over to him. "Hamczel, your little finger is dead. It's best we cut it off now, before it starts to rot and poison you. I'll do it, I'll be quick. You'll hardly feel a thing."

"What, you're going to chop off my finger?"

"I have to. You may lose your whole arm or die if I don't."

"Please, Barak, don't do this to me."

"Be brave little man, Peta is fetching Hanna. She will clean the wound and bandage it for you."

Hamczel tried to sit up but his chest burned as soon as he moved. He heard the door open again, and then the whispering voices of Peta and Hanna discussing something he could not make out. He shut his eyes when Barak gripped his hand. Barak spoke briefly. "I'm going to do it now, little man. Peta, hold his wrist tightly. Hanna, make sure you have the bandages ready to bind his hand."

Hamczel felt a hand gripping his wrist tightly, a moment later he felt a strong pull on his hand and heard the sound of bones cracking. In the first moment there was no pain – then it hit him like a wall of snow cascading down the mountainside. His hand felt as if it were being crushed under the trunk of a fallen tree – fire ploughed up his arm – his chest scorched with the contraction of his muscles and he cried – cried out so loudly everything around him receded into an abyss of pain.

Through the haze of his agony, he heard them speaking and felt his arm gyrate as Hanna wound a length of muslin around his hand. The intense burning sensation cooled to a deep throbbing, its rhythm keeping time with his pounding heart. He became aware that Barak was talking to him. "It's done, little man. A few days from now you'll be back to normal. Try to rest and get some sleep. I'll stay here with you."

"Where's my finger?"

"It's in a piece of cloth, don't worry I'll bury it later."

"No, keep it for me."

"It's only your little finger and the ice has destroyed it."

"I want to keep it, rest it next to Crista's toe so that at least part of us can be together for all of time."

Peta grabbed Barak's arm and led him away from the bed. He reached up and whispered into Barak's ear. "He's in shock, humour him for now and he will find it easier to rest."

Barak moved to Hamczel's side. "I will wash it and then wrap it in a clean cloth for you. Listen, little man, if you need anything, anything at all, just ask me and I will sort it for you."

"Thank you, Barak. Thank you for everything you have done for me."

Three days later, Hamczel stumbled out of his bed to his front door. The mountain air was cool and dry, the sky unblemished by clouds and sunlight tinged everything with its buttery yellow warmth. He looked up to the white tipped peaks that surrounded the village in every direction, hesitantly taking a step out into the open. Something caught his attention, two swaying blurs at the edge of his vision. He turned to his left, looked at two things that were swinging in the gentle breeze. Suspended in mid-air by pieces of twine tied onto one of his roof timbers, there were two small objects dancing side-by-side. It took a moment for him to realise he was looking at Crista's toe and his finger, held aloft against the backdrop of the distant, bluish tinged mountains. He recollected Barak telling him he would dry out the severed digits in the air, curing them the same way as they preserved strips of beef from a slaughtered cow. He took a deep breath into his tight chest and silently prayed to be at peace with Crista in some future time.

❊ ❊ ❊

The Vatican; 1436

Niccolo Cesarini patiently waited for the last of the *invited* Cardinals to arrive. He nervously drummed his fingers on the table as the last member took his seat. He stood up and blanked out the stares coming from pairs of cold grey eyes cast in his direction. "I have called this special meeting for reasons of which you are all aware of," he said, glaring piercingly into the eyes set on him. "Our Pope, Eugenius the fourth, is floundering in his efforts to retain power. His critics and enemies are closing in from all sides and soon he will take refuge elsewhere. The safety of our Pope is not the reason I have summoned you here today." He paused to look at the surprise on their faces and smiled.

"Despite the fact that Eugenius has shared half the wealth of the church with us, his beloved and closest followers, the future prospects for fiscal growth is dire unless we take action. I have with me today, signed orders from our Pope that will ensure the future prosperity of our church, and the purging of all who stand in the way of us delivering God's rule over humanity," Niccolo shouted, waving an open document at them.

"I implore each of you to return to your lands and double your efforts in motivating the Inquisitors to confiscate the properties, wealth and lands of every heretic. No village, town or castle must remain in the hands of those who do not offer total devotion to our great church. Not until every breathing man and woman renders their lives to God's purpose through personal sacrifice to our cause, can we rest. I urge each of you to gather intelligence as to where the heretics and their wealth are hidden. Enter the deepest valleys, climb the highest mountains and penetrate the darkest forests to unearth those that covet that which is ours."

Their eyes remained fixed on Niccolo as their thin lips broadened into wry smiles. One voice broke the cold silence. "How extreme should our methods be? There have been recent instructions to use gentle persuasion rather than the tearing and burning of flesh to purify the souls of the afflicted."

Niccolo paused. He looked at each Cardinal in turn, before replying. "You will each be given papers that include detailed instructions on how to make implements of purification. From this day forth the rack will tear limbs from their sockets, the wheel will crush bones, the pear will split open the wombs of witches and the press will crush skulls of sinners. All who confess to being a heretic are to be purified by reduction to ash at the stake. All properties and wealth are to be confiscated for the cause of the church. Half you will retain for your personal expenses and the other half will be amassed, through me, for the enlargement of our great church."

THREE

Henry tried to cast off the shades of guilt that were consuming him as he hovered outside 'D M Chaplin's' shop front. He looked up at the shop sign, painted in gold coloured, copperplate lettering. D M Chaplin: Purveyors and purchasers of antiquarian watches and clocks.

He slipped his hand into his pocket and touched the cool metal of the pocket watch that had been in his possession for less than twenty four hours. *What if it's worth a million pounds, maybe more? It would change my life, give me a chance to buy my own house, a new car and find a decent job I could enjoy.* He traced his fingertip over the face of the snake on the front of the watch, felt the two raised red jewels that gave access to the inner secrets of the timepiece, before he pushed open the heavy dark green door of the seductress baiting him with dreams of gaining a fortune.

The shop he had chosen was situated in a side street in Kensington, one of the wealthier districts of London. He'd spent most of last night studying the watch, and curious to see what it might be worth, started searching through the internet to see if he could find something similar, he'd not. What did catch his eye though, were the watches on sale in the shop he now entered. Many of the pocket watches for sale had asking prices of several million pounds and they didn't look half as good as the watch that great-uncle Roderick bestowed to him.

"Can I help you sir?" a diminutive, mousey-looking, bald-headed man who wore ridiculously heavy framed glasses, called out from behind a counter.

"Maybe, can you take a look at this and tell me if it has any value?" Henry asked, removing the watch from his pocket and carefully placing it on the glass counter.

The man picked up the watch and tried to open the case. "Press down the left eye then the right eye of the snake on the front," Henry said quickly.

"Oh very clever indeed, I'm impressed. I've seen something like that before. How odd, there are no hands."

Henry quickly explained what each of the concentric dials represented and how the watch showed the correct time and date.

"I'm just going to show this to Mr Chaplin, I'd like to get a second opinion," the man said, as he disappeared through a set of grey pleated curtains covering a doorway.

Henry heard the shop door opening and turned around to see a tall man wearing a black suit and top hat entering the shop. The man's face was framed with a neat and highly groomed beard that looked as if it were crafted by a barber of a different age.

"Are you buying or selling?" Henry said nervously to the man who was staring at him with his dark eyes.

The man removed his top hat and placed it onto the glass counter. "Neither, I'm just looking. What about you?"

"I've just been given a watch, it's very unusual. I'm just checking to see if it's worth anything."

The man touched the tip of his nose with his forefinger, closed his eyes and seemed to lose himself in his thoughts for several seconds before replying. "Certain objects have greater value then money."

The curtain behind the counter opened to reveal a heavily

overweight man who appeared to have difficulty in both breathing and walking. He heaved from side to side as he struggled to walk the two strides to the counter. "Good morning, young man, I'm David Chaplin, owner of this establishment. My colleague tells me you are looking to sell this timepiece."

"I'm not sure if I want to sell it, but I'm interested to find out more about it and to see if it has any value," Henry replied, aware that the stranger was looking directly at him.

"I've taken a good look at the watch. It is very unusual but I doubt it's more than a few years old. Have you noticed there's no winder and the back does not open? I suspect it's powered by a battery and made to look as if it is very old," he said, while turning the watch in his hands. "I can only imagine it has been made as a special order, possibly by a Chinese watchmaker, very clever some of these Chinese craftsmen. Because of its originality, I'm prepared to offer you eight thousand pounds cash for this item."

The stranger at Henry's side reached out and grabbed the watch from David Chaplin before he had the chance to move. He held the watch up to his face and studied the dials on the watch's face. "I beg to differ, but in my opinion this watch is very old and was almost certainly made in southern Germany several hundred years ago. As to its value, I think you've missed at least three, if not four noughts off the end of your offer. Here, put this in your pocket and join me for a coffee," the stranger said, handing the watch back to Henry.

"Five million, in your bank account by this afternoon," David Chaplin snapped back, his jowls wobbling hideously as he spat out his offer.

"Thanks but I think I'll go," Henry said, turning for the door.

Henry rushed outside and headed to the main street to collect his thoughts. He paused when he reached the busy road that was bustling with traffic and passers-by. *That strange man said three or four noughts. Does he mean it's worth tens of millions? They were trying to rob me, possibly that last offer was only a tenth of its true value. With that sort of money I'd never have to work again.*

Before Henry had time to move or fantasise about what he could do with such a large fortune, a strong hand gripped his upper arm. He turned to see the bearded stranger beside him, who yanked him in the direction of a nearby coffee shop.

The strange bearded man spoke quietly as he guided Henry into the coffee house. "Don't be alarmed, I'm a friend and all I want is for you to listen to my advice over the next few minutes."

"Who are you?"

"My name is Mont – Gomory."

"I'm not sure I want your advice Mr Montgomory."

"Sit down and listen. My name is not Montgomory, its Mont, followed by Gomory."

"God your name's worse than mine," Henry replied.

The man gave Henry a black stare and then smiled. "I don't think there's much wrong with the name Henry King. They're both strong names and flow well together. My name is very old. Mont means mountain and as for Gomory, you can check that out sometime."

"Hang on, how'd you know my name? I never told you my name."

"Maybe I heard it in the shop a few minutes ago."

"No, I never introduced myself to either of them."

"Maybe I know it because we met once before."

"I've never seen you in my life."

"Not in this life, not yet, but maybe in another one. We may have met in the past or possibly the future."

"Now you're talking weird."

"Order two coffees, have what you like, I'm buying."

One of the waitresses, adorned in a black dress and lace apron approached the table. "Are you gentlemen ready ta orda," she said, with an accent indicating she was from south of the river.

Henry blurted out a reply without thinking. "We'll have one large latte and a large cappuccino, please."

"Which are you having?" Mont asked.

"I don't mind. What's this advice you're going to give me?"

"Do you believe in fate?"

"Do you mean, do I think things are pre-ordained?"

"Let me tell you something about time," Mont said, bringing his hands together and interlocking his fingers. "Have you ever noticed how the world runs on repeated cycles? Each day the sun rises in the east and sets in the west. Over a year, the seasons change, but the cycle is repeated year after year. The moon waxes and wanes, the tides rise and fall, people are born and die, but life goes on."

"I know all about that but it has nothing to do with predicting the future. The cycles occur because of physics, nothing more. I don't believe in fate, what happens, happens because of previous circumstances," Henry said, feeling confident with his logical response.

"There are many cycles, some are obvious, some are hidden but there is always repetition. The watch in your pocket is a keeper of cycles and soon it will control an event it was built to ordain. You have become the keeper of the watch and are entwined in what's about to unfold. My advice to you is simple, hold onto the watch at all costs."

"You're weird. Are you telling me I'm some sort of keeper of an object that is going to change the world?"

Mont laughed out loud. "The watch is a keeper of time and enmeshed in its working are two fragments of the past. When these fragments reach a conjunction, a union that failed to happen long ago might, and I say *might,* with reserve, happen again. That alignment is set to take place soon and if you are the keeper of the watch, it is you that will be affected."

The waitress set the coffees on the table. "Is there anything else I can get yah?"

"No thanks," Henry said curtly.

"Which coffee are you having?" Mont asked.

"I'm not bothered, you choose."

"I'll take the latte. The froth on the cappuccino will stick to my beard."

"Are you telling me I shouldn't sell the watch?"

"I'm not telling you anything, I'm just giving you some advice."

"If I sold it, my life would change forever."

"If you keep it, it will change forever. Who is to say which change is the best?"

"I suppose I could keep it until this *conjunction* occurs and then sell it."

"That's for you to decide, but the watch always chooses its next keeper."

Mont pulled out a fresh ten pound note and placed it neatly on the table. "I have to go now. Remember, water can turn to vapour or ice, but eventually it returns to water and continues to flow. Time is like water, sometimes it dissolves into invisibility and sometimes it seems to freeze, but in reality it always flows."

"Will I see you again?" Henry asked, trying to take in everything Mont had told him.

"You may or you may not. I will leave you a card. Call this person if you want a new job. You'll not be so desperate for money if you follow her advice," he said, as he stood up and walked out of the door.

Henry sipped the last dregs of his coffee, picked up the card and reached into his pocket to feel the smooth coolness of the watch's surface.

* * *

Yasuf peered through the trees and watched the villagers going about their daily routine unaware their lives were about to change forever. While he waited for Akubar's orders to attack, he thought back to what happened four years ago.

It was on a hot day like this when he was playing with his brothers that they came without warning. His father owned a small garage and allowed them to borrow an old tyre to use as a toy. Just as his brother rolled the tyre towards him, the first whizzing noises broke around him, followed a second later by the sharp cracks of gunfire. Even before the tyre reached him, he saw something dark spray from the side of his brother's head – a sinister cloud he now knew was the hallmark of brain tissue erupting from an exploding skull. He wanted to run, but his legs rooted to the ground and through his open, but unseeing eyes, he failed to notice those around him falling to the ground.

Only when someone grabbed him from behind, did he come to his senses again. His upper arms burned as he was lifted in a tight grip and carried to the front of his father's garage. The man holding him forced him to kneel, before shouting at him. "Christian, watch what happens to your kind. Do you know this man?" he screamed, pointing to his father.

"It's my father. Dad, are you alright? Have they hurt you?"

The back of the man's hand lashed across his face. "I asked you if you knew this man, I did not give you permission to speak to him. Don't speak again."

He remembered watching as other men came from the back of the garage, each carrying a tyre. They forced his father to stand at gunpoint and lowered four tyres over his body before knocking him to the ground and tying his ankles together. Someone came out with a battered can and poured oil onto the tyre nearest his father's feet. One of the men rolled up a sheet of newspaper and pushed it between his father's legs and the oil-soaked tyre. He then struck a match and set it to the paper. The fire was small at first, consisting of a fist sized mass of boiling flame that wobbled under a rising column of black smoke. Suddenly his father began screaming as the first dribbling of molten rubber dropped onto his legs. In desperation, his father tried to roll himself over, but the flames grew larger as the oil ignited. The men who were watching started laughing and jostling each other as the fire engulfed the lower tyre, and his father vented his agony by screaming. One of the men stepped forward towards his father and began shouting at him. "Christian, this is what the fires of hell will feel like for all eternity. Denounce your demon god and sing praise to Allah now. Allah will take you under his arm in the next life if you accept his teachings now."

His father stopped screaming, took a deep breath and tried to spit at the man. It took nearly twenty minutes for the flames to reach up to his waist and the moment his cries of agony ceased, as his heart failed him. The fire burned for over an hour, and as the steel wires in the tyres uncoiled, their spreading amber net shrouded the charred remains of the corpse in their midst.

Just as he though his ordeal was over, a group of men dragged a screaming and kicking woman onto the garage forecourt and threw her onto the ground. "Look woman, this is what's left of your man. Now you have no man. Hey men, shall we give this woman a man. Who wants to go first?"

He wanted to close his eyes as the men took it in turns to rape his mother in front of him, but something made him look, take in the vileness of those animals, nurture his hatred and mould him, so that one day he could take revenge for what they did to his parents. When they finished, they grabbed him by the neck and led him over to his mother. He dropped down to the ground in front of her face and looked into her wet eyes. "Yasuf, my son. Tell these men you want to become one of them," she whispered to him. "Join them so that one day you can kill them," she hissed gently.

"Boy you have no family, what do you want us to do to you?"

He had stood up, turned and faced them. "Why do you do this?"

"We do this in the name of our God. Allah is the only true God and all who do not follow him must die."

"Is your God powerful, is he the one God I should follow?"

"You want to follow Allah?"

"If he is the true God, yes I do."

"You want to become a fighter for the Boko Haram after what we did to your mother and father?"

"Yes I do," he said, casting a glance at his mother.

"This woman is as good as dead. She is bleeding from her wounds and will soon die. Here, put her out of her misery and send her to hell," a man said, handing him a machete.

He turned to look at his mother and saw from the expression on her face she was telling him to act. "Make it quick," she whispered.

A moment later, without thought, he raised the blade and brought it down on her neck so hard that her head came away from her body and rolled to one side.

His mind returned to reality as he heard the order from Akubar. "Forward, take them. Kill all who resist."

None of the villagers were armed and after the initial killing spree, everyone was rounded up and segregated into groups. Akubar led Yasuf into a wooden building to the side of the church. Inside, Yasuf saw that eight young men were hanging by their arms from a heavy wooden beam that spanned the ceiling. Each man was standing on tiptoe and judging by the expressions on their bruised faces, they were struggling to catch their breath. Akubar removed a dagger from his belt and began cutting the clothing from one of the men. As he cut through the man's trousers, he spoke. "Yasuf, these men are all soldiers, but they hid their weapons and uniforms when we raided the village. They are all cowards," he shouted, turning his dark eyes onto each man in turn as he pulled the shredded trousers from the first man's legs. "I want to know where they're from and if there're any more soldiers nearby. I'm assigning you the task of interrogating them. Watch how it's done."

Akubar finished cutting off the last remnants of the man's clothing, tied a loop of rope around his ankles and then pulled his feet up level to his backside. "Watch how I truss him like a Yankee turkey," Akubar said, as he passed the free end of the rope around the front of the man's neck before looping it through the rope around his ankles and tying it off. "Listen, all of you and listen carefully. My friend here is going to ask you some questions," he said, pointing to Yasuf. "Answer him truthfully and fully. If any of you says 'I don't know' he'll cut off your balls. Now I don't know if you know what it's like to have your balls cut off so I'll show you. Yasuf come here and watch carefully."

Yasuf stepped closer, watching as Akubar cupped his hand under the man's testicles before tying a short length of string to act as a ligature.

"You must tie of their balls like this, but don't tie it too tightly or they will not bleed out."

Yasuf peered closer to watch how Akubar fastened the string. "What happens if it's not tight enough?"

"They'll bleed and die very quickly. Do it too tight and they'll survive. Let me tell you, it's best not to survive."

"I don't think I'd want to live without my balls," Yasuf murmured back.

"Grip them firmly like this and pull them down as far as they will go. See, look how the skin is stretched." Akubar shouted above the man's frantic screams. "Now pull them forward making sure you keep everything stretched and tuck your knife under his cock like this. Come closer, see how it's done. Pull the knife across and slice down at the same time, like this."

Yasuf had never heard someone scream so loudly. He wanted to push his fingers in his ears to cut out the screeching sobs of the writhing man. As Akubar cut, he saw an initial squirt of blood spray over the floor but no further bleeding. Akubar stepped back and held up his hand that contained the gory mess of amputated testicles and scrotum into the face of his victim, while rhythmic pulses of bright red blood began to jet onto the floor under the man. "I want all of you to look at him or I'll cut your balls off now," Akubar screamed at the other men. "Watch how long it takes him to die. That is what will happen to you if you don't talk. Yasuf, come outside with me for a minute."

Yasuf stepped out into the overwhelming heat of the late morning and vomited onto the dry and dusty ground. Akubar placed a hand on his shoulders. "First time you've seen something like that?"

"Yes, how can you do that to someone?"

"Listen Yasuf, I can do that easy. I was once a soldier and captured the same way they were."

"They didn't cut you like that though did they?"

"Oh yes they did. My balls were cut off eight years ago and I hung for three days before they cut me down. I was the only one who didn't die and they said it was because Allah spared me for their cause. I'm here because Allah wants me here. I may not be a strong fighter anymore, but I'm a good thinker. Allah provides me with medicine so I can fight his cause. Now go and question them. I'll send in some more men to make notes of what they say. Don't worry, they'll talk and tell us where the other units are."

"What do I do when I've finished questioning them?"

"Do exactly as I did, cut off their balls. If anyone is still alive after three days, he too has been chosen by Allah and will join our elite band."

"Do I have to do – that?"

"I need you to prove your commitment to Allah and the next time we capture some pretty girls, I'll allow you to have first pick for another wife."

That evening, Yasuf shuffled back to the main camp. He knew he was now one of them and there was no turning back for him.

In the church hall, Kalu hissed through his teeth in an attempt to ease the thumping pain in his groin and relieve the cramps growing across his chest. He craned his neck to gain a view of the others but saw nothing through the hazy mist obscuring his sight. "Can anyone hear me?" he cried out in desperation, hoping to hear a voice before death overtook him.

"I hear you."

"Who is it? I don't recognise your voice."

"It's me, Abeo. I can't believe they cut off my fucking nuts. I hope those bastards burn in Hell."

"We're going to die aren't we? I've prayed to Jesus to forgive them for what they've done. You should do the same, Abeo; Jesus will love you more if you forgive them."

"I'll try but I'm not sure I can. I'm frightened. I'm not ready to meet the Lord Jesus yet. I'm only eighteen and I've never been with a woman. Oh fuck, I'll never know what that's going to be like now they've cut my balls off."

Kalu wished he could block out Abeo's screams. It was bad enough to endure his own agony, but even worse having to listen to his comrades. *One more time, I'll pray to Jesus one more...*

FOUR

The following day, Hamczel asked Burak to help him dig a grave to bury Crista's remains.

"Do you want me to dig a full sized grave, little man?"

"No, but I want you to dig a deep hole. I want her foot to rest in peace for all time. Barak, can you make a small and strong box to place her foot in, something that will not rot and allow worms to enter to feed on her remaining flesh."

"I think I've already something suitable for that purpose. I've an old box my father made before he died, one lined with sheets of lead that will last for hundreds of years. What about her jawbone? Are you not placing that in her grave?"

"Don't think me strange, but I want to be able to look on what is left of her beautiful smile. Every time I look at that row of perfect teeth, it makes me think of the happiness we were destined to have. Barak, I cannot let that go from me."

"I understand how you feel now, little man, but you are young and time is a great healer. By this time next year, I expect you'll have found another to love and your life will move on to new beginnings."

"I cannot see that happening, Barak. Crista was and is my whole life. Her smile will remain with me until the day I die."

Barak studied Hamczel's expression and saw how deeply he was affected by Crista's death. *I'll need to do something to help him take his mind off Crista. I'll let him mourn for her for another week and then...*

"Barak, Hamczel, come quickly there's a large wolf skulking near the cowsheds," Pata cried out.

It was rare for wolves to come near the village as they normally kept well clear of people, knowing they were likely to be attacked with spears or arrows if they came too close. Barak ran into the timber shed to collect a large axe, while Hamczel followed Peta to the outskirts of their small village. They passed the cowshed and joined a group of men that were shouting and waving their arms in the air. Hamczel peered ahead and saw it. The massive black wolf was sitting upright, no more than fifty paces from where he stood. Thoughts of Crista's torn and eaten body coursed through his mind. *Are you one of the pack that ripped her beautiful body apart? You'd better run away now before I kill you.*

"Somebody, give me a spear and I will kill it," Hamczel cried.

Without looking, he took hold of the shaft of a spear someone pushed into his shaking hand. With his eyes fixed into those of the wolf, Hamczel walked forward. His steps never faltered until he stood two paces from the dark beast. The wolf watched him approach but remained still as he closed in on it, then without warning, it rolled onto its back and exposed its belly in a gesture of submission.

Hamczel raised his spear, but stayed his thrust as the golden brown eyes of the magnificent beast remained fixed on his glare. From somewhere ahead, a long drawn out howl eased his tension. Hamczel looked up and saw a white wolf slowly approaching. One of the villagers from behind him called out. "Hamczel, kill it now and we'll take the other one."

"No. I'm in no danger. I believe this animal has come to ask forgiveness for what it or its cousins did to Crista."

Hamczel looked down at the wolf, laid down his spear and placed his hand in front of its mouth. The wolf sniffed and then licked the back of his hand three times before climbing to its feet and slowly retreating. Three times, the wolf looked back at him, before joining the white wolf and running off towards a band of trees further up the valley. Hamczel walked back to the others, knowing in his heart he forgave the wolves for what they'd done, but sure in the knowledge that he would never love any other woman than Crista while he lived.

Later that day, he lowered a lead lined box into a deep hole and wept uncontrollably as Barak shovelled freshly dug soil back into the grave to hide Crista's foot for all of time to come.

Over the next few days, Hamczel entered a state of deep depression. He stayed in his bed until the early afternoon, ate little and sat outside his chalet until late into the night. The villagers were busy preparing for the onset of winter. Their main produce was cheese, many times more than they could consume and each autumn they gathered the excess stock, making it ready to trade in the nearby town of Harsburgh.

Barak was busy inspecting and repairing the seven wagons they used to transport their wares to the town. Two days from now, he would travel with some of the other men to Harsburgh and trade their cheeses for flour, dried meats, eggs, preserved fruits, salt and other essentials they needed to survive the winter. The cows were now safe in the sheds and enough hay was stored to ensure their survival over the long winter.

As he knelt to check the spokes of a wheel, Barak caught sight of Hamczel sitting on the ground outside his chalet. "Hamczel, come here, I need a hand to repair this wheel."

There was in fact nothing wrong with the wheel, but Barak spent the afternoon making a new spoke and pleaded with Hamczel to help him fit it as he'd pulled something in his shoulder. As he aligned the wheel to the cart's axle, an idea crept into his head. "Hamczel, you are a man now."

"I know."

"Have you ever been to Harsburgh?"

"I went once when I was a small child but I don't remember much about it."

"The day after tomorrow, I'm making a trip to Harsburgh with the other men. I could do with your help to unload and reload my wagon. This shoulder of mine is giving me a lot of grief right now."

"I don't think I'm up to doing much at the moment. There is a sadness eating at me and I can't make it go away."

"Please help me? I'm your friend and I need you to help me load and unload my wagon."

Hamczel looked into Barak's chubby but friendly face and realised he couldn't refuse his faithful friend. "I'll come, but I doubt I will make good company for you."

"I'm not worried about company, I just need a strong pair of hands to help me load the sacks," Barak said, as he lifted the side of the heavy cart and asked Hamczel to push the wheel onto the axle stub.

At a steady walking pace, it would take a person about eight hours to reach Harsburgh from Hamczel's village, but the group of men were not walking at a steady pace. When they set off at dawn the sky was clear. The early rays of the sun rapidly transformed the sparkling crystals of hoar frost into glinting droplets, clinging to the roadside grasses playing out their iridescent dance in the gentle morning breeze. They escorted seven heavily loaded carts drawn by castrated bullocks that seemed eager to reach their destination. By late morning, the blue sky was overtaken with darkening greys and a gentle breeze began to bite as it strengthened from an easterly direction. Then the light drizzle turned into cold rain that lashed their backs as they headed in a westerly direction. Without warning, the leading bullock decided it was time to stop for lunch. By the side of the winding road there were thick clumps of lush grass and the lead animal made a decision not to let it go to waste.

Barak walked up to the front of the line of stationary carts. "Johannes, we must move on or we will not reach Harsburgh before nightfall."

"I've tried everything, I've called him, beaten him with a stick, pushed him and offered him a fresh apple, but he will not budge."

"Let me try something," Barak said, walking up to the bullock that had its nose buried in the long grass.

Barak pulled the front of his leggings down and urinated on the grass where the bullock was eating. The bullock hesitated and then took a few steps forward to the next clump of grass.

"Everyone, come here and piss on the grass by the roadside. Spread out and cover as much of the grass as you can."

The bullock lifted its head and sniffed a couple of times before deciding to walk further down the roadway. Barak threaded a loop of rope over its face and pulled it tight. Using his weight, he pulled the animal forward and maintained a firm pull on the beast. The bullock seemed to forget about the grass and settled into a steady walk once again. Hamczel joined Barak at the front of the convoy. "Where did you learn that trick?" he asked.

"I didn't learn it anywhere. I just thought if I was eating and someone pissed all over my meal it would put me off eating my food."

"Barak, from what I've seen of you, nothing could put you off eating your food," Hamczel joked, laughing for the first time since Crista's death.

Compared to their village, Harsburgh was a massive settlement having a population of several thousand people. At that time, the land was divided into principalities, which were loosely governed by the King. In reality, the mountainous areas were under their own dominion and ruled by a collection of noble families that preferred to have union through wedlock, rather than fight weary battles that wiped out their bloodlines.

Harsburgh had become established as a centre of trade and culture, it supported numerous businesses and in the past decade many residential properties were transformed into shops. It was into this area, just before sunset that the weary travellers now passed through, seeking shelter for the night. Barak checked each building they passed, hoping he would soon spot an inn that could offer them a bed for the night, but all the fronts were closed with heavy wooden shutters. Ahead, he saw a solitary amber glow. "I'll checkout where that light's coming from," he called out before ambling ahead.

Barak stopped outside the open fronted building. The glow was coming from a blacksmith's forge. "Hello is anybody home?" he shouted out.

"Who is asking?" came back a gruff reply.

"I'm Barak, a traveller with a group of twelve other men and seven bullock pulled carts. We have come here to trade and are looking for lodgings for the night."

A man appeared from behind the forge. He was at least as large as Barak, but appeared bigger because of a long leather apron that covered the front of his wide body. Barak looked at the man's face and guessed he'd never taken a razor to his cheeks since he first started to sprout a beard. The man looked at him and spoke in a smoother voice than his first growled response. "Greetings Barak the traveller, I'm Michael the blacksmith. Do you have money?"

"No, but we have cheese. Do you like cheese?"

"Have you any strong cheese?"

"Plenty, would you like to try some?"

Ten minutes later, they led their bullocks and carts into a large stable behind Michael's premises and settled down into a straw filled barn. Barak explained that they could stay as long as they liked in exchange for one round of strong cheese per night.

"You struck us a bargain there," Peta said, grateful to be under a roof and have a chance to dry out.

The following morning they discussed what stock should be taken to market and by whom. Because of his inexperience at trading, Hamczel was told to remain behind for the morning. I'll come back for you in the afternoon and teach you how to trade at one of the smaller markets," Barak said, winking at Hamczel.

"What shall I do all morning?"

"Have a walk around the town. There are shops that sell things you've never seen before," Barak replied.

Once Hamczel finished eating his bread and cheese, he dusted himself down and walked out onto the main street. Everything had changed from the night before, the shutters were open and the shops displayed their wares and goods to passers-by.

Hamczel became lost in this strange new world. He gazed at strange looking clothes, stared at stone jars of fancy foods he'd never heard of and watched a man making a musical instrument that used metal wires to make sounds.

He turned into another road and inhaled appetising aromas of unknown foods baking in unseen ovens, studied finely painted cups decorated with lacy blue and white designs, but suddenly he stopped. The shop was like nothing he'd ever seen before. An elderly man worked at the rear of the shop, his face turned down, his eyes fixed on his craft. Set on two shelves behind the open shop front, the objects of his profession were performing their task in random unison. Hamczel stared trance like at the swinging pendulums, the oscillating wheels, the rocking animals and the glinting tiny pieces of metal that formed the hearts of the beautiful clocks.

The only clock he'd ever seen was the massive clock in the chapel an hour's walk from their village, the chapel he and

Crista was to have been married in. He stepped into the shop to take a closer look at the shiny mechanisms of the clocks, some smaller than his hand. He could see the perfectly formed gears and cogs, delicate springs and spindle like levers that combined to display the time of day in such an intricate way.

"Can I help you sir?" the old man said from his workbench.

"I hope you don't mind, I'm just looking. They're beautiful. How can you make such tiny parts?"

"I think most people wonder how a man with clumsy fingers can make such pieces as these. When you know how and have the right tools it's not as difficult as you might think, but it takes skill and patience to learn how to make keepers of time."

"I'm Hamczel, I come from a village in the mountains and we've come here to trade our cheeses."

"Well, Hamczel, I'm Guther, the clockmaker of Harsburgh."

"Would you trade one of your clocks for a round of cheese?" Hamczel asked, regretting his question the moment he asked it.

"Hmm not really, I'm not that partial to cheese. These days everyone deals in money. If you sold your cheese for money you could come back and buy one of my clocks."

"Money is of no use to us. You can't feed yourself through a long winter with money. We are exchanging our cheese for foods that will last us through the winter. Maybe one day I will leave the village and find a job that earns me money, and then I can buy one of your clocks."

"Do you have patience?" Guther asked, fixing his small grey eyes into Hamczel's.

"I have lost what I wanted in life and time is now a weapon that acts against me. If you mean do I have time to spare? Then yes, I have all the time I shall live to spare. Why do you ask?"

"No reason. It's just that I'm getting old and I've never married. I have no one to pass my skills to and they will perish when I reach my end."

"I don't understand what you mean."

"When you do understand, come and see me."

Hamczel left the shop feeling confused about what the old man said to him. *Is he suggesting that I should come and work for him? If so, why doesn't he just say it clearly?* Over the next few days, Hamczel learned the basics of trading. When all the cheeses were gone, he returned to the village with the others. It was a long and cold winter with short days and long nights. Through each and every night, Hamczel cried as visions of Crista haunted his twisting sleeplessness.

It wasn't until May that the first hint of spring reached their village. The elders called for Hamczel and told him because of his good work last year, they wanted him to mind the cows on the slopes again this summer. Thoughts of Crista erupted in his head and that night he packed a bag and crept out of the village. The following day he entered Guther's shop. He now understood the meaning of what old man had said.

※ ※ ※

Bavaria: 1437

Archbishop Ambrosius accompanied Inquisitor Balthasar down into the warren of cellars that composed the crypt of the recently refurbished cathedral. "My Lord Ambrosius, I believe you will be satisfied with what we have achieved in such a short time. I've had twenty of the finest blacksmiths in the district working day and night to produce the tools of confession I'm about to show," Balthasar said proudly as they descended the final staircase into the crypt.

"Balthasar, I'm not your Lord, I'm not any one's Lord. You may address me as your *Greatest Reverence*, though I feel more humble and comfortable if you use my name. These *tools of confession,* will they really work on the most stubborn of heretical souls?"

"My – Ambrosius, I can assure you no mortal man, or woman, will withstand the persuasion to bare all and confess his or her sins. Most succumb at the first stage – the rack. I believe it's when they hear their ligaments and tendons tearing just before their bones are torn from their sockets that most yield to our inquiries."

"That's all very well Balthasar, but I've heard stories of one noble Count who refused to confess even after both his arms were torn from his body."

"As I said, the rack is only the first stage. We have developed many implements of terror to aid the purification process of a sinner's soul. For example, the head press."

"Pray dear Balthasar, what does that involve?"

"Would you like to see a demonstration? I have a prisoner who confessed to murdering a priest before he stole Christ's golden cross from the altar. It took only a few turns of the rack to loosen his tongue. He is to be burnt at the stake tomorrow, but I'm certain his body hasn't given sufficient penance considering the gravity of his crimes."

"Will this *press* kill him?"

"I do not intend to kill him; he needs to be cleansed by fire if there is to be any chance of giving salvation to his soul, though after such an insidious crime, I'm certain he'll burn in the fires of Hell for all of eternity. We have found the head press a very useful tool if a reluctant confessor is made to watch its devastating force on another wretch."

"Show me, Balthasar. Let me witness your instrument of confession."

Balthasar shouted to a hidden monk standing in the shadows of a recess located in the vault's wall. "Gregar, fetch prisoner Helwig and secure him in the head press."

"Balthasar, I hope you understand the importance of what I

said to you earlier. It is essential that we clean up as much of the land as possible in the next few years. I understand from the King himself that there are many principalities and kingdoms still under self-rule. These pockets of corruption are ruled by demons, some openly worshiping Satan or his Dukes of Hell. We must eradicate this evil as quickly as possible."

Balthasar nodded urgently. "I couldn't agree more. These wretched little kingdoms are a stain on our morally noble lands. They suck the wealth from the common people like leeches devouring the lifeblood of a fish."

"When you are certain the main towns are clean you must build up your forces and venture into the countryside. There are many great castles high in the mountains that are inhabited by vile demons and witches that curse our faithful people. It is well known that the cause of the plague is due to the curses of such *foul* creatures," he grimaced. "Over the centuries they have looted the dead and amassed their riches in the deep dungeons of their stone towers. You must seek them out and recover the wealth, returning it back to the people through the mechanism of the church."

Balthasar briefly turned his gaze away from Ambrosius as he heard approaching footsteps. "I believe the prisoner is ready for our demonstration. Please, Archbishop, Ambrosius, come and watch how we extract the truth."

Ambrosius followed Balthasar through the darkness of the large vault that was intermittently lit by randomly placed torches playfully throwing their wavering light onto the surfaces of mysterious contraptions of torture. "You seem well equipped for the task ahead," Ambrosius commented, as he passed by a row of chairs set with a metal spike set in the centre of their seat.

"The chairs of submission are a very clever design. The spike is not quite long enough to penetrate any vital organ but causes acute agony to those embedded on its cruel barbed tip. Some have survived for several days while resting on one of those chairs and have confessed to a long list of sins. We are here. Behold, the head press."

Ambrosius looked at the terrified face of the man before him. His chin was held in a metal cup while the top of his head was covered by a shiny metal cap. Above the cap was a beam connected by two thick metal threads that ran down to the cast iron base of the apparatus.

Balthasar walked behind the equipment and began turning a wheel set atop one of the threads. "When I turn this wheel, the beam above the prisoner's head is forced down by the screw thread. I can do the same the other side, forcing the metal helmet over his head to descend a bit at a time," Balthasar said, as he turned a second wheel. "Normally, we would do this a little at a time, but listen to what happens when I force the beam down a bit."

Ambrosius watched as Balthasar moved from one wheel to the other, turning each several times before moving back to the other wheel. The man screamed at first, but as his mouth was clamped shut; his face took on an extraordinary appearance as it became increasingly squashed in the press. Through muffled screams, Ambrosius heard a series of noises that sounded like dry twigs popping on a hot fire. "What's making that crackling noise?" he asked curiously.

"It's the sound of his teeth breaking into his jaw bones. I'm told it's the most excruciating pain you can feel," Balthasar said, as he strained to turn the wheels harder.

Ambrosius watched in fascination as the man's face deformed further, his upper lip now being almost level with the lower part of his eyes. There were three or four loud cracks that came together and then the man shed tears. From the corner of his eyes red rivulets of blood streamed over his distended and deformed cheek. "What cracked?" Ambrosius asked.

"That was the bones around his eyes breaking up. I'm going to stop now otherwise I may split his skull into pieces. This one needs purifying at the stake tomorrow and it will be better for his soul if he is awake to feel his corrupt flesh melting from his bones before our almighty God decides his final destiny. God save his soul."

FIVE

It was four o'clock in the afternoon, two hours before Henry was due to start his next shift. Though he hated to be too early for work, if he didn't leave now, he'd catch the heavy traffic as everyone else travelled home from their work. If only I could have a normal job and work civilised hours, my life would be so much better.

A recent check of his bank balance had depressed him even further. He reasoned that even if he worked sixty hours a week, he was still about twenty pound a week short of his requirements. His car started on the fifth attempt and behaved as if it were running on kangaroo juice for the first mile of his five mile journey to work. Ideally, he'd prefer to use public transport and ditch the car, but there was no public transport when he finished his shift and taxi fares would cost more than running his car.

Two miles before he reached his place of work, he noticed a little orange light was glowing on his instrument panel. When he tried to accelerate past a taxi that stopped without indicating it was pulling in to a bus stop, his car slowed and juddered to a halt. This time it would not restart. He called work to say he might be a bit late and then spoke to a nice woman from the breakdown services, who told him it may be a couple of hours before anyone could come out as there were an unusually high number of callouts.

Dave, the mechanic, connected his laptop to something under the bonnet and asked Henry to turn on the ignition. "Your emu's died."

"I didn't know I had an emu under there, I thought it was an engine," Henry replied sarcastically.

"All cars have got emus these days. Technically they are known as the EMU or engine management unit. Anyway yours is as dead as a dodo."

"Are they very expensive?" Henry asked, already knowing the answer was going to be a 'yes'.

"Around five to seven hundred plus fitting, if we can get hold of one. This car's old enough to be a museum piece. I suggest you see what you can get for it as scrap and buy something a bit newer. I know a place not far from here that gives a good price for junk cars and I'll give you a tow there if you want."

Thirty minutes later, Henry walked away from Joe's cheap parts stores with a promissory note for seventy pounds when he handed in his car documents. He waited patiently for a bus, which came around thirty minutes after its scheduled time. He arrived at work two and a half hours after his shift was due to start. Just as he finished putting his uniform on, his duty manager, Steve, beckoned him to come over for a chat. "I didn't think you were coming in and I've given your shift to Dave," he said curtly.

"Sorry, but I did call in to say I might be late. My car died on me."

"I've covered your shift now so you can go home," Steve said, as he signed off a couple of receipts.

"But I need to work to pay my bills."

"Then you should get here on time. I'm not having you work this shift. The extra wages will come off my bonus."

Henry felt like calling his mother, he always felt like that when things were not working out, but he also knew he needed to make his own way in the world and not rely on others.

He thought about the pocket watch. If he sold it, his worries would disappear in an instant, but something that the stranger said entered his head. *What was his name? Gomory. Yes that was it. Gomory said I should keep the watch.*

When he got home, Henry opened the drawer he'd placed the watch in for safe keeping. He removed it and held it in his hand. Absently, he glanced down into the drawer and noticed the card Gomory had given him. For the first time he looked at it closely.

At the top of the card there was a logo showing an image of a camel with a woman sitting astride it. Under the picture was the company's name: *Dromedary Investments.* Under that were the details of the proprietor. *'Duchess' Gremory: Managing Director and Senior Investment Advisor. Past, present or future, who can be sure?* The only other information was a mobile phone number. Henry flicked the corner of the card with his finger until he found the noise irritated him. He opened his phone's keypad and dialled the number. A few seconds later, he heard a woman's smooth voice greeting him. "You are through to Helena Gremory, how may I assist you?"

Henry hesitated. "I have been given your contact details by..."

"Are you Henry King?" The voice interrupted. "I've been expecting a call from you."

"Yes, but how did you know it was..."

"Mont is a close friend of mine and he told me all about you. Can you come to my office at nine tomorrow morning so we can discuss your future position with us?"

Henry paused, there was something very disconcerting about the rapidity of this development, but he was desperate. "Yes that's fine, what's the address of your office?"

"I'll text it to you and see you at nine." She hung up.

His phone bleeped, indicating an incoming text message. He opened it and noted the address was for premises in Mayfair.

That evening, Henry rummaged through his drawers looking

for his one white shirt and two ties.

After consuming his last, slightly underdone frozen pizza, he tackled the problem of using, for the first time, the iron his mother bought him as a flat warming present. Eventually, he considered the shirt was wearable as all the deep creases were now only on the back part of it.

He decided to have an early night, set the alarm for seven on his phone and took out the old pocket watch. He studied the front of the case, fascinated by the myriad of minor scratches and dents. He rotated it and allowed the sharp flashes of ruby-red light reflected from the snake-eye jewels to enter his eye. For the first time, he noticed the case was not perfectly circular, but contained a complex asymmetry that suggested the watch casing had been distorted by violent incidents in its past history.

He rubbed his thumb over the case and allowed the sensations of its texture to evoke his mind. *I bet you hold more secrets than any living man? How old are you? What events have you witnessed with the passing of time?* He felt drowsy and reached for the card Mont gave him. He wondered if Dromedary Investments was based in the Middle East. The drawing on the card was simple, but even from the basic few lines used to produce the image; he could tell the woman sitting astride the camel was beautiful. Before he could think another thought, his heavy eyelids closed and he fell into a deep sleep.

His eyes opened in response to bright orange flashes that penetrated through his eyelids. The sky appeared on fire as dark clouds rolled above him to reveal fiery interiors that burned with a conflagration reminiscent of an intense volcanic eruption. Pinnacles of rock rose from the ground and appeared to waver in the flickering light cascading down from overhead. A blurry shape approached him, but its form eluded him as shadows clung around it, allowing no light to fall on its surface.

Only when it approached within a few paces of where he

stood, did the shadows fall away to reveal the rider and her beast, a one humped camel. He looked into the rider's face and couldn't draw his gaze away from her eyes. Her face was perfect, every proportion exact. Her eyes pulled at him, her mouth sucked him towards her, her nose inhaled his essence and when she smiled at him, he felt all his will to resist her impending consumption of him evaporating into the arid air.

He tried to speak to her, but every muscle in his throat went into spasm, his mouth boiled dry, his breath vaporised into a vacuum and his chest froze. She turned the camel around until her back faced him, and then she gestured for him to follow by raising her arm and curving it forward. As the camel advanced a few steps, shadows overtook it to obscure its outline. He rushed forward to catch up with her and as he drew near, the shadows pulled away to the sides to reveal another form.

A tall muscular figure with thick black hair and a neatly trimmed black beard stood before him. The figure pointed to him with one of its arms and the extended hand burst into flames. His body froze as two snakes with burning red eyes emerged from the flames and arched their heads nearer to his face. The snakes' mouths opened to reveal pairs of fangs and flicking forked tongues, then the figure held up his other hand and threw something high into the air.

Henry darted his eyes up to see what the object was. It was circular, spinning slowly and throwing out sharp flashes of red light. The spinning shape arced nearer to him and he held out his hand to catch it. In his hand there was a watch, a pocket watch, his pocket watch. He played his thumb over its surface and recognised the subtle distortions to its circular shape, the almost imperceptible dents and scratches rendered into its structure through countless centuries. Suddenly, the watch vibrated in his hand, the fire in the skies unfolded into drab greyness and the opening bars from *The Exorcist* played through his head. He woke to find he was grasping his phone, it was seven o'clock in the morning and his alarm had gone off.

The dream was still playing in Henry's head as he walked past the entrance to Dromedary Investments for the third time. The bus journey took twenty minutes less than he anticipated and he'd planned to arrive half an hour early, just in case. He checked the time on his phone and calculated it would do no harm to be ten minutes early. He climbed up the six black and white diamond latticed marble steps and pressed the only button set centrally on the door. He heard no audible chime or ring and wondered if he should press the button again. From somewhere behind the solid, navy blue coloured door, he heard a click and a clunk before the door silently opened inwards. He was greeted by an immaculately dressed man in his early thirties, whose appearance was spoilt by his unusual hair style that tried to disguise his advancing male pattern baldness.

"Good morning, the Duchess is expecting you. Please come in and I will show you to her office," the man said in an accent that could only have gained its embellishments from a public school education.

Henry tried to reply, but his throat froze and dark images from his nightmare flickered through his thoughts. He followed the man down a corridor the seemed to have no end and stopped outside a door drably painted in neutral beige. "Please go in, she is eager to meet you."

Henry stepped into the office, or was it a study. The room was large but filled with antique furniture that appeared to be part of a collection spanning every continent over several centuries. There was a single large window that must have been east facing. The morning sunlight flooded through it and reduced the outline of a woman sitting behind a mahogany desk to a silhouette.

Henry swallowed hard before forcing out a few words. "Good morning, Mrs Gremory, I'm Henry King, you're expecting me."

"Good morning, Henry. Please call me by my first name, Helena. When you are more familiar with me, you will call me Duchess. Don't be nervous, I'm not really a Duchess. It's just an affectionate nickname I picked up when I was at school. Come closer and sit down in front of me."

Henry looked at the small plain chair in front of the desk and stepped forward to sit on it. As he sat down, rays of sunlight cut into his eyes and temporarily blinded him.

"I'm so sorry. I forgot the sun comes in through the window at this time of the morning. I'll pull down the blinds and switch my lamp on."

Henry half-closed his eyes until he sensed the blinds were drawn. He still couldn't see what Helena looked like as the room was in near darkness. He heard the click of her lamp's switch and looked up to see the face of a woman he instantly recognised – the woman riding a camel in his dream – the woman with the most perfect face he'd ever seen.

He tried to work out her age without staring too deeply at her. She could be anywhere between thirty and fifty. She was not a girl – definitely a woman – he saw the faintest traces of age lines, but as she moved her face to speak again, they disappeared. "Henry, you're a good looking young man, a bit nervous but I can tell you have a pleasant demeanour. I think you're perfect for the position we have open at Dromedary Investments."

As she spoke to him, he switched his glance to her hands that were resting on the desk's surface. Slowly he tracked his vision up her bare arms to her shoulders. At first, he couldn't work out what was wrong. He looked at her face again and it hit him. *She hasn't got a single blemish anywhere on her skin. Not a freckle or a mole- it's unnatural. Is she wearing makeup all over her body?*

"Henry, how much would you like to earn?"

The question startled him. "As much as I can," was all he could think of replying as he studied her, hoping to discover at least one minor flaw in her features.

"Is ten thousand a month sufficient for you while you're training? If not, I could advance you another five thousand a month from your future earnings."

"How much – did you say ten thousand a month?"

"Yes, Henry. You are about to embark on a new phase in your life and become a very wealthy young man."

* * *

Chad: Present day.

Yasuf awoke with sweat pouring from every pore of his body. He moved his hand down to his private parts and breathed a sigh of relief when his hand contacted the moist warm skin that covered his testicles. For the third night in a row he dreamt a girl came into his tent and as she was seducing him, she pulled out a sharp knife secreted in her clothing and sliced his balls off. Since the incident, three days past, when he sliced the bags housing seven men's testicles from their screaming and squirming bodies, the thought of taking his wife or slave repulsed him. He crawled out from his tent into the hot humidity of another morning in the bush, slapped at the stinging insects that were already seeking him out and looked for Akubar.

He spotted him squatting beside the porridge pot, prodding at the glutinous contents with a thick twig. "Akubar, how are you this morning? Can I ask you something?"

"I'm good brother. What do you want to know?"

"I want to ask you something about your – condition."

"What you mean – my condition?"

"What's it like not to have any balls?"

"Oh that. Well brother, I suppose I'm used to it by now. It changed me but I guess you have to accept what you are. I take medicine every day to help me be a man. "

"Did it hurt much when they did it? Where you frightened?"

"Brother, there isn't any pain that could be worse. I was so scared. I thought I would definitely die. I could feel the blood pouring out of me and I squeezed my legs together as tight as I could, but I guess I was lucky they tied my balls off too tightly. You want some porridge, it's ready?" Akubar said, stirring the mixture in the battered pot.

"No thanks, I don't feel like eating at the moment. How long was it before they cut you down?"

"I think it was about three days. When you're hanging like that by arms, you can't breathe. It's hard to remember clearly. At some point the pain in my chest became greater than the pain…" Akubar pointed down to his crotch with the porridge covered stick. "Somewhere, I found something to keep me going. I prayed to God not to let me die, to give me one more chance to live. When they came to cut me down I was only half awake, but I remember someone shouting out that Allah had saved me for something special, that I was special."

"What happened then?"

"They gave me water and laid me down on a bed. I asked about Allah and they told me he was the true God. They asked me if I prayed to him and I said yes, I had. Listen brother, Allah is all powerful and if you serve him, he will look after you in this life and the next."

"Is it right we should be killing Christians the way we do?"

"Do you want to know about Christians? Let me tell you brother, for the last two thousand years the Christians have been killing our brothers in ways that are far worse than anything we do. They are disciples of the Devil and must be eradicated so we can all live in peace and give praise to Allah. Our God is greater than theirs."

"Do you miss going with a woman?"

"You can't miss what you've never had. My brother, we have an important visitor coming to see us today. He's a senior cleric and has been working with our brothers in other lands under the flag of the Islamic State. He is bringing us some special equipment and I have decided you are the one to use it."

"What equipment?"

"You'll have to wait and see. Now come, let's eat some of my delicious porridge."

SIX

Hamczel walked through the night along the meandering roadway that led to Harsburgh. It was by coincidence that he picked a night of a full moon to make the journey. The strong silver light gave him confidence to overcome any fears he had about walking alone in the dark. It was when the moon was at its highest point in the sky that he became aware of something moving parallel to his right. He stopped several times, but the dark shadow that shimmered at the edge of his vision merged into the shadows formed by trees and small hills in the outlying fields. He pressed on, quickening his pace and thought he heard panting sounds nearby. He whirled around and saw them.

For a brief moment, exposed in the full light of the moon, he clearly saw two wolves, one as black as the night sky and the other as white as the milky moon. They stopped and glared at him. The black wolf craned its head up to the sky, emitting a long drawn out howl that cut through his trembling flesh to expose raw primeval fears carried by humans since they first walked the Earth. Then they were gone.

He arrived in Harsburgh an hour after dawn and headed directly to the street he remembered Guther's shop was situated in. The street was virtually empty, a few people were shambling along the cobblestone road trying to avoid puddles that filled randomly formed potholes in the street's worn surface, but all the shops were still closed with their shutters fastened tight. Hamczel covered his mouth as he involuntarily yawned. He was about to take a stroll down the road in an effort to stave off the tiredness that crept over him, when he heard bolts being withdrawn behind the shutters of Guther's shop. Hamczel stepped up to the shop's front and wondered what he would do if the old man sent him away. One of the heavy wooden shutters swung open and the face of the old clockmaker stared out into the empty street. Hamczel smiled at him and stepped into the doorway. "Do you remember me? I spoke to you last autumn."

The clockmaker looked up and squinted before smiling back. "Yes, I remember. How can I help you – have you saved up enough money to buy one of my clocks?"

"No, I have no money. When I was here you told me you had no one to pass your skills onto and that I would understand what you meant. I now understand. Will you teach me how to make clocks?"

"Are you willing to devote your life and all the time within it to learning my craft?"

"If I stay in my village, my life and time will only prove to be a burden to me. Teach me your craft so I can master time and overcome the cruelty it hold over me."

"I cannot teach you to be a master of time, but I may be able to guide you to becoming a master of making time's keepers. There are many facets to making clocks, many skills to be acquired. If you are in no rush to achieve mastery of my craft, then I will take you on as my apprentice. I cannot pay you much, but I will give you board and lodgings for as long as you prove to be a deserving student."

"Does that mean you accept my offer then?"

"What is your name, remind me?"

"Hamczel."

"Come inside Hamczel. Have you eaten breakfast?"

"I have not eaten or slept since yesterday. I walked through the night to come here and my body is tired, but my mind is eager to learn. Start teaching me now."

"Hamczel, my boy, a tired mind and an empty stomach are like using flawed metal to make parts of a clock. In time they will fail in the task they are set to do. I will prepare you a breakfast of milk, honey and fresh bread. After you have eaten, sleep for a few hours and then we will make a start."

Over the next few days, Hamczel learnt the rudiments of time keeping. Guther taught him about cogs and gears, how the ratio of teeth affected their rate of turning. He instructed him on the designs of springs, both as methods of storing energy to make a clock run and as systems of oscillation to control the passing of time.

He detailed the workings of pendulums and discussed the merits of the properties of different metals used for making a clock's components. Hamczel was fascinated by the intricate machine Guther used to cut perfectly formed teeth into tiny cogs used for the smaller clocks. "Where did this machine come from?" Hamczel asked, as he watched Guther use the guides to aid him cut twenty four teeth into a gear wheel no larger than a small button.

Guther looked up and smiled. "I made it with my own hands. It took me ten years to cut and file all the parts, but once I made it, I could make smaller parts that are perfectly formed."

"How small can you make the parts?"

"With this machine, I can make a clock small enough to fit in your hand. I had hoped to make another machine that would make smaller parts, small enough to make a clock that would fit into a person's top pocket. My life is nearing its end, Hamczel. The spring that drives my body is nearly unwound. It is my hope that you may one day achieve my dream, to make a clock so small, it will fit into a closed hand."

Over the next two years, Hamczel became familiar with every

aspect of Guther's skills. Late one night, Hamczel tightened the last screw that held the chassis of his first clock together. He called out to Guther that he had completed building his first clock and waited for the old man to look at his work.

"Excellent work Hamczel. It is as good as I can make. I thought it would take you much longer to learn my craft than it has done. You have made me very happy."

The following morning, Hamczel woke up and made his way down the stairs to the shop. Guther was always up before him, but the old man was not there. He called out to Guther several times and hearing no reply, he went back up the stairs. Guther lay in his bed, he was very still and pale. Hamczel realised that the old man's spring had fully unwound.

For the next ten years, Hamczel continued making clocks, but every evening he spent a couple of hours working on making a copy of Gunther's machine, but smaller, much smaller.

Hamczel felt he owed it to Guther to achieve his dream of making ever smaller clocks, clocks small enough to fit into a pocket. One morning, as he was cutting teeth into a small cog, a man entered the shop. He looked up at the stranger and greeted him. "Good morning sir, are you looking to buy a clock?"

"Good morning. I've heard you are a very gifted clockmaker and I have a task for you."

"How can I help you sir?"

"I have a timepiece, but unfortunately one of the parts has broken. Do you think you can make me a replacement for me?"

Hamczel looked more closely at the stranger. He was well dressed. His jacket looked as if it were made from the finest black silk, his leggings were also made from a similar material and his boots were manufactured from perfectly stitched black leather. The man's angular face was framed with a finely trimmed beard and thick black hair brushed back over his head. Hamczel felt uneasy as the man's dark eyes fixed onto him. "Can you show me your clock and I'll see what I can do?"

The man reached into his pocket and removed a small circular silver case, which he placed onto Hamczel's workbench. Hamczel looked in puzzlement at the object in front of him. He'd seen something similar before, a small metal case used to hold fragrant herbs that could be sniffed to ease the symptoms of a cold or fever. "I don't understand?"

The man spoke calmly. "There is a clasp on the side that opens the front and back. Open it and you will understand."

Hamczel depressed the clasp and opened his mouth in shock. Under the front cover was a small clock face with a single hand. Running around the edge of the clock face were Roman numerals from one to twelve. It was what he saw when he opened the back cover that made him shake. He looked down in disbelief at the array of tiny gears, almost too small to see clearly. "Where – what – who made this?"

"It was made for me by a clockmaker in Italy but sadly the man has passed away. There is a small coiled spring that drives the mechanism and it has broken. I will pay you handsomely if you can make me a replacement."

"It's very small but I think I can make the part. It will take me a couple of days though."

"I'm in no rush, time means very little to me. I will come back in three days."

The man turned and left without saying another word. Hamczel picked up the tiny clock and incredulously looked at the small parts. It took him all of that day to partly dismantle the timepiece. Firstly he needed to file down the tips of his smallest screwdrivers to fit into the cuts in the tiny screws.

Eventually that evening, he reached the stage of withdrawing the broken spring. There was nothing remarkable about the design of the tiny clock, in fact it was a very simple, having just a single hand to denote the time of the day, but he failed to conceive how such tiny parts had been formed by the craftsman who built the object in front of him.

He spent the next day cutting and hardening a thin strip of iron, heating it in the small forge he used to change the malleability of metals and then plunging it in cold water. After several hours, he felt confident the strip of metal had the same dimensions as the broken spring. It took him most of the night to fit the spring and reassemble the parts.

An hour before dawn, he carefully wound the small knurled knob on the top of the timepiece and smiled as the one of the small wheels rotated back and forth on its hair thick pair of springs. He held the object up to his ear and felt his pride swelling as he listened to the rhythmic ticking of time passing by.

On the day after, early in the morning, the stranger walked into his shop. Hamczel looked up into the man's dark eyes and smiled. "I have repaired your little clock. It's as good as new."

"Such devices are not called clocks," the stranger replied.

"What are they called then?"

"This is a watch," the stranger said, picking up his timepiece. "A pocket watch as it's small enough to put in your pocket."

"I've never seen anything like it. Are there a lot of them in Italy?"

"This is the only one I know of that exists at the moment, but they will become common place in time. You should make watches like these; it will make your fortune. You will become rich and marry a beautiful woman, raise a large family and live in a big house."

Hamczel flicked his eyes up to the stranger. "I will never marry, I love only one woman and I can never marry her."

"If you were rich, she would surely have you?"

"It has nothing to do with money, she's dead."

"If you could meet her again in a different time, would that make you happy?"

Hamczel stood up and leant forward, resting his hands on

the workbench as he spoke. "I would give anything to have the chance of being with Crista again, anything."

"Do you really mean that?" the stranger asked, returning Hamczel's dark glare with his black eyes.

"Who are you? I don't even know your name. Why are you making me think about Crista?"

"You ask many questions at once. I am Duke Gomory, the last line of a very old family. I'm not forcing you to think of your lost love, you are doing that of your own volition." Gomory slipped his hand into his pocket and pulled out two gold coins, which he carefully laid out on the workbench. "Here is my payment for your work. I have another task for you if you care to undertake it. My payment will come in two parts. Fifty gold coins for each year you work for me, and the promise that in the future you will find your love again."

Hamczel felt his blood draining from his face. With cold sweat breaking out on his skin, he tried to absorb the last words the stranger said. Fifty gold coins like the two in front of him were more than he could expect to earn in a lifetime, no two lifetimes. It was the last words the stranger had spoken that made him reel and withdraw into an abstract reality. "How do you mean, find my love again?"

"Time is a strange traveller. She has a past and a future, but what we know, what our essence feeds on is *now*. Already, what I've said has moved from now to the past, and what I'm about to say is the future. All parts of time are one. Have you noticed how past events happen again. How the hands of a clock sweep over the same path they did the day before," Gomory said, drawing a circle in the air with his hand.

"Of course I have, but what has that to do with bringing Crista back?" he asked.

"When the winter snows and ice melt away they are not gone, they return in the following year. At the end of each day, the sun fattens and reddens, slipping from our awareness through the darkness of night, only to return in its brilliance and rekindle our waking world the next day," he said, closing his hands together before spreading his arms wide. "My friend, if you do as I ask, one day your essence and that of your lady will conjoin in a new phase. It will not be your life or hers, but the essence of each of you will come together again and what you could have had, will be fulfilled in different lives in a new cycle."

"How can this be achieved?" Hamczel cried out.

"You will make me a watch, a watch like no other."

"I don't understand."

"I will guide you, provide you with the materials, shape the design and empower you to gain mastery over the cruelty of your loss. All I ask is for you to work for no more than two hours a day, every day, until the watch is complete. I will pay you in advance," Gomory said, lifting a bag from inside his jacket. "Here are fifty gold pieces, your first year's wages."

"What if I don't have the skills I need to build your watch?"

"I will teach you everything you need to know."

"When do I start?"

"You will start straight away. The first thing you must do is make a new machine to form the smaller sized parts. The machine you have over there," Gomory said, pointing to the machine Hamczel took years to make. "It is too large. You must make a copy, but one quarter the size."

"But that will take me years."

"I estimate no more than five. I will return in exactly five years with four bags of coins. If you have completed making your machine by then, I will pay you for your work and give you drawings of how to make my new pocket watch."

Before Hamczel had the chance to ask any more questions, Gomory turned around and walked out of his shop. Hamczel ran to the opening, but the stranger was nowhere to be seen.

For the first few days he counted the coins over and over, arranged them in piles of fives, then tens, but he did not start to build a new machine.

On the fifth night after Duke Gomory visited him, he dreamt of Crista. He was in a strange town filled with tall buildings like nothing he'd seen before. The surface of each tower was like the smooth surface of a tranquil lake that reflected images of nearby buildings so that they looked as if they were part of its walls.

He walked down a wide street and ahead saw an approaching figure dressed in white. As he neared, he could see the figure was a woman, but when she drew close to him she pulled a veil across her face.

She stood directly in front of him before taking his wrist in her hand. She raised his hand until his fingertips touched her veil. He noticed his missing little finger was grown back. He briefly curled it to check his new reality. He clasped the veil and pulled it from her face, it was Crista. He moved his hand to the back of her neck and pulled her to him, felt his lips press against the soft yielding tissue of hers. For what seemed a time with no end, he tasted the familiar scent of her warm breath as their mouths coupled in conjoined union. He woke – alone – cold – empty.

Over the next few weeks, Hamczel worked on building his new machine. Every day he visited the blacksmith's workshop and gave him orders for metal parts he would take back to his workshop. He worked with fine files to shape and form each part, used his older machine to make smaller and finer worm gears for progressing each cog through a fraction of a turn.

The weeks turned to months and the months to years, until, four years and eleven months later, his miniature machine was built. He was unsure, to the day, when it would be exactly five years since Gomory visited him.

For three days he fidgeted nervously, frequently stepping out from his shop into the road hoping to catch a glimpse of a stranger in a dark suit. After one of these brief excursions into the world outside the confines of his workshop and display area, he returned to his task of completing a wall clock ordered by Count Vladimir.

Just as he was aligning a section of the sub-chassis holding the chiming mechanism, he realised there were two people standing in front of him and watching him closely. He looked up into the faces of two of the prettiest young ladies he'd ever seen in his life. He coughed lightly to try and hide the flushing heat he could feel spreading across his cheeks.

The girl on the left smiled at him, displaying a row of immaculate petite teeth that reminded him of Crista's. "Good afternoon Hamczel. I am Gertrude and this is my friend Maria. We have come to buy one of your best clocks," she said, pointing to a row of the smallest and most ornate clocks on display in his shop.

Hamczel studied the two girls before replying. The one who spoke to him, Gertrude, was incredibly pretty. Her blond hair was tied into braids, which she had arranged in winding coils on her head. He flicked a glance into her green almond shaped eyes, traced his vision down her long but delicate nose and drank the image of glistening moistness in her full, soft and pink lips before admiring her shapely and well defined feminine jawline.

He turned to look at the other girl, who was smiling alluringly at him. She had a darker complexion enhanced by large liquid brown eyes that seared into his fluttering chest. He roamed through the folds of her glossy, almost black hair, followed the definition of her cheek bones supporting her flawless smooth skin and coughed once more before replying. "Are you looking for anything in particular?" *How does she know my name?*

"We're looking for something pretty – delicate – ornate. That one there, the one that looks like a little house covered in flowers. Can I take a closer look?"

"Of course," Hamczel said, moving awkwardly from behind his work bench to the display shelf. "I'm afraid it's rather expensive though, the clock parts are made from the finest metals and each flower is centred with a precious gemstone."

Maria spoke for the first time. "The price is of no consequence, our – guardian has told us to come here and choose whatever we desire."

Hamczel was taken aback when he heard her speak. She spoke with a foreign accent. Her voice was deep but somehow enticing. He could not imagine any man refusing to do as she asked. "Is your guardian coming to my shop?"

Gertrude giggled and nudged Maria with her elbow. "He's not really our guardian, he's our – lover."

"What both of you?" Hamczel asked, before he realised how inappropriate his question sounded.

"Both of us and he satisfies us in more ways than you could imagine," Maria said, as she lifted the clock off the shelf to examine it more closely.

Hamczel turned away from the women and came face to face with someone he recognised, Gomory was standing directly behind him. "I'm sorry. I didn't hear you come in. How long have you –"

"I've been here long enough to hear you talking with these two women," he interrupted.

Hamczel studied Gomory's face for a few seconds, trying to work out what was different. His thick dark hair was the same, his beard was immaculately groomed, but there was something strange about him. He looked into Gomory's eyes and noticed what was different about him from the last time he saw him. There were no fine lines to date the age of his skin, no furrows on his brow, no creases tracing down from the edge of his nose to his mouth – he looked younger despite the passing of five years. "You're looking well," was all he could think to say.

"I am well, Hamczel, very well. I see you have met my two companions, lovely creatures, aren't they?"

"Yes delightful, you are a lucky man," Hamczel replied, glancing at the two women.

"It is not luck, Hamczel. These ladies have had the good fortune to be chosen by me," Gomory said, moving away from Hamczel and nearer to the two young women. "Tell the clockmaker how lucky you are to be chosen as my companions."

Maria spoke first. "Before I met the Duke, I was working in a merchant's tavern. My parents became ill and I became desperate to find work. By day, I served the merchants food and beer, but at night I surrendered my body to old men that took but gave no pleasure. I made just enough money to feed and clothe myself. One day, the Duke entered the tavern and asked me if I would join him on his travels. He promised me fine clothes and all I could eat if I would keep him company. Now I want for nothing and when I say nothing, I mean nothing. The Duke knows how to please a woman more than any other man."

Gertrude then told her story to Hamczel. "I was born into a noble family that came into hard times. My father forced me to marry Count Hiedrich, who was a very wealthy, but very old man. For a year the Count made me do vile things to his withered body, but he suffered a weakness in his manly regions and I remained intact as he could not break into me. The Count's health failed and he died. The Duke appeared at the funeral and offered to look after me if I joined him and Maria on their travels. At first I was unsure, but when the Duke showed me how a man can love a woman, I knew I never wanted to be apart from him."

Hamczel felt his face burning with embarrassment as the girls told their story. He'd never heard anyone talk so openly about their personal life before and felt an urge to press his fingers into his ears to block out the tales he was hearing.

"Maria, Gertrude, I have business to discuss with this clockmaker. I will purchase the clock you have chosen. Why don't you find a dress shop and chose something special to wear, something you think I would like to see you in later tonight," Gomory said, in such a way the two women left Hamczel's shop without delaying.

"Now Hamczel, I have some drawings that I want you to take a look at," Gomory said, holding out a long silk covered object he was carrying.

Hamczel watched as Gomory carefully remove a length of rolled up parchment from a fine black silk cover. Gomory slowly rolled the parchment out flat onto the top of Hamczel's workbench before gesturing to him to take a closer look. Hamczel glanced at the first sheet of parchment, observing there were detailed drawings of more than thirty gear wheels and cogs of different shapes and sizes. The second sheet was covered with drawings of levers and springs, but hidden under the top two sheets of parchment; Hamczel saw there were at least another six sheets. The top sheet fluttered briefly as a cold gust of wind drove in through the open shop front.

Gomory held the sheets flat with his smooth hands. "The drawings detail the components you need to engineer to make my pocket watch. I have drawn everything exactly a hundred times larger than the actual size of the parts. You can see I've added notes to tell you which metal to use for each piece you will make."

"This will take me years to complete and where will I find the metals you describe?" Hamczel said, realising the enormity of the task that lay ahead of him.

"I have under my cloak, five bags. Four hold gold coins, my payment for work you have completed up to now. The fifth bag contains the pieces of metal you will need to make these parts. I have calculated that if you work for one hour a day, ten years from now, you will be ready for the next stage."

"What is the next stage?"

"For you to assemble these cogs, levers and springs into the internal workings of my watch. Ten years to this day, I will return with the next set of drawings." Gomory then reached inside his cloak and pulled out five black silk bags that he carefully placed on top of the unrolled pieces of parchment.

At first, Hamczel worked on the parts of the watch for several hours each day, but found his eyes grew tired as he strained to focus on the tiny teeth of the gears he was making were accurately cut. The weeks turned to months and the months to years, until the day came that every tiny piece was made.

This time, Hamczel kept a careful check on the dates and sat back in his chair satisfied that he still had five days to wait before Duke Gomory was due to make his next visit. Just as he was about to retire for the night, he heard a heavy knocking on the closed shutters of his shop front. "Who is it?" he shouted.

"It's me, Duke Gomory. I have come with the next set of drawings."

"You're five days early," Hamczel called out, rising from his chair.

"So are you. As you have completed the first stage, I thought I would also come early."

Hamczel was about to ask how he knew he'd finished his work, but thought better of it. "Wait there, I'll open the shutters."

Hamczel pulled back the bolts on one of the shutters to let Gomory enter his shop. Even by the light of the single wavering candle flame, Hamczel saw Gomory had not aged a day since he last met him. His bearded face showed no traces of lines or wrinkles that mark the passing years of mortal men.

Gomory seemed to be anxious to complete their dealings as quickly as possible. Before Hamczel had the chance to welcome him, he'd unpacked and laid out the next set of drawings.

Hamczel listened as Gomory explained how the drawings detailed each stage of assembling the watch's workings and how the case was to be constructed. It was then that Hamczel realised how different the watch would be from a normal clock. Instead of having hands, the time was displayed by a set of nine moving concentric rings. Each ring had one or more holes in it and exposed symbols on a back plate. As Gomory talked rapidly about the intricacies of the watch's workings, a thought tore through Hamczel's mind.

"Wait, stop for a moment. What has this got to do with me and Crista? You told me that one day I will be reunited with Crista, but what part can this watch play in that?"

"I've been waiting for you to ask that question," Gomory said, looking deeply into Hamczel's eyes.

"Well I've asked it, so what's the answer?"

"Did you notice that two of the gears I asked you to make have fine grooves cut into them?"

"Yes, I wondered about that," Hamczel said slowly.

"If you truly want to enter the cycle that will bring the essence of the two of you into union, then you must do as I say."

"What must I do?"

"Do you have anything that is of Crista?"

"I don't understand. What do you mean?"

"Do you have a lock of her hair, a clipping from a fingernail or a tooth from her childhood? Do you have any part of her?"

Hamczel pictured the piece of jawbone he kept under his pillow. "I do, but I don't want to destroy all that I have left."

"Listen, Hamczel. Those two gears do not continue to turn in one direction, they move back and forth with the cycle of the stars. Those two grooves will align in some distant time and if they hold a part of you and a part of the girl you seek, then when they are aligned, you will be conjoined with the one you seek."

Hamczel remembered that in his drawer there was a piece of muslin that protected Crista's severed toe and his little finger.

He had placed the two digits side by side, kept them together as the only union he and Crista could have. "Would a sliver of bone from each of us do?" he asked.

"Do you have that in your possession?"

"I do."

"That would be perfect."

Over the next ten years, Hamczel assembled the workings of the watch and etched the intricate relief on the front casing. When he finished, he admired the single letter 'G' that was partly engulfed by a coiled snake wound around it.

The hardest task had been making the complex levers that released the casing when each eye of the snake was depressed from left to right. The eyes were made from small rubies that proved difficult to mount into the ends of hidden bars secreted behind the front case.

Hamczel spent many days trying to calculate when the hair thick strands of bone he had painstakingly shaved from his finger and Crista's toe would align inside the watch. But the workings were so complex, with off centre gears changing the directions of different parts of the gear train frequently, he lost track of their progress after the passing of more than a couple of centuries. When he started making the parts he was baffled by the inclusion of three tiny lead weights that were free to swing like tiny pendulums. Now the watch was complete, he realised that with every movement, the lead pendulums acted to wind up the main spring that drove the mechanism. This watch would never need to be wound if it was moved around by its owner once every few months.

Ten years to the day since he last saw Gomory, Hamczel waited anxiously for his visitor to return. As the day wore on, the thought of ever parting with the watch he'd made haunted his wondering mind. Just as the sun was setting, Gomory walked into the small shop looking no different than he had twenty years earlier.

Hamczel gained comfort from this, realising for certain that Gomory was no ordinary man. "The watch is complete except for the back casing. Also, I'm not sure how to set the time and align all of the rings into the correct position," Hamczel said, without first greeting his visitor.

"Good afternoon, Hamczel, I trust you are keeping well?"

"Sorry, I didn't mean to be discourteous, it's just that I've devoted over half my life to making this watch and I was impatient to tell you of my progress."

"There is no need to be sorry as I understand your feelings concerning this piece of work. Give me the watch and I will set the dials into their correct positions. When I have finished, I want you to fit the back casing in place. I have a small bottle of liquid I will give you. I want you to smear the liquid around the edge of the casing before you fit the back on the watch."

Hamczel raised his eyebrows and frowned heavily. "Why?"

"Once the watch is set in motion it's essential that its workings must never be tampered with. The liquid I'm giving you is a resin from a very rare tree and once it dries, it will form a seal that can never be broken."

"Are you going to take the watch away with you?" Hamczel said, feeling a sense of panic rising through him.

"No, I'm leaving the watch in your safe hands. I want you to look after it for me until my next visit."

"When will that be?"

"I don't know, that depends on you," Gomory replied, as he rotated the gears in the watch. "The workings are in position. Here is the bottle of resin, remember to do as I said. Make sure you keep the watch in your pocket, it will remain fully wound if it is moved a little each day."

Hamczel noticed Gomory was reaching inside his cloak for something. Gomory tugged at something around his waist and lifted a heavy black bag onto Hamczel's workbench. "This is the remainder of what I owe you for your labours. Use the money in whatever way you deem fit."

"I'm forty five years old and already have more money than I can ever spend. You don't need to pay me anymore," Hamczel said, pushing the heavy bag back towards Gomory.

"It is yours. Do with it as you will. I must go now but I will return when the time is right."

Over the next hour, Hamczel applied a coating of the resin to the edge of the back casing and gently tapped it in place with a small hammer. He waited for another hour before placing the watch in his pocket, picking up the bag of gold coins and climbing the stairs to his bedroom above the shop.

Over the next ten years, Hamczel concentrated on making pocket watches. These were much simpler than the one he made for Gomory, featuring nothing more than minute and hour hands. The watches were wound by a knurled knob set in the top of the casing and would pass the time for two or three days after each winding.

In time, word about this wonderful new invention spread through the valleys and Hamczel found his order book was filled with the names of various Dukes, Counts and Princes. When he turned sixty years of age, he found his eyesight was failing him and he was no longer able to craft the small intricate parts he needed to make his watches. He returned to making clocks, but found his passion for producing time-keeping artefacts was waning alongside his vision. Early one morning, an elderly man with thick silver hair and a trimmed white beard entered his shop.

"Good morning, Hamczel. I have returned," he said, as he passed through the doorway.

"Do I know you?" Hamczel asked, squinting through the hazy fog of his cataracts at the man's face.

"You have something of mine in your possession, a pocket watch."

"Surely, you can't be."

"Duke Gomory, I am."

"But you're so…"

"Old? I use the nature of time as it best suits me and it suits me to be old at present."

"Have you come for my – your pocket watch?"

"You are correct, it is *my* pocket watch. Listen to me carefully, Hamczel. It will, for all time, be my watch, but it's not meant for my possession. You must look after my watch until you die. The watch will know how to find its next keeper and the one after that. Make sure you care for my watch, if you act irresponsibly you will affect future conjunctions and your meeting with the woman you desire so much will be tainted. You will not see me again during your lifetime as we must part on separate pathways. I bid you farewell."

"Wait. How long before I see Crista again?"

"The question has no meaning. You will never see her in *your* time, but in another time," were the last words Hamczel heard from Gomory's lips.

For the next couple of years, Hamczel passed the time by repairing clocks that had worn or broken over the ages.

The winter of his sixty-second year of life was particularly harsh, with deep snows blocking the roads and penetrating frosts that ate down into the bones of the elderly. Hamczel found it too cold to work, and spent most of his days lying under the covers of his bed in an attempt to fend off the biting chill that etched through every fibre of his body.

With little to occupy him, he passed the time gazing at the slowly moving rings of the pocket watch and thinking of what might have been if Crista had not died out on the glacier.

As the months passed, the first hint of spring broke through the icy fog that had enshrouded the town of Harsburgh all that winter. Hamczel woke in his bed to see a shaft of warming sunlight breaking into his room. He stirred under the covers and heard a loud rapping noise coming from the shop below him.

As he pulled himself out from the comfort of his warm bed, he heard a voice calling his name. He pulled a blanket around his shoulders and eased his way down the steep flight of stairs leading to his shop.

"I'm coming, wait there," he called out as the shutters shook again.

With difficulty, he pulled back the two stiff bolts that secured the shutter before lifting it into its open position. An old man stood in the doorway, releasing voluptuous torrents of steaming breath into the cold air as he exhaled. "Are you Hamczel from the hamlet of Thewa?"

Hamczel thought back. The village he'd grown up in had a name but nobody used it. They'd just said 'our village' or 'the village, 'but a distant recollection came to him. "Yes I am he. Who wishes to know at this early hour?"

"I do," the man said, pushing past Hamczel.

"Who are you and what do you want?" Hamczel said abruptly, feeling rising annoyance with the intruder.

"I am Albert from the village of Purin. You've heard of Purin?"

"Yes," Hamczel replied, recalling that was the name of Crista's village.

"I understand you were promised to be married to a girl from my village."

"Yes, her name was Crista but she…"

"Was my wife."

"You are mistaken. Crista was going to marry me. She was returning over the glacier to be with me when…"

"She was returning over the glacier to tell you she had married me. She never wanted you, but thought I didn't want her. When she told me she met you I asked her to marry me, and she accepted. We were married three weeks before she travelled over the pass to tell you she would not be yours."

Hamczel stood back and took a deep breath. "You're lying.

Crista was going to marry me. She loved me."

"She liked you, but when I bedded her, deflowered her, and showed her what a man can do for a woman, she turned her love to me."

"Get out, go," Hamczel screamed.

Through that day, Hamczel paced around his shop and repeatedly opened and closed the pocket watch. He felt the watch in his hand, thought of the two parts, pieces of him and Crista that were inside the watch he laboured to make through all his adult life.

As the afternoon matured to evening, the skies darkened. Their impending dissolution into night was broken by harsh flashes of approaching lightning. As the first rains cascaded down, Hamczel threw open the shutters of his bedroom window and cast the pocket watch into the muddy street below.

Albert walked steadily along the mountain pass. For over forty years he carried the burden of Crista's rejection. As he aged, his bitterness consumed his every waking thought until today. Finally he'd found the courage to confront the man who took Crista from him. The hurt that passed though him when she refused his proposal because she loved another had severed his boyhood dreams of what it would be to become a man.

He could see how his lies had cut through Hamczel, destroyed what remained of his life, and it felt good. He quickened his pace as the rain fell harder and headed for the shelter of a large conifer. A burst of lightning straddled the sky and Albert froze as he saw the outlines of two wolves in the overhead sky.

Formed from clouds, he was certain he saw a black and a white wolf sitting side by side. He reached the shelter of the tree and looked up at sky again. A fork of lightning seared from cloud to cloud, from the black wolf to the white one, before a white light burst from the black wolf's mouth and scorched down through the branches of the tree under which he was taking shelter.

Hamczel made a decision: tomorrow he would set off and make his way to Albert's village. He had to know the truth, know for sure that Crista had given herself to another. Since he met Gomory all he cared about was meeting Crista in some future life. But if she loved another and did not want him then his life had been in vain. The years spent making the watch, wasted. The watch, he'd thrown away in a moment of anger.

What had Gomory said? *The watch will know how to find its new keeper.* Had he, in throwing it away before he died laid a curse on the watch? Hamczel walked over to the open window and looked down at the sodden roadway that was intermittently visible in the flickers of nearby lightning flashes. He contemplated going down to look for the watch, but the intensity of the rain increased and his head span with dizziness. He fell back on his bed and almost at once fell into a deep sleep.

Hamczel knew he was in a dream despite the intense reality of what was around him. He was walking along the mountain pass that led to his village. He recognised the familiar shape of the mountain range ahead of him and surged forward up the steep climb that would take him home. Through the lines of pine trees to his left and right, he caught fleeting glimpses of something moving.

To his left, a white shape flicked behind the compact cover of closely knitted tree trunks, while to his right, a black darkness stole through the shadows without showing itself. He stopped abruptly and turned to his left, just catching an outline of a white wolf disappearing behind a thick clump of trees. He waited for a few minutes, but there was no sign of the animal.

Turning to continue his walk, he saw something was coming down the path ahead of him. At first, he thought it was a rider atop their horse, but the movement of the animal was unlike anything he'd seen before.

As the rider approached, he saw it was a woman mounted on a strange beast. The animals face was shorter and more rounded than that of a horse, and its legs were thinner and longer, giving it a top-heavy appearance. As it neared, he saw the animal was deformed with a large hump on its back. Something to the side of the woman's waist glittered in the sunlight and though he'd never seen a royal crown before, he recognised it for what it was from boyhood memories of stories he heard about kings and queens.

He called out to the woman. "What animal you are riding?"

She answered back in a voice he instantly recognised. "It is a camel, a horse of the desert."

He felt his heart thumping violently in his chest. The woman's voice, it was Crista's. "Are you who I think you are?" he called out, holding his chest.

"Yes my beloved, I have come to give you a message."

"Were you true to me?"

"I was always true to you and I will be for all time. Follow me. I want to show you something."

She turned the camel off the track and headed towards a thick clump of conifers.

"What are you going to show me?"

"The result of deceit and lies. Do you see the tree that has been struck by lightning? Walk to it and see what lies on the ground under it."

Hamczel walked forward, clutching his chest, which felt as if it was about to explode. On the ground at the base of the burnt out tree was a man. He looked as if he was sleeping but when Hamczel drew nearer; he saw the man's face was missing. Where his eyes, nose and mouth should have been there was a dark hole exposing the inside of his empty and blackened skull. "Who is he?"

"Look at his clothing and all will be clear to you."

Hamczel looked at the tattered tunic, the worn leggings and the scuffed boots. "They are the same clothes as worn by a man that visited me earlier today. Is this Albert?"

"Albert no longer exists. Look into my face Hamczel."

He tore his eyes from the gaping hole that was once Albert's face and looked up into the beautiful face of the woman mounted on the strange beast. "Crista, it is you. Why are you here?"

"You were recently wronged and I have come to undo that wrong before I continue on my journey."

"Did you ever love this man? Did you let him touch you? Did you marry him?"

"No, I never felt anything for him while I lived. He wronged us, Hamczel. Now he has paid the price for his evil, and what remains of him, will shortly be consumed for all eternity from this Earth. Move away from his body so they can finish what they are here to do."

From his left and right, he saw the pair of wolves approaching. He took a step towards Crista, but the thumping in his chest stopped and day became night.

On the fifth day that Hamczel's shop did not open for business, his neighbours broke the main shutter down and entered his property. As they began to climb the stairs, they started to gag on the overpowering stench of death. Outside, a passing traveller noticed something glinting in the morning sunlight. He bent down to see what it was that was partly buried in the dried out mud of a deep rut in the road. Using his thumb, he swiped the clinging debris from the front of the object and saw the bright red eyes of a snake coiled around a letter 'G'.

✸ ✸ ✸

Bavaria: 1480

Burgermeister Clemens of Gothburgh wiped his beard to remove the juices spilling from the ribs of a suckling pig he was chewing. He surveyed his two guests, checking they were relaxed now they had feasted and drunk liberal quantities of the finest ale. He felt confident about the way things were progressing with Archbishop, Jander, but the young Franciscan monk troubled him.

What was his name? Kunrat – yes that was it. He felt disturbed at what the man had said a few minutes ago. *You must understand, Burgermeister, no one can be excluded from being a heretic, no matter what their position or level of hierarchy in society.*

To discover that this man, barely older than twenty had been appointed Chief Inquisitor for this region troubled him. He decided to pick up the conversation again by addressing the Archbishop. "My Grace, I trust everything is in order. May I ask how long you intend to stay in Gothburgh?"

"That depends on how long it takes us to complete our task, Burgermeister. As I explained to you earlier, we are under instructions from the Pope and King Frederick to discover and eliminate all heretics from this region. I cannot stress how important it is to purify the population and enable good catholic people the opportunity to devote their lives in the praise of God. This is only possible if they are not distracted by false teachings and the influence of the greedy and corrupt. Do I make myself clear?" he said, reaching for his cup. "Have you another bottle of that excellent wine you served us earlier? It really is quite a delightful tipple to accompany a serious conversation." Archbishop Jander raised his nearly empty cup and drained the last dregs of Burgermeister, Clemens' finest wine.

"I'll send my servant down to the cellar and see if we have another bottle. If not, I'm sure he'll select something equally delectable. I agree wholeheartedly with you my Grace. I'm sure we will all become better citizens once you have finished your work."

"Burgermeister, I am led to believe there are several families of great influence living in castles set in the higher lands of the mountains. We have found that these families are more often than not the centres of demonic practices, a remnant from the days when demons ruled these obscure lands."

"I have heard such rumours, my Grace, but I have never had dealings with these hidden elite. As far as I know, there is only one such family in this area, residing in Gothburgh Castle. Despite the commonality of the names, our pious town has no dealings with this family. It is my understanding they control all the lands that extend beyond the castle, including the three main valleys that form the lower regions of the mountain range you see to the east of us."

"I'm glad to hear that Burgermeister. When we have identified and eradicated all the heretics from your town, we will march on this castle, destroy the demons within and claim all the lands for the purposes of our great Church and the glory of God. I ask you to accompany, Inquisitor Kunrat, to the preliminary trials of your town's heretics. While you do so, I will sip your wine and consider how best to assign you a suitable role to assist God's salvation of your wretched people."

Kunrat sat with his head bowed as if in silent prayer. Slowly, he slid his hands forward across the table and rose to his feet. He turned and raised his head so that his features were visible in the candlelight. Clemens studied the cold hard features of the man's face: His long pointed nose, deep set emotionless eyes, thin lips framed by a narrow angular chin and the shadowed craters of his pock marked cheeks.

Clemens considered him to be one of the most unsavoury looking people he'd seen with the exception of a few he'd come across bearing the final stages of leprosy. Kunrat pulled back his lips in an attempt at a smile. "Burgermeister, please follow me. It is time to reveal the heinous devilment and delinquency of your town's people."

Clemens walked two paces behind Kunrat, as they crossed the small square to the town hall recently requisitioned for the interrogation of the first wave of heretics identified by the Inquisition. They were still a minute's walk away from the large wooden building, when he heard the piercing screams coming from within the hall. With each step, he picked out the sound of a different person screeching like a maimed cat.

Above all the cries and shouts of agony, he trembled at what must be happening to one particular woman, as her shrieks were so discernible above the others it made him cease the ruminations of his imagination in an effort to mask out her cries of torment.

Kunrat passed through the open doorway and Clemens hesitantly followed. The main part of the building consisted of a large central hall that provided an open space for meetings, wedding parties and other ceremonial gatherings. There were three tiers of open balconies set on the side walls and it was these that initially caught Clemens' attention.

Fastened to the rails of the uppermost balconies there were at least a dozen sets of large pulleys. From each pulley there was a person suspended by a rope. By the light cast from numerous blazing torches, Clemens watched as the naked bodies of hanging men were pulled level to the upper balcony before being dropped. The men were fastened to the ropes by their wrists, which were cruelly contorted to a position above the back of their heads. A quick glance was enough for him to see that the elbow and shoulder joints of each man was already dislocated, while those more advanced in the progress of the process showed signs of the impending dismemberment of their upper limbs.

He turned his attention to the source of the incessant screaming, but could only see a group of robed figures crowed around a table. One of the figures appeared to be struggling with something as his shoulders writhed from side to side. Once again a long wailing scream drowned out all other cries.

"What is going on there?" Clemens called out to Kunrat, while pointing to the group gathered around the table.

"We discovered a most terrible witch dwelt among you. She tried to escape her fate by offering herself to her captors. It is essential we make her confess her sins before purifying her soul at the stake. Come I will show you how this is done."

Clemens swallowed and let Kunrat lead him to the table. As they approached, Kunrat waved the men aside and Clemens saw a sight that remained with him until the day he died.

The woman was about thirty years old and had been stripped of all her clothing. She was tied down to the table by thick ropes tightly bound around her waist. Her legs were raised and forced into an open position. Protruding from her bloody crotch was a long metal rod with a wheel set at the end. Fastened to her, there were two metal implements set with three sharp talons that were buried into the soft fleshy tissue of each of her breasts. "What are you doing to her?" Clemens shouted to Kunrat, so he could make himself heard over the surrounding wails.

"It is the standard method of interrogation for witches. The device inserted into her is the pear. As the wheel is turned, four petals open up inside her. Each petal is set with a sharp barb to cut into her flesh," Kunrat hissed, before running his tongue over his lips.

"The thought of it makes me feel sick," Clemens said, leaning forward to take a closer look at the implement.

"This creature is temptress of Satan and her womb must be destroyed to ensure she can never give birth to a demon should she arise from her ashes after burning at the stake. Her breasts are soon to be torn from her body, so she can never provide milk for her demonic spawn. As you can bear witness, it's no easy matter to be one of God's Inquisitors. Burgermeister,"

"Yes, I can see you have to put a lot of effort into extracting the truth from these creatures."

"I advise you look closely at what happens to those deemed to be a heretic. As this town's most important citizen, I'm sure you want give us your complete cooperation and prove your loyalty to God and his Church. I would hate to think of the consequences should you be suspected of holding heretical views. Do we have an understanding?"

Clemens took one more look around him, but did not look at the woman again. "I understand and assure you I will cooperate with you in any way you desire."

SEVEN

Henry walked away from the ATM clutching a mini-statement in his trembling hand. He had read the balance of his account at least six times in the past minute, but still could not believe this was happening to him. All that money and I've not even done a minute's work for it yet. As he thought more about what was happening, his anxiety levels rose higher. What if I'm no good at the job, will she want the money back? What is the job? What will they want from me?

He hesitated to look up at the shop signs. Helena, or the Duchess, had instructed him to go to an Italian tailors in Savile Row. Tonight he was to dine with her at a swish restaurant he couldn't pronounce the name of to discuss his future employment role.

She had impressed on him how important it was to dress appropriately for every occasion, be it business or pleasure, and handed him a card with the name and address of a bespoke gentleman's outfitters. He looked down the street and spotted the sign for 'Corrionno's Gentleman's Apparel' a few shops ahead of where he stood.

As he approached the entrance door, he caught sight of his reflection in the main window, and shuddered at the contrast between his misshapen fleece and over-washed jeans to the impeccably cut suits on display in the window.

A diminutive man with slicked back dark hair and a pencil thin moustache approached him before he was fully through the doorway. "Good afternoon, how can I help you sir?"

Henry fumbled in his pocket and pulled out the card the Duchess gave him. "I've been told to come here and buy something suitable," he said, taking a deep breath.

The man turned the card over and raised his perfectly shaped eyebrows when he saw the hand written note on the back of the card. Henry had been tempted to translate the short message, written in Italian by Helena before she gave him the card, but he found it impossible to make out the exact lettering of her flowing writing. "Is the occasion business or pleasure?"

"What do you mean by occasion?" Henry asked.

"Sir, the note on this card says, 'Dress this young man so that he will dazzle me at dinner tonight'."

"I think its business, I'm just starting a new job with this lady's firm and she's going to tell me what I have to do."

"Not to worry sir, we'll take care of everything and ensure you're covered for both options."

Henry felt uncomfortable about what the man said. The Duchess was an outstandingly beautiful woman but not his type, or rather he felt, he was not her type.

Before he could think further, he was dragged to the back of the shop. From seemingly nowhere, a horde of men dressed in black suits and white shirts gathered around him. As he tried to ask what was going on, his clothes were unpeeled from his body and a seething mass of tape measures were wound along and around every part of him.

In some sort of coordinated unison, the men scribbled violently on spiral bound jotters with gleaming silver pens. The man with the pencil thin moustache faced him, smiled and spoke calmly. "All of your measurements have been taken and our tailors will begin making your suit straightaway sir. Please put on this robe and come into our waiting area. Would you like a cup of coffee sir, or maybe something a little stronger?"

Two hours later, as Henry downed his third cup of coffee laced with an Italian liquor he'd never heard of, the man with the pencil thin moustache approached him. "Please follow me through to the fitting room sir. Your apparel is ready for your approval."

Henry looked at his reflected image in the tall upright mirror and took a few steps back to admire the unrecognisable handsome stranger staring back at him. He scanned the image from the patent black leather shoes, up through the immaculately hanging trouser and onto the white shirt and grey tie framed by a perfectly shaped jacket. "You certainly know your stuff," Henry said to no one in particular.

"It's the combination of the cut and the way the silk is woven to make the fabric of the suit sir. Can I take it that sir is happy with our endeavours?"

"It's fantastic but how much does it cost?" Henry asked, as he recalled the four figure price tags on the display suits.

"Not for sir to worry about. Everything has been placed on Madam Gremory's account according to her wishes. The rest of your new wardrobe will be ready for collection the day after tomorrow."

"The rest?"

"Madam Gremory gave instructions in her note that you should be fully equipped for any occasion. Do you have a car or shall I order a taxi for you when you come to pick up your clothes? It is a considerable collection."

Henry wondered if he was still inside the dream he'd had. This sort of thing just didn't happen to people outside a book or a film. "I'm in the middle of changing cars and I haven't had time to pick up my new one yet," he said half-truthfully.

He still had four hours to pass before he met with the Duchess and estimating that his flat was about an hour's walking distance, he decided to break in the new shoes hugging tightly to his feet.

When he reached his flat, he showered and shaved to complete the final preparations for his new image. At 6 o'clock, he called a taxi to take him to the restaurant. He paused briefly to consider how his life had changed so dramatically after receiving the pocket watch. Without knowing why, he opened his dresser drawer and reached under his holey socks for the little watch.

He glanced at the front of the case briefly, admiring the bright reflections thrown back from the small snake eyes and dropped the watch into his inside breast pocket. His phone buzzed and he assumed his taxi had arrived early. The phone broke into a ringtone, someone was calling him – he hoped it was not his mother. He checked and saw it was his boss, Steve, from the burger bar. With everything that had happened he'd forgotten about his *real* job.

"Hi Steve," he said nervously.

"I need you to come in early, Shaun has called in sick."

"I can't come in early. In fact, I'm not coming in tonight as something has cropped up."

"What do you mean you're not coming in tonight?"

"Actually, Steve, I'm quitting."

"You have to give a month's notice. Now get your arse into gear and be here in the next thirty minutes or I'll…"

"Sack me. That's fine sack me." Henry shouted as he dabbed the red phone icon with his finger.

The phone buzzed again but when Henry looked at it, he realised it was a text telling him his taxi was waiting.

Steve called him three times before he made it to the taxi door, but he cut off each of the calls on the second ring before setting his phone on silent. He arrived at the restaurant Osteria Francescanario ten minutes early and wondered if he should go in or wait until it was precisely seven o'clock. He went in.

He was greeted by a very pretty Italian girl. "Good evening sir. Would you like to book a table or do you have a reservation?"

"Err, I'm meeting someone."

The girl looked at him with her large lightly mascara coated eyes and smiled. She waited for a few seconds. "What name?"

"Henry, Henry King."

He watched her slide her perfectly manicured olive coloured finger down the reservations book. "I'm sorry sir but I don't have a reservation for anybody by the name of Henry King. Are you sure your friend booked here for this evening?"

"No, Henry King is my name. The person I'm meeting is a Mrs Gremory, Helena Gremory."

"Oh you mean the Duchess. She arrived a few minutes ago. I'll take you to her table."

Henry tried to put out of his mind the little demon thoughts that were sneaking into his consciousness. *You've made a cock up already. Why did you give her your name when you knew she'd booked the table? You've quit your job and the way it's going you won't have this one for long. You're a loser and always will be.*

There must have been over eighty tables and most were already occupied. Henry glanced through the mass of tall silver candelabras trying to catch a glimpse of the Duchess, but he failed to see where his enigmatic host was seated.

"You are booked into one of our private rooms, this way," the young Italian girl said, swaying her slender, but shapely hips tantalisingly in front of him as she led Henry towards a partly opened door.

Helena Gremory rose from her chair in such a way that Henry was reminded of a cobra posturing itself ready to strike its victim. He reached for her out stretched hand, ready to shake it before he realised, as she pushed it in the direction of his mouth, that she was offering it to him for a kiss. Delicately, he kissed the back of her hand. "You look dazzling, Henry. Please sit down, opposite me. My other two guests will be arriving in a few minutes."

"Your other two guests?"

"I want you to meet two of my employees. I will put you under the wing of one of them until you find your own feet."

"Mrs Gremory, or should I call you Duchess? Can I ask you what it is I will be doing in my new job?"

"My title is Madam Gremory, my ancestors were from Germany but they settled in France a few centuries ago. Please call me Duchess. I'm more comfortable with that name. Let me tell you a bit about my business. In this world there are many people who have a lot of money, more than they could ever spend in their lifetime. It's a peculiar habit of these people to want to make more money and that's where Dromedary Enterprises provides a service. You've heard of stocks and shares, the currency markets, hedge funds and investment consortiums I take it?"

"Yes, but I know nothing about them," Henry replied nervously as the Duchess fixed her enchanting eyes on him.

"You don't have to. I have other people who look after that side. Investing money is usually a risky business. The value of any investment can go up or down. The clever part is to know when it's going to go up or down."

"I wish I knew the answer to that," Henry said, hoping his interruption was not ill-timed.

"There are many factors that will cause fluctuations in the value of any commodity but these are due to past, present and future events. I have assembled a team that have developed a series of algorithms that merge these three facets of time into one. The world is ruled by a series of cycles and my company has unravelled enough of these cycles to bring the future into the present. Quite simply, we can double the value of any ones investment in less than a year. The rich and wealthy are queuing up to hand over a large proportion of their assets to my company" she said, winking almost seductively at him.

"I think I get the gist of what you do, but where do I fit into this?"

"You are to become one of my frontline people. You possess three important gifts: Your naïve charm will relax my clients, your good looks will seduce hesitant investors and your passion to succeed will motivate people to follow your advice."

Henry paused. "I'm not sure I have a passion to succeed or any of the other qualities you mention."

"Oh you do. You just don't realise it yet. Here are my other guests. Let me introduce you."

Henry rose to his feet, noticing a young couple had entered through the partly open door. He glanced at a tall, dark haired man who was a little older than him and then felt his insides churn as he looked at the most beautiful girl he'd ever set eyes on. The Duchess also rose to greet her guests. "Henry, this is George Prince. A bit of a coincidence about your two names don't you think? George, this is Henry King, possibly he will rank over you one day," she said, laughing lightly. "This, Henry, is one of my best protégées. She is a distant relative. Her family can be traced back to Germany and were part of the same line I'm descended from. Meet Cristina Smith."

Henry took Cristina's hand and delicately raised it to his mouth. As he touched the back of hand with his lips, he caught the faint scent of her natural odour and felt his heart beating powerfully in his chest. As he sat down, he moved his hand inside his jacket to calm his throbbing heart, but his fingers slipped inside his breast pocket and connected with the pocket watch.

Unseen, inside the watch, two of its tiny gears imperceptibly rotated. Atom by atom, two slivers of bone crept towards an alignment.

* * *

Akubar told Yasuf to wait near his tent until *their* guest arrived. Yasuf wondered what the special equipment would be. He felt pleased that he had been chosen to be responsible for operating whatever it was and let his mind drift.

He had been with this Boko Haram group for over four years, but only recently joined the elite force that undertook missions to attack Christians. He was pleased with the way he had become a *brother* and been accepted by his fellow jihadists, but the brutality measured out to the infidels was haunting him.

Since he had castrated the young men in the church hall his dreams had become disturbed. The thought of entering either his wife or the slave bitch and ejecting seed from his balls into them made him squirm with discomfort. Maybe he should try to give the bitch a good hammering and overcome his nervousness by releasing his fear, anger and sexual juices against her. She was after all a Christian, a heretic worshiping God through a false prophet.

Twice he offered her a chance to become his second wife – but she refused to convert. He had threatened her, telling her he would rent her body out to the younger soldiers who had never been with a woman – but still she remained fixed to her misguided beliefs.

They were currently in Chad, but Akubar informed him that in a few days they would cross back into Nigeria and attack a Christian school thought to hold over a hundred young girls.

Yasuf said the men needed comfort because of the harshness of the war they were raging against their enemies. Just as he began to relax and feel more comfortable with his situation, Akubar called out for him to come to the operations tent.

"Yasuf, this is Musalfa, a most important cleric from the Daesh. He has travelled from a country called Syria especially to meet with us. He has come with some special equipment and wants to teach you how to use it."

Yasuf looked at the three boxes laid out on the rickety table in front of the main tent's opening. The first box was about the size of a small suitcase, but made from a light silvery metal that had a pattern cut into its surface. The second was a long, oblong, black box that he thought might contain a grenade launcher or similar weapon, while the third box was cube shaped and made from shiny grey plastic.

He looked up to Musalfa, who was very tall, his face almost completely obscured by a thick grey beard that grew down to his waistline and a white head cloth that was thickly wound over the top of his head. Akubar waved Yasuf towards the table and spoke softly to the cleric. "This young man has proved to be one of our best fighters, but he is also very clever. I think he would be perfect for what you have in mind."

Musalfa turned to Yasuf and spoke in a grating voice that filled him with fear. "Come here. Let me see you more closely. Are you faithful to Allah? Are you prepared to give up your mortal life so that the word of our God will be spread to all men across the Earth?"

"Yes," Yasuf replied fearfully.

"Open the silver box and lay its content on the table."

Yasuf struggled with the two sprung catches, unsure of how to unclip them. As the second catch clicked open, he slowly raised the hinged lid of the box. He peered inside and saw a flat, rectangular object that he recognised was some sort of laptop.

"It's a satellite computer that will link you to many branches of Daesh. It's easy to use and I'll show you how it works shortly. This box," Musalfa said gruffly, pointing to the black oblong container "holds the antenna that will connect you to the satellite."

"What's in the small box?" Yasuf asked, pointing to the grey plastic container.

"That is your camera. You are going to make films for us Yasuf. Fear is our friend. We've discovered that if our enemies see how we intend to crush them, they lose their will to fight against us. The more frightening the films they see, the easier they give up their resistance and join our great cause to create an Islamic state that will dominate the world."

"How will I know what to film?"

"Remove the laptop from its case and open the lid. I will show one of our films so you'll know what I expect you to produce. Akubar, it's most important you watch too. I want you to use these ideas to inspire you. Next time you capture some Christians, I want you to plan how you will kill them. The more terrible you make their death, the longer you draw out their agony, the greater the fear you'll install into all the other Christians."

Akubar grinned. "The Christians have delivered many terrible deaths to our people, it will be good to return their favour."

"Your young warrior will film their executions and send the images to us from this laptop. We'll then broadcast the edited films back to the Christians. There are some gifted members of Daesh that are able to hack into their websites allowing us to disseminate these films to them. Yasuf, move aside and let me show you some ideas."

Akubar and Yasuf watched on as the cleric dabbed at the keyboard. The screen lit up and haunting music played as the picture of a waving black flag and strange words they did not understand appeared on the screen. The scene opened with a shot somewhere in a bleak desert.

There was one blue coloured plastic barrel and two metal oil drums standing in a row. Six men dressed in black robes began walking around the barrels speaking in a strange language that neither Akubar nor Yasuf understood. From the side, a yellow vehicle appeared. It was some sort of mobile crane marked with the letters J C B. A man was dangling by his arms from the end of its jib.

As the machine advanced towards the blue barrel, the man swayed like a pendulum. The machine stopped and the driver waited for the man to stop swinging before gently lowering him waist deep into the blue barrel. Akubar and Yasuf leaned closer to the screen, watching as the man writhed and screamed in terror. "What's in the barrel?" Akubar asked, as he stared at the screen.

"It contains concentrated Nitric Acid. It is dissolving his skin and has triggered his nerve endings to fire signals of pain to his brain. He would die in minutes if he was left in there. Watch what happens next."

They watched as the man was lifted from the first barrel and dipped into the second.

"What's in that barrel?" Akubar asked, as he kept his eyes glued to the screen.

"Just water to remove the acid," Musalfa said calmly.

They watched as one of the men dressed in black robes approached the third barrel and threw something into it. Bright orange flames erupted from the top of the barrel and at the same time the vehicle began lifting the man out of the second barrel. Yasuf's eyes popped open when he saw there were large sections of skin hanging down like torn curtains from the man's lower body and legs.

The yellow crane inched forward until the man was held over the burning barrel. Musalfa distracted them as he burst out laughing. "You should see your faces. Your eyes look like they are going to pop out of their sockets."

"Is he going to be burnt alive?" Akubar asked, keeping his gaze fixed on the screen.

"No, he's being held high enough above the flames not to be burnt, but the heat is invoking a deep agony in him. Look how he writhes and is trying to pull away from the flames. Watch what happens next."

A minute later the machine reversed back and lowered the

man into the first drum of acid. Musalfa reached forward and stopped the recording. "The film is over two hours long as that's how long it took for him to lose consciousness. When he showed no signs of waking, he was held over the flames to burn. I know you have limited supplies here in the jungle, but you are resourceful people. The next time you take prisoners, I want you," Musalfa said, pointing to Akubar, "to dream up something inspiring. Show me a death so terrible that even I would convert from being a Muslim to a Christian rather than endure that death. In this way, every Christian we capture that has seen how they will die, will willingly convert to our side and join us in our jihad. There were six other prisoners watching that man die. Each thought they would suffer the same fate, but when they were offered the chance to join our cause, all happily consented."

"Is this what you want me to make films of?" Yasuf asked nervously.

"It is. Through the sacrifice of that one man, six others were saved. Yasuf, my brave young man, if you perform the task I'm setting for you, you'll help to save thousands of lives."

EIGHT

Nine days before Hamczel's demise, Prince Vladrek set of with an escort of eight men from Castle Boese. His home was located high in the mountains close to the Swiss border and had stood perched on the ledges of a natural cliff face for centuries. Over the last hundred years, his father and grandfather added seventeen turreted towers to the box like structure, turning it into a masterpiece of gothic obscenity. Vladrek's father's words still rang in his ears as he eased his horse down the rocky and twisting pass into the lower valley.

The times of small kingdoms such as ours are coming to an end my son. It is for this reason I command you to marry Princess Czyelle, daughter of King Murak of Gothburgh. Only by uniting our great families through this act, will we remain strong enough to resist the gripping talons of those who seek to seize our lands and obliterate our bloodline forever.

Vladrek knew his father, Malius, was referring to the Catholic Church. Since he was a little boy, the stories of the havoc reaped by the Inquisition that passed through the lower lands had played their evil games out in the nightmares of his nocturnal world.

He vividly remembered the story told to his father by a man who escaped from one of the towns in the lower valleys. How the men were gathered and stripped of their possessions including their clothes. How each man was stretched on a rack or broken on the wheel and then, when they confessed to being heretics, their broken and dislocated bodies were burned on a stake as they struggled to breathe their last tortured breath. Of the women, raped by the inquisitors and then by their guards, their breasts torn from their bodies by three pronged, red-hot breast rippers heaved on by those who violated their tenderness. Those who survived were made to endure final moments of extreme cruelty, their wombs being split open from within by a device only the Devil himself could have conceived.

All of these acts of gross abomination coursed through Vladrek's mind as he departed from the safety of his home. So he was to marry Princess Czyelle, but why him? Why not his older brother, Burgolt, his sibling and tormentor? He knew he would always take second place to his elder brother, but why couldn't his father insist that Burgolt marry first. Maybe it was because Burgolt held a strong influence over his father that the burden of marrying a woman rumoured to be ugly and fat fell on him.

Anyway, his brother seemed content with his current position, free to claim the maidenhoods of all the prettiest girls who worked as servants in his household. How many bastards had he now sired? Everywhere he looked there were hundreds of little brats running around the castle wearing the distinctive features of his brother's snake-like eyes and beaked nose.

At the end of their first day's travelling, Vladrek and his escort set up camp for the night. While his men erected the simple tents that would be their shelter for the night, Vladrek wandered down to a small stream to refill his water flagon. As he crouched to lower his leather bottle into the bubbling icy water, a full moon broke free from the shrouds of slowly drifting clouds. With his bottle still submerged in the gurgling water, Vladrek looked up to see the craggy, almost vertical slopes of the valley sides expose their cruel and twisted contortions through the illuminating effects of the freshly exposed moon. *This is a place of malevolence if ever there was one,* Vladrek thought as he rose to his feet. He was just about to return to the campsite, when something caught his eye.

On the other side of the stream, just below the rocky cliff face, two creatures were slithering through the shadows. He raised his hand to shield out the dazzling moonlight and caught a glimpse of two shapes, one dark and the other light, disappearing behind a large fallen rock. He turned and half ran back to the camp. "Do wolves roam through these valleys?" he called out to his escorts.

"Why? Have you seen something?" one of his men shouted back.

"I'm not sure, but I thought I saw two animals creeping about around the bottom of that slope," he said, pointing to where he saw the outlines of crawling beasts.

"It's unusual for wolves to come this far up into the mountains," another of the men called out.

"What did they look like?" another said.

"I thought I saw something dark, maybe black and another, it was light in colour, possibly white. I only saw them briefly but I'm certain they were some sort of animal."

"I'll take a look," one of the escorts said, checking his sword slipped easily from its sheath.

The man returned a few minutes later. "Whatever you saw isn't there anymore, but one of us will keep watch through the night just in case.

When Vladrek woke the next morning it was already daylight, but the sky was heavily overcast and a fine drizzle seeped through the air saturating everything it touched. They abandoned their attempt at breakfast when their fire stubbornly refused to light and water penetrated through their clothing.

As the cold and dampness seeped into him, Vladrek felt increasingly apprehensive about his future. If she was really fat and ugly would he have to be intimate with her? Would he have to see his fine blood mingle with hers to produce a tribe of fat and ugly children? Would she nag and scold him if he didn't love her?

The drizzle turned to rain and Vladrek's mood darkened with the sky. The clouds seemed to sink down from overhead and fall around them obscuring the path they were taking. One of the escort's horses became jittery, dancing from side to side and threatening to break into a gallop. From a hidden point came a rumble of thunder heralding an approaching mountain storm. "I think we'd better set up camp for tonight as the weather's getting worse," one of the escorts called out.

They pitched their tents where they stopped and hurried under the fabric to take shelter from the rain, which now fell in torrents. Vladrek had his own tent, but wished he was in one of the other two tents with his men. He tossed under his blanket, longing to feel dry.

Everything felt sodden, as if it could not hold another single drop of water. The rain pounded on the stretched cloth of his tent, its drumming noise reminding him of stampeding horses.

Then, he realised he could hear horses, not stampeding horses, but distressed horses. Their horses were neighing, displaying through their staggered shrieking a primeval fear that only animals sense.

He crept towards the flap of his tent and peeled back the soaked material. From somewhere, there was deep almost inaudible roar and it was growing louder. Vladrek sprinted out into the rain and ran to where the horses were tied up. He placed his hands on the waterlogged back of one of the animals to calm it down. As the horse yielded to his attempts of pacification, he sensed something rising up through his feet. It felt like a tremor, almost imperceptible, but its intensity rose alongside the subsonic roar eating into his ears.

From somewhere out of his range of vision, in the darkness of the night, the subliminal background noise transformed into a sound Vladrek had heard before. Not far from his home there was a waterfall. Most of the time the water fell in happy leaps down a cliff face, but when there was a storm the waters turned brown and roared in anger as they tumbled down to feed the cataracts below.

He untied the horse and shouted loudly to warn his men of the impending danger. In a moment of terror, he mounted the horse, which took it as a signal to flee from what was coming. Vladrek clutched onto the animal as it bolted into the darkness, unaware that a wall of water and stones twice the height of a man had just ploughed through the camp his escorts were, until a moment ago, interacting with characters that were part of their private dreams.

Despite the almost pitch darkness and torrential rain, the horse below Vladrek thundered sure footed down the valley maintaining a safe distance between it and the wall of water behind them. All Vladrek could see were odd snatches of the valley's sides when a lightning bolt blazed overhead. In the last flash, he observed the valley was wider and the ground more level. He eased himself back in the saddle to be more comfortable and was caught unaware as the horse jumped over a small ditch. As the horse landed, he rocked forward and slipped up to the horse's neck. Before he could regain his seat, the horse bucked under him causing him to roll over its back and crash into the soft muddy ground.

At first he feared to move, wondering which limbs may have been broken, but little by little, he raised his arms and flexed his legs without any serious pain. As he was about to sit up, he became aware of a something crouching over him. For a brief second, the moon's rays found a hole in the clouds and Vladrek saw he was staring into the face of a large black wolf.

He shut his eyes and swallowed, felt his mind disconnecting from his limbs and prayed for sleep to take him before he was torn to pieces. Something pushed under the back of his head, forcing it to tilt forwards.

Then he felt wet jaws and hard teeth slide under the back

of his neck. He wanted to scream, but every part of him was paralysed. He felt the wolf's head push under him a bit further before it jaws clamped shut. There was no pain, no tearing of flesh, instead, he realised he was moving, being dragged backwards. He felt his upper garments tighten across his chest and knew the wolf had gripped his clothing in its jaws. *Is it taking me to its den so it cubs can eat me? Why doesn't it just finish me now and let me escape from my terror?*

He opened his eyes as a new sound broke into his ears. He could hear the wolf panting but there was a loud rippling and gurgling coming from around him. With his eyes open, he realised the wolf was dragging him to higher ground out of the reach of rapidly rising water. He considered rising to his feet to make his own escape, but his mind slipped out of consciousness as it fled from the ordeal of what had just occurred.

Vladrek awoke to the sensation of the sun's rays burning into his face. He opened his eyes and squinted when the white light of the fireball in the sky saturated his vision and obscured his surroundings from view. He was sitting upright, his back propped against a boulder.

Below, as his eyes accustomed to the brilliance of the recently risen sun, he saw a swollen river swirling down the valley bottom. Overhead, the blueness of the sky was unblemished, without a single fleck or wisp of cloud. Everything from last night flooded back to him and he jerked up looking for signs of the wolf – and his horse.

A stark reality drove into him. He was alone, he was lost and all he possessed were the clothes on his back. He gathered his thoughts and stood up, shielded his eyes and scanned down the valley looking for any signs of civilization – there were none. He walked the rest of the day, deviating down to the river to drink a mouthful of water from his cupped hand. As evening approached, he reached the mouth of the valley and spotted faint orange lights twinkling from far below. The descent to the lower ground was by a steep path that snaked down a mountainside, something he could not manage in the dark.

He sought out a rudimentary shelter under an overhanging rock and lay down on the long grass. That night he dreamt he was at feast in his home, cramming meats and cheese into his mouth alongside his father and brother. When he awoke in the morning, he realised he'd never felt *real* hunger before.

It took Vladrek all of the next day to reach the small town he'd spied out the previous evening. As he entered the town's perimeter, he noticed people were staring at him. He approached a group of three men who were playing a game that involved tossing small stones. "Pardon my intrusion into your game, but I'm Prince Vladrek from Boese Castle. I've lost my horse and my way. I've not eaten for two days. Could you tell me where your ruler lives so I can gain some assistance in my plight?"

"You look more like a wandering beggar than a prince, be off with you," a bearded man said, who was about to toss a pebble into a circle drawn out on the bare ground.

"Don't be so abrupt, Marsk, he don't speak like a beggar. I've never heard what a prince talks like, but I can imagine it'd be a bit like he talks," the second man said.

The third man looked Vladrek up and down before speaking. "I can see your clothes were once very fine before they were dragged through the mud. We have no leader here. Each man does his bit to make sure we are well fed and have comfortable shelter. I know what it is to be hungry and without a home. You're welcome to stay in my house for the night and I'll ask my wife to prepare some food for you."

"That's very kind of you. What is your name?" Vladrek asked, turning to face the man who was no more than thirty years old.

"I'm Gamrul, gifted in the craft of making the finest cheese you'll ever taste."

"That he is," the first man said, running his soil-ingrained fingers through his thick beard. "Maybe I was a bit harsh with you. If you are a prince then you're in a sorry state. What happened to you?"

Vladrek told his story as they walked into the small town, but he omitted the part about the wolf as he felt these strangers might think him some sort demon.

After eating a meal of bread, cheese and apples, Gamrul led Vladrek to an outhouse filled with sweet smelling hay. "It's not much, not for a prince, but you'll be warm and dry in here. Where are you heading to?"

Vladrek realised he'd forgotten about his quest, forgotten he was making his way to meet his future wife. "I was on my way to Gothburgh, my father has arranged for me to marry a princess but my escort has gone and I don't know my way."

"I think I know where that is. You'll need to pass through a town called Harsburgh, it's about three days walk from here. I go there sometimes to trade my cheeses for food and clothes to keep us warm in the winter. I'm sure once you reach Harsburgh, someone can tell you the way."

Vladrek spent the next two days recuperating. Gamrul supplied him with enough food for a three day hike and gave him clear directions to Harsburgh.

Three days later, early in the morning, Vladrek walked into the centre of Harsburgh. He was unsure who to ask for directions, and as he cast his eyes along the street, he spotted something glinting in the heavily rutted road. He wondered if it was a piece of jewellery that someone had dropped and stooped down to pull it out from the dried mud. As he rubbed the encrusted dirt from the object, he noticed two points of sparkling red light. Using his thumb, he swiped from left to right and looked in awe as the casing opened to reveal nine concentric rings that shimmered iridescently in the sunlight.

Vladrek walked deeper into the town hoping to find a dwelling that belonged to a Count or Burgermeister he could ask for help. He stopped when he spotted a large stone building surrounded by wooden scaffold. Even though it was early, there were at least forty men working on the building. Vladrek turned to a man who was also watching the building work. "Whose house is this?" he asked.

"It is the house of God," the man replied without looking in Vladrek's direction.

"Do you mean a church?"

"I do."

"Why is it in such a poor state of disrepair?"

"Because it's hardly ever used, but all that's about to change."

"Why?"

"There's news that the Inquisition is heading this way. We'll all need to show we obey the word of God and spare no expense in maintaining his house, even though the old and the weak will go hungry. They say that if the Inquisition suspects you are not faithful to God's word, they'll stretch and break your body and then burn you alive. None of us wants that so we're rebuilding God's house."

Vladrek felt a gentle tap on his shoulder. He swung around and faced an old man with thick white hair and a neatly trimmed beard. The man looked at him for a few seconds before softly speaking to him. "I understand you are making your way to Gothburgh."

"Yes I am – but how did you know that?"

"I know much, Vladrek, son of Malius. I'm intending to travel in that direction and offer to be your aide and travelling companion. Your journey will be much safer if you allow me to guide you."

"You seem to know a lot about me. How can I trust you?"

"If you were to leave now and take the main road to Gothburgh, the Inquisition will intercept you. You'll be searched and when they discover what you are carrying in your pocket, the small object you picked up earlier, you will be denounced as a hand-servant of Satan. They will cut off your manly parts, slice open your belly to expose your innards and burn you alive."

"Tell me, what do I carry in my pocket?"

"You carry my watch, but it is yours to keep. The future, all futures are open to me and what I offer you is a safer path for the final part of your journey."

"Who are you?" Vladrek said, looking closely into the face of the stranger.

As the man replied, "I am usually known as Duke Gomory, but others know me by a different name," Vladrek noticed for the first time how smooth and unlined the man's skin was. If his hair and beard were not white, he could easily pass as a young man.

"How do you intend we should reach Gothburgh *safely*?"

"There is an old roadway that has fallen into disrepair. It is not passable by wagon but is still easy to negotiate by foot. If you wish to accomplish your task we must start our journey now and not rest until we reach Gothburgh this time tomorrow. If you delay by even a single day, the inquisition will reach your destination before you do. Once they see the maiden you seek, they will use her for their own entertainment until she is with child. It is the practice of these demons to dispose of their unwanted chattel by the use of fire."

"Are you telling me they will burn Princess Czyelle alive?"

"With her unborn child still inside her. It is the way of these men."

"Do they not act in God's name?"

"They use his name but are not part of him, whoever you believe God is."

Vladrek's mind spun in circles at the thought of a young

woman suffering in the way Gomory described, even if she was fat and ugly. For the first time in his life, he felt he had a purpose, a challenge that was worthy of his bravado. "Come, let us go and do as we must," he said, placing his hand on Gomory's shoulder.

The old road from Harsburgh to Gothburgh was constructed in Roman times and ran in a straight line across valleys, over hills and forged streams. The original blocks of stone and clay that made up the once smooth surface of the road were now long gone, leaving a path littered with ruts and potholes waiting to snap the ankles of unwary travellers.

Through the daylight hours, Vladrek easily kept up with Gomory's long strides and sure footedness, but as twilight morphed to night and the path penetrated under the canopy of a thick forest, he found the unpredictable footing too hazardous to proceed any further. "Gomory, stop. I will break my ankle if I fall down another hole."

"We have to continue if we are to reach Gothburgh in time. Move to the edge of the road and I will take your hand to guide you."

Vladrek crept forward, searching through the darkness for sight of Gomory. "Where are you, I can't even see you?"

"I'm here, at your side," Gomory said, as he clutched Vladrek's hand in his.

Vladrek felt a hand close around his: a cold hand that offered no heat, a hand that felt it was made of polished marble rather than living flesh. He involuntarily shuddered. "You are cold."

"No, I am preserving energy. I have reduced the flow of blood from parts of my body that do not need them. I never know when I will next find food to eat, and in this way, I endure for days at a time without taking nutrients."

As the night passed, Vladrek realised Gomory was pulling him harder and faster along the uneven path with greater urgency. "Are we not moving fast enough? Are we going to be too late?" Vladrek hissed as he lost his balance in a dip.

"The Inquisitors are making better progress than I anticipated. We must reach the castle at first light."

"How can you know that? We are on a different road, aren't we?"

"Yes we are on a different road, but they lead to the same point in place and time. Now hurry."

Vladrek decided not to pursue his line of questioning. He looked up into the tree canopy and felt relief when he saw silhouettes of branches were visible against the lightening sky. They broke from under the tree covering into an open field. Ahead, perched on a hillside, was the outline of a large castle. "Is that the castle Princess Czyelle lives in?" he asked, turning to look at Gomory.

"It is and you must announce your intentions without delay."

"What intentions?"

"That you wish to marry the princess. You must persuade her father to allow you to leave at once. Request that you are given an armed escort and the best horses to make your escape."

"Don't be ridiculous, look at me. I look more like a beggar than a prince. What notice will they take of me?"

"Show the head of this little kingdom what you have concealed in your pocket. While you prove your honourable intentions, I will talk with the head guard to warn him about the arrival of the Inquisition."

"Will they try to fight the Inquisition?"

"If they do they are all doomed. The Inquisitors are escorted by a large army of ruthless fighters that receive a share of the spoils, including the women. Their outward intention appears to be the saving of souls but the reality is different."

"How is it different?"

"They seek only to claim all lands and wealth in the name of the Church, but they are the Church. There are some who also seek an inner pleasure by feeding on the torment of tortured bodies. If you're ever in a situation where you know you will be captured by the Inquisition, use this," Gomory said, pulling a long thin object wrapped in cloth from his inner pocket.

Vladrek took the offering, unwrapped the cloth covering and held the small stiletto blade point upwards. "Am I meant to defend myself with this?"

"No, use it to kill yourself. Do you see the two fine grooves running down the blade? They are laced with a potent poison that will spare you any suffering."

Vladrek followed Gomory up a narrow, almost hidden path that snaked up the steep hillside to the base of the castle towering over them. As they neared the dark grey stone that formed the base of the castle wall, Vladrek noticed a small wooden door that appeared to have been made for a child to enter or exit the castle. "Are we…"

Gomory whipped around and placed his upright index finger over Vladrek's lip. Slowly he moved his finger back to his lips making it clear to Vladrek he must remain silent. Then he placed his flat hand on Vladrek's chest, slowly moving back to indicate to him he should not move. Gomory turned and half ran to the door.

Vladrek leaned forward trying to see and hear what was happening as he watched Gomory whispering to someone who had just opened the small door. Suddenly, he turned and waved for him to come to the door. As Vladrek approached, Gomory spoke to him. "I have explained our situation and I'm certain we will shortly be admitted into the castle. Don't speak to anyone until I tell you to."

"Do you know these people, have you met them before?"

"I do not know them and I have never met them before, but they know me."

Vladrek was about to ask Gomory to explain what he meant but though better of it. Where are we going?" he asked instead.

"You will be taken to the King and it's most important you tell him you need to take his daughter away with you now. Don't forget to ask for good horses and an armed escort."

Vladrek felt bemused. He was about to meet a king he'd never met before and rather than follow the usual protocol of exchanging compliments, feasting and building diplomatic bridges based on lies, he was expected to say, 'Hand your daughter over and give me your best men and horses'. Before he could think anymore, Gomory gripped him firmly and pulled him into the little doorway.

On the other side of the doorway were four heavily armed guards, each holding twin-bladed axes set on long poles in their right hand, heavy broadswords in their left hand and wearing grim faces that said 'we'll use these if you try anything.'

Two of the guards ushered Gomory to walk with them into a dark corridor. Vladrek then felt his arms nudged by the other two guards and followed several steps behind the route Gomory had taken.

There was no conversation or discussion as they tramped up endless flights of steps. Vladrek thought he saw Gomory being taken through a door to his left, but when he reached the spot, there was no doorway to be seen. They climbed several more flight of stairs before reaching a pair of large wooden doors. One of the guards stepped forward, opening the doors before the other guard guided Vladrek into a large room that was well lit because of the many windows along three of its four walls. The guard spoke to Vladrek. "Kneel before the King. State your name and purpose."

Vladrek looked at the man sitting in front of him. He was still quite young, no more than fifty years of age. His brown hair was neatly cut and his face clean shaven, which meant he had access to fine steels that were only available to a few. "Majesty, I am Vladrek from Castle Boese. My father, Malius, has arranged with you that I should marry your daughter, Czyelle. I have come for her hand in marriage. Unfortunately these are not good times. I understand from my travelling companion that the Inquisition is making for this castle as we speak and..." Vladrek stopped speaking as a messenger ran up to the king and spoke in his ear.

"Continue with what you were saying," King Murak said.

"It is most important I take your daughter away from this danger. In fact, if you wish, you could flee with me," Vladrek added.

"Are you saying I should abandon my home and people because of a few monks? Do you think me a coward?"

Vladrek knew in his heart his last statement was a mistake. "I didn't mean it that way. I was only thinking of your safety."

"You are young and naïve, Vladrek, if you *are* Vladrek. You smell and look like a beggar. How do I know you are who you say you are?"

Vladrek tried to remember what Gomory had told him. Just as he was about to speak, another messenger arrived to speak with King Murak. This time the conversation lasted for what seemed like an eternity. As Vladrek brushed his hands down his front to try to even out the creases in his clothes, he felt the slight bump of the pocket watch. The messenger nodded several times as the king spoke to him and left in a hurry. "Majesty, please take a look at what I own. I'm sure you'll realise that only a wealthy prince would own such a treasure as this," Vladrek said, holding out the opened watch.

King Murak rose from his seat and walked up to face Vladrek directly. "You may stand. I have received news about the Inquisition and it seems you may be right. Even now they are within an hour's march of my castle and their numbers are great, too great."

"What do you intend to do?" Vladrek asked, closing his hand over the pocket watch.

"I'm told they come with over a thousand soldiers and will

outnumber us five to one. I've given orders for horses to be made ready to take you and my daughter far away from here. I will place you in the care of my best ten men. Vladrek, it's time for you to meet your future wife, the Princess Czyelle. Daughter, come here."

Vladrek slipped the watch back into his pocket and turned in the direction Murak was facing. He watched as a young woman emerged from a shadowed doorway.

As she stepped into the shafts of sunlight beaming through an array of windows set in the longest wall and advanced toward him, he felt his heart racing in his chest. She moved elegantly, her long trailing blonde hair flexing like a young sapling yielding to a brisk summer breeze, her blue eyes radiating an inner mystery like the sky seen from a high mountain peak and her smile – her smile that revealed a wall of whiteness that would seduce a traveller to climb such a peak to touch its frosted crown.

When she spoke her first greeting to him, "Vladrek, I'm so lucky you have chosen me, you're so handsome," he felt his body dissolving into a quivering broth of gurgling emotions. His heart thumped in his chest and nearby, the little pocket watch ticked unnoticed, playing out a line of time, guiding two fragments of bone towards an alignment that would be cruelly postponed, as the teeth of an off-centred cog engaged to reverse the motion of the seventh ring of time.

※ ※ ※

Kunrat settled back in an old chair he placed near the open fire so he could warm his chilled body. He was unused to the cold drafts of air that swept down from the surrounding mountain slopes, and had already decided to postpone his assault into the mountain valleys until the coming winter was spent.

He closed his eyes so he could recapture the images of the twenty heretics he watched burn at the stake an hour earlier. Most of the men were too weak to fight the ravages of the flames that cleansed their bodies of the evil contaminating them, but two had resisted, pulling their twisting torsos higher up the wooden pole they were fastened to. One had tried to hold his breath as the flames licked his face, desperate not to draw in the hot air that would scorch his lungs and snuff out his live force.

Soon, the last of the heretics in Gothburgh would be gone, reduced to light-grey ash to be dispersed by the autumn winds. As he watched the final grimace of one man in his mind's eye, a messenger broke his waking dream.

"Master Kunrat," how he loved the term *master*, "we have discovered a coven of witches. They were hiding in an old house just outside the town."

Kunrat opened his eyes and looked directly at the messenger. "Where are they now?"

"They have been taken to the main hall of the Inquisition."

"Has their interrogation begun?"

"Not yet, Master. We are waiting for you to assign the methods best suited for each of the witches."

Kunrat raised himself from the chair and stretched his arms in the air. "Tell me, is it still cold outside?"

"Yes Master, there is a bitter wind coming down from the east."

"Pass me my robes," Kunrat said, dreading the thought of stepping out into the cold air.

Huddled together with their hands tied behind their backs, seven women watched in fear as a robed figure approached them. Frena, the youngest of the group whispered to the woman next to her. "We must convince them we're not witches, tell them the truth that we were frightened we were going to be raped by an invading army."

The woman next to her, Agnise, coughed heavily before replying. "We can try, but I've heard that once they believe you're a witch they will torture you until you confess. You are young and pretty, maybe they'll believe you."

"I don't see how they can think I'm a witch. I'm just a young girl. I've never been with a man and I know nothing of spells or curses," Frena whispered back.

One of the guards stepped forward. "Silence, don't talk. The Master is here to inspect you. Stand up straight and look directly at him so he can see what you are."

Kunrat glanced along the line of women, most were old and fat, but among the group, one stood out as the most exceptionally beautiful girl he'd laid eyes on. "You, what is your name?"

"I'm Frena, just a simple girl."

"Are you a witch?"

"No sir, I'm just an ordinary girl who lives – lived with my parents on a small farm."

Kunrat studied the girl. As he took in the shape of her vibrant eyes, high cheekbones, dainty nose, long dark curly hair and lush mouth, he felt a disturbing awakening of arousal under his robes. "You will address me as Master. I hold dominion here and it's me who will decide if you live or die. I am going to interrogate you and if I discover you are a witch, you will be burned alive at the stake. Do you understand?"

Frena thought about what he'd just said to her. Though she was a simple girl, she was wise to the yearnings of men. She knew men were attracted to her. How many times had she tactfully turned down offers from wealthy merchants willing to pay her half a year's wages to deflower her honour? She prided herself she that she was still intact – a virgin, saving her precious gift for a man she would love until death.

She looked at Kunrat's beady eyes, watched them tracing up and down her body, observed the way his thin lips pushed together, and then parted, before he ran the pointed tip of his tongue over his lower lip. She recognised that he wanted her and shuddered at the thought of surrendering her body to this despicable creature.

At the same time as she was almost overcome with revulsion of what might happen, her primeval urge to survive surfaced. *If I hold onto my pride I will die – die horribly. Surely it can't be that bad to suffer this vile creatures needs for a few hours?* "Master, I understand and will submit willingly to any tests you wish to subject me to so I can prove my innocence to you."

The familiar feeling of dominance rose through him. Again, a person who would not have even passed him a glance a few years ago, now offered her complete submission to his power.

Two years earlier, Kunrat was destitute, without a home and only in possession of the rags on his back. He came by chance to the doors of a monastery and welcomed the comfort of the shelter and kindness shown to him. Lacking any opportunities to progress in the outside world, he gave his spirit to Christ along with a vow of celibacy. In exchange for food and lodgings, he sacrificed his rights to know of the pleasures of carnal gratification. In a few months he discovered how intelligent he was, how easy it was to manipulate those in authority and gain power with his current position.

Now, in front of him was the most exquisite creature he'd ever seen, creating a conflict that seemed to have no solution with an honourable outcome. If he took advantage of the situation, he would surely condemn his soul to the eternal fires of damnation. Then, an idea, a grotesque idea formed in his clever mind.

"I will subject you to an intense interrogation. This will be done in private. Depending on the outcome of your compliance to my demands for the truth, you will either be set free or condemned to burn. Guards, take this one to the interrogation cell in my quarters," Kunrat ordered, pointing directly at Frena.

"Do you wish us to remove her restraints?" asked one of the

two guards who stepped forward to separate Frena from the other women.

"Removing everything except the bindings that secure her hands behind her back."

Frena shivered in the cold air as she was led across the square to the large house used as a temporary residence by Kunrat. She looked from side to side as she passed through the opulent main room that was reassuringly warmed by a large open fire, but shuddered as the guards pushed her into a small room that was barely furnished with nothing more than a simple bed and plain wooden chair.

One of the guards forced her down onto the chair and checked her hands were securely bound before he moved to stand in the open doorway. Shortly after, she heard footsteps approaching and tried to free her mind of what would happen next.

"You may leave us now. Wait at the end of the corridor and only come if I summon you. I have a challenging task ahead of me and I don't want to be disturbed by anyone under any circumstances," Kunrat shouted at the guards.

Frena looked up and waited for him to speak. He pulled off his robes and threw them on the bed. She saw he wore a plain white gown that hung down level with his knees and reeled back in the chair when she noticed a protrusive bulge under the thin cloth.

He moved directly in front of her and dropped down onto one knee so his scrawny face was level with hers. "Are you a witch? You are such an alluring animal and you are driving me insane with your cunning charms," he said to her.

Frena opened her eyes wide and looked directly into his. "Master, I'm not a witch. I'm just an innocent girl, a virgin. I sense what you want from me and I don't want to die. I want to have a life, have children, to see them have children. Master, if I can live by giving you something in exchange, then I am willing to humble myself to your authority."

She felt his cold hands as he pressed them on her warm cheeks and tried not to tremble as he slowly pulled her face to meet his. She opened her mouth slightly to accept his cruel lips, held her breath so as not to smell or taste the rank odours of his yeasty tongue that probed the moistness of her mouth.

He pulled back and smiled, but not a friendly warm smile given by one lover to another, more of a sneer that foretells a victim they are in the grasp of their dominator. She jumped when he spoke abruptly at her. "I have taken a vow of celibacy and I'm forbidden to place this, "he said, standing and lifting his robe to show her his standing manhood, "in your sweet offerings, but I am enchanted by you my girl. If you wish to live you will comply with my desires. Do you understand?"

Frena stared at what he held directly up to her face, wishing she could will herself away from this room, this man and what she knew she had to do. She thought of the children she would bear in later life and how this sacrifice would give lives to those children.

She closed her eyes, shut down her thoughts and opened her mouth. Slowly, she leaned forward and allowed him to guide her quivering lips onto the end of a fleshy stalk that would save her from the devouring flames that would rob her of all her desires for the future.

As he gripped her hair and pulled her onto his engorgement, she pictured two giggling girls and a laughing boy running over ripe green fields, the smell of autumn apples and the aromas of a dewy spring morning. She withheld gagging and spitting as his satiation engulfed her, instead picturing babbling mountain streams that poured frothing waters to feed the bright coloured flowers that clung to life at their edge.

Kunrat stepped away from her and fell onto the bed behind him. His mind frothed in turmoil. He thought his release would render him free from the dark desires overwhelming him, but almost as soon as his quivering ecstasy passed, he wanted to feel her smooth skin in his hands, feel her soft breast yielding to the playing of his tongue and bury his throbbing organ into her untouched orifice. He began to recite the Lord's Prayer in his head and repeat the vows he made to Christ, but to little avail, as when he briefly opened his eyes, there she was within in his grasp.

Frena wished her hands were free so she could wipe the smell of him from her lips and chin. At least it was over now, and soon she would be set free to return her home and parents – if they were still alive.

He stood up and walked to her. She saw him reach out to grab her by the arms and before she could move, he pulled her from the chair and gently lowered her onto the bed. She felt him lifting her gown and then his fingers touched her – touched her intimacy. She didn't resist but decided she must acquiesce to what was inevitable. As he pushed her to turn her onto her back, she rolled willingly.

She closed her eyes as he placed his mouth over her left breast and surrendered to what was happening. She did her best not to wince when he pushed into her, easing her hips up slightly and concentrating with all her might to relax. As he slowly stroked himself inside her, she adjusted her position and masked out the feelings of guilt as her sensations of pleasure began to grow. For a brief moment she reflected on how it could be that she was enjoying being taken by the hideous monster above her.

He took her three times through the night and she felt defiled and dirty, but also confused. Rather than being the horrendous experience, she had enjoyed every minute of his *affections.*

She woke to find him standing over her with a guard at each side. One of the guards was holding a strange looking metal object in his right hand and looking at her with a face that displayed disgust towards her. Kunrat turned to the guard and spoke in a voice filled with authority. "I have no doubts this woman is a witch. She has the ability to cast spells with her tongue that no man can resist. Fit the bridal to her mouth so she cannot utter another word and take her to the stake for burning."

Frena tried to cry out and tell Kunrat he was wrong, but before she managed to say more than a few words, the metal plate of the bridal held down her tongue and pressed into the back of her throat making her retch. As they pulled her upright, she felt the warm fluids of Kunrat's pleasure dribbling down her inner thighs adding mockery to the humility and despair of her situation.

Kunrat squashed a swelling wave of guilt rising in his mind by applying crisp logic of what *really* happened. There was no doubt the woman was a witch, she had cast a spell on him that caused him to break his vow of chastity. *I must burn this witch before she destroys me. It wasn't me that sinned. I'm just an innocent victim of her witchcraft. I know I have to kill her in case she tells of what I did. She can't talk now with that thing on her head. If only things were different I could be with her for always. No, she is a witch and that's why I have to be rid of her.*

You're killing an innocent girl because of your lust. A voice said.

No, she made me do it.

"Master, will you be attending the burning?" one of the guards asked.

"Yes, I will light the pyre that will cleanse her soul. Take her from me. Tie her to the stake now and make sure you use wood and straw that is dry so she has a quick death.

Frena felt the cold air bite into her naked body as the guards dragged her out into the open. For a moment she wished she was a witch, if so she would cast a spell, no, *many* spells to curse the vile man that robbed her of her innocence and was now claiming her life.

She shut her eyes tightly and tried to blank out the reality of what was happening to her. She felt them lift her up onto a platform and push her back against a hard pole. She made gurgling noises through her throat to mask the sound of rattling chains being tied around her waist and hoped the flames would rapidly extinguish her existence.

Then she heard *his* voice, calling out for someone to pass the torch to *him*. At first she caught the scent of singeing straw, then the gentle warmth of air rising up around her body. For a few seconds, her mind relinquished the churning turmoil of her fear and hatred. Then the flames burst over her naked skin and began their cruel consumption of her body and mind. She wanted to scream but the warming bridal cramping her mouth choked her of her last wish.

Kunrat gazed on trance-like as he saw the thick dark curls of her beautiful head of hair shrink to a tight fitting hood around her contorted face. He watched abstractly as browning blisters erupted over her smooth torso and breasts. Already an idea was taking shape in his mind.

We will come across many covens of witches and now I have the secret to uncovering them. If I select the beauty amongst them for interrogation and she seduces me as this one did, then I will know they are witches. He turned to the men around him and snapped out an order. "The other women found with this one are also witches. Spare no efforts to extract the truth. Apply the pear and breast rippers on each of them until they confess, then burn them."

NINE

Henry heard every word Cristina said to him, but his mind only analysed the subtle nuances of the way her mouth formed the sounds. As he registered each subliminal lisp, every tiny explosion of a tongue pressing on the roof of a mouth and lips breaking apart simultaneously, he could only think of exploring the sensuous soft organ modulating the sounds with his own.

God how he wanted to kiss her engorged moist lips, taste the flavours of her mouth in his, feel her jaw rippling as she consumed his irrational desires.

"Henry, do you understand why it's essential you remain aloof with these particular clients?"

"Sorry I was miles away," Henry replied to Cristina for the fifth time in an hour.

"Is something bothering you? Are you ill?"

"I think I'm sick."

"What's the matter?"

"I can't say."

"Is it something serious?"

"I don't know. In a way I hope it becomes serious."

"I think we should take a break. I've been trying to tell you about the nature of some of our clients, where their money comes from and why you must never ask any awkward questions."

"Do you mean the drug traffickers and offshore internet casino operators?"

"Yes. So you were listening."

"Sort of."

"Henry, please tell me what is bothering you?"

"You might not like it."

"Listen, I'm not fazed by anything, I've been doing this job for over three years now and I've met just about every slimy shit you can imagine."

"What if I were to tell you that you're the problem, the reason I can't concentrate."

"I don't see what I've done that would cause a problem between us."

"It's not anything you've done," Henry said, pausing to take a deep breath and hoping the sweat breaking out on his forehead was not yet visible, "it's just you. Cristina, my heart wants to tell you I've fallen in love with you, but my logical side tells me I'm just totally infatuated with you. All I can think about when you talk to me is the way your lips move, how they would feel pressed against mine, what it would be like to hold you close and…"

"Are you trying to say you want to fuck me?"

"I'm just trying to tell you that I can't stop thinking…"

"Because if you are, my answer is yes," she interrupted. "I've liked you from the moment I first met you. Look, I have to teach you everything you need to know about this job and if you can't take any of it in because you're too busy wondering what it would be like to fuck me, then let's do it."

"What now?"

"My flat's only ten minutes from here and it's a lot more comfortable than this office."

"Are you sure?"

Cristina leant over to Henry and just before she reached for his mouth with hers, she whispered, "Let's have a two minute warm up first."

All that had happened over a week ago and now Henry was apart from Cristina. The lessons had gone well, but the love making was exceptional. He'd spent the last eight nights with her but not tonight.

He lowered himself into his first-class seat and opened the black brief case containing the notes Cristina prepared for him. The train jerked in the way that only trains do, as it eased its way out of Euston Station.

Henry pulled out the file Cristina printed for him yesterday and tried to focus on the details of how Dromedary Investments dealt with the transfer of millions of dollars or whatever currency from overseas accounts to its own investment platform. In four hours from now, he was set to meet his first client and all he could think of was how he would mess it up.

As the train picked up momentum and began clacking through the myriad of junctions in north London, Henry tried to dismiss the urge to empty his bowels for the third time that morning. He knew this day was coming, the day he was sent to interview a potential client, but it had always been something that was going to happen – a distant hurdle he would have to leap over in a future removed from current reality. It would have been fine if they gave him a little job for this initiation, but no, the Duchess had emphasised to him over the phone that Mr Garcia was an important client, one who was interested in making a massive investment.

He abstractly reviewed the paragraphs detailing the automated multiple purchasing of Bitcoins – through a host of off-shore money transfer organisations – that could only be accessed through the dark web on untraceable browsers. He flicked on a couple of pages to check through the summary statements, detailing how Dromedary Investments used state of the art software and insider sources to enable profitable investments in every transaction. The thought of demonstrating this to Mr Garcia on his tablet was sufficient to cause him to rise from his seat and make his way to empty his bowels one more time.

Henry inhaled a long slow draft of air into his rigid body as he passed through the doorway into the decadence of Hotel Gotham in Manchester city centre. He hardly absorbed the retro ambiance of the reception area when he approached the desk to announce his arrival. "Henry King, I have a reservation," he croaked.

The receptionist, a young woman attired in a uniform from the previous century smiled pleasantly at him. "Good afternoon Mr King, let me check. Ah yes – I see you are booked for two nights in a junior suite. If you could just sign in, I'll arrange for a porter to take your bags to your room."

Henry nervously scrawled his details down on the sheet of paper, turned around and noticed two men with dark complexions were watching him. He looked in a different direction, passing his gaze through the twenty or so guests milling around the reception area and suddenly felt very alone.

For the last eight days he had been in the company of the most wonderful person he'd ever met. Thoughts of Cristina, her smile, her laughter, her intimate nuances and infectious humour coursed through him in this moment of isolation. He was on his own now, about to face the greatest test of his young life and he was scared.

"Excuse me sir, may I take your bag up to your room," a young porter said, who wore a dark uniform brightened by a double row of silver buttons that twinkled like perfectly aligned stars.

Henry hesitated as one of the swarthy looking men walked over to him. "I think so," he said to the porter as the man stepped up to face him.

"Excuse me, are you Mr King?" the man said in a deep voice.

"Yes I am. Can I help you?"

"Yes sir, you can. I am Pablo. I work for Mr Garcia. He has booked a meeting room and is ready to see you – now."

"I've only just arrived. Is it okay if I go up to my room first?"

"The porter will sort out your bags. Please come with me now, Mr King. Mr Garcia is a very busy man and does not wait for anybody."

"Well, in that case, I'll come with you now," Henry said with a smile.

Henry soon realised that Hotel Gotham was like a maze. There were side-turnings off every corridor which led to seemingly endless rooms adorned with art deco fittings. Within a couple of minutes, he lost his bearings and realised his bladder was calling to be emptied.

Pablo opened a door and ushered Henry into a small meeting room. Sitting at the end of a retro designed table was a thick set man, who remained seated as Pablo pulled back one of the chairs and deployed his arm to indicate to Henry that he should sit down. "Mr Garcia, he has arrived. This is Mr King," Pablo boomed with his deep voice, before stepping back to stand with his arms folded across his chest in front of the only door in or out of the room.

Mr Garcia was definitely in his fifties. His brushed back thinning black hair, dark complexion, wide full mouth and broad jawline aided Henry's impression that this man was a South American gangster who would not hesitate to have him assassinated, cut into small pieces and dispersed around Manchester's refuse bins.

Mr Garcia fixed his beady dark eyes on Henry's face and spoke with a much higher pitch voice than Henry was anticipating. "Mr King, I'm very pleased to meet you and hope our transactions will be successful. You are much younger than I expected."

Henry was about to say 'I'm new and you're my first client' but Cristina's voice entered his head and he remembered the basics of her coaching. "Dromedary Investments has a policy of recruiting its agents for expertise and business acumen. I can assure you, Mr Garcia, that despite my youthful appearance, I am an expert in many areas of business and finance."

"So you have experience of *turning things over* I take it?"

"I have indeed, I've *turned things over* many times in my working experience to date," Henry said, picturing how many burgers he tossed in the last few months.

"Show me how your company works. I have several lucrative businesses in many parts of the world, but I'm very reticent about paying the excessive taxes demanded from me. Currently, I have most of my capital in off-shore accounts but they charge between two to five percent to look after my money."

It was clear in Henry's mind that he must never ask a client for details of their business activities and should derail his clients if they offered too much information. "It's best if I show you how we will invest your money on my tablet," Henry said, as he fumbled to open his brief case. "I'll just need to log in to the hotel's Wi-Fi. Do you happen to know the password?"

"Pablo, do you know the password?" Mr Garcia called out.

Pablo reached to his inside pocket and threw a business card onto the table. "It's written on the back of that," he bellowed.

Henry typed in the password and opened the first link on his list. Over the next twenty minutes he explained to Mr Garcia how a large number of relatively small withdrawals would be made over a four day period until the fully agreed investment amount was transferred into Dromedary Investment's account.

For the next two hours, Henry showed how the money would be invested in shares, currency markets, gilts, bonds and hedge funds. He opened up details of anonymous clients' accounts and saw Mr Garcia's face light up as the figures showed their assets doubling every few months. Finally, Henry showed him flow charts to explain how the money could be returned through multiple accounts and pseudo business fronts.

Mr Garcia rubbed his wide firm jaw with his thick hairy fingers. "Everything seems very plausible. I need to verify everything you've told me before I make a decision. I'll call you on your mobile when I'm satisfied that what've you said is correct. Pablo, write down Mr King's phone number and contact Raymond."

Henry left the room and followed the signs to the reception area. He approached the desk and asked for his room number and where the nearest toilet was. After unpacking his new designer clothes that the Duchess had organised for him, he decided to change out of his suit and wear something more relaxing.

He picked out a black top and noticed for the first time the logo of the Duo Wolf brand. Finely embroidered on the inside silver label were the heads of a black and white wolf. He briefly admired the quality of the stitching that brought the wolves' eyes alive. He was just about to leave his room and head to one of the restaurants to eat, when his phone rang. He didn't recognise the number but answered.

"Mr King, it's me, Mr Garcia. I've had my colleague check out a few things and I want to do business with you. I have a question for you. Will an investment of two hundred million dollars be possible, or is it too large a sum for your company to handle?"

"Sorry, did you say two hundred million dollars?" Henry asked, as he calculated how much his two percent commission of the total sum invested by a client would amount to.

"Yes, I am interested in having someone manage that sum."

"Mr Garcia, can I call you back in five minutes. I will just contact my director to confirm there won't be any issues with an investment of that size."

"I'll await your call, Mr King."

Henry scrolled through his contacts and prayed that the

Duchess would answer her phone, she did.

"Hello, it's me, Henry. Mr Garcia wants to invest two hundred million dollars. Can we handle that amount?" Henry asked as he paced around the room.

"Well done, Henry, I knew you had it in you. Of course we can. In fact the larger the sums the easier it is for us to manipulate the markets. That's a very healthy commission for you on your first job."

"I know I can't believe it, four hundred thousand dollars for a day's work."

"Henry, you are mistaken, it's not four hundred thousand, it's four million. Make sure you keep Mr Garcia happy."

Henry sat on the edge of his bed and wondered when he would wake up. *This has to be a dream it can't be happening.* He looked down to his phone and swiped the screen to recall Mr Garcia. "Hello, Mr Garcia. I've some good news for you. There is no problem with your investment. When would you like to go through the paperwork?"

"We can do all that tomorrow. You've taken a great weight off my mind young man. I've been worried sick about that money sitting in those accounts. I want to celebrate this evening, so let's go and hit the town as they say. Mr King, I assume you will receive a handsome commission for your work so you can do me a simple favour. I want you to book us into a whore house for tonight. I prefer them with big breasts and fat arses so make sure you don't line me up with any skinny ones."

"A whore house?"

"You know what I mean. What do you call them over here, is it a brothel or massage parlour? I just want to get laid tonight and you are joining me. Make sure you don't disappoint me."

"Oh fuck," Henry said to himself. *Shit, what shall I do? I haven't got a clue where to find a whore house. Cristina, oh my God. What about Cristina?* Henry looked down to his phone and swiped his finger over her contact details. She picked up after three rings.

"It's me Henry," he said, tapping his fingers nervously on his knee.

"Hi, how is it going?"

"Good I think. He wants to invest two hundred million but there's a problem."

Cristina frowned and wondered what the problem might be. "What, does he have some doubts about the security of his money?"

Henry paused to think. *If only that was the problem.* "No, it's nothing like that. He wants me to go out with him tonight."

"You don't mean he wants you in exchange for agreeing to make the deal?"

Henry wiped the image of Mr Garcia's fat lips kissing his out of his mind before replying. "No, it's even worse. He wants me to book us into a place for some entertainment."

"Henry, can you be precise. I can't help you if you don't tell me what's wrong."

"Look Cristina, what he wants me to do is book some time with some prostitutes in one of those places that prostitutes do their thing," he replied, placing the phone down on his lap briefly.

"Oh is that all. It comes with the territory. Just book something you think he'll like."

"Right, how do I tell you this? He wants me to go with him," Henry said with trepidation.

"Are you worried what I'll think? Just make sure you wear something to protect yourself and think of me while you do your thing. I have to be honest with you, Henry. I'm really fond of you, in fact I think I am falling in love with you, but the type of people we meet in this field of work will have what they want. I've had to sleep with a few of my clients to close the deal. Don't worry about what I'll think of you, and thank you for telling me, you're so sweet."

"Cristina, there's one other problem. I haven't got a clue how to find a *whore house.* To be honest, I wouldn't know where to find one or what to ask."

"I'll tell you what, give me a few minutes and I'll sort it out for you. What's he after?"

"Big and beautiful I think."

"Do you mean fat or curvy?"

"Curvy."

"Consider the job done. I'll email you a link in a few minutes so you know where you're going later. Have fun, but don't enjoy yourself too much."

* * *

Nigeria: Close to the border with Chad.

Akubar clamped Yasuf's shoulders with his hands and shook him like a young child. "Brother, we are going to be famous after this raid. We have ninety two young girls in our care. You can now have six wives and a couple more slaves just like King Henry."

Yasuf cast his eyes to the eight men sat in a huddle. He could tell by the whites of their eyes they were terrified about what was going to happen to them. "What are we going to do with them?" he asked, pointing to the men.

"They are all going to become stars of your film. I have already planned how they will die. It's time you set up your equipment. I think it's best if you pan the camera to those who are watching the first man die, try to capture their fear so we can show it to those who resist us. These good men will perform one last deed to help promote the glory of Allah."

"How are you going to kill them?" Yasuf asked, flicking his eyes from Akubar to the men.

"That is simple. I've come up with an idea that will bring them a long and painful death, one that will overcome each man with a fear so terrible, anyone who watches it will surrender to us without a fight and join our cause."

As he unpacked his camera from its case, Yasuf fought to hold back his tears. From somewhere deep in his head a voice was screaming at him, telling him that what he was doing was wrong. *Allah, I know in my heart this is not what you want, but I have no choice left to me. Please Allah, save me from what I have become.*

Later that evening, Yasuf blinked several times in an attempt to remove the red mist covering his eyes. In desperation to remove the images and sounds of those he filmed earlier, he entered the tent of his slave girl.

She sat impassively, tethered by a length of rope to the central pole supporting the worn canvas of the simple shelter. He realised he didn't even know her name as he'd never asked her in all the times he used her.

He pulled off her gown and pushed her onto her back. He didn't look into her face as he pulled off his smoke ingrained clothing, didn't touch her body as he moved to mount her and didn't touch her with his hands as he pushed firmly to enter her. He thrust himself rhythmically into her yielding body and released his anguish repeatedly over the next hour. Occasionally, he felt her squirming underneath him, but dismissed any thoughts of her discomfort from his head. Her only purpose was to quench his needs. After his third release he paused, propping himself up on his elbows. He looked at her face and saw she was studying him intently. "Do you hate me for what I do to you?" he said, wishing at once he'd not broken his veil of silence.

"I did the first few times, but I've become accustomed to you and what you do. In fact I love it when you take me like you just did. Is that wrong?"

Yasuf withdrew from her and sat up beside her. "You like what I do to you?"

"I know I shouldn't, but you make me have nice feelings inside."

"What in your head?"

"No inside me. It feels so good. Can't you feel me shaking sometimes?"

Yasuf looked down at her face and was shocked to see she was smiling at him. "What's your name?"

Before I became yours, I was called Susan. My mother named me after a sister who cared for my older brother when he became ill with a fever. I want you to give me a new name."

TEN

King Malius gazed absently through the arched opening of his private room set high in a turret overlooking the only route into Castle Boese. Certain that his younger son Vladrek, was dead, he mused over the prospects for his family's bloodline. It had been his intention for Vladrek to become the successor to the throne rather than his older son, Burgolt.

He pondered on the difference between his only two sons. Burgolt had his unfortunate physical and emotional deficiencies. Vladrek, on the other hand was a younger version of himself, handsome, thoughtful and intelligent, although he lacked confidence because of the torment he suffered from his older brother. And now the older brother was concerning him. Only yesterday he received discrete reports of how three more servant girls had been found dead, and all of them bore the familiar trademark of Burgolt's doings.

As Malius considered his options for *dealing* with his troubles, he observed, but did not see a group of horse riders climbing the ascent towards his home. Only when he finished fantasising about different methods of removing Burgolt from the realm of the living, did his mind register that uninvited guests were making their way to the main entrance of the castle.

He jumped out of his chair and peered through the opening,

wiping his white hair from his eyes with one hand while propping himself up with the other. He quickly counted – there were twelve riders on horseback, ten were armed men, one a hooded rider and the other a young woman – surely it couldn't be?

Two weeks earlier, one of the escorts accompanying Vladrek on his journey to Gothburgh had returned, informing him that the whole party was lost in a flood. The man who returned was in a bad way, his ribs were broken along with his right arm. He'd said that everyone, including the horses were swept away, that he'd only escaped by managing to grasp an old tree trunk that was swept up to higher ground.

He had gone on to recall how he searched for survivors over the next three days, but only found the corpses of perished men and horses left in the flood's trail of devastation. Malius craned his head down to watch as the robed rider dismounted far below him. He called out through the opening, "Vladrek, is that you?" and leapt back with joy as the tiny figure pulled back his hood and looked up at him. Malius nearly fell over his chair as he turned around and headed for the series of staircases leading down from the turret.

Burgolt pushed the girl off his bed, grabbed her discarded clothes and threw them onto her naked body. "Next time you try to resist me, I'll use a larger one on you. Send in the next girl," he ranted as he kicked her thigh and caused her to roll towards the door. As she pulled her chemise over her head, there was a loud rap on the door.

"I'm not ready for you yet, wait until you're summoned," Burgolt shouted at the door.

"My Prince, I have a message from your father. Your brother has safely returned," a muffled voice called through the closed door.

"Tell him I'm busy and will see him later. Send in the girl

standing outside my door."

Burgolt pulled the device from his body and placed it under the bed, checking it was within easy grasp for when he might need it later.

A young, pretty girl stepped into the room and nervously looked into the tearful face of the girl who was tying her skirt around her waist. Burgolt looked at the girl and tried to remember who she was. "Have we had the pleasure of meeting before?" he murmured, as he envisaged what lay underneath her loose fitting garments.

"No my Prince, you passed through the kitchens where I work yesterday and gave orders that I should attend your room at high sun today."

"You are a delectable little thing. What is your name?"

"I'm Libeste."

Burgolt rose to his feet and stepped up to the trembling girl. "Do you know why you are here?"

"I am told that my Prince likes pretty women."

"Are you a good lover, Libeste?"

"My Prince, I don't know as I've never been with a man."

Burgolt pulled Libeste's blouse from the waist band of her skirt and slipped his hands underneath it onto her breasts. "My girl, I'm going to teach you how to become a great lover. Now, kneel before your Prince so you can receive your first lesson."

King Malius drew in deep breaths as he reached the bottom of the final flight of steps. For a moment he steadied himself, taking in several long slow gulps of air to ease his dizziness and the sharp pains biting into his chest. *My time is nearly at a close, I must make a decree soon. Vladrek, my son, you will be crowned the new King when I die.* "Where is he, where is my son?" Malius yelled, as he stepped painfully with an upright posture into the main entrance hall of the castle.

One of his senior servants, Balrek, ran into the hall from a side doorway. "He's here your Majesty, in the guest hall. He's returned with a princess and she is very beautiful. Shall I order a feast to be made in the kitchen to welcome the return of Prince Vladrek?"

"Yes, order a feast. Tonight I will celebrate. We'll all celebrate the return of my son." Malius cried back.

Malius swept his hair from his face, straightened his cloak, and strode upright through the doorway into the guest hall. Vladrek was sitting on one of the large chairs and next to him, Malius saw a beautiful woman. Standing either side of them was a group of heavily armed men. Vladrek and the woman stood up as Malius entered.

Vladrek spoke first. "Father, this is Czyelle, daughter of King Murak. We had to leave in a hurry as the army of the Inquisition was on us. Father, we must prepare for the worst as I do not think it will be long before we are attacked."

"My son, I take heed of your warning, but tonight we will celebrate your safe return. I thought you dead, but I can see you have more about you than shows from the outside. Your Princess is very beautiful and I am already excited at the prospect of having grandchildren that are not – like – never mind that for now. Where is Burgolt, why is he not here to greet his brother's return?"

"He is attending to some business," a servant called out from the back of the guest hall.

Corrupting more servant girls and making more of his hideous spawn, Malius thought, as he contemplated making his decree here and now. "Please forgive my ignorance, Princess Czyelle. You must be tired after your travels. I will have my servants attend to your needs. Vladrek, you too must rest after your adventures, but before you do, I want to have a quick talk with you about a matter that has been troubling me a great deal."

After eating, bathing and dressing into clean clothes, Vladrek lay on his bed, the bed he and Czyelle would be sharing in a few days from now. He picked up the pocket watch and pressed the snake's pair of haunting eyes to reveal the prismatic sheen of the watch's hidden inner face. He placed the watch up to his ear and listened to its gentle beat, allowing its regular ticking to bring order to his meandering thoughts.

He was still felt shaken by his father's words. 'Son, I have decided that you are to be the next King of Castle Boese. Your brother has proved himself unfit to lead us through the troubles that lie ahead of us.' He wondered if his life with his new bride would be long and happy or fraught with disappointments and possibly death in these changing times. Why couldn't they be left in peace to live their lives as they wanted? How was his brother going to take the news that he would not ascend to power? Why, when his future seemed so bright, was he filled with a sense of dread, of impending doom?

For a moment he allowed the gentle ticking from the watch to distract him from his troubles. He closed his eyes and pressed the watch into his ear, but jerked out of his trance as the door to his room burst open and crashed against the stone wall.

Burgolt walked into his room and stepped up to the head of the bed. "So you survived the flood. We had news that you were dead. I hear you have brought back a bride for yourself. Is she fat and ugly?"

Vladrek looked up at his brother and tried to brush aside the creeping unease brewing inside him. "Yes, I just managed to escape. I think the horses sensed something was about to happen and they woke me up just in time. As for my bride to be, she is very beautiful, and I'm very lucky to have found her," Vladrek replied, as he set the watch down on a small table at the side of his bed and closed the casing.

Burgolt's eyes caught a glimpse of the pearly iridescence reflecting from the watch's face before two glints of sharp red light forced him to blink. "What is that you have there, brother?"

"It's something I found on my travels. It's a small timepiece like nothing I've ever seen before."

"Let me have a look," Burgolt snapped, as he reached out and picked up the watch. "How does it open?"

"Do you see the snake's eyes? Press down the left one and then the right."

Burgolt's small beady eyes grew larger as he studied the face of the watch. "What does it do?"

"It measures the passing of time and more. The inner rings show the positions of the wandering stars and track the moon. It's a wonderful creation, but I've no idea who made it."

"Can I have it? This is something made for a king and it won't be long before I am King. Did you know our father's health is ailing? This should be mine and if you love your brother as a brother should, you'll give it to me."

"I'm not sure I can. I met a stranger who said it was his watch, but I'm to keep it safely for him," Vladrek replied, wondering if this would be a good time to tell his brother that he was not going to become, King.

"You are tired brother. Sleep well tonight and tomorrow, I will talk reason into you and explain to you why you must give this to me," Burgolt said, snapping the watch's casing shut before placing it back on the table.

Burgolt bowed before turning around and leaving the room. He shut the door behind him and stomped down the stone corridor.

Later that evening a great feast was held in the main hall of Castle Boese. King Malius sat at the head table with his son, Vladrek, to his right, and his bride to be, Czyelle, to his left.

Burgolt, still in his room, reached from a kneeling position to grasp his favourite toy from under his bed. He looked down to the semi-conscious girl under him and considered slapping her face to rouse her from the slumber he induced on her by strangulation. He decided she might fight against him again, so he strapped on his device first, before gripping her cheeks and shaking her violently. As she came too, he pushed onto her and stifled her screams with the flat of his hand. Twenty minutes later he realised she was no longer breathing.

Burgolt entered the main hall, putting all thoughts of what had just passed out of his mind. By now the girl's body would be floating down the stream that cut through the nearest valley.

He looked at the main table to check where his seat was and caught his first glimpse of Czyelle. *Brother, you didn't tell me your bride to be is the most beautiful woman in the world.* He checked to see where his empty chair was on the head table, but all the seats were filled. Walking past the other tables, occupied by members of the court and senior servants, he fixed his gaze on his father. "My King, please accept my apologies for my late arrival. Where am I to be seated?"

King Malius put down the beef rib he was chewing on, wiped his mouth and stood to his feet. "Burgolt, we assumed you were too busy to share the celebrations of your brother's safe return. I gave your seat to Duke Fredrick, as he is good friend and wished to congratulate your brother on his forthcoming marriage and ascension to the throne."

Burgolt hesitated before replying, carefully calculating the words spoken by his father. "What throne is my brother going to occupy?" *Has he inherited another kingdom?*

"No, Burgolt, he has not inherited another kingdom. I have made a decision. My health is failing and in a week's time, I am stepping down as King. Unfortunate events are happening outside and soon the Inquisition will come knocking on our doors. You are not strong enough to see us through these times, but your brother has demonstrated great strength. Vladrek will be crowned King of Castle Boese on the day of his marriage to Princess Czyelle."

Burgolt looked around the large hall. He cast a quick gaze at the hundreds of faces turned in his direction, looked through the endless pairs of eyes focusing on him to see how he was reacting to his father's words. "My King, madness has consumed you. I will not challenge your words now, but will wait until tomorrow, when I'm sure you will have recovered your senses."

Burgolt wanted to turn and run, but as he looked at his father, brother and Czyelle, a sense of determination overtook him. Taking strong and deliberate steps, he walked up to the head table and stopped at Czyelle's side. "My Princess, my brother told me you were a very beautiful woman, but he did not do you justice. You are indeed a fit prize for any man. Please let me kiss your hand as a token of my appreciation and wish you success in your forthcoming marriage."

Princess Czyelle rose to her feet and held her hand out towards Burgolt. He took it in his and raised it to his mouth. Czyelle felt his wet tongue slide over the back of her hand before he pulled her closer to him. With his mouth against her ear he whispered, "You are not destined for my brother, but will wed the true King, me."

Czyelle pulled away from him and sat down. Both Malius and Vladrek saw something had happened, but waited until Burgolt walked away before asking Czyelle what was wrong.

"What did he say to you?" Malius whispered, while Vladrek leaned over to catch her reply.

"He said he was going to marry me and that he will become King. I don't understand."

"I think he's shocked by what he's just heard. You have nothing to worry about, he's just jealous of his brother," Malius replied, wondering if Burgolt was plotting something.

When the feast was over and the guest were leaving, Malius pulled Vladrek to one side. "Son, I'm worried about your brother. He is bitter about what I've decided and I want you to be on your guard."

"You don't think he'd do anything to me do you? He's my brother and shares my blood."

Malius brushed away a strand of hair that hung over his face. "There is something evil, something corrupt that lurks inside your brother. I think it best if you are wary of him."

"I will take notice of your advice, father. I admire your wisdom and following in your footsteps as King will not be easy for me."

Vladrek climbed the two flights of stairs that led to the floor of his rooms and noticed a guard was standing outside his bedroom door. He gave the guard a curious look, but before he had a chance to speak the guard glanced at him and said, "The King has ordered me to stand watch over you."

Vladrek entered his room and prepared for his bed. The cloak he'd worn on his travels was still cast on the floor and as he picked it up, he felt something hard in one of its concealed pockets. He reached inside the cloak to see what it was and pulled out a thin object wrapped in cloth. He remembered the stiletto blade given to him by the stranger, Gomory.

With care, he wound the cloth from the knife before slipping it under his pillow. The copious quantities of food and drink he consumed through the evening caused him to fall asleep as soon as he lay in his bed.

In the small hours of the morning, a girl crept along the corridor outside Vladrek's chambers. She spoke softly with the guard before escorting him down the passageway into an empty room. Burgolt watched from a safe distance.

Shortly after, Vladrek awoke, realising that someone was astride him, pinning him down on the bed by kneeling on his covers. "Don't worry brother, it's only me. I want to talk with you."

"What are you doing here? What do want?"

"I'm here to give you some advice. Leave now. I'll give you a large bag of gold coins so you can start a new life far from here. I'll tell our father that you were too frightened to become our King."

Vladrek tried to push Burgolt from him, but the covers restricted him from moving easily. He twisted hard, but only succeeded in turning over onto his stomach. Burgolt bore down on him with all his weight. "Brother, I'm taking that watch, it's mine. I'm also going to take your Princess. If I'm to be King, I will need to have a Queen, and she is perfect. Do you understand me?"

Vladrek managed to ease his right arm up through the covers and slip his hand under the pillow. "You no longer frighten me, brother. There is a guard outside my room and if I call he will come in here to kill you."

"Your guard is currently with one of my little whores. At this moment he's more interested in what her pretty mouth is doing to his cock. I will get what I want, brother, even if I have to kill you."

Vladrek closed his fingertips around the handle of the knife and flexed his limbs in an effort to work out how he could throw Burgolt from him. "Let me up so I can face you eye to eye."

Burgolt slipped back a few inches and pulled the cover down from Vladrek's shoulders. "Don't do anything stupid or I will kill you. I have a heavy stone in my right hand and I will bring it down on your head and break your skull if you try anything."

Vladrek knew he must act soon. He doubted his brother intended to let him live, so he practiced his next move in his mind. If he swung back his right arm, he should be able to stick the blade into his brother's ribs. Gomory had told him the knife contained poison in the two groves running down the blade, so if he could just make one stab it might be enough.

Using all his strength, he forced his body up with his left arm and swung out with his right. He felt Burgolt react as soon as he began his move. A knee crushed into his back before he could complete his swing, then his brother's hand gripped his right wrist and twisted his arm until he lost grip on the knife. For a second he felt his brother's weight shift, before the covers were pulled back from his body and a searing pain shot up through him. He just had time to realise Burgolt had stabbed him between his buttocks, forcing the poison blade up his rear passage, before a cool numbness seeped into empty blackness.

Burgolt released his tight grip from the knife's handle and climbed off the bed. He crept slowly up to the head of the bed, checking for any sign of life in his brother's body. Why was he not breathing? How could such a small blade have inflicted a mortal wound? He'd not intended to stab his brother in his anus – that was just where the knife ended up.

With hesitation, he half rolled his brother over onto his side and saw his eyes were open and unmoving – he was dead. Burgolt walked down to the end of the bed and reached out to grip the knife's handle. Slowly, he withdrew the blade, anticipating a rush of fresh blood would pour from the wound, but there was none. He raised the blade close to his face and ran his fingertip over the congealed sticky coating, noting that the blood had already set into a stiff jelly. *Something made his blood clot very quickly, is it this blade?*

He walked back to the head of the bed and set the knife down on the small table next to the pocket watch. For a moment he hesitated, then, he picked up the watch and slipped it into his pocket.

Hanging from the wall, he noticed a small neck-scarf and reached out for it. He used it to carefully wipe the cleavage between his brother's buttocks and found there was only a trace of blood smeared on the white scarf. To be certain, he spat on the scarf and wiped one more time before concealing it in the same pocket as the watch. He gently pulled back his brother's buttocks and checked to see if the wound was visible – but all he saw was a slight tear deep in the dark recess. He grabbed the covers and carefully draped them over his brother's body, his thoughts already putting together the mechanism for covering up the murder. Burgolt realised the only person who knew he was here was the servant girl. He paced to the door, reasoning he could easily dispose of her later.

What about the guard? Burgolt panicked before he remembered the guard should have been at his post and knew he would be too terrified to admit what he was doing. He turned to look back at the unmarked body of his brother. The way he was lying in his bed looked as if he had died naturally from some hidden illness in his sleep. Everything was perfect.

Burgolt looked around him and spotted the knife on the table. He grabbed the knife and wrapped it in the scarf before placing it into his pocket. He calmly walked to the door, opened it and shouted. "Help, come quickly. It's my brother, there's something wrong. I can't wake him."

A moment later, Burgolt heard the sound of someone running towards him. The guard had emerged from a room further up the corridor and was now running as fast as he could while trying to pull up his leggings. "My Prince, what's the matter?"

Burgolt rushed into his brother's room and shouted to the guard. "I just arrived. I wanted to discuss the wedding plans with my brother but I cannot wake him. I think he's dead."

The guard pulled back the covers and checked Vladrek's face. "Oh God, how can this have happened?"

"Were you not meant to be on duty?" Burgolt asked.

"Yes, my Prince, but I only left my post for a minute, I needed to relive myself."

Burgolt thought about what he should do next. "I will go and summon help. Check his body and see if you can find any signs of foul play. If someone has harmed my dear brother I will burn them alive after I've skinned them."

An hour later, Burgolt leant against the stone wall of the corridor outside Vladrek's room. His brother's room was filled with every member of the castle who professed to know some medical knowledge, and judging by the murmuring he could hear coming from the room, they had reached a general consensus that his brother had died from a sudden failure of the heart.

As he waited, he planned what he must do next. He would visit Czyelle, commiserate with her on her loss and inform her that they would marry in three days from now. He would have to dispose of the servant girl, something he could arrange tonight. He would summon her to his room and take care of her in his usual way.

His father was the awkward one to deal with. He was certain his father would suspect him of being responsible for Vladrek's death, but what could he do? The old man was at the end of his reign and needed a successor. There was no one else but him. His thoughts were cut off by the call of one of his father's servants.

"Prince Burgolt, your father wishes to speak with you now. Please hurry, he says it's urgent you attend him at once."

Burgolt swallowed hard, drew in a deep breath and followed the servant. He was led to one of the court chambers and was surprised to see his father seated in a large upright chair surrounded by a dozen members of his court. Burgolt bowed and spoke quietly. "My King, is this audience not going to be held in private?"

Malius set a grim face onto Burgolt. "I feel safer if all that we have to say is witnessed by others."

"What do you mean, safer?" Burgolt asked, feeling it was better if he went on the offensive.

"I know not what you did with your brother, but I'm deeply disturbed that it should be you who discovered him."

"I just paid him a visit to ask if there was anything he wanted me to do for his forthcoming wedding."

"Just as the guard disappeared, how convenient for you. I'm sure you know I cannot sanction your ascension to the throne while I have a breath left in my body. I will remain King until I perish. You are the rightful heir, but that does not mean I have to witness you take over my kingdom."

"Father, I know I have disappointed you, but I'm going to make up to you before you die. I have decided to change my ways. I am going to marry and provide you with grandchildren to carry on your bloodline."

"Which whore have you chosen?"

"I am going to marry Princess Czyelle. In fact, I plan to tell her when I finish talking with you. We will be wed three days from now."

"And what if she doesn't want you?"

"That, father, is not her decision to make."

Malius rose to his feet and stepped towards Burgolt. "By all the power in me, I wish you'd never been born. I forbid…"

Malius stopped speaking. He reached out with his right hand to grasp something that was not there and brought his left hand up to grab at his own chest. He opened his mouth one more time, but instead of speaking he made a noise similar to a baby gurgling as it explored the novelty of hearing its own sounds. Burgolt watched in curiosity as a purple coloured wave spread over the old man's face, and stepped back as his father dropped to the floor.

Two hours later, Burgolt stood over Czyelle as she sat tearfully in a chair. He had informed her of the sudden tragic deaths of Vladrek and his father, and now turned his conversation to what he intended to happen. "In three days from now, the period of mourning will conclude. I am to be crowned King of Castle Boese and you my dear, will be crowned my Queen.

We will marry in the morning, ascend to the throne in the afternoon and consummate our union in the evening."

Czyelle looked up into Burgolt's beady eyes that looked more rat-like because of his large hooked nose. For a moment she imagined kissing his cruel thin lips, feeling his scrawny body against her soft flesh. Her men were still here – maybe if she could find them, they would help her escape from her forthcoming horror.

Burgolt spoke with her one last time before they were married. "I'm not sure if you are aware, my lady, but I have a considerable appetite for the pleasure of the flesh. I'm going to appoint one of my servants to attend to you. She is experienced in my needs and will advise you on what I will expect from you. Do not disappoint me."

※ ※ ※

Kunrat walked to the rear of the line of men heading up the hill to attack Gothburgh castle. He lifted his right hand up to his chest and gripped the crucifix hanging from his neck.

Inwardly, he tried to pray to Christ, asking for guidance about the thoughts spiralling through his head. Since the witch had cast a spell on him to commit several acts of fornication with her, the thought of his next interrogation of a witch consumed his every waking thought.

Soon the leading army would engage with the guards of this heinous castle filled with vile demons of hell. He was certain they would discover a large coven of witches inside its dark walls, and in the cause of his God, he would root out and uncover the witchery within.

He felt the sharp corners of the metal cross bite into the soft skin of his hands as he clutched the symbol of sanctity tighter, in effort to cast out the rising lust growing in his loins.

As he forced his body up the steep incline, crushed the crucifix with his hand, he tried to make peace with his beliefs by applying sensible reasoning to what would happen.

A commotion of screaming and swords clashing stirred Kunrat from his thoughts. He knew the head of the column had engaged with the castle's defence and the battle had commenced.

He slowed his pace and looked ahead, but a turn in the path blocked his view of what was happening at the main gate leading into the castle. A few minutes later, progressing like a slow wave across a deep lake, repeated calls came rippling down the line of monks, priests and armed soldiers.

"The gates are breached and they have surrendered."

Kunrat threw back his shoulders and pushed out his chest as he walked into the castle's main hall. He scanned through the huddled groups of terrified men shackled together and dumped in heaps around the perimeter walls of the huge room. "Where are their women? Where are the witches that inhabit this foul edifice?"

One of the guards mingling around the prisoners shouted back, "So far we've found no sign of any women, Master."

"What have you found?"

"These men and their King, but also, Master, we've found two chests filled with gold."

Kunrat paused, rubbing his thin chin with his long fingers. "How many gold crosses, how many crucifixes have you found?"

"None so far, Master."

"I thought not. These people are godless and we must teach them a lesson. Bring in their King, strip his clothing from his body and lay him out on that table," Kunrat shouted, pointing to a large table set in the middle of the hall.

He then walked slowly around the hall, stopping to stare into the faces of the shivering prisoners. "Is there any man here who is skilled in using a forge and can cast metals? If so speak now and I will spare you from interrogation if you pledge your allegiance to Christ."

From the other side of the hall, a single voice called out. "I'm the castle's blacksmith and know the craft of forging and casting metals."

"Who spoke?" Kunrat snapped.

"I did, my name is, Peter," a man called back, rattling the chains securing his wrists and ankles.

"Guards, release that man and bring him to me," Kunrat yelled across the hall.

As the guards unscrewed the bolts locking the shackles to the man's wrists and ankles, another man was dragged into the room. "Master, this is King Murak. What do you want us to do with him?"

Kunrat walked over to the table. "Lay him out on the table. Arrange him in a crucifixion position and tie him in place. One of you, find me a piece of charcoal."

"Where am I going to find charcoal in here?" one of the guards said, staring back at Kunrat.

"Look for a fireplace and pick out a piece of charred wood. I want to make a sketch."

As Kunrat finished speaking, two guards escorted the blacksmith to the table. Kunrat turned to address the man. "So your name is, Peter. That's a good Christian name."

"I am a Christian, my Lord."

"I'm not a Lord. You may address me as, Master."

"Sorry, Master. What do you require from me?"

"I'm going to mark out the shape of a cross on this heathen, I want you to melt down all the gold and cast it into the shape of a crucifix exactly the same size as the cross I draw on this man."

The guard returned with a black stick that he held out for

Kunrat to take. "Master, this is all I could find."

Kunrat reached out for the stick and grasped it in his right hand. A moment later he screamed and dropped the piece of charred wood onto the floor. "You fool, it's still burning. You've made me burn my hand."

"It's all I could find, Master."

"Give me your dagger."

"I'm sorry, Master, please don't kill me."

"I'm not going to kill you, though I'm tempted to burn out your eyes with hot coals. Hand me your blade."

With a shaking hand, the guard pulled a dagger from his belt. "Here you are, Master, but be careful as I always keep this little beast very sharp. One never knows when one might need to slit a throat or two."

Kunrat took the dagger and walked up to King Murak. "Peter, watch how I mark this man. The cross I wish you to make must be the exact size as the cross I'm going to draw on him." Kunrat placed the point of the dagger onto Murak's forehead and slowly drew the blade down the centre of his nose, over his lips and down onto his chest until he reached the Kings genitals.

"You – lift that thing to one side," Kunrat spat out to a nearby guard. Dextrously, Kunrat traced the blade pass the base of the King's flattened phallus and sliced through the skin of his scrotum. He then took a step nearer to the table and used the knife to score from one wrist to the other across the King's chest. "Blacksmith, measure the size of the cross and return within an hour with my golden crucifix."

"Yes, Master, but the metal will not have cooled by then."

"I don't want it to be cool. In fact I want it as hot as possible. Carry the cross here by whatever means you can the moment the metal has set. Take as many guards as you think you'll need to help you. Now go."

Kunrat placed his hand on King Murak's chest and parted the

slit skin with his fingers to expose a blood filled valley traversing down his torso. "My King, most men would have screamed out loudly when I did what I did to you. "Are you brave or mute?"

"I am neither. I know I have no choice but to surrender to your desires, *Master.* We are an innocent people living in harsh conditions. By my governance as King, no man hungers and all are cared for. If you decide I'm not worthy then do as you will to me, but spare my subjects as they have only followed what I commanded them to do."

"That is for me to decide, *King Murak.* Tell me where you are hiding your women and I will deal with your subjects as leniently as I deem God will allow. Continue to hide from me where they are concealed, and I will unleash the full forces of the Inquisition on you and your subjects," Kunrat said, releasing his hold on Murak's parted wound.

King Murak thought of his daughter, Czyelle, surely by now she would be safely away from danger. "All I know is that the women I love have already fled far from here."

Kunrat raised his arm and rested his chin in his hand. Taking a few steps away from the table, he spoke aloud so that all in the large hall would hear his words. "Heed my warning. Shortly, I will demonstrate how I deal with heretics and those who hide witches." He swirled around, glaring at the shackled prisoners."Guards, raise the prisoners to their feet and bring them nearer so they can see how their King dies. I want you all witness the fate that awaits you if you do not cooperate with my requests. The first man who reveals where the women are hiding will be set free and given a bag of gold coins, along with the choice of selecting one woman who is proven not to be a witch." He paused before smiling benignly at the men being raised to their feet by the guards. "The rest of you will be interrogated as suspected heretics and forced to confess your sins before purification."

Kunrat walked away from the table, turning to face the approaching prisoners, fixing each man with his glaring eyes. He repeatedly looked directly at every man and made a mental note of who was likely to reveal what he wanted to know.

An eerie silence descended on the waiting group in the great hall, only to be broken by a series of grunting noises seeping in through an open doorway. Accompanied by scuffling sounds of shambling footsteps, a group of ten guards sidestepped into the hall, struggling to hold their heavy burden with long metal tongs.

Kunrat turned and noticed the air between their heads shimmered, casting distorted views of what lay beyond the group.

A short distance behind the guards, Peter hovered nervously, shielding his eyes with his hand in an attempt to keep a distance from those looking at him. Kunrat stepped forward. "Is it done?" he shouted across to Peter.

"It is done, but the cross is very heavy and can only just be lifted by these ten men. Where do you want them to rest it?"

Kunrat took a step forward and shouted, "You men, lift the cross higher and hold it over the King. I will guide you to its final resting place." Kunrat moved nearer, gesturing to the men to adjust the position of their cargo until he was satisfied with its placement. He held out his hands, palm down, waving them slightly as a signal to lower the golden cross.

The first sound Kunrat heard was a gentle hiss, followed by a series of crackling pops, along with the gasps of those witnessing the unfolding event. On taking in his second deep breath, Kunrat inhaled a mixture of acrid singeing and aromatic cooking as the vapours released from Murak's flesh wafted across the hall.

Within seconds, Kunrat saw the cross had sunk deeply into the torso and face of the shaking King. "Lift it from him, he dies too quickly," he screamed at the guards standing around the table. The men grappled with their tongs and raised the crucifix into the air. The prisoners wretched and coughed as they saw strips of melting skin and dripping fat cling momentarily to the gleaming symbol of Christ. "Cut away his bindings and cast his body onto the floor. Take that man and tie him to the table," Kunrat screamed, pointing to a man who had stared back at him with steely determination. "If necessary I will have every man suffer the burden of supporting this cross of Christ unless one of you tells me where the women are hiding."

From somewhere behind him, Kunrat heard a voice. "Master, I will talk with you."

ELEVEN

As the train jolted out from Piccadilly Station, Henry checked his phone to see if there was any change to his personal account with Dromedary Investments. Using his thumb and forefinger, he expanded the screen, and turned the phone in his hand to display a landscape view of his new balance.

Mr Garcia had only completed authorisation to drain his bank accounts of two hundred million dollars a couple of hours ago, but already four million dollars had been transferred into his personal account. How could it be possible to make so much money for a day and a half's work, a third of that time spent sharing four buxom whores with a fat and hairy middle-aged man? What would Cristina really think of him? After all she arranged it, so she shouldn't be that put out, should she? Henry reasoned he was only having flashbacks of last night's shenanigans because of sleep deprivation.

He rotated his phone, closed the page informing him he was a multi-millionaire and sent a short text to Cristina, letting her know his ETA. He then sat back and contemplated how he'd reached his current age without having any knowledge of what he learned from last night's experience. His thoughts flicked to Cristina. He wondered how many clients she'd slept with to swing a deal.

Cristina picked up her phone and smiled when she read Henry's text message. Just as she put her phone down, it chimed with a unique ring tone, indicating the Duchess was calling her. "Good afternoon, Duchess. How are you?"

"I'm very well, Cristina. I thought I'd let you know our newest recruit has a result, a very good one."

"That's a coincidence. I just received a text from him. I will be seeing him in about three hours," Cristina replied, as she sat on the edge of the bed

"The real reason I called, is that I have another client lined up for Henry, but I don't think he's ready for what will be needed from him. The client is a gentleman by the name of Saddam Al-Hanna-Qarta. He is a very wealthy investor from the middle-east and has his toes dipped in many murky puddles. Cristina, this gentleman has preferences that make Henry the ideal front-liner to engage in a deal with him."

"Are you telling me he has a preference for young men?" Cristina replied, raising her left hand to her mouth and brushing her lips with her fingers."

"Search him out on Erickson's website on the dark web and you'll have a better idea. I gather you know Henry in many ways. Do you think he's ready for this type of encounter?"

"To be honest, no I don't. Henry is a very sweet guy and from what I can gather he's had four moderate length monogamous relationships in his entire life. I think Henry's idea of adventurous is to leave the bedside lamp switched on. Though after last night, he may be more worldly wise than he was."

"I suspected that might be the case. Can you do anything to help? The meeting will not be for another week. If you can assist me in any way, I will reward you with one percent of the commission."

Cristina drummed her fingers on her knee as she thought through the Duchess's request. "What size investment are you expecting this client to make?"

"It could be in the nine figure region, Saddam has skimmed the cream from a very large number of massive middle-east investment programmes over the past ten years. We need to snag this one, Cristina."

"Leave it to me. I have a very good friend I'm going to introduce to Henry, one who is perfect for broadening his horizons and bank balance. I'll call you when I've set everything up. Give me a couple of days."

"Thank you, Cristina. I knew I could count on you."

Cristina put her phone down and wondered how she would introduce the idea to Henry. She would let him rest tonight, after they made love, and broach the subject tomorrow.

She stood up, walked out of the bedroom and into the kitchen. While deep in thought, she flicked on the kettle, but after placing a heaped teaspoon of coffee granules into a mug, she picked up her phone and ran through her contacts. *It has to be Mark, he's ideal. I hope Henry likes him.* As the kettle clicked off, she spoke to Mark. "Hi Mark, I have a huge favour to ask you. Can you come over tomorrow night? I have a friend I'd like to introduce to you. His name is Henry and…"

As he climbed the single flight of stairs that led to the flat he and Cristina were sharing near Oxford Street, Henry felt rising apprehension climbing up from the pit of his stomach. There was a sense of guilt growing in him as he mounted each step, guilt that last night had been awesome, guilt that he'd never enjoyed a sexual encounter so much before in his entire life. He pressed his key into the lock and pushed against the door to break it from the clutches of its tightly fitting draft-proof frame. "Cristina, I'm back. Are you there?"

"I'm just coming out of the shower, I'll be with you in a minute," she called back.

Henry dropped his bag to the side of an armchair and

hovered nervously. He looked up as he heard Cristina pad into their lounge. Her long wet hair was tied back showing off her gorgeous face. She was wearing a thin and short light cotton gown that accentuated her small waist and clung to her damp breasts. "You look great," he said, trying to lift his eyes from the protruding blimps of material that marked the position of her nipples.

"You don't, you look shattered."

"I've not had a lot of sleep."

"So, how was it?"

"A lot easier than I expected. Once I showed Mr Garcia how his money would be invested and managed, he was up for it. It was like taking the proverbial candy from a baby."

"I wasn't asking about Mr Garcia," Cristina said, folding her arms under her breasts.

"Sorry, I'm not following you," Henry said, glancing down to Cristina's toes.

"How was last night, the entertainment I organised for you and Mr Garcia?"

"Oh that. It was okay I guess."

"Okay, only okay. I hope it was a lot better than just okay. By the way you owe me twelve-thousand pounds."

"Sorry, what for?"

"That was how much the special service cost. Each of those women charge three thousand pounds for a night's work and as I booked four, so that comes to twelve thousand."

"I had no idea they were so expensive. No wonder they were good," Henry said, suddenly realising his guard was down because of his tiredness.

"So they were good, how good?"

"Look Cristina, I'm not that experienced in, you know? I had my eyes opened a bit by those women. After all they professionals so they know what to…"

"I won't embarrass you any more on one condition," Cristina whispered.

"What condition?"

"On the condition that you take a shower and come join me in bed. I want you to show me what you learned from these very expensive professionals," she said, throwing open her robe.

It was mid-morning when Henry was woken by Cristina climbing over him before sitting astride him. "Good morning sweetie, how was your night? Mine was wonderful," she greeted, laughing lightly.

"My night was pretty good too. What are you doing?"

"I fancy a quick snack before breakfast and having a shower?"

"Are you hungry?"

"Oh yes, and you're on my menu."

When Henry emerged from the shower, he caught the scent of freshly ground coffee, hot toast and grilled bacon wafting through the air. With only a towel wrapped around his waist, he walked into the kitchen and saw Cristina was busy looking at her laptop. "Work or recreation?" he asked, looking to see where the food was.

"A bit of both. I've been researching information about a potential client, but I've come across something very disturbing. Normally I wouldn't watch this type of thing, but it's all over the dark web."

"What is? Is there some breakfast for me?"

"There's bacon and toast in the oven, I've put it on low heat to keep it warm, and the coffee jug still has a mug full left in it. I can't believe how evil some people are. You should see what these sick bastards are doing."

"What are you watching?" Henry asked, as he dropped a hot plate of bacon and toast onto the worktop.

"It's a video that's been put out by a terrorist group showing members of Boko Haram executing a group of Christians. It's really sick."

Henry searched for a tea towel so he could carry the plate over to where Cristina was sitting. "Is there a message with the video or is it just a film of the executions?"

"Oh yes, there's a message and someone's gone to a lot of trouble setting up over twenty different language options."

Henry set the plate down near Cristina and poured some coffee into a mug before sitting on a bar stool beside her. He glanced at the screen and noticed the picture was highly defined, rather than the usual blurry image he saw on mainstream television. The picture showed a man hanging by his arms and suspended a few inches above the ground. "Is he one of the men they're going to execute?" he asked Cristina, as he bit into a slice of crispy toast and sprayed breadcrumbs over his white towel.

"Make sure you clear that up after you've finished or we'll be invaded by plagues of cockroaches," she laughed. "Actually, I think this is their second victim. They forced the others to watch as they killed the first man and then picked him out from that group. I think he knows what's going to happen to him – watch."

Henry looked at the screen and saw a man carrying a metal cylinder with a pipe protruding from it approach the suspend man. "What's that he's carrying? It looks like some sort of fire extinguisher."

"I think you'll find it's just the opposite."

Henry watched as the man pointed the nozzle on the end of the pipe at the man's feet and sprayed something on them. Another man ran over carrying a flaming torch and dabbed it on the man's feet. Henry recoiled as he watched the man writhe in agony as flames erupted from his feet.

At the same time, the camera panned over to five men, forced at knifepoint to watch what was happening. Over the next twenty minutes, Henry watched open jawed as the victim's lower legs, thighs, genitals, abdomen and face were systematically sprayed and set on fire. During the process, messages scrolled across the screen warning all Christians this was the fate awaiting them when the revolution reached them. "He's not dead yet is he?" Henry croaked to Cristina.

"No, there's worse to come."

"I don't think I want to watch any more of this," Henry said, rising from his stool.

"Me neither. Come on let's get dressed and spend some money. We can stop somewhere for lunch."

"Yes, it would be good to get some fresh air. How can one person do something like that to another human being?"

"I don't know. I suppose we don't really know what happened to these people to make them like that. Maybe cruelty breeds cruelty."

"Cristina, can I ask you a question?"

"The way you put that sounds ominous. What do you want ask?"

"How many of your clients have you slept with?"

"Oh, that's easy to answer, five."

"Did you enjoy any of the men you slept with?"

"Henry, out of the five, two were women."

"Women, you've had sex with other women?"

"Yes I have. I'm not orientated that way and the first time was really scary for me. Listen, let me tell you something. This job I have, you have, it pays us a fortune for very little work."

"I know that and it worries me. If the figures are true then we're earning more in a week than most people earn in a life time."

The reason we've been selected for this job is because we send out the right signals. We're the front-liners, the first direct contact between ruthless and powerful people and the might of Dromedary Investments. These clients we meet, they're only wealthy because they're confident in everything they do. They see themselves as superior to the rest of us, and in particular, to you and me."

"But does that mean we have to submit to them in – that way?"

When we meet a client, it's essential we let them feel they have dominion over us, and in some cases that means acquiescing to their demands. I really like you, Henry, and one day, when we've made enough money, we may end up together and, who knows, raise children or something. For now, we mustn't pass moral judgements on each other, but accept that each of us must do what needs to be done to achieve the goals of our current employment."

Henry looked deeply at Cristina. He'd never heard her speak like that before and suddenly the reality of what he'd entered into in his new life hit him. *We are just little pawns on the board of life.* "I liked the bit you said about what we may do when we've made our money. How long before we get there do you think?"

"If we're hooked up with the right clients, I think a year will do it. I've worked out fifty million is plenty to have a good life and provide for your children's future needs."

"How much have you earned so far?" Henry asked, hoping her answer was going to approach her target figure.

"I'm about half way there."

They spent the day trailing around the up-market shopping areas in London and returned back to their flat around four in the afternoon. Cristina put down her shopping bags and opened the cupboard door they kept their meagre wine reserve in. "Henry, can you do me a favour? You know the wine merchants around the corner, can you go there and buy a couple of bottles of some really good quality red?"

Henry frowned and looked across to Cristina. "Why, you don't normally like to drink red wine?"

"An old friend of mine is popping around this evening and they like good quality red wine."

"You didn't say anything about a friend of yours coming around. What's her name?"

"Actually it's a *he* and his name is Mark."

"Is he – an old boyfriend?"

"Do I detect a hint of jealousy in your voice? He's an old friend, but not a boyfriend. He's not that way inclined."

"Do you mean he's gay?"

"Mark is a very attractive man, in fact he's stunningly attractive, but he's only into other men. In fact you're just his type."

Henry felt a burning blush rising up over his face. "Well, as you know, I'm one hundred percent straight."

"So am I, Henry, but I have also experienced what it's like to be with a woman."

"You said it scared you. You didn't enjoy it did you?"

"The first one, no, but the second one was an older woman who was very experienced. I felt comfortable and safe with her. I found it easier to let go of my inhibitions. It was fantastic, one of the best experiences of my life."

Henry thought about asking her if it was better than with him, but changed his mind. "What country?"

"I think she was Russian."

"No, I meant what country of origination would you like the wine to be from?"

"You choose, you're the man and red wine is a man thing."

Henry rose nervously from the sofa when Cristina led Mark into the room. He saw at once what she meant by attractive. He was tall, with a slim but athletic build and facially, reminded him of a young Omar Sharif he'd recently seen in the old movie, Doctor Zhivago.

Henry held out his hand as Cristina introduced him to Mark, noticing that his large deep brown eyes were playing up and down his body. Mark took a firm grip of his hand and held it firmly as he spoke. "Cristina has told me all about you, but she didn't tell me how gorgeous you are. Such a waste for a good looking man."

"Have you known Cristina a long time? Would you like a drink?"

"Yes. Yes. That answers both questions. It you ever tire of him, Cristina, let me know and I'll convert him to my cause."

"Mark behave yourself, you're embarrassing poor Henry."

"Sorry, please excuse my manners, but your Henry is wasted on women."

Cristina grabbed Henry's arm. "He's only playing around because I told him you were totally straight."

Mark grabbed Henry's other arm and gently pushed Cristina away. "No one is totally straight, it's just that some people like to think they are purely all-man or, all-woman, when in fact we are all a bit of both."

As the evening progressed, Henry was impressed by Mark's conversational aptitude. Through a haze of constantly refilled glasses of red wine, their discussion resolved most of humanity's problems. As they concluded that the only way forward was to eradicate poverty and establish a system where every person could take responsibility for their life by having gainful employment, Mark stood up and edged his way to the door leading to the bathroom.

"Cristina, love, would you mind if I had a shower now? I think I'll be too pissed later and who knows what damage I might do if I fall over," Mark asked, winking at her.

Cristina picked up a large glass of red wine and sipped from it before replying. "Yes that's fine. We'll carry on the conversation without you. Have you got your own towel? If not, I think there's a clean one in the cupboard that's next to the bathroom door."

"Thanks, Cristina, but I've got one in my bag," Mark said, picking up a large black bag Henry had not noticed earlier.

"Is he staying the night? Where's he going to sleep?" Henry asked in alarm.

Cristina turned to Henry and placed her hand on his knee. "Of course he's staying the night. He lives in Liverpool and has travelled down by train especially to see me."

"How did you meet him?" Henry asked.

"We were at school together and have always been friends. Do you like him?"

"I suppose I do. God this wine's gone to my head. How much have we drunk?"

"I'm not sure, how many empty bottles are there on the table?"

"Henry shut one eye and counted. "I think I can see six, but I only bought two."

"Mark came well supplied. I think he had a few bottles in his bag. Henry, have you ever tried Viagra?"

"No, I don't think I need help just yet."

"Did you know it can heighten your sensation of pleasure? Do you want to try some?"

"What, now?"

"Yes now. Mark always spends ages in the shower. Here, take this with the wine left in your glass. It takes about twenty minutes before you'll feel the benefits and I can tease you first." Cristina said, handing him a blue pill.

"Where did you get that from?"

"I was going to surprise you with it later, but I'm feeling very impulsive. I think it's the red wine that's affecting me; it always makes me super horny when I drink it. Please, Henry, I want you and I want you now," Cristina said, as she popped the pill into her mouth before twisting around and kissing Henry.

Henry felt her push the pill into his mouth with her tongue, felt her hand slip higher up his leg and felt her grab his other hand and push it onto her firm breast. She released her lips from his and held a glass of wine to his lips." Sip this now and sip on me later," she whispered, as he took a gulp of wine and swallowed.

"What about Mark? We can't do anything, he might finish his shower before we've finished."

"Come on, Henry, be daring. It'll be more exciting if there's a risk of being caught in the act." Cristina said, undoing the top button of his jeans. "Let him come out to play with me."

Henry felt himself slip into a reclining position on the sofa and surrendered to Cristina's passionate kissing. As soon as she touched him, he knew he'd lost. He raised his buttocks slightly to help her ease down his jeans and moved his arms so he could reach the bottom of her T-shirt. She didn't wait for him to undress her, but pulled off her clothes in a matter of seconds before yanking him out his jeans and pulling his top over his shoulders.

There lovemaking became intense, rapid. She switched position, changed again and again. Guided him to a hectic rhythm, sedated him to a stationary thrust, forced him to sip from her cup, enclose on her engorged nipples and swallowed his pride.

He was unsure which drug caused him to surge with such supreme lust, blue pill, red wine or wild woman?

She rolled onto her back on the seat of the sofa, opened her legs wide and pulled him into her as he knelt before her. He felt her legs wrap around his waist and pull him even closer, restricting him, urging him in every limited move. She forced his mouth onto her breasts, pulled him up and burrowed into his throat with her tongue, gnawing his open mouth with her soft lips. She used her legs to dominate his movement, ease him back, crush him in, hold, squeeze, relax and squeeze. Squeeze. Relax. Push. Squeeze.

Through the mist of exquisite pleasure and unparalleled libido, Henry sensed a hand playing over his back, a hand that could not be there, should not be there, as Cristina was massaging his abdomen with both her hands as she held him in her grasp.

He lifted his head, looked to his right and realised Mark was there. As he tried to protest, Cristina tightened her grip on his waist by clamping him to her tighter and moving her hands up onto the back of his head. She gave him a long drawn out kiss and lifted his head slightly before speaking gently to him. "Henry, I want you to do this for me. We can stop this anytime you want, but please, for me, try to move with the flow."

"I don't understand. What do you want me to do?"

"I don't want you to do anything, just let me guide you. I won't let you come to any harm."

Before he could reply, Henry felt Cristina move her hips, move them in such a way, squeeze in such a way that he was consumed by a primal urge to follow her lead. Her motion became more frantic, his impending need to release rippled through his lower body with such urgency he felt he was about to explode – then she slowed – stopped.

He felt Mark's hands rest on his lower back – sensed the touch of familiar engorgements brush delicately against his crevice. She began to move again, move him, drawing him deeper into a honey trap with no escape. He knew he should pull out, resist, decline, but as she pushed his head down to the tissue of her breasts while Mark moistened his clutched opening. He surrendered.

Trapped between his two lovers, yielding to the sucking pulls and pulsing pushes, penetrating and penetrated, Henry entered a mesmeric state of discomfort and pleasure. Through the night, his will to resist succumbed as he delivered and took pleasure from both of them.

Cristina woke in her bed, stretched out her arm to reach for Henry, but he was not there. She was always the early riser and since they shared a bed, he'd never risen before her. She sat up and recalled the events of the previous night. "Henry, where are you?" she yelled.

She eased out of the bed, taking her time as her legs ached after her exertions over the previous night. "Henry, are you in the lounge?" She called out as she passed through the open door.

She saw he was sitting on the sofa, staring at something he held in his hands. "Henry, are you alright?"

He turned to face her and she saw he was crying, had been crying for a long time, his eyes red raw at their edges. "What's the matter? Talk to me about it."

Henry fumbled with the object he was holding. "What was that all about?" he blurted out tearfully.

"Do you mean last night?" she asked, knowing that was exactly what was upsetting him.

"Of course I mean last night. Why did you make me do that?"

"Before I answer that question, can I ask you something?"

"What?"

"Please answer me honestly. Did you enjoy what happened?"

Henry looked down at the object he was holding, turned it in his hand and then looked up to her with his bloodshot eyes. "Yes I fucking did and I shouldn't have. What would my mother say if she found out? What would my friends think if they knew I'd enjoyed what I did?"

"Do you think it was wrong?" Do you think someone is going to judge you because of what happened? Do you think I will think differently about you? I think I love you, Henry. In fact I know I love you."

"Well don't get to attached to the idea because I'm never

doing anything like that again."

"I will never ask you to do anything like that again. I had a reason for opening you up to that experience, a very good reason."

"What, to find out if I'm gay or bisexual?"

"No nothing like that. It was to do with work."

Henry stared at her. "Are you sure it's not to get even with me?"

"What do you mean, even?" Cristina said, stepping closer to him.

"Well you've been with – a woman – in fact at least two. Maybe you think I should have some sort of similar experience."

Cristina clenched both her fists and stood upright. "Now you're being ridiculous. If you must know the truth it's to do with a client you're going to meet in the next few days."

Henry turned back to look at the object in his hand, before turning to face Cristina again. "What client?"

"I don't know how she does it, but the Duchess has a gift for matching her clients with us front-liners. She has a client lined up for you to meet."

"What has that to do with last night?"

"This client has a preference for people like you, Henry. He will be attracted to you and may want to, how should I put this? Get to know you better."

Henry tightened the grip on the object in his hand. "Do you mean I will have to go with a man? I'm not doing it."

"This client is very special. If you persuade him to make an investment it would mean we'd have enough money between us to quit."

"What are you saying, Cristina?"

"I hate this job. Every time I meet a client, I know I might have to sell myself. Henry, you have no idea what I endured with one of the clients, it's not something I care to even think about. The

Duchess has offered me a percentage of the commission if we can hook this one."

"Hang on a minute. You said the Duchess matches her clients to us. I've only dealt with one client, Mr Garcia, and there's no way he was attracted to me, he just wanted to fuck women with big tits."

"Who pleasured those women more, you or him?"

Henry paused and frowned. "I suppose I did, I think he spent more time watching what I was doing."

"Precisely, don't you see it? He was trying to re-enact his youth and you were the young stud he used to be. The reason he wanted you there was to relive his past times of conquering women."

"Are you sure?"

"Yes, I'm sure."

Henry took a deep breath and looked down to what he held in his hand. "Do you know what this client is like?"

Christina hesitated before sitting next to him. "I do, I searched him out on the dark web. He goes by the name of Saddam Al-Hanna-Qarta, but that is definitely an alias. He purports to be middle-eastern, a devout Muslim and a beneficiary to humankind. In reality he's very fat, very ugly, very corrupt and extremely wealthy."

Henry twisted around to face Cristina and pulled back from her. "Are you telling me I have to have sex with some fat and ugly criminal?"

"I don't know if it will come to that and you always have the option to pass this client on to someone else. The Duchess believes you are the right person to host this man. Henry, if you succeed in this deal, it will make us at least thirty million if not more. I'm going to tell you something, but please, don't repeat it to anyone. I've been checking out the Duchess, she doesn't exist on paper or the net."

"What does that mean? Is she just another criminal?"

"I don't know. I've tried to make an estimate of the amount of money tied up with Dromedary Investments and the figures are staggering, it's not just the amount of investments, but the size of the transactions. I really don't think it's sustainable for much longer. In theory, its assets are expanding at a rate which will consume all free flowing money in the world economy in the next year. It's like a balloon that's being over-inflated and eventually it will burst. I really think we should make what we can as quickly as possible and pull out our funds."

"What would we do then?" Henry asked, placing the object in his hand down on the coffee table.

"Move away and start a new life. We could take on new identities and see how it goes. My hope is that we are right for each other, but we've only recently met. I'm willing to pool our resources and give it a go with you. I've had a couple of really bad experiences with clients and know how you feel, but it's no more than one day of your life and it could change everything for us," Cristina said, mildly distracted by the pearly sheen reflecting from the object Henry placed on the table.

"Basically, last night was really your attempt at trying to prepare me for a meeting with this, Saddam bloke."

"I couldn't let you go in blind. I knew if I told you what would be involved you'd either refuse or be so nervous, you'd mess it up. At least now you have some idea of what it's like to have physical contact with another man, though this one's not as pretty as, Mark."

"I don't know whether to thank you or despise you for what you did, but thanks for being honest with me now."

Cristina leaned forward and reached out for the object on the table. "What's this, it's beautiful."

"I'm not sure exactly what it is. I recently inherited it from my great-uncle, it's some sort of watch, but like nothing I've seen before. From the day this came into my possession, my life has changed drastically."

"Does it work?" Cristina asked, holding the watch up to her ear.

"It seems to work. Can you hear it ticking?"

"I can," replied Cristina, unaware that two slithers of bone were currently turning toward an alignment preordained centuries ago.

❊ ❊ ❊

Through the day, Yasuf patrolled the perimeter of the camp but could not stop thoughts of Susan passing through his head. Finally, as darkness overtook daylight, another soldier relieved him from his duties.

An hour after sunset, he crept into a small tent and whispered, "I'm here."

"Yasuf, you've come to me again. Don't you think you should spend the night with your wife, you've slept with me every night for the past three weeks?"

Yasuf flicked on his small torch and shone it into the girl's face. "I don't want to be with her, I want to be with you, Susan."

"I don't understand you. Your wife is very pretty, much prettier than me, she's converted to Islam. I'm a Christian and you hate Christians."

Yasuf pointed the torch's beam up to his face. "I don't hate Christians, I was one once one."

"Then why do you kill Christians?"

"I don't want to kill Christians, in fact I don't want to kill anyone, but I have to do as I'm told or they'll kill me."

"Wouldn't you rather die than do something you hate?"

"I don't know. I'm not brave enough to make that kind of decision. Susan, what if we ran away together? We could travel to

Kenya or head north and try to get into Europe."

"You mean you want to be with me, but not here?"

"Yes, I want to be with you and live as a man and wife do. I have to get away from here. When they burned the last prisoners, bit by bit until they were nearly dead and then splashed bleach into their open wounds, the cries of those men reminded me of what they did to my father." He wiped the tears streaming down his cheeks away and reached for a piece of cloth to wipe his nose on. "They burnt him alive, from the feet up by putting him in old car tyres. I vowed I would kill them all, but I never found the courage. I'm not strong or brave enough to kill them, but I'm brave enough to run away. Will you come with me?"

"When do you plan to go, Yasuf?"

"I have it all planned. We'll leave tomorrow night. I know where Akubar hides the loot he takes from the prisoners, gold rings, watches, money and other valuables. Tomorrow, I'm going to take some of it and hide it out in the bush. If we leave this time tomorrow night, we can be miles from here before they discover we're missing. Please tell me you'll come with me?"

Susan sat up and reached for Yasuf's head. As she pulled him onto her, she whispered, "I want to be with you, make love to me now."

It was still dark when Yasuf and Susan were awoken by the sounds of an explosion, followed by intense gunfire. "What's happening, are we under attack," hissed Susan.

"I don't know, it sounds like it's coming from somewhere outside the camp. Wait here, I'll go and see what's happening," he said, pulling on his camouflaged uniform.

Yasuf ran into the centre of their camp, but it was deserted. To the north, he saw a fiery glow breaking through the trees and headed in that direction. There was still the odd single pop of a gun going off, but it seemed that if there was a battle, it had now finished. Ahead, he heard voices shouting and the crunching of branches and twigs breaking underfoot. Shortly after, a group of men broke through the heavy undergrowth and he was relieved to see the group was headed by Akubar. "What's happening?" he shouted.

Akubar walked up to him, his white teeth glowing as he grinned. "So my little brother has woken. Did you not hear the helicopter flying overhead earlier?"

"No, I must have been sleeping."

"You must have been sleeping very deeply. You are spending too much time shagging that slave girl. Anyway, we fired a rocket propelled grenade at the helicopter and hit the tail-rotor. You should've seen it. The whole thing began spinning around like a mad witch-doctor casting a bad spell. It came down about half a mile from here and caught fire, but not before this lot tried to escape," Akubar shouted excitedly, pointing to a line of uniformed men bound together with a long rope."

"Who are they? They're all white except one," Yasuf said, seeing the men for the first time.

"Marines, American Marines. Oh Yasuf, we're going to make such a fantastic film when we execute these prisoners. I'll have to plan something very special for these boys."

As the predawn light strengthened, Yasuf watched on as the prisoners were stripped naked and tied in a kneeling position. Each man was held in place by having his arms bound to an overhead pole supported horizontally by a pair of uprights. Most of the men were injured, but the gashes on their bodies did not look too deep or life threatening. When the men were securely bound, Akubar called everyone to gather around before he started to speak.

"My brothers, today we have made a great catch. We will use these men to show the world that we are a force to be feared," he shouted, pointing to the prisoners. "Tomorrow I will execute these men one at a time by cutting off their heads with this knife," he ranted, holding up a short bladed dagger. "The blade of this knife is blunt so it will be a long and hard task for me. Brothers, these are some of America's finest soldiers and we must humiliate them and America through their deaths. They fight against Allah so they must suffer before they die. Now I ask you brothers, what is the worst thing that can happen to a man before he dies?"

Someone shouted out, "Having your balls cut off."

"No brother, there are things more terrible than that. I'll tell you what these men would hate more than anything, what will make them wish their mothers never gave birth to them. These men are going to be taken by men before they die," he shouted, thrusting violently with his hips. "We'll defile their souls by raping their bodies before their execution. I ask you all to go from here and return with more men who will offer their service to Allah through committing an act of sodomy on these demons. I want at least six men to take each prisoner before he dies. We will film this and send it to the Americans to show them how we'll destroy their armies."

Yasuf saw the shock in the faces of the assembly as Akubar's words sunk into their heads. For a moment the men turned to each other and then someone shouted, "Fuck the Americans. Fuck the Americans."

Unseen, at the edge of the bush, a camera and long range microphone relayed images and sounds of what was happening. Several hundred miles away, at a military base near Abuja, a group of uniformed commanders listened to the transcript of Akubar's speech and watched the images relayed back of the captured men. One of the uniformed men rose to his feet and addressed everyone in the room. "I'm calling Washington. Mobilise every airborne unit, we're going in to get our boys back."

Yasuf waited until everyone, except a small guard delegated to watch over the prisoners, left to follow Akubar's orders. He checked no one was watching him and crept into the main supply tent.

A few weeks earlier, when he was trying to find Akubar, he'd gone to the tent to see if he was there, but before he entered, he spotted Akubar crouching over an old ammunition box. He waited until Akubar finished what he was doing before disturbing him and that is when he saw the hoard of treasure.

Akubar was emptying a bag of gold rings taken from some recent captives into the box, but at the same time he picked out and held up some of the other items of contraband. When he finished, Akubar locked the box and placed the key under a small rack that held ammunition for the worn out AK 47s. Now that everyone was on an errand except him, Yasuf thought he would never have a better opportunity to steal some of the treasure.

Twenty minutes later, he crept into Susan's tent. "I have taken what I need. I have gold and a big bundle of American Dollars. We must go tonight before they discover what I've done."

Susan looked at him and reached out to touch his face with her hand. "Are you sure this is what you want? It's not too late; you can still put it back before someone discovers it's missing."

Yasuf touched her hand and squeezed it firmly. "I'm sure. They have something planned for tomorrow and I don't want to be here. I'm going to hide our treasure in the bush. I'll be back in about an hour. Tomorrow we will both be free people to do as we want."

Susan squeezed his hand back. "Take care. I don't want to lose you now."

Yasuf stepped out from the tent and looked carefully in every direction. Apart from a few women strolling around to collect water or perform some other domestic duty, there was no one else to be seen. He already knew where he would hide the treasure, under a fallen tree that lay just beyond a stream that cut across the eastern path.

Staying alert, Yasuf walked casually around the perimeter of the camp until he reached a dark opening that led directly into the thick bush surrounding them. The pathway reminded him of being inside a tunnel, with thick branches forming an arched roof overhead. The stream was about twenty minutes walking distance from the start of the path, which only led to uninhabited open plains to the east. He was confident it would be currently deserted.

As he followed the descent into the small valley the stream ran through, he experienced a disconcerting feeling he was being watched by someone. He stopped and looked in every direction but saw nothing. Just as he was about to take a step, something glinted momentarily to his right. He dropped down to a crouching position and stared in the direction he though he saw a brief flash of light. The overhead canopy was thick and very little light penetrated down to where he waited. Just as he decided he'd imagined seeing something, he saw a movement of something or someone slipping away through the thick vegetation. He waited for a few more minutes and decided it was most probably just an animal foraging for food in the undergrowth. He continued, and shortly after reached the stream. Ahead, part way up the other side of the valley; he picked out the fallen tree in the gloom of the jungle shadows.

With his bag now securely buried in the soft soil exposed by the tree's torn out roots, he headed back to the camp. Twice, he thought he saw something moving to his side, the second time he was sure it was a man wearing a camouflage suit, but when he stopped to look, he could not detect his stalker. He reached camp and boldly walked through the randomly arranged shelters until he reached Susan's small tent.

She jumped up when he entered. "You frightened me coming in like that without calling out."

"Sorry, I've been creeping about so much for the last hour; I forgot to greet you first. Has anyone been looking for me?"

"No, it's been very quiet here. I don't think any of the men have come back yet as I've not heard any shouting."

Just as she finished speaking, Yasuf heard jeering noises coming from several men who had entered the camp. "I'd better go and see what's happening. It's important I act as normal so as not to arouse any suspicion. I'll come back before nightfall."

Yasuf walked into the centre of the camp where the captives were being held. He noticed the prisoners were showing signs of the effects of the heat and lack of water. Their sunken eyes and pale, chapped lips displayed the characteristics of dehydration. Realizing the one black prisoner was not with the others, he scanned around the open clearing until he spotted the outline of a solitary figure tied the same way as the other men, but under the shade of a large tree. The men who had recently arrived were walking around the line of captive Americans and jeering at them. Akubar appeared, clapped his hand and summoned everyone to gather around him. Yasuf stepped forward to join the gathering.

"Brothers, I'm so glad you joined us. These are the Yankees I told you about. Look at them, don't they disgust you. Tomorrow I want you to fuck these whores of Satan, despoil these haters of Allah. They are not a pretty sight, but we're going make them look better by giving them some water and food so they are fully awake and aware when you stick your fat black cocks into their meat." Akubar walked up to one of the prisoners and kicked him in the face. "Did you hear what I said Yankee? Are you looking forward to having your white arse fucked by our black cocks?"

Yasuf watched as the man wearily lifted his head up to look directly at Akubar. Slowly he moved his lips as if to speak, but instead, with steely determination, he spat what precious moisture he could conjure directly into Akubar's face.

Akubar stood motionless for a moment, before wiping the spittle from his face with his hand. "This one will be fucked first and die last. Give all the prisoners food and water, and while they're eating, show them what you've got in your trousers. Let them see what they are having for their last meal before I cut off their heads."

Akubar looked in Yasuf's direction and beckoned for him to come and join him. "Little brother, are you looking forward to tomorrow's entertainment? You'd better be up early and sort out your equipment. We're going to make the best film ever. I wish I still had my balls, I'd love to pay back that Yankee personally before I cut his head off."

Yasuf smiled at Akubar before replying. "I have everything sorted and planned for tomorrow. Everything will be perfect."

"That's good to hear brother. Tomorrow will be the best day of my life."

As the sun sunk towards the horizon, Yasuf felt it was safe to return to Susan's tent. Akubar was too busy taunting the prisoners to notice him and it would be dark in an hour. As he reached the opening to the tent, he called out to Susan. "It's me, I'm back."

"Are we really going tonight? If so, you might want to know that I've collected enough food and water to last us for several days."

Yasuf rubbed the top of his head with his hand. "Shit, I'd not thought about that. Not only are you very pretty, Susan, but you're very clever."

"How long before we leave?"

Yasuf was about to say 'about an hour after sunset', when the outside of the tent was lit up with an eerie orange glow, followed by series of crackling explosions. He spun around and put his head outside the tent.

At several points around the camp's perimeter, bright orange fires burned where previously there had been wooden shelters or canvas tents. As he absorbed the images of the burning fires, streaks of glowing vapour trails traced across his view before terminating in bursts of white fireballs that lit up the whole area. A cacophony of high explosives detonating assaulted his ears, forcing him to duck back into the tent.

"What's happening?" Susan screamed at him above the deafening noise.

"We're being attacked. Grab the food and water and let's make a run for it. I'll show you the way," he yelled back as a shockwave shook the flimsy tent.

Yasuf gripped Susan's hand and pulled her along the edge of the camp towards the opening that led east. Something detonated to their left and everything around them lit up with a white light that cast black shadows along the ground. Yasuf felt, rather than heard the first round fired in their direction, a zing that passed his face and pressed hot air onto his lips. "Susan, run, they are shooting at us."

The opening in the undergrowth was just ahead, a black hole leading to safety, a new life, escape and adventure. He tightened his grip on Susan's hand and pulled her harder. "Run for your life," he screamed at her.

"I am, and I'm running for your baby's life. I am carrying your child, Yasuf."

He couldn't reply, not now. He moved so he was behind her, shielding her from the bullets that stung through the air around them, urging her on, faster, quicker to the safety of the opening a few steps ahead of them.

They passed into the blackness of the gap in the undergrowth and blindly ran until the flashes and thumps were left behind. Only when all traces of the battle were out of sight and sound, did he feel safe to stop briefly. He faced her in the dark, placed his hand on her shoulders and drew her near to him. "We've made it. Soon we'll reach the stream and I will retrieve our treasure."

"Do you think we'll be happy one day," Susan said, pulling his head down so his lips met hers.

He put his arm across her back and drunk the taste of her kiss. She jerked. Before he had time to find out why, his mouth was engulfed by a hot, salty and metallic sensation. As she slumped in front of him, he unravelled the messages his brain received from his senses. The way her back rippled under his fingertips, the push he felt in his abdomen, the taste of blood in his mouth and the bright green spot of light hovering on the centre of his blood covered chest.

He sensed something had penetrated into him, but blind panic erased the stinging in his chest and abdomen. He dived to the ground and listened as two hisses passed over him. He reached out and found her neck, edged his fingertips to the place that played out life's pulse, but found only soft, inert tissue. He wanted to stand and scream at them, let them know he lived and would one day seek them out for retribution, but he was not strong or brave enough yet.

TWELVE

Czyelle looked out onto the rolling green fields through the narrow window in her room. Summer was reaching its height and the surrounding countryside proudly displayed its full awakening, but she was imprisoned in the shady gloom of her room, locked in like a prisoner awaiting a fate she feared more than death.

When Burgolt informed her of his plans yesterday, her first thought was to discover what happened to her ten escorts, but before she could speak to anyone, two armed guards had taken her to this room and locked the door from the outside. Three days from now, she would be married to the most disgusting man she'd ever met and have to endure his advances on her. She moved away from the fresh breeze permeating through the only open slit that gave her access to the outside world, sat on the edge of her large soft bed, and attempted to hold back tears bursting for imminent release.

The sound of the door rattling as it was unlocked caused a shudder to pass through her body. *Has he come to demean my spirit?* She was relieved to see her visitor was a young woman no more than twenty years of age. The woman, dressed in black, walked slowly into her room and glanced at the furniture and fittings before turning to face her. "Good morning, my Princess. I am, Amalie, sent to you at the bequest of Prince Burgolt. I am here to give you instruction on what the Prince expects from you on your wedding night and subsequent times of intimacy. Please, can I sit beside you on your bed?"

Czyelle took a deep breath and fought to hold back an urge to burst into tears as another tremor passed through her body. She turned to look at the girl standing in front of her, briefly taking in her striking features. She looked into her large, dark eyes that displayed both sympathy and kindness, followed the line of her strong nose down to her wide, warm and friendly lips, drank in the softness of her face's oval outline and felt envy as she studied the reflected sheen radiating from her long, auburn tresses of wavy hair. "I've been dreading this moment. Yes, please sit beside me," she replied apprehensively.

"My Princess, we can talk openly as no one is listening. The guard who is supposed to have his ear to the door is standing ten paces down the corridor. I have promised him I will visit him later, if you know what I mean."

Czyelle felt a wave of shock pass through her. How could this woman be so free with her favours? "I thank you for coming, but I fear every word you will tell me. The thought of what is going to happen to me is… is too terrible for me to contemplate. I know I will have to find a way to pass through this, but I don't know how. Tell me, how can you bare for him to touch you?"

Amalie placed her elbow on her knee and rested her chin on her hand. She looked at Czyelle with her large eyes and smiled. "The first time I went with him I was innocent and didn't know what to expect. One of the other girls warned me of what I should do. I was very frightened, but did as I was advised and it wasn't that bad. Now I am his favourite, he only uses my services about once a week and in exchange, I have a room twice the size of this one, I eat what I want, when I want, and I'm free to come and go with who I want."

"What will he do to me on our wedding night?" Czyelle blurted out, allowing pressurised tears to pour down her cheeks.

Amalie placed her hands on Czyelle's shoulders and gently squeezed them until Czyelle looked directly at her. "He will want you to do the same as every other girl he takes for the first time. Do you want me to tell you what will happen?"

"No, I don't really want to know, but I suppose it's better if I do. I'm so frightened."

Amalie twisted to face Czyelle and put her arm over her shoulder. "Have you ever been with a man before?"

Czyelle sat back and glared at her contemptuously. "I am a noble Princess, not a common whore."

"I take it that means no. Have you ever seen what a man looks like, without his clothes on?"

Czyelle shut her eyes. "Yes, I have a brother who is two years younger than me. Last year one of my hairbrushes disappeared from my room and I knew my brother had borrowed it before. I entered his room without knocking and he was lying on his bed and playing with his thing. I know this may sound stupid, but how can something that big fit into a woman without damaging her?"

"My Princess, is that what is scaring you?"

"Partly, but Burgolt, he's so ugly and mean. The thought of being close to him makes me feel like vomiting."

"I'm going to tell you a few things. At first, it will sound worse than it actually is."

Czyelle pulled away from Amalie and lay back on the bed. "Tell me now so that I know what I will have to endure. I'm shutting my eyes so I can picture every vile moment."

Amalie lay down next to her. "To start with, he'll expect you to kiss his manhood. You must tell him how proud and strong it feels. He'll want you to take it in your mouth, draw as much spit up as you can and you won't notice the taste. When he starts moaning, tell him how it fills your mouth, tell him how good he tastes and how you want it inside you. Beg him to take you, he likes that. When he enters you, gasp, when he strokes you moan as if you are in ecstasy. When he's finished beg for more. He'll then lick your breasts and touch you down there," Amalie said, gently tapping Czyelle on her crotch.

"You touched me."

"Only a light touch. You will have to become used to more than being touched."

"Yes, I suppose I will. The thought of having his – thing in my mouth and then inside me disgusts me."

"You'll hardly notice."

"What do you mean? I saw my brother's and I would notice if that was in me."

Amalie placed her arm under Czyelle's shoulders. "Sit up. I want to show you something. I am a free woman in this castle and I've been intimate with quite a few men. They're all different shapes and sizes. Now the bigger ones, they can be as long as this," Amalie said, holding up her right hand and running her finger from her fingertip to below her wrist. "As for Burgolt, well he's like this." She held out her thumb and wiggled it.

"Are you telling me he's small down there?"

"Very, but never tell him that. Just pretend you're really enjoying it. He'll be all over you for the first week, then the novelty will wear off and he'll be back to deflowering young maidens who know nothing about what a normal man is like. Seriously, never let him see you're not satisfied, he has something else he uses on women that do not show their appreciation, something that can and has killed many girls."

"I'll remember that. Can I ask you a favour?"

"Of course you can, I'm here to help you."

"When I was brought here by Prince Vladrek, ten men from my father's castle escorted us. I've not seen them since my arrival. Can you find out for me if they are safe, and if so, where they are?"

"I'll see what I can do, several of the guards owe me, if you know what I mean," Amalie said, winking with one of her large eyes at Czyelle.

"Do you enjoy being with a man?"

"With a real one? Yes. There's nothing better than lying with a strong man who knows how to please you. I'll give you time to think on what I've told you so far. I'll come and visit you at the same time tomorrow."

Czyelle watched Amalie move gracefully across her room and exit through the door. As soon as she closed the door, a loud clunk from the lock reminded her of the predicament she was in. The memory of finding her brother playing with his thing caused her to think about her family. Were they still alive? What had become of her father, her brothers and everyone else she knew? If only Vladrek had not died suddenly, her outlook would have been so different. If her escorts where still in the castle, then maybe she could escape, as the thought of being married to Burgolt was too horrendous to bear.

Burgolt held the open pocket watch in his hand as he sat on his bed. He watched the almost imperceptible turning of the outer ring, wondering if he'd made the right decision to marry this Princess. She was beautiful, but the castle was full of beautiful women and over the past years he'd come to know them all.

Deep down, he knew that once he completed his consummation of her body he would soon tire of her, but this time he would be bound inseparably to her through the bond of matrimony. Did it matter? He would be crowned King, ruler of his people and free to do as he wanted. There was no reason why he should change his routine, there would always be new girls brought into the castle, and his supply of fresh flesh would still be there for him to take at his will.

He held the watch up to his ear and marked the passing of

time with each rhythmic tick, letting his mind roam – tick – tick – tick. He jerked involuntarily as an extra click occurred between the regular ticks. He disregarded the aberration that signalled the counterturn of a gear that followed the retrograde motion of Venus, unaware that deep inside the movements of the watch, two slivers of bone began to creep away from each other. He put the watch down and relaxed on the soft bed, falling into a deep sleep.

Burgolt was stirred by urgent rapping on his door. "Prince Burgolt, may I come in, I have important news about a visitor."

Burgolt raised his head from one of the many soft pillows that cushioned him. "Did you say a visitor?"

Through the closed door, Time, one of the now dead King's messengers, shouted back his response. "A stranger has arrived and asked to have an audience with you. He has come from Gothburgh castle and is asking for you by name."

Burgolt pivoted off the bed and stumbled to the door. "Who is this stranger?" he shouted back, before opening the door.

"My Prince, he says he is a Duke, Duke Gomory, but I have never heard of a Duke Gomory.

"What does he look like?"

"He is very tall, has thick black hair brushed back over his head and wears a neatly trimmed beard. He is dressed in black clothes that look to be made from the finest Chinese silk."

"How old is he?"

"Do you know, I'm not sure what age he is? There's something odd about his appearance, but I can't fathom it out."

Burgolt looked at the old messenger and wondered if his eyesight might be failing him because of his advanced years. "Go down and take him to my study. Have a dozen armed guards watch over him. Tell him I will meet with him shortly." Burgolt opened a large chest near his bed and selected a mauve silk jacket that he knew made him look regal. Before leaving his room, he picked up the pocket watch, shut the casing and dropped it into one of his jacket pockets.

As he climbed down the three flights of stairs leading to the ground floor of the castle, Burgolt thought about what the messenger had said. This stranger had asked for him by name. Why not his father or brother? Surely news of their deaths could not have travelled so fast? Anyway, he'd soon find out what this was all about. If the stranger was going to cause a problem, it was something he could quickly resolve by ordering his guards to execute him. He pulled his hunched shoulders back, pushed out his chest and strode arrogantly into his study. The stranger stood near a large fireplace with his back facing him. "I understand you wish to speak with me, Duke Gomory?"

Burgolt watched closely as the man turned to face him. Time's description had been accurate, he was tall, he did have dark hair and a beard, and there was something unusual about him. He studied his features as he spoke to him.

"Prince Burgolt, it is my pleasure to see you in the flesh."

Burgolt's mind whirled. There was something unusual about the man's face and now, something strange about what he said. "May I ask what your business with me is about?"

"It is about something of mine that is in your possession."

"Do you mean the Princess Czyelle?"

"No, she is not mine. You have in your pocket an object that belongs to me. Don't worry, I have not come to take it from you, but I need to give you advice about how to safe keep that, which is in your possession."

Burgolt looked at Gomory as he spoke and realised what was different. The man's face was smooth, unlined. As he spoke there were none of the usual signatures of expression, no frowns, no creases around the eyes and an absence of laughter lines. "My Duke, I am at a loss to what you are referring about. Tell me. What of yours do you think I have in my pocket?"

"My pocket watch – the watch you took from your brother

shortly after his untimely death."

Burgolt felt a shockwave pass through his body. He looked at the stranger and weighed up the risks of letting him live. He could have him executed with one command, but first, he wanted to see what game he was trying to play. "You said you have come to advise me about the safe keeping of this watch. What is your advice?"

"Simply to care for and keep the watch for as long as you live. The watch will find a new keeper when the time is right. It is essential you never cast this watch away or thoughtlessly pass it on to another."

"My Duke, I have no intention of giving this watch to anyone. May I ask if you have any other business?"

"That depends on you. For now you are safe, but early next summer a grave darkness will fall onto your small kingdom and many will perish at the hands of a plague that is covering our lands. I'm willing, with your consent, to offer you guidance and protection when the time comes."

"Are you talking of the Black Death?"

"No, something far more terrible, the Inquisition will be at your doors and they will show you no mercy. All who inhabited your future wife's home have now perished, or become slaves to the tyranny spreading through these lands."

"Can you stop them?"

"I can protect a few."

"Can you protect me?"

"Only time will answer that question. I can leave now or stay as your guest. The decision is yours to make."

Burgolt's mind wavered. Could he, should he trust this stranger? How did he know about the watch? How did he know he was going to marry Princess Czyelle? Did he have special powers? "Tell me exactly who you are?"

"I am Duke Gomory. I am here because some use my name,

my being, as a purpose for their own end. I am what you wish to make of me."

"How old are you?"

"How old is an oak tree? Does its span of time begin when it was an acorn or earlier, when that acorn was not yet grown from its parent tree? Or is it when the acorn pushes forth the first shoot in late spring? There are questions that have no closed answers and my place in time also has no set position."

"I do not understand what you say, but I sense you may be of help to us in the future. For now, I have decided you may stay, but if I have reason to doubt your sincerity, I will cast you out or have you killed. Do you still wish to remain in Castle Boese under these conditions?"

Gomory held his hand out to Burgolt. "If that is your position, then please have someone show me to my room."

Czyelle's heart leapt when her door burst open early in the morning. She was relieved when she saw it was Amalie, but wondered why she had come so early. "I wasn't expecting you until later. For a moment, I thought it was him."

"Sorry, I didn't mean to alarm you. The guard outside your room opened the door when he saw me coming. I have some news for you."

Czyelle pushed her cover down and swung her legs out of the bed. "Have you found out where my escorts are?"

Amalie's expression changed, her smile wilted and her eyes seemed to grow larger. "I think I know where they are, or at least where their bodies might be. I managed to persuade one of the guards to tell me what happened. The same day you arrived, Burgolt ordered their execution. I gather their bodies were thrown into the same river he uses to wash away his other victims."

"No. It can't be. They were all good and loyal men who had never harmed anyone."

"I'm sorry but it's typical of Burgolt. I have news about someone else you know?"

"Is it my family, are they safe?"

"I've not heard anything about them, but a visitor came to the castle yesterday. His name is Duke Gomory and he's staying here."

"He's the man who helped Vladrek reach my home. Vladrek told me about him. He said there was something strange about him and the he might have special powers."

"He must have something special about him. Burgolt has accommodated him in the royal guest suite and given him freedom to come and go as he pleases."

"Do you think I might be able to see him? He may know what's happened to my family."

"I can ask. Have you had time to think over what I told you yesterday?"

Czyelle stood up and walked to the narrow window. She gazed out onto the limited view of green fields, sighed and turned to face Amalie. "I have, but after what you've told me, the thought of sharing a bed and my body with Burgolt is unbearable. I wish this window was wider."

"Why, so you could see more?"

"No, so I could cast myself out of it and bring an end to my predicament."

"You must not think like that. It's really important that Burgolt believes he can satisfy you. Do you pleasure yourself?"

Czyelle let Amalie's words echo through her mind to check she'd heard correctly. "What do you mean?"

"Have you discovered the pleasure of touching yourself, like your brother did?"

"No, it's not something I know how to do?"

"Surely you must have tried?"

"My matron of honour always told me I should not touch myself there in case I broke my maidenhood. She said my future husband would think I had already given myself to another man."

Amalie stepped up to Czyelle and placed her hand on her shoulder. For your own sake you need to know what it feels like to reach the pinnacle of pleasure. Burgolt will expect it of you and if you don't react properly, he'll use one of his toys on you. Lie down on your bed, pull up your gown and allow me to show you what you will have to pretend to feel when you lay with Burgolt. I promise you, I will keep you intact."

"You want to touch me?"

"I am only doing this for your protection, my Princess."

Czyelle's chest was still heaving up and down as the door lock clanged into position. At first, she shook with fear when Amalie touched her, but with each passing caress, she gave in to the waves of joy cascading up through her body until it happened. As she writhed in exquisite bliss, she felt Amalie's lips find hers. She wanted to push her away, but the soft warmth of her full mouth caused her to open her mouth, accept the fleshy tongue probing into her. Hesitantly, she surrendered when Amalie moved down her body, probing her breasts and her belly with her gorgeous moist mouth. As Amalie moved nearer to the point of her throbbing ecstasy, she responded by pulling at her clothing, peeling off the fabrics covering her tutor.

Overcome by sensations she never knew existed, she responded in kind and feasted on the forbidden fruit of her mentor. As the morning evolved into afternoon, she lost count of the times she and her teacher screamed in capitulation to the demon of lust. Finally, Amalie pulled away from her. "Remember, move and shout out like that when you're with Burgolt, and you will come to no harm."

Czyelle awoke the next morning, but did not stir from her bed; instead she allowed billowing thoughts to flutter haphazardly through her mind as she contemplated her current reality. It had always been her dream, as a princess, to marry a handsome prince, live in a grand castle and raise a family of beautiful children – but she was to marry Burgolt. And Amalie – what happened – it wrenched her heart to know the strength of gratification possible with another person – and she – doomed to share her bed with a man as pathetic in mind as body. There had to be a way out – something to cling to that would release her from what fate ordained her future to be. What about Gomory? Could he – would he rescue her from the living hell she was about to endure.

Throughout the day, Czyelle jumped every time the door clunked, each time she prayed that Amalie had come to visit her, but it was only the guard sliding in a tray of food that she could not bear to touch. The afternoon faded to evening and the evening dissolved to night, but Amalie did not come.

The following day, Czyelle climbed out of her bed and pushed her face into the slit that opened her view to the outside world. This was the last day before her marriage, her last day uncorrupted by Burgolt. She openly wept as she thought of her family, of childhood memories and childhood dreams. The door opened, she turned and froze – he was here.

"I trust you are well rested. I want to explain what will happen tomorrow, take you through the procedure," Burgolt said coldly.

"Before you do, can I ask you one question. Am I to be locked away in a room after we're married or will I have the privileges of a true queen?"

"That depends on you. If you demonstrate to me that you are a loving and faithful wife, I will grant you freedom to go as you please within the confines of this castle. On the other hand, disappoint me, and you will remain in a smaller windowless room then this one and your only amusement will be when I come to ravish your body."

Czyelle swallowed the bile that rose from her empty stomach, thought of what Amalie had told her and stepped up to face

Burgolt. "You are to be my husband and I will be a dutiful wife. I eagerly wait to feel your touch, my Prince." She then lowered her hand, gently stroked the slight bulge of Burgolt's crutch and briefly pressed her lips to his.

"That is good to hear, my Princess. What was I saying?"

"You were going to tell me about tomorrow's procedures."

"Ah yes. Early tomorrow morning you will be attended by several maids. You will bathe in hot water and adorn the perfumes provided for you. You will then be dressed in your bridal gown and escorted to our chapel. There you will undertake the vows to be my faithful wife."

Czyelle cringed at the thought of what that involved, but looked at him affectionately.

"We will attend a small feast before changing into the gowns of the King and Queen. We will be crowned in the main hall and then attend a sumptuous feast to celebrate my ascension to the throne. Once the feast is underway, we will retire to my rooms for a night of unbridled passion and consummate our bond of matrimony."

Czyelle stared into Burgolt's eyes but did not look at him. Somehow she found a way of blanking out his hideous features. "My future husband, I cannot wait for that moment."

Czyelle retreated from reality through the rest of that day and the next. Everything that happened seemed no more than a wispy dream: the speeches, the lavish food, the pomp and ceremony, all where a fantastical illusion that was not really happening.

Even as she pulled off her gown and stood naked before him, knelt when he pushed down on her shoulders, took him in her mouth, lay back and let him enter her, all was not real. She listened to her moans, her gasps, outwardly felt her body writhing as it did when Amalie touched her, but she was on the outside and nothing could touch her.

He barely endured, shuddering and grunting as her hips

shook in the sham of prostituted orgasm. She lay back, watching her body from outside, waiting for him to recover and seek out her solitary moist harbour, but he fell into a deep slumber and the first sailing was complete.

Over the next few days, Czyelle familiarised herself with the layout of the castle, introduced herself to the senior servants and endured Burgolt's brief interludes of passion.

She discovered the more passionately she received his attentions, the shorter they lasted. After the fifth day he did not come to her bed. As the hour grew late, she decided to visit the castle kitchens as she was hungry. Passing through a long corridor, she caught sight of a women approaching, but could not see her clearly as there was a flaming torch behind her. The woman suddenly called out her name. "Queen Czyelle, I was on my way to see you."

"Amalie, what are you doing here?"

"I thought I might visit you and ask you if you had anything that needs attending to."

"What do you mean?"

"Can I be honest with you?"

"Of course you can, Amalie," Czyelle said, wearing a puzzled expression.

"Your King, he will not be with you tonight. He has given orders for six girls to be taken to one of his rooms. Does he satisfy you?"

Czyelle hesitated, initially shocked at the boldness of Amalie's question. "I don't think that man is capable of satisfying any woman. What needs of mine are you referring to?"

"Your needs as a woman, my Queen."

"Are you suggesting we should do as we did when you showed me how to satisfy the King?"

"Only if you want to, my Queen."

Czyelle looked at Amalie's full mouth and raised her hand to stroke her lips. "I would like that very much. My body yearns for release and I will never find that with my husband. Are you coming to my room or am I going to yours?"

As summer ebbed into autumn, Czyelle tolerated her existence. Burgolt demanded his matrimonial privileges no more than once a week and Amalie fulfilled her needs at least every other day. It was not what she hoped her life would be, but better than she expected a few months earlier. On a particularly cold night, as she huddled under her blankets, there was a gentle tap on her door. Thinking it must be Amalie, she shouted, "Enter."

At first she didn't recognise who was entering her room as they held up a candle level to their face. "Who is it?" she said apprehensively.

"I am Duke Gomory; a mutual friend informed me you wished to see me."

"Yes, but that was some time ago before I married…"

"The incumbent King?"

"Yes, I hoped you might help me to…"

"Escape?"

"You seem to know what I'm about to say. Why are you here?"

"My Lady, would you mind if I set my candle down on your bedside table and sit on the edge of your bed? There is a cold draught blowing through your window and it will be more comfortable to talk with you if I were seated."

"I don't think it's advisable, my husband might still come."

"He is not in the castle. He's left on a hunting expedition and will be gone for at least three days."

"Hunting, this time of year, what is he hunting?"

"It seems there have been sightings of two wolves roaming near the cattle at the far end of the valley. The cowherds are too frightened to move the cows for fear of attack, so a hunting party has set off to find and kill the wolves. Your husband insisted on being the one to capture and kill the wolves."

Czyelle looked into Gomory's face and felt her chest flutter as his smouldering eyes fixed into hers. "You didn't answer my question. Why are you here?"

Gomory leant over her and rested his hand on the thick bedcover. "I feel responsible for what has transpired. I brought Vladrek to your home and urged your father to let you run away with him. Now circumstances are different and I have come to see if I may offer you my services."

Despite the thickness of the covering, Czyelle could feel a light pressure from his hand pressing against her breasts. Already she could sense her nipples engorging as the silk lining pressed against them. "I find it hard to know what you could do for me," she replied, studying his face in the flickering candlelight and thinking how handsome his smooth features were. "Can I touch your beard? I've never touched a man's beard before." As soon as she spoke she thought, *why did you say that?*

"Of course you can, though that is not what I was expecting you to ask from me."

Czyelle slipped her right arm from under the covers and reached out to touch his beard. "Oh, it's so soft and gentle. I thought it would be firm and rough to touch."

"Not everything is as it seems," Gomory said, moving his face closer to hers.

Czyelle felt the slight change in pressure on her breasts and realised she was becoming moist. "Would I be wrong to ask if we could have one kiss? I've never kissed a man with a beard." *Why am I saying these things? What's wrong with me?*

Before Czyelle took her next breath, Gomory lowered his head and pushed his mouth onto hers. She felt the warmth from his lips, the soft tease of his beard stroking her chin and a flowing ripple pass down her throat, through her chest into her lower belly, which now ached to feel the touch of a hand. She slipped her left hand down between her legs and contacted the warm emissions of her needs. She shivered suddenly. Gomory pulled away from her. "Are you still cold?" he asked.

"I don't know what I am. Maybe I am cold and need warming."

"It is for you to invite me into your bed, I force myself on no woman, but I will give to those who willingly seek what I have to offer."

Czyelle tried to stop an uncontrollable shaking that passed through her. She knew she should not lie with this man, but every sensitive part of her body throbbed to be touched and stroked by this bearded stranger. "Remove your clothes and let me see what type of man you are." *I can't believe I said that. What's happening to me?*

Czyelle watched intently as Gomory unpeeled his layers, she gazed wantonly at his firm and contoured chest, she wanted to reach out and touch his abdomen that exposed the structure of firmly developed muscles under his smooth skin, and she felt her mouth fill with saliva as he revealed a magnificent manhood from under his silk leggings. "Does my Lady wish me to replace my garments or join her in her bed?"

Czyelle pushed back her covers and opened her arms and legs to him. She shut her eyes as he climbed onto her and opened her mouth to accept his kiss. She lost count of how long he held her mouth with his, before he moved down, slipping the soft warmth of his beard over her breasts. She felt like she danced with angels as he pressed his warm wet mouth on each of her breasts and she reached out to feel for his excitement pressed against her thigh. He moved down to her urgency, his beard soothing the hunger in her groin, his tongue whetting her appetite for what must follow. She gripped his arousal and for a moment she was consumed with doubt. "I want this to happen but I feel it's wrong."

Before she could speak again, he moved up to kiss her. He pressed his thumbs lightly against her nipples, drew her mouth into his and slowly pressed against her wetness. All at once, visions exploded in her mind, she felt everything he did to her, but her mind's eye pictured a pair of wolves atop her.

One was black and the other white. At first the black wolf licked her, gently, rousingly, teasing and stimulating her until she thought she would burst apart with the desire for satiation. Then the white wolf pushed the black wolf aside and clenched her in its jaws, drove into her rampantly without mercy, consumed her cravings until waves of unbearable pleasure tore through her arching body. Then, as she tried to capture her breath, the black wolf licked her wounds, pushed air into her lungs and revived her will to feast on cardinal lust again. Each time she felt satiated by the white wolf, the black wolf restored her yearning for more until she screamed to the white wolf to take her again. At some point she opened her eyes and saw the sunlight streamed into the room. "Is it morning already," she asked.

"No it's late in the afternoon," replied the white wolf.

❊ ❊ ❊

Kunrat turned and peered through the hanging mist lingering in the air, the remaining evidence of Murak's partial evaporation by the cross. He picked out the man who shouted to him, and listened, as the shaking prisoner explained how it was possible to gain access to a secret room in the basement of the castle. Now that he knew where the women of the castle were situated, he barked his orders to the surrounding guards. "Take this man with you and follow his directions. If you locate the women, bind their hands and bring them one by one to me. I will be in the room at the back of this hall. If you don't find any women, cut off his manly parts, open his belly, pull out a loop of his bowel and bring him back here. I will have him suffer the burden of supporting the cross once it has been reheated."

Kunrat walked to the rear of the great hall and turned to face the remaining guards. "What are you waiting for? It's time to start the inquisition. Extract confessions from these prisoners by whatever means you deem fit. When they confess, prepare them for purification by fire tomorrow morning. As for those who do not confess by this evening, break them on the wheel and raise them on poles outside so the crows can finish them off."

He then drifted into an ante-room, which he assumed was used by the King to entertain important guests. He sat in one of the two raised and large seats that were ornately decorated, suggesting they were ancillary thrones for a king and queen to sit on while they greeted their guests. He sat back and waited for the women to arrive.

As he waited, Kunrat tried to reconcile his dark thoughts of what a *witch* was about to do to him against his moral instincts. He had sworn an act of celibacy in front of a Cardinal, so was it a sin for him to put himself in the position of being cast under a spell by a witch, enabling her to force him to break his vow? Was it not his charge to unearth these crones in Satan's service and expose them for what they were? Had he not already rid the world of hundreds of evil sorceresses, whose only purpose was to corrupt good men and condemn them to eternal damnation? But if he succumbed to their charms, would he not also be damned? Memories of the last witch, the first one he tested by allowing her to seduce him, flooded back to his mind and he felt the fabric under his cod piece tension as it tried to contain his arousal.

His thoughts were broken by the sound of a woman shouting and cursing. Shortly after, three guards entered the room, struggling to hold a woman who tried her best to bite and kick them as they dragged her before him. "Master, this is the first of them. We found about twenty women hidden in a suite of rooms in the basement. This one is very spirited," the guard grunted as a large woman twisted in attempt to break his grip

213

of her.

"Pull back her hood so I can see her face," Kunrat growled.

"She's not the prettiest thing you'll ever set your eyes on," the guard said, as the woman lunged to bite his hand.

Kunrat retreated back into the chair as the hood fell to reveal an older woman. He looked on in horror at her large curved nose and felt sick as he saw her three remaining teeth were blackened, enlarged and protruding at a distorted angle from her foul mouth. "Why do you show me a hag? If ever a woman was a witch, this one is. Get her out of my sight."

"What shall we do to her?"

"I don't want our confessional devices tainted by her foul juices. Burn her now. She is obviously a witch most foul. Only a whore of Satan would issue such contemptible language as she does," Kunrat shouted over the rants of the woman as she compared him to a leper's penis.

The next three women brought before Kunrat were all old and ugly, each he condemned to the processes of extracting confessions before their reduction to ashes. "Are all the women like this?" he called out to the exiting guards.

"There are some younger ones, but they resisted when we tried to bind them. It took a while to secure them without harming them, Master. We assumed you wanted them whole without missing limbs or heads."

Kunrat waved away two more hideous old crones and looked up to the ceiling as the next woman was brought in front of him. Before he looked at her, he cringed as she screamed abuse at the guards holding her and directed an obscene comment to him. "I see God did you no favours when he created you. Looks like he used my grandmother's backside to make your face," she called out to him.

He looked down from the ceiling and stared at the buxom redhead. Her tunic had torn at the shoulder and barely covered her ample chest. The lower part of her skirt hung on the ground and through the gash in its side, he followed the sumptuous curves of her muscular calf and thigh. *She is a descendent of the Norsemen, a fine specimen. I wonder if the rumours about these women are true?* "What is your name?"

"I am Vassal, daughter of Harder. What business do you have with me?"

"Are you a witch?"

"No. Are you the Devil?"

"You will not address me like that. I am the *Master*."

"You resemble what I shit out of my arse, Master."

Kunrat gripped the arms of the chair tightly and leaned forward as his stomach muscles cramped. He took a deep breath and considered what he'd like to do with this harlot. As he entered a brief fantasy, reality crept over him. *She is too wild, too dangerous.* "I believe you are a witch. You will be interrogated and encouraged to confess your sins. Guards, take her away."

As Vassol was dragged from the room, two guards escorted another girl to face Kunrat. He looked at the young girl and smiled. She was very pretty and dainty. "I am the Master of the Inquisition. You will address me as, Master, at all times. Do you understand?"

"Yes, Master," she replied softly.

"My purpose here is to ascertain if you are a witch. Are you a witch?"

"No, Master."

"What is your name?"

"Margaret, Master."

"Margaret, if you are found to be a witch, the only course I can follow is to have you burnt alive at the stake. Will you submit to my questioning so I can determine you're not a witch?"

"If you believe it's necessary, then yes, Master."

"Good. Guards, take this one to my private interrogation room on the first floor."

Kunrat waited a few minutes before rising from his chair. He felt certain this girl would do everything – anything to save her life. As he climbed the stairs to the small bedroom on the first floor, he silently said a short prayer to ask for forgiveness for the sins he was about to commit.

Later that evening, Kunrat descended the staircase one step at a time. Everything around him seemed remote, unreal, without form. He made his way to the great hall, but failed to hear the screams of the condemned as they passed unheard through him.

Only when he entered the great hall to witness a man's screams, as his legs and arms were crushed between a heavy wheel and thick wooden poles, did his mind accept a new truth. One day, he too would join these unfortunate souls in the eternal flames of Hell.

As he wondered through the maze of tortured and broken bodies, the same thoughts circled through his mind. *All she had to do was follow my lead. Why could she not make such a small sacrifice to save herself? Why did she make me do that to her.* He knew the truth, knew what he'd really done. She refused every chance, rebuked his subtle advances until he couldn't contain his lust any longer. God had witnessed him rape her, not once, but many times before in anger, he squeezed out her innocent life essence by throttling her throat with his bare hands before ripping her neck open with his teeth. One of the guards approached him. "Master, have you finished interrogating the witch?"

He turned to face the guard – pausing briefly before replying. "I have. Unfortunately she turned out to be a very powerful and dangerous sorceress. I had no option but to destroy her at once. Remove her body from this building and see to it that her remains are reduced to ash."

THIRTEEN

Henry opened his eyes as the haunting opening bars of Tubular Bells stabbed through his dream. He sat up, reached with one arm to tap his phone and stretched out his other arm to pat the mound in the bed that was Cristina, but realised he was pressing down on a lump of empty scrunched up duvet. "Cristina, are you up already?"

From the kitchen, he heard her echoing reply. "Of course I'm *up*. That's why I'm not in bed."

"Why are you up so early?"

"I'm making some coffee and I've made you a packed-lunch so you don't have to eat the crap they serve on the train."

A nauseous wave rose up from the pit of Henry's stomach. Today was the day he had been dreading. Somehow, time seemed to stop over the last few days, but now the day was here. He picked up his phone and glanced at the time. In ten hours from now he would be booking into a Glaswegian hotel and encountering his nemesis, Saddam Al-Hanna-Qarta. "I think I'm going down with something, I feel sick," Henry called back.

Cristina bounced into the bedroom and grabbed the duvet off the bed. "Don't be such a wuss. Come on, I've made some fresh coffee, picked the mouldy bits off the bread and made toast. You're only feeling queasy because you've hardly eaten these past two days."

"It's easy for you to say, but you're not about to go and meet half a ton of blubber that wants to…"

"Actually, I've got an assignment and it may be worse than yours."

"What do you mean? You've not said anything about it."

"Actually, I tried on several occasions, but you were too preoccupied with what Saddam might want from you to take notice."

"Is that when you said the Duchess had contacted you?"

"Yes. I'm meeting with three exiled Russians tomorrow. Apparently they've defrauded the Russian health programme of several billion dollars and are seeking a safe haven for their nest egg."

Henry twisted out of the bed and opened his sock drawer. "That sounds very unethical."

"Henry, what are you doing?"

"Putting my socks on."

"Shower first. You can't meet your client coated in the remnants of our bodily fluids, or have you forgotten what we did last night?"

Henry absently gazed out of the train window at the sheep grazing in the fields. *Those sheep are so lucky,* he thought, *all they have to worry about is where the next clump of grass is coming from.* He turned to a woman sitting opposite him. "Excuse me. Do you know where we are?"

"We're nearly at Oxenholme Station."

"Where's that? Is it in Scotland?"

"No love, it's in Cumbria, near the Lake District."

That's too close to Scotland, thought Henry. He struggled to unravel the film wrapping from the sandwiches Cristina had made for him, wondering what she had found in their nearly empty fridge that he would appreciate over the processed ham baguettes available on the train.

On first glance, he thought the sandwich was filled with chicken mayonnaise, but it didn't smell like chicken mayonnaise. He took a small bite from the middle of one of the triangles and desperately tried not to spit out the mush that was in his mouth. *What has she put in these sandwiches?* he thought, as he pulled the top layer of bread off the partly eaten triangle. *Christ, she's given me lemon yoghurt and sliced banana filling.*

"Are you feeling alright?" the woman sitting opposite him asked.

"Yes I'm fine. It's just that my sandwich is not what I was expecting it to be."

As the train slowed into Glasgow Central Station, Henry gazed out of the rain streaked window. The sky reflected his mood, gloomy and getting darker. He reached up for his overnight bag and reluctantly shuffled along the central aisle of the carriage, stepped onto the platform and shivered as a blast of cold air displaced his thick blonde hair.

In a trance, he followed the exit signs and made for the nearest taxi rank. He failed to notice the skyline, instead counting down the number of people in the queue, until it was his turn to grab a cold wet door handle and issue instructions for his destination. "Radisson Blu Hotel please."

In no time, he was paying the driver, booking in at reception, and rising in a smooth elevator before sitting on the edge of a king-sized bed. It all seemed like a distant recall of a partly forgotten dream. His room phone trilled sharply, jarring him out of his quixotic world. He picked up the phone and listened.

"Mr King?"

"Yes, speaking."

"I understand you are meeting with Mr Al-Hanna-Qarta. He wishes to let you know he is now available to meet with you and requests you to join him in the restaurant bar."

"Thank you. Tell Mr Al-Hanna-Qarta, I will be down to meet

him shortly."

Well this is it, now or never. For a moment, he felt he was standing in the middle of a jousting field. One charging knight representing the fortune he would make for this deal, the other urging him to flee from the area and escape the terrors that lay ahead.

He spotted Saddam the moment he entered the bar, a vast mound of rounded flesh that was precariously perched on the slim lines of an elegant bar stool. Saddam sat with his back to him, his white shirt painfully stretched across his wide shoulders and struggling to support the aeroplane-tyre contours above his trouser-line.

Henry continued his approach, but slowed with each step. Just before he was in hailing distance, Saddam turned around. Henry smiled briefly at the man with a ruddy complexion, button nose and pig-like eyes obscured by folds of excess tissue that didn't belong there. As Saddam spoke, his jowls wobbled disconcertingly, sending wavering pulses to the flesh hanging under his chin. "Mr King? Henry King?"

"Yes, good evening. I'm Henry and I take it you are…"

"Saddam Al-Hanna-Qarta, a pleasure to meet you Mr King. Would you care for a drink? They have a magnificent collection of single malts here. Would you like me to pick one for you?"

Henry was perplexed. Saddam was definitely not an Arab; he looked more like a Cornish farmer than a sheik. And surely that was a glass of whiskey in front of him; did Muslims drink whiskey? "Thank you. I'll trust your choice."

Saddam raised one of his heavy arms into the air to attract the barman's attention. "If it's alright with you, I thought we'd have a couple drinks, eat at the restaurant and then retire to my rooms to discuss our business. I have the penthouse suite on the top floor and it has a good sized office we can use to discuss our business."

Henry sipped from his glass. "This is really good malt, Mr

Al-Hanna-Qarta, a good choice," Henry said, wondering how anybody could like something that tasted like a dissolved oak table.

"Please call me by my first name. We can drop the formalities for now."

"That's good, Saddam. And please call me Henry."

"Actually, my name is not Saddam, it's Frank."

"Oh, okay then, Frank."

"And I'm not really a Muslim. It's a lot easier to gain the trust of the Arabs if they think you are one of them. You wouldn't recognise me when I've got my spray tan on, along with my prosthetic nose and glued on beard."

Henry quickly wanted to change the subject; his client was giving him too much information. "Was there any particular reason you chose Glasgow for our meeting?"

"Yes, I like the food at this hotel. Shall we go and eat, I'm starving."

Henry scooped the last traces of triple-chocolate truffle from his bowl, focused briefly on the enormous belly of the man opposite him, and wondered how it was possible for one person to consume at a single sitting, more food then he could eat in a week. Saddam, or now Frank, dabbed his moist mouth with his napkin and sat back in his chair. "Now what did you think of that? Is that not the finest food you ever tasted?"

Henry clamped his mouth shut and coughed lightly to disguise the belch rising from his bloated stomach. "Yes, I don't think I've ever tasted better," *or eaten so much.*

"Shall we adjourn to my rooms and discuss our business?"

"Yes, that would be good. I'll need to collect my laptop from my room first, so shall I meet you up in the penthouse suite?"

"Okay Henry, but don't be too long, I'm dying to get down to business."

I bet you are, thought Henry as he rose from his chair.

Henry realised it was the first time he'd ever seen in reality how the other half lived. The penthouse was enormous, covering nearly half the roof space of the hotel. The main living area was glazed on both sides and gave an impressive view of the sprawling city below. Saddam, or Frank, was sprawled back in a massive armchair; Henry wondered if it had been especially brought into the suite to accommodate such a massive man. Henry was surprised when the door was opened by a young man who looked as if he was of North African descent.

"Good evening mesture King. We are being expecting you. Please do go in, mesture Al-Hanna-Qarta is ready to do you," the dark skinned man said as he opened the door.

"Thanks," Henry replied nervously.

Frank rolled forward out of the chair, executing the manoeuvre in such an eloquent fashion as he'd surely done many time before. "Henry, that was quick. Come into the office and show me what you've got."

As he passed into a smaller room furnished with a good sized table with eight chairs surrounding it, Henry unzipped his laptop bag. Over the next hour, he took Frank through the sales patter of Dromedary Investments as he displayed graphs and charts showing the yields expected on a client's investment.

Frank listened attentively, interlocking his fat, glistening fingers ever tighter as the graphs extrapolated an invested sum to more than double in a ten month period. "Henry, I'm impressed. I can see how this works and it's fabulous. Now, I need to ask you a question and I don't know if you think you can go along with this, but it's essential if we're going to do a deal."

Henry waited for him to ask the question, but he didn't. "What did you want to ask?" he said quietly.

"I am in a position to do a deal with the major oil cartels. The sums of money are huge and for a day, just a single day, there will be a balance in my bank account that is equivalent to the GDP of Columbia. In case you don't know how much that is,

I'll give you an indication. It's a few hundred billion US dollars. Why have I mentioned Colombia you may ask? The answer is simple. If we can do a deal, on that day, Saddam will disappear, Frank will disappear, and so will a sum of money equivalent to the GDP of Columbia. That my boy; will be my new home."

Henry suddenly felt very small as he looked at Frank's massive frame. He wanted to pinch himself and wake from this dream. It had to be a dream. "What do you want me to do?"

"I will need your company to sift these funds out of my account in less than six hours. If you can do that then we all become fabulously wealthy. It will be the largest fraud of all time. Don't you see it; your company is perfect for this job? All your accounts are hidden, untraceable and an investment of that size will make it easy for you to manipulate the markets to make even more money. Can you do it?"

"I'll need to make a call, in private," Henry said, rising from his chair.

"Feel free, I'm not going anywhere," Frank replied, as he slipped his bloated fingers apart.

Henry walked into the main room of the suite and crossed to the opposite side. He realised he was shaking as he scrolled through the contacts on his phone. He touched the icon to call the Duchess and waited for the phone to answer.

"Henry, how are you?"

"I'm good. I'm with a client and need to ask you something?"

"I was expecting your call. If the question pertains to the transfer of a large amount of money in a short period, the answer is, yes."

"You know about it?"

"I do. Oh Henry, if you are asked to do some follow up work, I want you to think about one thing. This deal is very important, so important that ultimately it will lead to three billion of the Earth's population benefiting from a massive increase in their quality of life. I cannot stress enough how important it is that you do everything necessary to close this deal."

Oh shit, Henry thought, as he returned to the office and Frank. Frank looked up at him as he entered through the open doorway. "Well can it be done?" he asked calmly.

"I am assured it's not a problem. Do you want to proceed with the deal?" Henry asked, before sitting down in front of his laptop again.

"I guess I've nothing to lose. You see it's not really my money I'm investing. There's a plan afoot by the middle-east oil cartels to hike up prices by reassigning production rights. The men behind this are just out for what they can get and I'm just a middle man they trust. Can you imagine their faces when they realise they've lost everything, including all the assets accumulated over the past thirty years. I trust you Henry, don't let me down though boy, because I've got friends everywhere, if you know what I mean."

Henry looked into Frank's piglet eyes and silently swallowed down his rising fear. He was so out of his league and the thought of him playing a part, any part in a *theft* of this magnitude terrified him. "I understand what you're saying. Let's sort out the boring admin side of this first. I'm going to need details of how to access the bank account Dromedary Investments will secrete the funds from. There are several documents you'll need to sign for by fingerprint coding, along with a recorded voice agreement. Are you comfortable about that? All the documents will be fully encrypted and only accessible by the CEO of Dromedary Investments."

Frank replied without hesitation. "By that you mean the Duchess. She's been around a good few years and made some of my acquaintances very wealthy men. I gather there have been several searches made to discover her true identity for more than twenty years, and still she remains an enigma. I wouldn't be here unless I felt certain about the merits of her company, which by all accounts doesn't appear to exist."

Two hours later, Henry closed the lid of his laptop and sat back in his chair. He noticed Frank was staring at him and shuddered as he remembered what might be next on the agenda. "Well, Henry, it's getting late and I have something I need to attend to. Did you see my Algerian friend, lovely young man and he adores my attention, or at least does a good job of pretending to. Maybe the two thousand US dollar salary I pay him each day spurs on his affections for me. To be honest, I couldn't give a fuck, but he is a good fuck. Everything is set up as I told you, so don't let me down."

Henry breathed slowly as he left the penthouse suite and as his muscles relaxed, he realised just how tense he'd been. When he reached his room, he called Cristina but she didn't answer. Then he remembered she was meeting with the three Russians and wondered if she was having as easy a time as he was. On the train journey home, Henry tried Cristina's phone several times, but it switched to voice messaging the moment he called.

When he arrived at the flat, Cristina was not there. He wondered if there could be anything wrong and realised he had no idea how long a deal might take to complete. After a couple of hours of flicking through all the television channels and checking every corner of the fridge for anything that might still be edible, he called the Duchess. "Hi Duchess, it's me. The deal is done."

"I know Henry. Each document comes directly to me when it's signed."

"Do you think the deal I've done is ethical? It's going to ruin a lot of rich people."

"Henry, those who are going to be *ruined*, ruined a lot of people to get where they are. Don't concern yourself about ethics; leave that part of the equation to me. Why did you really call me?"

"Do you know how Cristina's doing? She's away meeting

some clients and I can't get hold of her."

"Don't worry about Cristina. I can see she's very busy now, in fact, as you speak, I'm receiving documents from her end, and it looks as if her deal is on a par with yours if not greater. You two are going to have massive assets in your accounts. You should start to plan what to do with your fortunes." She hung up.

Henry thought about ordering a takeaway, but a recall of what he'd eaten the previous evening dampened his appetite. He made his way to the fridge, removed the last carton of lemon yoghurt that was three days past its 'eat by' date, took a brief shower and climbed into the large, lonely bed.

It was still dark when Henry felt the bed shaking as someone climbed into it. "Cristina, is that you?"

"I hope so. You're not expecting any other women to creep into our bed while I'm away, are you?"

"No of course not. Are you okay?"

"I think so. My dealing with the Russians was very strange. Actually, I'm bit concerned about the whole thing. Something's not right with this one."

"What do you mean by not right?"

"Firstly the deal was too easy, but secondly the sums of money involved are massive and when I say massive, I mean massive."

"How massive?"

Cristina switched on the bedside lamp and looked down at Henry. "Sit up for a minute, we need to talk."

Henry eased up to lean back on the headboard of the bed, ignoring the annoying creak that had started after a round of rampant lovemaking last week. "What's bothering you?"

"The amount of money these Russians want to tie up with Dromedary. I don't have an exact figure yet, but it's going to be over a trillion US dollars."

"If that's the case, your commission will be…"

"I don't even want to think about it. It's more than I could spend in a lifetime. What about your deal?"

"It was big. A similar amount to the GDP of Columbia he said."

"That's nearly four hundred billion dollars."

"How did you know that?"

Cristina reached down to her bag and pulled out her laptop. "I want to show you something. I've been checking out loads of stuff on the world economy and trying to estimate the likely wealth of the company that employs us. If I'm right, Dromedary Investments is currently controlling around ten percent of the world's GDP."

"Is that a problem?" Henry asked, feeling he should feel alarmed, but unsure why he should feel alarmed.

"Not if the finances are used to aid productivity and generate global trade, but – and this is a big but – if these funds were used as a form of self-destruct, then the domino effect would render every currency and bond as worthless."

"Why would anyone do that?"

"Maybe because they could. I'm really worried, there's something not right here."

Something clawed at the back of Henry's mind. "Earlier tonight I called the Duchess, I was worried about you."

"Were you?"

"Yes. Anyway, she said something to me about *our assets* and how we should plan what to do with them. The odd thing is she hung up at that point."

"Do you think she was warning us about something?"

"I don't know. Maybe we should start to withdraw some of the money."

Cristina dabbed at her laptop. "Have you ever read the small print about withdrawing from our commissioned funds?"

"No, the cash I'm making from my basic salary that's paid into my bank account has been more than I need at the moment. Besides, I've only been at this for a few weeks and it's not sunk in yet."

"Well I have studied the small print. Look. We are only allowed to withdraw at the rate of nought point one percent on each and any day."

"That's a bit of a con."

"Actually, it's not that bad. Have you checked your balance recently?"

"What since I did the deal last night?"

"Has that gone through yet?"

"No, it's a few days until that happens. Anyway, what do you mean by *it's not that bad*?

"If we start withdrawing our maximum amounts each day from now, in a few weeks we'll have enough to get out of this. The only problem is where to invest."

"We could just put it into a bank account."

"Henry," she said, causing him to look directly at her. "If we suddenly start depositing huge amounts into a UK bank account we will attract the attention of the tax people, the fraud squad, if such a thing exists, and every other Tom, Dick and Harry who monitors dodgy dealings. Besides, if the system goes down our assets will be worthless. I need to give this some thought. By the way, how did it go with the big guy, did you have to..?"

"No, thank God. He's employed some poor other sod for that part of his life."

"Oh, that's good. My Russians weren't interested in anything but money, and I think they prefer to spend their time on their own, preferably with a few women at once. I saw one of them meet up with a gang of classy escorts when our meeting finished. Now, let's make that headboard creak again."

※ ※ ※

Yasuf slipped along the path on his belly in the darkness until he felt the ground slanting down to the stream. He slid silently down the bank, clutching at his wounds that were now biting into him with each movement he made. As he lay in the pitch black, he used the spike on his belt buckle to prise out the fragments of a bullet that had shattered as it passed through Susan's spine. The sharp splinters of metal had only penetrated a few millimetres into his flesh, and as the grey light of an approaching dawn crept through the overhead canopy, he could feel there were only two fragments remaining under his skin.

He nearly vomited as he tried to dig out a hard lump near his navel, the piece of shrapnel seemed to have a sharp spike protruding from it and tore at his flesh as he tried to lever it out. He eased it to the surface and managed to grip it with his fingernails. When he finally managed to coax it out, he held it up in front of him to see what he was holding. It was not metallic, but looked like a piece of splintered bone. In a moment of horror, he realised he was looking at a fragment of Susan's spine or rib that had entered him when she was shot.

He threw the blood covered slither of bone into the stream in disgust. With the last piece of metal withdrawn from his body, he lay on his back and considered his options. He could climb up to the other side of the bank, retrieve the hidden treasure and try to make it to Kenya, or go back and see if anyone survived.

As he felt his strength returning, he decided to venture back along the path and find Susan's body. She should at least be buried before her remains were consumed by scavengers. He couldn't give her a Christian funeral, but maybe he could say a prayer to God, whoever he was, to send her on her way to whichever heaven she was destined for.

He eased himself up onto his feet and limped back along the path. He was disorientated and unsure where Susan had fallen, and as he rounded each bend, anxiety crept up into his throat in the form of acid refluxes emanating from his guttural fears.

Creeping through the shadows, he saw something ahead, a dark discarded heap spread out on the forest floor. He slowed his pace, padded each foot more gently into the soft yielding leaf littered soil. It had to be her. Why did she look so black? She moved. Yes there was movement. He crouched and waited. Too frightened to call out, he hesitated and watched. She did not stir, but something wavered over her, rippling like small leaves disturbed by the first gusts of an approaching afternoon storm.

He clamped his fingers tight and summoned courage to fuel his progress. Step by step, he drew nearer. Ants, fucking ants and millions of them swarmed over her body. He reached up and grabbed a branch, turned and twisted his body to tear it from its host tree. His torn flesh burned, his fear rose, his courage and determination nearly capitulated, but the branch cracked as it spilt and came away, free in his hand.

Frantically, he swept at the ants, brushed their pulsing mass aside. He flicked their columns and ranks into chaotic disarray as the swarm spread in diluted and disorganised anarchy. Through the remnants of writhing and broken ants, he stared into a gaping hole that had once been her flat brown belly. A belly he had caressed and lain upon as he filled her with his physical lust, but also was the smooth covering of their unborn child. Now it resembled a bloody crater, an open cancer of raw dissected flesh, but within, something caught his eye. Nestled among the torn meat, resting in deep slumber, no larger than his thumb, he saw his child.

He ran, ran as far and as fast as his shaking legs could pound. Inside, he screamed, outwardly, he drew gulping breaths as he feed oxygen to his adrenaline fuelled body. In an eternal instant he entered the clearing that was once their camp.

At first, the smell of burnt flesh assaulted his nose and mouth, then the sound of a carrion bird flapping its wings, before he saw the carnage around him. Everywhere he looked, there were body parts strewn around like discarded chaff from wheat stalks that had been beaten against hard stone. He stopped, listened – silence.

Aimlessly, he wandered around, bypassing the deep craters marking the point of impact of bombs, missiles, mortars or whatever they used to blow apart the lives and people that were his family.

He stopped to look at the remains of someone he no longer recognised, transfixed by the image of a blackened, upright torso, with one of its arms bent at the elbow so the hand rested peacefully on the top of its bloated charred head. He pictured how blasted metal had cut away their lower body, scattering everything below their waistline into hidden recesses at the edge of the bush. How their upper body had fallen upright to the ground, an arm flailing in the air and falling to rest with its hand slapping to a halt on their head. There was nothing here for him, no survivors to aid, no enemies to fight and no one to share his grief. He turned to head back to where Susan lay, but something on the ground caught his attention.

It was an ammunition box, one that was familiar to him, Akubar's box of treasure. The padlock was secure but the side was ripped open. He picked it up and shook it. On hearing the jangling of its hidden contents, he pushed his fingers into the gash and began to ease out the precious contents. At his feet lay a pile of gold trinkets and wads of currency. He looked around him for something to wrap his loot up in and spotted a dismembered leg lying a few feet away. He shuddered as he peeled off a tube of camouflage patterned trouser covering a lower piece of leg that was severed at the knee. Without any idea of what he would do next, he gathered up the items that might give him a future and headed back into the jungle to bury Susan.

Just before he reached the edge of the clearing, he noticed a handgun lying in the dirt. He picked it up and released the magazine from the pistol to check if there was any ammunition in it – and saw there were still six rounds remaining. He clicked the safety lock on and tucked the pistol into the waistband of his trousers.

When Yasuf reached the place Susan's remains had been, he froze. She was gone. There were drag marks in the ground that terminated under a bush in the thick undergrowth. He pulled back the branches, but there was no trace of her. Casting out memories of her smile, her laughter, the way she looked at him, he continued to the stream and retrieved the rest of his treasure.

FOURTEEN

The warmth of the sun breaking through an east facing window in Czyelle's bedroom roused her from a dream. She had been on horseback, clamping her legs tightly to remain atop the galloping beast weaving tenaciously to avoid the gnarled trees as it charged through the night in an ancient forest.

Behind her, a roar of water bursting through the undergrowth, tearing younger trees from the anchor of their loamy support as it surged forwards, goaded her to urge the beast into a gallop. To her side, one to the left, the other to the right, a pair of wolves raced like precursory waves guiding her flight from the following flood.

She opened her eyes and memories of what he did, how he rode her and satiated her hunger, burst through like the sun discovering a rent in towering storm clouds. Her body felt relaxed, untouched, defying the recall of his unending passion – his animal releases into her soft craving womb. She lifted her head and peered through the valley of her up-thrust breasts resembling a pair of smooth sunlit hillocks. She focussed on the tangled dewy forest that lay beyond her breasts, fascinated by the pinprick reflections emanating from the fruits clinging to the woven branches nestling between her thighs.

She turned to her side and saw all evidence of his visit was gone; it was almost as if he was never there, but the memories of what he did, burned indelibly into her soul. Who was this Gomory? He was surely not a mortal man, though all she had known of men was Burgolt, and he was, by Amalie's account, not a real man.

The thought of having to endure Burgolt's feeble fumbling again, caused her to feel more wretched than she'd ever felt before. She would find Amalie and ask her to tell Gomory to take her away. Yes, that was it. She would run away with Gomory, even if she had to share him with others, as she knew she could never satiate his lust alone. She rose from her bed, pulled on her clothes and set off to roam the castle until she found either Amalie or Gomory.

Burgolt rode in through the main gate of the castle in a dejected mood. For two days they roamed the lower regions of the valley searching for the wolves. It seemed that with each new reported sighting they just missed them and then, last night, he had come face to face with them.

He had been dreaming he was caught in a flood, the churnings waters dragging him through a desolate forest until a surge of water lifted him to safety on a piece of higher ground. All around him, the waters boiled and seethed angrily, their waves rising like white spirits ready to consume him.

Then, from the frothing maelstrom, he noticed something forming and emerging onto the dry land. The dark shadows crystallized into the outline of a horse and rider. As the horse stepped nearer, he saw the rider was a naked woman with eyes that burned like hot coals. The horse reared up onto its hind legs and called out with a shriek that cut through him like a sharp sword slicing through the soft flesh of an un-ripened child. At that point he awoke, but the horse's shrieks did not abate.

He crept out to the opening of his tent and saw one of the horses rearing and calling out in distress. He reached back and felt for his sword, gripping the hilt tightly before stepping out into the cold night air. Before he had taken two steps they confronted him, a pair of wolves, one as dark as the night, the other as white as freshly fallen snow.

The pair drew nearer, stealthily padding closer until they were within range of the arc of his sword swing. As he raised his sword, their eyes lit up like the woman on the horse. He lost all courage, urinated into his clothes and fell to the ground in a quivering heap. No one had seen what happened, but he knew the wolves were a portent of a terrible adversary to come, one that would destroy him.

Czyelle considered visiting the Royal Guest Suite where Amalie told her Burgolt had roomed Gomory, but caution warned her to steer clear in case she was seen. She would have to find Amalie as no one would find it suspicious if she sought out her advisor, her confidant and *her illicit lover*. As she roamed through the maze of rooms at the back of the castle, the rooms used by servants to prepare all kinds of produce for the consumption by the ruling class, one of Burgolt's servants called to her. "My Queen, we have been looking for you everywhere. Your King has returned and wishes you to attend to him."

Czyelle pushed down the rippling panic rising in her chest. "Has he been hurt?"

"No, not at all my Queen. He rests in your room and wishes to see you at once. What are you doing down here?"

"I am – was looking for Amalie. Have you seen her?"

"I have not and you really must go to your King. I believe he is becoming rather fretful that you are not there to greet him on his return."

Czyelle bit on her lower lip as she climbed the stairway to her room. What if he wanted to be amorous with her? She'd not bathed since her liaison with Gomory, so he'd surely know she had been with another. Maybe if she told him she was ill, he would seek his release elsewhere.

She saw two guards were posted outside her door, which lay slightly ajar. Hesitantly, she pushed the door open and looked down to see Burgolt, scrubbing himself with a cream coloured sponge in large tub of steaming water. "Husband, it's good to see you have returned safely. Did you manage to capture and kill the wolves?"

"Never mind the wolves. I have missed you attentions. Remove your clothes and climb into my bath. You can finish cleaning the detritus of my travels from my body and then I will give you the pleasure of my attentions."

Czyelle coiled up into a foetal ball as soon as he left. When they climbed from the tub and lay on the bed, still wet and covered with the slippery lather from the scented soap, she had surrendered to his demands. She inwardly prayed he would finish quickly, but as the time passed he became more aggressive and his exertions seemed frantic.

Her mind was filled with Gomory, of how he sought to discover every part of her that responded to his touch and kisses, and only as she lay impassively, did she remember what Amalie had said. She jerked into her role: Gasped and moaned, told him how good a lover he was, quivered and trembled, writhed and twisted, clutched his back and dug her nails into his skin, before venting a scream of empty bliss that secured his release, the release she so desperately sought.

It was over a month before Amalie visited her again. She was gazing out of her window watching the fall of the first snow of the encroaching winter. The high peaks surrounding the castle had unfolded their white crown lower and lower over the past week, but this was the first coating of winter that had sprinkled this far down into the valley.

She turned as she heard someone enter her room without knocking. It was Amalie. "Why have you not come to visit me?

I've looked and asked everywhere, but no one has seen you."

Amalie opened her large eyes wider and smiled briefly. "Your beloved husband has had me locked up in a room for weeks. He's been teaching me how to appreciate his sensational qualities as a lover."

Czyelle gave Amalie a quizzical look. "I thought you were his favourite and knew how to please him."

"So did I, but something happened to me and I forgot. He nearly used his toys on me, but I begged him not to and told him I was ill. He insisted on testing the truth of what I said by having me locked up and then visiting me three times every day."

"That must have been terrible for you. You said something happened, what?"

"I don't know how to describe it. I was approached by a man and I couldn't resist his charms."

"You've had many lovers, why was this one so different?"

"With this man I rode with the wolves. I reached for the tops of the mountains and climbed to new places I didn't know existed. Then, when Burgolt wanted me, I felt empty. I forgot how to respond to him and he came close to killing me."

Czyelle shuddered as electric shocks tingled down her back and through her lower belly. "This man, was it Gomory?"

"Yes, how did you know?"

"I have also ridden with the wolves."

Amalie smiled. "Which did you prefer, the white wolf or the black one?"

Czyelle reached out and pulled Amalie to her. "I did not have any preference for either, but rather it was the combination of the two that gratified me beyond my expectations."

Amalie locked her eyes into Czyelle's "Would you like to touch and kiss as the wolves did?"

"More than anything," Czyelle whispered back, as she stroked her first touch on Amalie.

Hours later, as the two women lay side-by-side; their bodies covered with a sheen of exuded moisture that only lovers know, Amalie traced a line in the myriad of droplets clinging to Czyelle's belly. "You are putting on a bit of fat, this used to be flat," she said, gently prodding Czyelle just below the naval.

"I know and I'm eating like a horse, two even. My breast are growing too, I think I'm becoming a true woman."

"When did you last bleed?"

"I'm not sure, not for a while."

Amalie sat up. "I think you are with child."

"Surely I can't be, can I?"

"Burgolt may not seem like a man, but this castle if filled with his bastard offspring."

Czyelle sat up next to Amalie. "Have you…?"

"Had one of his children? No thank God. I don't think I can have children."

"If I am with child, maybe it's not his, maybe it's Gomory's."

Amalie frowned. "How many times have you been with him?"

"Only once, but it seemed like many. I tried to find him, but I didn't want to arouse any suspicions. Have you seen him recently?"

"No and do you know what's odd? I'm sure he's found a way of leaving the castle. After we… met, I tried to find him. I looked everywhere and asked everyone if they knew where he was, but not one person could recollect seeing him in the castle."

"Do you think there's a secret exit we don't know about?"

Amalie suddenly jumped off the bed and crept to the door. She put her ear to the cold wood and listened. Slowly, she walked back and whispered into Czyelle's ear. "I can hear breathing on the other side of the door. I think someone is listening to us."

"Do you think they heard us earlier?" Czyelle whispered back.

"I don't know. I hope not. I'd better get dressed and go. I'll see you later."

As winter's talons gripped the lands around Castle Boese, Czyelle's body filled and rounded in preparation for the offspring she carried. For the first time, she noticed the rat like juveniles racing through corridors, scampering down staircases and littering the workrooms as their mothers paid for their existence by toiling through the dark days.

Inwardly, Czyelle prayed her child was not one of his vermin, but an immortal conception of Gomory's. Burgolt had left her alone, there were rumours he'd found the favours of a new whore, but Czyelle only felt relief to be left alone with *his* child. The more she thought about the swelling in her stomach, the more she knew it had to be *his*.

Spring arrived earlier than usual and after three warm days of clear skies, most of the winter's snows trickled as silvery streams down to the white crested waters of the surging river that ran to the side of the castle. On that third warm evening, Czyelle's door burst open and Burgolt stood on unsteady feet before her. "Wife, I have been guilty of neglecting you. Come to my room so I can show you how much I love you," he shouted, as he fumbled for the doorframe to regain his balance.

"Are you drunk?"

"I have sipped on some wine. I'm celebrating the end of a dark period in my life."

Czyelle pulled her covers over her engorged breasts. "What dark period?"

"I'll be honest with you. I have been under the spell of an evil witch. She seduced me with her charms, but all the time she shared her favours with my armed guards. She tried to turn them against me, but my men are loyal. I have just come from cutting off her head with my own sword's strike, and it's as if a veil has been lifted from my eyes. I realise now, you are my only true love and tonight I will take you as you've never been taken before."

Czyelle pulled the cover a little higher before speaking. "Husband, I am carrying a child and cannot lie with you tonight."

"You will come with me now. We both know the truth; There is no danger my manhood will harm our child. It is after all, 'just a little thing'. That's what that bitch said just before I cut off her head."

Czyelle knew Burgolt was agitated and therefore, very dangerous. She wanted to ask who the unfortunate girl was, praying it was not Amalie, but she also didn't want to rile him further. She sought deeply to find enough courage to face her predicament and threw back the covers. She eased out of the bed and stood naked before Burgolt, thrusting out her swollen breasts and belly to accentuate the advancement of her childbearing. "Husband, I will lie with you, but show consideration for our unborn child."

Burgolt stepped up to her, picked up her discarded gown and laid it over her shoulders. He gripped her tightly by the arm and pulled her towards the doorway leading out of her room, saying, "You are my wife and it's your duty to ease my tensions. Tonight you will show me that you are worthy to bear my child and will do as I command." He then hauled her into the landing and urged her forward towards his room by clamping tightly onto her upper-arm with his right hand.

Czyelle withstood the foulness of his deviant fetishes for over an hour, but when he knelt on her stomach and threatened to urinate over her face, she pushed him off and tried to run from the room. He caught her and threw her face down on the bed before tying her wrists with a leather strap. "You ungrateful whore, if you were not the Queen, I would have you beheaded now."

Czyelle rolled onto her back to face him. "I would be grateful for that service, at least then I would never have to suffer the taste of your puny manhood. You are nothing more than a streak of slime, husband, and I will never give myself willingly to you again. Go ahead and take me, you're right, your *little* thing' is not capable of reaching deep enough to harm *my child*."

Burgolt stared darkly at her, but did not speak. He then reached down under his bed and withdrew a girdle composed of leather straps. Czyelle watched as he strapped the device around his waist with his back to her. He turned to face her and she gasped in horror at what she saw. She felt a rising nausea creep over her as she took in the size of the dark-brown leather phallus rising up beyond the level of his naval. She tried to push back away from him and cried out. "Please no, you will harm the child."

Burgolt crawled onto the bed and put his mouth to her ear. "It is time you felt the joy of one of my toys. I am a kind husband, for this is the smallest one and my only intention is to tame you. If you ever defy me again, I will use larger ones on you. Now lie back and take what you deserve."

Czyelle crawled into her own bed and curled up into a ball like she did when she was a child. She wiped a stray tear from her eye breathed out slowly. He had relented at the last moment. Her cries, begging and pleading seemed not to affect him at first, but she persevered, becoming hysterical about her precious baby and something gave in him. She felt him pull back from her and rest a hand gently on her face. "I'm sorry, I don't know what came over me," he murmured. She seized the moment and promised that once the child was born she would give him her undying devotion, and it worked. He told her to go and look after their child. Oh how she hoped it was not his child. Cocooned by her own body, Czyelle slipped into a deep sleep.

There was something in her room, she raised her head in the dark and tried to follow a scurrying sound running along the floor near to the far wall. For a moment it was quiet, then, she heard the scratching of sharp claws slipping against the stone floor. Her night candle had long since expired and there was no trace of light showing in the windows that were hidden in the pitch-blackness of the room. It moved closer to her bed, the something had run across the floor and was now under her bed.

She froze, stopped breathing and listened. It moved, scrabbled under her bed towards the foot end. She wanted to climb out of her bed onto the floor, grab a fresh candle and make it to the door that led to the outside corridor. There she could light her candle from one of the large ones that burned through the night, but she was too frightened. It was on the bed.

Something was padding on her covers near her feet. She kicked out, waiting to hear it land on the floor, but there was only silence after the cover slumped back onto her feet. She felt something moving, a disturbance slipping up the bed under the cover, an invisible pulsing crawling near her left leg. She sat up and tensioned, ready to leap from the bed and blindly find the door.

A white light shone through one of the windows, moonlight that had broken free from the obscurity of its cloudy shrouds. She looked down to see a small bump under the silk cover edge up level with her hip. Gripping the edge of the cover with both hands, she threw it back to expose the uninvited guest that was tormenting her. The rat, it surely was a rat as she'd never seen a mouse this large, ran underneath her. She threw herself off the bed and slammed down onto the hard stone floor.

For a moment she lay still, allowing the hard stone to sap heat from her skin and add to the tremors shaking her clammy body. Slowly, she raised her weakened body from the cruel sanctity of the cold stone and stood upright near the bed. The door was only a few steps away and as she made to take her first stride, she felt something moving under her nightgown.

Instinctively, she looked down over her breasts and saw what appeared to be a rippling hand playing over her swollen abdomen that was hidden under her nightdress. She frantically pulled the gown over her head and stepped back, but saw nothing scurry away into a dark corner. It moved, moved on her child filled torso. She looked down again, stared open eyed at the undulating bump writhing on her front as it twisted and writhed under her skin. It was inside her, rummaging next to her child. She tried to grab at it with her hand, digging her nails deeply into her skin, unconscious of the pain tearing her apart. Apart, she was apart, apart from it, her baby. They were no longer one.

Czyelle opened her eyes to scream, but nothing came from her mouth. Her skin burned red-hot, her body was soaked with sweat that seeped from every pore and her lower belly felt as if it was torn open. It was day, light streamed in through the windows and something was terribly wrong.

As soon as she moved, she felt it, a warm sticky wetness that spread down her legs and seeped into her lower back. She pulled off the covers and a white wave of sickness raced up her body as she looked down at the blood, so much blood. Everything, from her breasts downwards was soaked in a fresh scarlet coating, resembling strawberries that had been minced and crushed to make a puree. She rolled to the side of the bed and clawed up to her feet. There was something in the middle of the bed, some animal or parasite that had burrowed into the congealed strands of her seeping haemorrhage.

She took several deep breaths and approached the blood cover thing in the middle of her bed. With abstract trauma, she began to wipe away the sticky web of blood soaked membranes that coated the object of her fascination. With each stroke of her finger, she exposed the rat sized creature, cleared the strands of bloody debris to expose its tiny arms and delicate fingers. Bit by bit, she opened its body to the life giving light entering her room until only its head was covered by a hood of light pink tissue. Using her fingertips, she pinched a fold in the obscuring covering and peeled it back to expose the tiny face.

Now she knew it was Burgolt's. The aborted child's face wore the familiar hallmark of the other rat-like creatures infesting the castle. Carefully, she scooped the little creature up into her open hand. "It is better for you, my child, that you did not enter this world. You were not meant to be and you have a release I can never have."

Czyelle walked slowly across to the largest window and using a chair, climbed onto the inner-ledge. She crawled forward with her arm outstretched, until her head was out of the opening. She looked down to the smooth grass and light-grey stones far below and twisted her arm to release the burden in her hand. Absently, she watched as the small parcel spiralled through the air, buffeted and tossed by the updrafts climbing the stone side of the castle walls, until it stopped as an almost invisible smear on the ripe green of heavily grazed grass.

If only, she thought. *Maybe I can,* she thought. The window was narrow, but with a twist of her body, Czyelle eased her shoulders past the rectangular stone frame. With a further twist, her hips slipped through and she was free. Nothing touched her: she felt weightless, free and fearless. She felt a light tug from the air rushing through her hair; a hiss of passing wind that turned to a roar. For a brief moment she heard the sounds of breaking bones and tearing flesh, but no pain, just release and then silence.

* * *

All around him, Kunrat heard the cries of those being stretched on the racks, crushed in the presses and impaled on spikes. *Is this what I'll hear in Hell,* he thought. It was a certainty he would go to Hell, there could be no forgiveness for his most recent sin.

Briefly, he blocked out the shrieking screams of a man being forced to sit on a chair with a barbed spike set at the centre of its seat. Harsh logic coursed through his thoughts and he made a decision. If he was going to spend all of eternity suffering torment from the demonic spawn of Hades, he might as well gain pleasure from the remainder of his mortal life. Maybe the memories of earthly gratification would help to see him through his forthcoming spiritual despair. He turned to see some men were dipping newly made torches into a cauldron of oil. "Give me one of those torches," he shouted to the nearest man.

"Do you want me to light it first?"

"No, just make sure it's heavily soaked in oil. Give me another torch as well, but one that's lit."

Kunrat walked over to the man impaled onto the chair and stood over him with one torch blazing in his hand. He spoke to one of the soldiers standing next to him. "What is this man's name?"

"I believe he is called Kirstan, Master."

"What has he confessed to?"

The soldier shifted from one foot to the other. "Nothing yet. He claims he is innocent, but he was heard praying to a pagan God."

"Kirstan, are you a pagan, do you worship false gods?" Kunrat screamed into the man's screwed up face.

"I've never done anyone any harm. Please let me off this chair," gasped the man.

Kunrat took one step back and spoke softly to the man. "You are not tied down and can rise anytime you want. I should warn you though; the barbs on the spike will hook to your entrails and pull them out through your arse if you choose to stand up. Confess your sins to me, admit to following a false God and I will end your misery."

Kunrat watched impassively as the man began to scream and cry, he then turned around and shouted for everyone to listen to him. "Halt what you are doing and listen to your Master.

These people are making fools of us all. They follow false Gods, possibly Satan himself. We must loosen their tongues by using Satan's own tool against them. Watch as I free this man from his demonic prison."

Kunrat turned back to the man and dabbed the unlit oily torch onto his chest before bringing the burning torch into contact with the oil. The man screamed as thick yellow flames licked up his chest into his face. The fire burned for several seconds before the flames flickered out. Kunrat bent forward so his face was directly in front of Kirstan's. He spoke again, loudly and clearly so everyone in the hall heard his words. "Do you worship false Gods?"

The man grimaced but did not answer. Kunrat lowered the unlit torch and pressed the oil covered cloth at its tip into the man's groin. "Kirstan, that is your name, isn't it?

"Yes," the man replied feebly.

"I will ask you again. Do you worship false Gods? Answer me truthfully and your torment will come to an end. Lie to me and I will burn you a piece at a time until you relent." Kunrat bellowed, as he lowered the lit torch between the man's knees.

"Yes, I pray to a false God," squealed the man.

Kunrat pushed the burning torch up to the oil soaked genitals of Kirstan and stepped away as he screamed in agony. "You see how easy it is to make these heretics confess," he shouted over the cries of the writhing man.

Kunrat returned to Kirstan and pushed the burning torch into his open mouth, holding it firmly in place until his muffled screams died. "Prepare fresh torches. We will turn this place into a fiery Hell for all of these followers of the Devil. Burn them all until they confess. Give them a taste in this world of what awaits them in their next world."

Several inquisitors came forward to question Kunrat. "Master, is this to be the fate of all the prisoners, including the *witches*?"

Kunrat hesitated for a moment. "Are the witches still whole in body or have they been broken?"

"All the witches are untouched except those you ordered to be burned at the stake."

"Take me to the witches. I will see if any require a more detailed form of inquisition."

Kunrat looked at the terrified group of women huddled into a single cell. He began by selecting the oldest and ugliest of the women, condemning them to torture by fire until they confessed.

Woman by woman, girl by girl, he eliminated those that did not appeal to his requirements, until just four remained. Turning to the guards and pointing at one of the remaining women, he said, "There is something evil in that girl's eyes. Strip her from her clothing, bind her wrists tightly and take her up to my interrogation room. I will arrive shortly to begin the process of extracting a confession from her."

Over the next week, all the previous inhabitants of Gothburgh Castle succumbed to fire. The two guards summoned by Kunrat to remove the body of a fourth witch from his interrogation room, whispered to each other as they wrapped the bloody body of a young woman in a hessian blanket. "Did you see her neck? It's just like the other three, bitten wide open at the side. Do you think he's drinking their blood?"

"I don't know, but I'm not asking him. Will you?"

"What, and end up broken to pieces on a wheel and put out for the crows to feast on? No I'm not asking anybody anything."

Over the winter, the members of the Inquisition established themselves in the castle and calculated the financial gains of their conquest. As the administrators transferred land deeds to the joint ownership of the Holy Roman Emperor and the Catholic Church, Kunrat became increasingly restless.

He regretted killing the women so quickly, regretted not

keeping at least one of them alive for his amusement. Next time, he would tell the others that he had captured a powerful witch who would be useful to keep alive as a tool against the dark powers.

He hated the winter, the penetrating cold that permeated into the thick stone walls of the castle, sucking out the heat from the air and his bones. As the days began to stretch out and the snow covered ground shed its thick covering, he called for a meeting to plan their next conquest. He had sent out scouts to investigate where they were needed next and the latest report aroused his interest.

At noon, on a day in mid-March, Kunrat summoned a meeting of the Inquisition. He rose to his feet and addressed the assembly. "I have received information about a small kingdom that lies to the east of a town called Harsburgh. Under the slopes of the great mountain range there is a castle occupied by a family with the name of Boese. That indeed is a black name if ever there was one," he hissed, as he interlocked his bony fingers and glanced upward in a mockery of prayer. "The King of the lands surrounding this castle is rumoured to be in league with Satan. There are stories aplenty of him ravishing young virgins and filling his castle with demonic spawn. It is said his offspring resemble creatures that are half rat and half hobgoblin." He paused to see the reaction of his audience before pulling a face that resembled a demon.

"I can't believe there are devils living so close to us," an Inquisitor called out in disgust.

Kunrat smiled briefly. "I gather the population of Harsburgh are extremely devout and God fearing people and of no concern to our mission, but the pestilence inhabiting the valleys to the east must be eradicated. As soon as the snows clear, we will march to this place and rid the world of the polluted corruption that breeds without restrain below the mountains. I order you to conscript all of the fit men living on the lands we have acquired. Offer them a share of the spoils we will gain as an incentive for their good service."

The members of the assembly cheered and waved their arms on hearing Kunrat's news. They began to chant in unison. "Long live the Master. Long live the Master."

A few weeks later, as a two thousand strong column of men rode up through a valley leading to Castle Boese, a rider approached Kunrat. "Master, we have noticed a lone rider galloping away to the south. Shall we pursue him?"

Kunrat steadied his horse before replying. "What did this rider look like?"

"It is strange, but he appeared to be wearing a King's robes and wore a golden crown."

"In that case, I'll join you on the pursuit," Kunrat replied, urging his horse forward.

FIFTEEN

Over the next few days, Henry felt neglected as Cristina spent most of her time surfing the net, using all four of her devices at once. As she jumped from desktop to laptop, to tablet and then to phone, he tried to find out what she was up to. "Would you like a coffee? What are you looking at now?" he asked inquisitively.

"I'm just checking through some stuff. I'm really busy with this at the moment, but I'll tell you all about it as soon as I've finished checking something."

Henry felt a sulk coming on, he'd not felt like this since his mother snubbed him for three days when he had gotten drunk on his fifteenth birthday. He reflected on his relationship with his mother. She was always there for him and when his father died suddenly, just after his eleventh birthday, she had gathered an inner strength that saw him through his loss. Now he had fled the nest, they still talked at least once every few days, but the conversation was always trivial. He'd tried to tell her about his new job, about Cristina, but his mum just said, 'Good for you, by the way, did you know next door's cat was run over last week? They're very upset about it'.

He picked up the pocket watch and depressed the snake eyes to open the case. As he looked abstractly at the nine concentric rings on the watch's face, he noticed something unusual about the alignment of the small holes. The set of circular apertures in the seven inner-rings were almost arranged into a symmetrical pattern. As he wondered if there was any significance about this alignment, Cristina shouted out to him. "Henry, come here, I want to show you something."

Because of the urgency in her voice, he put down the watch without shutting its casing and dashed over to her. If he had waited a few seconds longer, he would have heard the single, crystal clear chime, the first ever emitted from the watch as the two inner rings entered a long awaited conjunction.

Cristina had tuned to face him and he saw she was bursting to tell him something important. "What is it, have you found something?" he asked as he sat on the stool next to her.

"I'm sorry I've been ignoring you, but I found so many connections and wanted to check out all the correlations before telling you what I've discovered."

Henry glanced at the tables and graphs on the screen and wondered what great secrets they held. "Why don't you start from the beginning and tell me exactly what you've found out."

"Okay, I guess that's a good place to start. I began by looking at how the global stock markets have performed over the last few years and compared it with Dromedary Investment's transactions over the same period. Look at this graph. The red line shows our company's activities and the blue line the effect on world share prices. Do you notice anything special?"

"Like what?" Henry said, resisting the urge to scratch his head.

"It's so obvious. The changes in the red line are directly affecting the rise or fall of the blue line. Quite simply, over the past ten years, Dromedary has been directly manipulating the value of world share prices."

"Are you sure? Couldn't it be coincidence or a bit of insider trading that has produced these *correlations* as you put it?"

"No, the *correlation* is perfect and the changes in world

stocks have followed Dromedary's transactions. The amounts involved in the transactions are relatively small, but each time they have produced a cascade affect that has shifted share trading values by double digit percentage points."

"What else have you found?" Henry said, trying to sound enthusiastic, as he didn't really understand what she meant.

"Each time an event occurs it's larger. It's a bit like a spiral that is growing. Look at this graph, it's an extrapolation of what I predict will happen over the next few months."

Henry looked at the image that showed what looked like little waves starting from the left of the screen. As he looked across, the waves grew larger reminding him of a seismic monitor depicting the growing shockwaves of an earthquake. To the right of the screen, the wavy line rose nearly to the top before dipping down and off the screen. "What does this show?"

"It shows the collapse of the world's economy. Everything of fiscal value reduced to nothing."

"How can that happen?"

"At the moment the total debt in the world is about one third of its total assets. If a sequence of collapses were initiated in certain ways, then that debt could become larger than the assets. In effect, all currencies would have a negative value."

"That sounds crazy. What would happen then?"

"I don't know the answer to that."

Henry paused to think. "So are you saying that if this happens we will have lost all the money we've earned over the past few weeks?"

"Most definitely as all currencies, shares and bonds would be worthless."

"So we've no hope if this happens?"

"I've got an idea. There's one commodity that will still be of value?"

"What's that, gold?"

"I'm not sure about gold, but the one thing that will retain value is land. People will still need places to live, food to eat and I'm certain civilization would not collapse, just reorganise to a new set of values."

Henry tried to imagine what might happen, but quickly lost his track of thought. "So are you suggesting that we start buying land?"

"I am. I think we should acquire as much agricultural land as possible. The one thing that is crucial for our survival is food. Whether we would be allowed to keep the land after such an event, I don't know, but nothing else will have any real value at first."

"The whole thing sounds implausible to me, but then again what's happening in my life is implausible. I came into this with nothing and if I leave with nothing, then I guess I've lost nothing."

"Too many nothings and you missed something out of your logic," Cristina said, nudging him in the ribs.

"What did I miss out?"

"You missed out the most important thing in your life, me. At least you gained me in all of this."

"So I did. I don't pretend to understand anything you've said, but as long as I have you, I know everything will turnout right. So what are we going to do next?"

"I've been transferring some money into an offshore account I set up. Let's buy a few farms."

As Cristina opened two new sites on her screens, her phone rang. She looked down to see who was calling and jumped to her feet. "Sorry, Henry, this call could be important. I'm going to take it in the bedroom. Start looking for any promising agricultural land for sale. I've already accumulated over sixty million dollars in the account."

Henry heard Cristina say 'hello' before she closed the bedroom door. He was briefly tempted to put his ear to the door and eavesdrop on her mysterious caller, but after what she said to him, he felt he could fully trust her. Over the next hour, he successfully bid on three large plots of land spread across Europe, which halved their bank balance.

Cristina returned, looking stern faced. "Henry, I have to go away for a few days. While I'm gone you need to keep transferring the maximum amount you can from both of our Dromedary accounts. I'll show you how to do that before I leave."

"Where are you going, is it a client?"

"It's to do with business but not a normal client. This is an important meeting for me and I hate to be secretive about it, but it's better you don't know who I am seeing or where I am. I'll explain everything to you when I get back. Now, let me show you how to transfer the money into our account."

Henry hadn't heard from Cristina for two days and for the fifth time in an hour, his thumb hovered over her contact link on his phone. He'd just finished transferring their daily allowance from the Dromedary account and decided he would search for more land to purchase after having another coffee.

As he waited for the kettle to boil, he switched on the television and thought about his future. Being apart from Cristina made him realise how big a part of his life she had become. He couldn't imagine what it would be like to live without her now. The rumblings and creaking of the boiling kettle muted out the voice of a newscaster emotionally delivering a story, but as Henry glanced at the screen, he saw an image of a large building being doused by firemen and turned his attention to the red strip at the bottom of the screen.

Breaking News: At least 51 dead in suspected terrorist attack on a London Hotel.

Henry turned up the volume and listened as a newsreader issued sketchy details of how six men carrying suitcases had entered the hotel seconds before a huge explosion. As the story unfolded, it seemed the hotel was hosting an award ceremony to jointly decorate members of the British and American Special Forces for their daring missions against Boko Haram.

Henry remembered a recent story about a rescue operation to release a group of America marines and kidnapped civilians on the Nigeria and Chad borders. A sudden wave of panic passed through him and he tried to call Cristina. Her phone did not answer, but immediately directed him to her voicemail. He pulled up the lid of her laptop and with a few taps on the keyboard, entered the dark web.

In seconds, he located the newsfeed site he sought, the one that displayed uploaded videos and personal accounts with no censorship. The hotel bombing was second on the list and there were already more than forty video links available for viewing or downloading. He put aside his thoughts of how some people *got off* on watching scenes of carnage and felt physically sick as he watched the film pan over what was left of the main foyer of the hotel.

Whoever filmed this had paused the panning every time their phone camera centred on grotesquely twisted body parts. For a moment, Henry felt his face whiten as he looked at the upper half of a young woman that resembled Cristina.

She had been cut in half at the waistline, the lower portion of her body was gone, but the rest of her looked normal. There was no blood, no parts missing and she almost looked as if she was smiling. He shut the laptop down and glanced at the television, noticing the confirmed death toll had risen to over one hundred and twenty. He picked up his phone and sent Cristina a text, asking her to text him back to let him know she was okay when she saw the message. As he put the phone down it rang. He snatched it back up and swiped at it without looking.

"Hello, Henry, have you seen the news? I just called to make sure you're okay."

"Hi mum, yes I'm fine. I've just seen it on the news, it looks really bad," he said, wondering what his mother would think if she knew he'd looked at the graphic images on the dark web.

"Are you keeping well? There's a nasty flu virus going around. Do you remember Mrs Dickson, the big woman who lives a few doors down from us?"

"I think so. Is she the one who fell over on a bus a few years ago?"

"Yes that's the one. Anyway they took her to hospital in an ambulance yesterday morning and she died in the night. Eric from next door says she died from the flu."

An hour later, Henry put down his phone. Much as he loved his mum, he found talking to her for any length of time very draining. He knew he should try to make some land purchases, but he couldn't put the thought that something might have happened to Cristina out of his mind.

He looked out of the window, at the strong sunlight that brightened the outside world, and decided to go for a long walk to clear his head. As he opened the door to leave his flat, he though he heard two faint chimes coming from their lounge. If he had returned he would have noticed that the central three rings of the pocket watch were now perfectly aligned.

On the fifth day of Cristina's absence, his phone chimed to inform him he had a message. Frantically, he opened the text and felt dizzy with relief.

Hi, Henry. Sorry I've not been in contact earlier, but I've been staying in a remote area and could not get a signal. I am making my way back home now and should be back in London later this evening. Hope you are well. I missed you and am really looking forward to seeing you. Love C.

For the rest of the day, Henry flicked from one task to the next, finding his level of excitement made concentration almost impossible. He performed the ritual of transferring the money, something he did like clockwork every day, but couldn't focus on the task of searching for land to purchase.

He wandered around the flat and tidied up by putting things into cupboards or drawers, though he was not sure he put everything in its right place. Later, in the afternoon, he popped out to buy some food and wine. He'd only cooked Cristina one meal since they met, lasagne made the same way his mother made it, but Cristina said it was the best homemade lasagne she'd ever tasted, so tonight he decided to make his signature dish. He heard the door clunking open as he searched, under his folded socks and the missing television remote in one of the kitchen drawers, for the whisk he needed to help dissolve the lumps in his cheese sauce.

"I'm back," Cristina called out.

He ran out to greet her and was shocked by how tired she looked. "Are you okay?" he said.

"I'm good, just very tired. I've not had a lot sleep over the past few days and it's such a long train journey from the Scottish Highlands."

"You've been all the way up there?"

"Yes, I've been staying in a very old castle. It was wonderful."

"Was it with a friend?"

"No, it was with an acquaintance I've come to know. I'll explain later, but this person has given me so much guidance on what we need to do to protect our future together. Did you remember to transfer our assets each day?"

"Yes, I've transferred the full amount from both our accounts every day since you've been away."

"Have you bought any more land?"

Henry wondered why she was so intent about their finances. He simply wanted to hug her and tell her how much he missed her. "No, I couldn't concentrate. I was worried about you and after that terrorist attack on the hotel, I couldn't focus on anything."

"That's okay. I now know what we need to look for. What's

that burning smell?"

"Oh shit, it's my cheese sauce for the lasagne I'm making for you."

"Henry, don't think me rude, but I really need to go to bed and sleep. I promise I'll be fine in the morning, but I've barely slept since I left here five days ago. There was so much I had to do and he wanted to teach me many things. I'm exhausted."

Henry wanted to ask who *he* was, but thought this was not the right time. "Okay, you go to bed and I'll clear up here. I don't feel hungry anymore anyway. I'm so glad your back, Cristina, I really missed you."

"And I really missed you. I'll make it up to you tomorrow."

Cristina was fast asleep when Henry crept into their bedroom. He could smell that she had showered and loved the way she exuded a fresh scent of her natural odours combined with fruity aroma of her shower gel.

He was about to climb into bed when he heard something chiming from the lounge. For a moment he wondered if Cristina had left her phone there, but saw it was on her bedside cabinet. He dithered, wondering if he should check, but the relief of having Cristina back with him had released the tensions of the past days. He climbed into bed and almost instantly fell asleep.

When he woke the next morning, Cristina was already up. He put on his dressing gown and walked into the kitchen. Cristina was sitting on a stool and rummaging through the contents of a glossy cardboard box. "You're up early, did you sleep well?" he said, sitting next to her.

"Like a baby, though from what I've heard, most babies are awake half the night."

"What's that?" Henry said, leaning over to take a closer look at the box.

"It's a DNA testing kit. Well actually it's an over packaged box that contains a sterile swab and a small glass tube to put it in.

The rest is just leaflets and a padded return envelope."

"Why have you got that?"

"I've been thinking. Suppose there is an economic crash and the medical system become overwhelmed. If I, or you, are carrying a genetic defect, it will be difficult to obtain treatment or have access to any drugs that might help. I think it's best to be cautious and have a test. If we do need anything in the future, we can buy it now, while we still have the resources and it's still available."

Henry gave her a puzzled look. "What made you think of that?"

"It was something someone suggested to me. It only takes a second. Come on, open wide and I'll take a sample of your cheek cells without you even knowing it," Cristina said, waving something that looked like a cotton bud in front of Henry's face.

Henry sipped on his coffee as Cristina sealed the two envelopes containing their DNA. "Do you really think something bad is going to happen?"

"I don't know if it'll be bad, but I think everything's going to be turned upside down for a while. Now let's buy some land. I know exactly what we need to look for."

Later, that evening, when Henry went to bed with Cristina, she made love to him like she'd never done before. Through the small hours, Henry entered a physical and emotional bond he knew he wanted to last forever.

Over the next month they extracted a fortune from their Dromedary accounts and amassed a few million hectares of land across the globe. Henry felt his life could not be better and then, Cristina hit him with a bombshell he thought he'd never recover from.

"Henry, I have to go away for a couple days."

"Why?"

"I'm pregnant."

"That's fantastic. Why do you have to go away?"

"I'm having an abortion."

"Sorry, what did you say?"

"I said. I'm having an abortion."

"Why, don't I have a say in this? You can't… you just can't without talking with me first."

"I am talking with you. Henry, it's not yours."

"Not mine? Whose is it?"

"That's not important. One day I want us to have children, but this child is not for this world. I cannot have this child, it wouldn't be right."

"Please tell me, whose is it?"

"I will tell you one day. You must trust me. It's too complicated to explain just now, but it's not what you think."

"I don't know what to think at the moment. I feel like you have destroyed me, destroyed our love. I don't think I can cope with this."

"Henry, you will. I know how hard this is for you, but you must believe me. I want to be with you, I want us to grow old together more than anything. This is something that has happened that shouldn't have happened. I could have lied to you and not told you, but I have, because I respect and love you."

Henry let his head sink into his hands and felt a warm wetness creep down between his fingers into the palms of his hand. With the salty taste of tears in his mouth, he turned to look at Cristina. "Why?"

"This sounds so stupid," she said, releasing her own tears. "I had no choice, he's too powerful, but what I gained from him will save us. If I had not taken the path I did, we would both die in the near future."

"I don't know whether to believe you or not. Just go and leave me for now. This is too much for me to take in. Why didn't you say anything earlier?"

"I didn't say anything earlier because I was terrified of losing you. One day soon, you'll understand what all this is about. I'll go now and see you in a couple of days. Henry, please be here when I get back."

* * *

Yasuf dug through the soft earth at the base of the fallen tree and pulled out the treasure he had hidden earlier. He could feel moisture seeping from the wounds on his abdomen and bit his lip as he climbed onto his feet. He turned to face the east and limped along the path that would lead to the open plains. The jarring pain of each painful step motivated him to continue, to find his destiny, his only remaining goal in life, to kill as many of those who belonged to the race that had taken Susan and his child from him.

Three days later, thirst, hunger and exhaustion had taken their toll. He sat in a small area of shade under a solitary withered tree and looked at the assembling vultures. The hunched birds swivelled their heads to check he was still moving, one of them advancing closer to see if its next meal was ready.

Yasuf picked up a small stone and threw it at the bird, shouting out, "I'm not dead yet and if you come any closer, I'll shoot you." He pulled out the handgun from his trousers and wondered if he would feel any pain when he pulled the trigger to put a bullet through his head.

He closed his eyes to escape the scene of a shimmering horizon and listened to the buzzing of the flies that gathered to lay eggs on his dead body. Through the sawing buzz, he thought he heard a throbbing sound, the rumbling chug of a tired diesel engine.

He opened his eyes and shaded them with his hand to scour

the landscape. Dust, a trail of dust was evaporating upwards to his left. He jumped to his feet, waved his arms and shouted as loudly as his weakened body could muster. They had seen him. The pickup was turning, approaching. He tucked the pistol deep into his trousers and held up his hands in a gesture of surrender. The battered Toyota juddered to a halt in front of him and a man in military fatigues jumped out, pulling out an AK 47 on him.

"What are you doing out here?" the man shouted.

My village was attacked and everybody was killed. I escaped but I have no food or water, please help me?"

"Are you Christian or Muslim?"

Yasuf wiped the dust from his eyes and looked at the man for a clue as to which side he was on. Behind the man, he noticed a glint of light reflecting from a crucifix hanging from the interior mirror of the pickup. "Christian, our village was attacked by Boko Haram."

The man turned back to the pickup and shouted to the driver. "Sylvestre, have we room for a passenger?"

The driver opened his door, but stayed in the pickup. "Ask him if he has the fare to pay for a lift."

"Do you have any money, boy?"

Yasuf sensed he was not safe and would need to be very cautious. "I have a little."

"Show me and I'll see if we can do a deal."

Yasuf reached into his bag of treasure and picked out a small wad of notes. "I have this," he said, throwing the money at the feet of the man. As the man bent down to pick up the money, Yasuf pulled out the handgun, slipping the safety catch off. He squeezed the trigger and winced as the recoil jarred his wrist.

Before the man had fallen fully to the ground, Yasuf discharged the gun at the driver who was reaching for his weapon. Both men were still alive. The first man rolled on the ground clutching the side of his face which had been torn open by the bullet. Yasuf walked up to him and shot him in the head.

The driver had fallen out of the vehicle and was kneeling, holding his bloody stomach and cursing. Yasuf stepped up to him and completed the execution. He gathered his belongings and threw them on the passenger seat of the pickup, grabbed a bottle of water and slowly sipped on the life giving fluid.

It took Yasuf nearly an hour to fathom out what each pedal did and how the gears worked. Eventually, he drove the vehicle a short distance away from the dead men and stopped to watch the vultures tear the flesh from their bodies. He lifted the crucifix from the mirror, kissed it and threw it out of the window. Looking at the position of the sun in the sky, he turned the vehicle and headed north. Akubar had once told him that Europe lay north and Europe was full of Christians.

SIXTEEN

In one of the ground floor rooms of Castle Boese, Berchtold craned forward to help him read the last digit of a sum, which was at the bottom of a column of numbers. It was so unfair that he should still have to work as a bookkeeper at his age, constantly straining his eyes to make out the illegible entries of others.

He pushed his ledger sheet across the desk so it was closer to the large window and easier for him to read. As he recorded the taxes collected over the past month, a passing shadow, followed by a hollow thud, caused him to look up and peer out of the large window in front of him.

At first he thought a large bird may have flown into the castle wall, but as his weary eyes fought to focus on an out-of-place heap resting on the ground a few footsteps from his window, he made out the crumpled form as being the body of a person, in fact, the body of a woman.

He eased his body from his chair, and moving as quickly as his stiff joints allowed, shambled across the room to its doorway. He shouted out several times before anyone heard him, but eventually a young boy came running up the corridor. "Quickly, find the guards and tell them someone has fallen from a great height," he yelled at the boy.

"Fallen where?" the boy shouted back.

"Outside my window. Just come back here with a guard as

quickly as you can."

Eberhard climbed onto the desk and pushed his head and shoulders through the window's opening to gain a better few of the body in front of him. He could see at once it was a woman, but felt sickened by the way her limbs radiated at unnatural angles from her ruptured torso. A sudden gust of wind disturbed her blood soaked hair, lifting it briefly from her hidden face. Eberhard realised he was looking at the body of the Queen. He jumped back off the desk, scattering Berchtold's papers across the floor. "When did she fall?" he shouted to the old bookkeeper.

"It was only a few minutes ago. I saw a shadow flash pass my window and heard her hit the ground. Do you know who she is?"

"I do and this is a tragic day. The woman who has fallen to her death is our Queen. That is the body of Queen Czyelle. I must go and rouse the guard. The King, he must be told of this at once. Stay here and watch over her body. Make sure she's not picked at by the crows."

Burgolt knelt over the lifeless body of the girl on his bed. For the first time a wave of guilt surged through him as he recalled how her face had taken on the form of Czyelle's, as he drained her life essence through the grip of his hand across her soft throat. He tied to snuff out internal voices that told him he was ill, nothing more than a creature of depravity because of his own short comings and an unworthy soul to inhabit this Earth.

When Czyelle had pleaded with him, something inside him had broken. Her beautiful face and glistening tears had tormented his soul, rendered him destitute in front of the woman carrying his child. He should have let her go and climbed into his own bed to sleep off his rage, before reconciling with her the next day. But no, he gave in to the dark anger and summoned a girl, vented his anguish by using his toys on her until her screams ate into his turmoil, causing him to abate her calls of terror through stifling her cries with his hand.

A shockwave of panic erupted through him as someone urgently rapped on his door. "My King, let us in, something has happened to the Queen."

He instinctively shouted back. "Wait, do not enter, I am not clothed. I'll come to the door in a moment."

"Please hurry, it is a matter of the greatest urgency and I must speak with you at once."

Burgolt climbed off the bed and grabbed the edges of the cover, which he pulled to him before folding it over the body of the dead girl. He hastily put on the nearest clothes to hand and partly opened the door, before slipping through the gap into the corridor and closing the door behind him so no one could see into his room. "What is it that is so urgent to rouse a King from his bed?"

"My King, something terrible has happened, the Queen's dead," the elderly messenger mumbled, backed by over a dozen anxious looking guards.

"Did you say she was dead? But how?"

"She has fallen from a great height and lies outside the castle. We don't how this happened, but I have sent a party of guards to check on her room."

As the messenger finished speaking, four more guards came running down the corridor. The leading one spoke urgently. "Her bed is blood soaked, it looks as if she might have been stabbed and then thrown down, but the window is very narrow and I don't think her body could have been passed through it."

The elderly messenger gave Burgolt a dark look. "Check to see if she was carried onto the roof and thrown from there. Look for any traces of blood or torn clothing on the steps leading up to the roof. If she has been murdered, we must find the culprit and bring him to justice."

Burgolt returned the glare of the messenger. "She was well when I spoke to her earlier and I've been in my room since then."

The messenger gave a wry smile and replied, "My King, I would never suspect you of killing your own wife. She was after all a member of the royal court and not a disposable peasant."

"Is she still lying outside the castle," Burgolt asked, in an attempt to take control.

"I have ordered for her body to be brought into the castle. I will have someone examine her to see if there is any sign that she was killed before falling."

Burgolt shifted from one foot to another and bit his knuckle as he pondered his next course of action. "I will dress in suitable attire and come down the courtroom. Go down and wait for me there."

"As you desire, my King," the messenger said, bowing slightly before turning around and walking away.

Burgolt selected his darkest clothes and kept his back to the bed as he dressed. The voices in his head seemed to be playing a cruel game, one suggesting the Queen had killed herself because of what he threatened to do, while the other told him she had been murdered by someone who intended to usurp his position.

He pulled his shoulders back and thrust out his chest as he entered the courtroom, keeping his eyes ahead and not looking at those who glared accusingly at him. A young guard ran into the room and in a panicked voice, made an announcement that caused those present to assume a grey pallor.

"My Lords, my King. I have come from the castle's roof. While we were searching for signs of foul doings, we saw something terrible in the distance. There is a dark army marching on us. They approach by the north valley and their numbers are great. They carry the flag of the Inquisition."

One of the seated lords stood and spoke. "When you say great army, how many men are you suggesting there are in this army approaching us?"

"I do not know exactly, but suffice to say the column extends back up the valley as far as the eye can see. I would estimate more than two thousand men and we have only four hundred able bodied soldiers to defend the castle."

The lord rubbed his beard with his hand and turned to face Burgolt. "My King, it appears we are heavily outnumbered, what do you suggest we do?"

Burgolt had never felt so alone, so in need of someone to stand at his side and guide him, then, he remembered his guest. "Where is Duke Gomory? He has told me he will assist us at this time of our need."

One of his administrators stood, bowed and addressed the assembly. "I understand the Duke has not been seen for several days. There are rumours that he left the castle one night, mesmerising the guards as he did so. Some say he is an advocate of the Devil."

Burgolt sensed the pairs of eyes burning into him and his mind felt numb. He'd never expected this day would come. His was a small kingdom and remote at the edge of the mountains. Why did they want to bother him? Why couldn't he just flee from this predicament and live out his life in peace? *Flee? Peace? Live?*

An idea crept into his head. "I will go and meet with this army and negotiate the safety of you all. I do not know if these are men of reason and will welcome me. Whether they will listen to my plea for clemency or kill me before I utter a word, I do not know, but I must try. For this reason, I will ride out to meet them alone. I am your King and it is my duty, even though it may cost me my life, to defend my subjects. Prepare my horse while I adorn my regal robes."

Burgolt smiled as a rush of whispers spread around the courtroom. He turned to face those sat on the tiered seats and bowed in turn at each section of his court. "I will now go and prepare to meet this adversary and pray that I will return with news of your safekeeping."

He strutted from the courtroom and climbed the stairs as fast as he could. In his room, he opened one of the wardrobe doors and reached behind his thick gowns until he located the small lever he sought. With a quick pull, he heard the hidden flap fall open. His shaking hand contacted the soft cloth of the bag that would buy his new life the other side of the mountains.

He felt his tendons straining as he pulled the bag of gold coins from its hidden shelf. He tied the bag to his belt and wrapped a thick, fur edged robe over his body. He was about to leave when something made him stop, he'd forgotten something, but could not think what it was. As he thought, *you haven't much time,* the image of a clock appeared in his mind's eye. *The pocket watch you fool, you nearly forgot the pocket watch.*

Burgolt struggled down the stairs, uncomfortably aware how his heavy bag of concealed gold caused him to walk in an askew manner. He adjusted the bag to the front of his belt and loosened the robe to disguise the burden pressing against his manhood. He strode aggressively into the courtyard behind the main gate and stepped onto the box aside his horse. "Aid me to mount my horse as my heart is so heavy with the grievous task that lies ahead of me," he commanded to his footman.

A soldier came forward with his sword and strapped it to his saddle before reciting what he'd been told to say. "My King, it has been an honour to serve you and I pray for your safe return."

Burgolt urged the horse towards the rising portcullis and held up his arm as a gesture of his personal bravery. He halted the horse as someone made an urgent cry.

"My King, wait. You've forgotten something."

Burgolt turned to see a member of the court holding out his

crown.

"My King, your crown. You must wear your crown, so these men know you are a King and not just a simple messenger sent to dissuade them from their intentions."

Burgolt reached down for his crown and set it on his head. He smiled at his followers and rode through the gate to meet with the advancing army.

The road from the gate led to the main route that ran in a north-south direction. To his left, the road would take him to the advancing army, but to his right it led south to a fork in the road. The left fork climbed up over the mountains before dropping down into the valley beyond, while the right fork descended into the old forest that was a refuge for criminals and scoundrels.

Burgolt reached the end of the road leading from the gate and turned his horse to the left. He advanced a few paces and swung the horse around, before setting it into a gallop southwards and away from the advancing army. He reckoned it would take him less than an hour to reach the fork and if he made good progress up the pass, he could make it to the next valley, and safety, by the next day.

After a few minutes, he slowed the horse to a steady canter and dreamed about his new life. It would be easy to establish himself as a merchant, he had sufficient gold to purchase a large house and employ servants, preferably impressionable young wenches happy to exchange favours for a gold coin or two. As he considered how many gold coins could be forged from the crown on his head, his horse became jittery.

At first, he couldn't see any cause for the animal's hysteria, until a shadow passed between the bushes to his right. There was an animal tracking him, a spectral smudge that darted from cover to cover of the undergrowth. An animal he'd seen before, a wolf.

He reached down and gripped the hilt of his sword for reassurance and looked ahead. The fork was visible by virtue that he could see the winding snake-like path twisting up the mountains to his left. He dug his heels into the horse's flanks and forced the animal into a moderate gallop.

As he reached the fork and pulled on the rein to guide his horse to the left, a white wolf slipped out from behind a rock and stood in the centre of the path. His horse reared and neighed in alarm. Burgolt patted the animal to calm it down, but just as he settled the horse, something growled from behind him. He felt the body of his mount bolt forward from under him and clawed at the reins in a desperate attempt to remain seated atop his beast, but the weight of the gold tied to his belt shifted to his right side and losing his precarious balance, he fell to the ground.

The horse turned and stampeded to the north, heading back the way he came. He climbed to his feet and heard the clunking of coins tumbling from his ruptured bag onto the stony road surface. Before he could bend down to scoop up his future, the pair of wolves edged closer to him and drew back their dark lips to expose wet pink gums and glistening white fangs. With his heart thumping like a whore on heat, he ran.

The wolves responded, not coming directly at him, but closing down on him from both sides to direct him onto the right fork that descended into the gloom of the forest below. As he ran down the path and under the cover of the trees' canopy, he heard the agile footfall of the chasing wolves.

He wanted to stop and draw his sword, cut off their monstrous heads, but it was strapped to the saddle on his runaway steed. For what seemed like an eternity, he scrambled down the steep path, often sliding onto his backside before regaining his footing and charging away from the demons chasing him. He became aware that night had fallen, in his panic and under the gloom of the forest, he'd failed to notice the light had seeped away as the day came to a close.

Finally, he stopped descending and as he paused to catch his ragged breath, he sensed he was alone. There was no sound of following footsteps, no hiss of expectant panting and sight of the pair of wolves that forced him to his wretched state. He checked the torn money bag, it was empty. He raised his hand to the top if his head and felt only his hair, his crown was gone. Slipping his hand into his pocket he felt for his last treasure, it was there, he still had the pocket watch.

As the minutes advanced, Burgolt could not even see his own hand that he held out in front of his face. He felt his way cautiously through the springy branches and wondered how long this night would last. Just as he decided to rest at the base of a large tree, a pinprick of bright orange light, like a spark rising from a bonfire, glinted momentarily to his right.

He edged his way in the direction of this glimmer of hope and after a few steps, he caught site of the flickering beacon that offered escape from his current isolation. As he neared, he heard voices. *Who are they? Will they kill me or offer me food and water?* He then realised how thirsty he was, how dry his mouth had become. Step by step he approached, treading carefully and silently, until, under foot, an invisible and brittle twig succumbed to his weight and issued a snap loud enough to raise the dead. The voices snuffed out leaving only a deathly silence in the windless night.

Burgolt's first awareness of the strangers was when a bag fell over his head. He collapsed to the ground as someone sat on him and squealed as several feet kicked into his ribs at the same time. Before he could fight back, his hands were tightly bound at the wrist with a twine that cut into skin. In desperation, he yelled at his unseen attackers. "I am King Burgolt from Castle Boese. Untie me at once. I demand you release me and treat me with the respect you must show to a King."

He felt pairs of hands grip his clothing, before he was dragged over the rough ground. His ordeal of being dragged like a dead animal ended as he felt the heat from an open fire scorching one side of his body. Someone gripped the sack that was over his head and jerked it off violently, causing his cheeks to burn as the rough fabric eroded his soft skin. Five men stood over him and jeered before kicking him again.

"What have we got here? Ugly looking thing, is it a rat?" the man standing in front Burgolt shouted to the others.

"It's some sort of vermin. Should we toss it into the fire and roast it?" another man said.

"Check its pockets first, it may have something valuable in them, especially if it's a King," the third man called out.

Burgolt tried to struggle as two of the men began feeling inside his clothing for valuables.

"I've got something."

"What is it?"

"Don't know. Some sort of little round box. Hey, vermin, what's this?"

Burgolt saw his only chance of hope. "It is a King's watch, a keeper of time small enough to place in one's pocket. It opens, press down the left eye of the snake and then the right."

"He's right, it does open, but I don't see how it tells the time, it hasn't got any hands. Shall we cut off his hands? Then the handless watch would have been owned by a handless King."

Burgolt tried his last gambit. "It is but a small trinket from my vast hoard of treasure. If you return with me to my castle, I will reward you with a pile of treasure greater than you could imagine."

"If we let you take us back to your castle you would have our heads cut off, but I don't reckon you have a castle, otherwise you wouldn't be out here in these woods. I reckon you're no more than a petty thief who stole this, whatever it is, from a noble gentleman. Did you cut his throat to get this?"

One of the men spread out his arms and eased the others men away from him. "I think we should hold a trial and decide if this man is guilty. I charge him with murder and theft. What is the verdict of the jury?"

The other four men spoke in unison. "Guilty as charged."

"The prisoner is found guilty as charged. There can be only one sentence passed for such heinous crimes."

"What are you going to do to me?" Burgolt squealed in terror.

"Well it's a pity to let a King's flesh go to waste, so you can do one good deed before you die and satisfy Sophie's appetite," the leader of the group said, pointing to a dark area a few paces away. "Strip him naked and hang him from that tree."

"Do you want us to hang him by his neck?"

"Don't be so stupid, you know Sophie likes her meat fresh. The more it kicks the more she likes it. Hang him by his arms, but not too high. Try to hang him so she can reach up to about here," the leader said, patting his stomach.

Burgolt tried to resist, but the men kicked him in the ribs the moment he struggled. Dejectedly, he surrendered and allowed them to strip him from his clothes and retie him. He watched as one man threw a rope over a tree branch and cried out in agony as he was hoisted into the air. He was suspended with his feet dangling about four feet above the ground and hoped his demise would be over with quickly. He was certain he was going to die, but his overwhelming fear was about the method they intended to use to end his life. The man who was the leader had gone over to a pile of supplies and seemed to be searching for something.

"Here it is. Who wants to rub this into him?"

"What are you talking about?" the man who was staring up at Burgolt replied.

"The honey, you know how she likes her honey."

"I will," the man standing near Burgolt's kicking feet replied.

"Make sure you rub it in good and hard. Spread it out from above his knees up to his waist and make sure you put plenty on his tender little bits," the leader said, walking with a pot held in his outstretched hand over to where Burgolt was hanging.

"You're right about little bits. This one's only got a little wiggly worm between its legs. Look, have you ever seen such a small one."

Burgolt tried to kick at the man, but two others came over and held his ankles firmly. He felt a rough hand rubbing something sticky over his inner thighs and tried to jerk away as his private parts were covered with the sickly greasy stuff they spread over him. Eventually, the men agreed they had spread sufficient honey over Burgolt's body and moved back.

The leader came up to Burgolt and said, "I want to give you a little advice. Sophie is a baby and she loses her temper if you kick her in the face. Whatever you do, don't kick her face. Now she's not had any meat for over a week, so I'm not sure how long she'll wait before starting her main course. She likes to have something sweet first, so let her enjoy the honey. When she starts biting you, feel free to scream as much as you like. It's very boring living out here and we don't get much in the way of entertainment. You all like hear to a good scream, don't you men."

"The louder the better," one of the men called out.

The leader gripped Burgolt's ankles and pulled down hard, making him wince as his shoulders strained to stay in their sockets. "I'm going to fetch Sophie over now. Remember what I told you."

Burgolt watched as the man walked over to the dark area and bent down to untie something. As he neared the light cast from the fire, Burgolt saw a black shadowy shape walking on all fours alongside him. Only as they passed the fire, did he see the mechanism of his death.

Sophie was a half grown mountain bear. Burgolt resisted the urge to lash out with his feet as the bear reared onto its hind legs. She carefully wrapped her forelegs around his waist. He closed his eyes as he felt the sharp points of her long claws press into his skin at the small of his back.

He waited for the first surge of pain, but all he felt was the warm wetness of a long tongue lapping up the inside of his leg. The licking seemed endless, her tongue engulfed his thighs and then she laced her tongue over his fear shrunken private parts.

He opened his eyes again as she pulled her head back and looked up at him her beady eyes. Without warning, her long, razor-sharp claws speared into his flesh and he squirmed, kicking out with his right leg to push her away. The first bite was hallway up the inside of his thigh, he felt and heard his flesh tear as she ripped a strip of raw tissue from him and dribbled down his leg as she swallowed.

She bit again, slightly higher. He drowned out the sound of his skin and flesh being torn from his body by screaming as loudly as he could. He continued screaming, shrieking into the dark forest air and praying to God to bring his nightmare to an end. As he was engulfed with further agony, when she ripped off his humble manhood, a determination overtook him.

He lost his fear of death, overcame the searing pain and finally understood the meaning of bravery. He would be brave, have no fear and relish the final moments of his awareness. She stretched up and dug deeply into him, he felt something inside give way and through the red mist that formed in his vision, he smiled at Sophie.

* * *

Kunrat dug his heels into his horse's sides and called out to those accompanying him not to lose sight of the fleeing rider, but soon, all sight of the rider was lost in the twist and turns of the roadway. "Keep going, his horse will soon tire if he rides at this pace," Kunrat shouted, punching his arm forward.

Just as Kunrat sensed his horse's rhythm was slowing, he caught sight of his objective, now cantering at a moderate pace. He slowed his pace by squeezing on his horse's flanks and pulling gently on the reins, until he gauged his speed matched that of the fleeing rider. For nearly an hour they followed, keeping a good distance behind the lone horseman so that he could not espy them following him.

A rider at Kunrat's side suddenly called out to him. "There's something wrong with his horse. Do you see how it's hesitating? Something is disturbing that animal."

Kunrat looked ahead to see the horse was now rearing up and trying to turn around. "Do you see anything?" he asked.

The rider shielded his eyes with his hand to gain a clearer view. "No, Master, I cannot see what troubles the horse. Wait, it's thrown him and the horse is bolting back in our direction."

"Come, let's see if we can catch him before he disappears," Kunrat yelled as he urged his horse into a gallop.

As they closed in on their quarry, they saw him drop down onto a path the led into a forest below them. When they reached the point they'd seen their fugitive fall from his horse, they realised they would have to dismount from horseback and continue their pursuit on foot.

Kunrat waved some of his men on and followed behind them, but ordered others to follow behind him in case they were attacked from the rear. "These old dark forests are inhabited by the refugees of crime. They are the shelter of those with a bounty on their heads and we must be careful to keep our guard. Keep a lookout for any signs of these vile and wretched creatures and if you see anyone watching us, destroy them with a well-aimed arrow."

As they penetrated deeper into the forest and darkness fell, Kunrat knew his men were uneasy about advancing further. It was becoming almost impossible to make headway in the pitch dark, but just as Kunrat thought about giving the order to call off the chase, they heard voices. Slowly, a step at a time they weaved through the tangle of young trees and mature shrubbery, until they caught sight of the flickering flames of an open fire.

Kunrat dropped onto his belly and crawled tentatively through the rotting leaf litter until he was in a position to look down at the unfolding events. Over the next hour, he salivated as he watched and heard the tortured screams of a man being eaten alive by a bear.

The first hint of an awakening day seeped through the few gaps in the overhead canopy, causing a surge in the morale of Kunrat's men. One of them crept alongside Kunrat and fixing an arrow into his bow, whispered, "Shall we kill them now or wait until they sleep?"

"If you think you can kill them all at one go, do it now, but do not kill that bear. I have plans for that beast."

Five men sat around the dying embers of their fire, still laughing about the night's main event. Their leader held a pocket watch in his open palm and turned his gaze from the watch's face to the hanging remnants of their entertainment. From below the remains of Burgolt's untouched head, arms and upper chest, long slithers of bloodied skin began to waver in the early dawn breeze.

The leader was just about to joke about Sophie's latest snack, when his speech was cut short by an arrow piercing his right cheek, its head slicing through his tongue, before punching out from his left cheek.

As the other four men turned to look at why he stalled, each felt a shockwave of pain as barbed heads from silent arrows cut into their vital organs, severing the flow of their life giving blood.

Kunrat waited patiently until the last man ceased his frantic twitching. He pulled himself up onto his feet and advanced to the five bodies, each lying in a thick puddle of their own blood. One by one, he kicked each corpse, while an archer stood by with a loaded bow ready to shoot a sharp pointed arrow through the head of any who might have survived.

As Kunrat rolled over the leader with his booted foot, he noticed something unusual throwing back an iridescent sheen from the man's hand. He stooped down and lifted the object from the dead man's hand and became mesmerised by the spectral eddies swirling over the face of the object. He lifted it to his ear and heard the almost imperceptible tick of passing time.

Later that night, Kunrat held the watch out in his open hand and looking up to the heavens on a cloudless night, he said, "You indeed are a precious find. Surely you are Satan's watch delivered to his most faithful servant."

Kunrat turned around to re-enter the castle, smiling at the thought of what was to come. There were few innocent virgins here, but plenty of witch whores for him to consume before feeding them alive, to his new pet.

SEVENTEEN

Henry felt like his mind was about to explode. All he could think about was Cristina being with another man. Every time he closed his eyes, his mind conjured up an image of how exhausted she looked when she returned from her mysterious trip to the Highlands of Scotland.

Why wouldn't she tell him whom she'd been with? She'd said he was too powerful for her to resist, but what she'd learned may save their lives in the future. Was this a lie? Was it a fabrication to try and let him down gently from the hurt he felt about her infidelity, or was it her way of trying to keep him on her side while she used him?

All his other relationships had been straightforward, boring, but straightforward. Each in turn fizzled out as a lack of emotional commitment led to a gentle drifting apart of two disinterested entities, but this was different, Cristina was different, he'd entered a new and dangerous chapter of his life and he loved it. He couldn't conceptualise being without her. The thought of not being together anymore stung him with so much pain he cried.

A shrill ring interrupted his thoughts. Where had he left his phone? Was it Cristina? Had something gone wrong? He jumped up and chased the noise; it was coming from the bedroom. He pulled at the crumple duvet and his phone fell to the floor. It was withheld number. Could it be the clinic she'd gone to? He answered.

"Am I speaking with Mr Henry King?" a man's voice chimed.

"Yes, who are you?"

"It's Mr Garcia, I met you a few months back and we did a deal."

"Oh yes, I remember. Is everything alright?" Henry said, remembering that Mr Garcia had his number.

"I don't know. That's why I'm calling you."

"Sorry, Mr Garcia, I don't understand."

"I'm calling you because the value of my assets has fallen by over eighty percent in the past two days. Can you please verify there's not a problem, that this is a temporary aberration before they recover their original value?"

Henry gritted his teeth as he tried to think how to reply to this question. "I'm certain it's a re-adjustment of investments, before a sequence of major acquisitions re-establishes the previously trending growth of your financial capital," he replied confidently, thinking how his ability to bullshit had grown over the past weeks.

"I would be grateful if you could confirm that with your superiors. I will call back in a few hours. Mr King, I am a very tolerant man, I tolerate the success of others without reservation, but I reward failure without reservation. If I lose my fortune you will regret ever being born. Do you understand me?"

"Yes, I'll find out what's happening and look forward to your call."

Henry was tempted to call Cristina straight away, but she would, or should, be back this afternoon. Instead, he called the Duchess. Her phone answered and switched to voicemail. "Hi Duchess, it's me Henry, Henry King. Could you call me back as soon as you can?"

Henry wandered out of the bedroom, into the kitchen, stopping in front of Cristina's desktop and laptop. She had taken her phone and tablet with her, but he was used to using her laptop for transferring their funds on a daily basis. He switched on the desktop and waited for the screen to load. Hoping she used a common password across her devices, he entered the password for her laptop. 'Cameltoe69'. There was something about her weird sense of humour he adored. The computer opened.

He'd seen her checking through the archives of Dromedary's investments, achieved by using hundreds of fictitious satellite companies that had seemingly legitimate bases in the World's more dubious countries. He thought he recognised the file he wanted, but when he tried to open it, he was asked for a password. Cameltoe69 did not work. He tried to remember when she last used this file. He'd watched her open it and he was sure she typed something first, but he'd not been paying attention at the time. He made a couple of attempts, using the name of her shower gel and her favourite perfume, hesitating when he thought he heard a knock on the front door. What might she have used as a password? As he was about to type in 'Duchess69', he felt a hand land on his shoulder, causing him to jump up from his stool.

"What are you doing?" Cristina exclaimed.

"You're back."

"Yes I'm back. Are you trying to go through my personal files?"

"No, well only the Dromedary one. I don't know the password so I was trying to hack into it. How did it go?"

"If you mean the abortion, it's done. Why do you need to go into that file?"

"I've had a phone call from one of my clients, Mr Garcia, his portfolio has fallen by eighty percent in the last two days and he's not very happy. I tried to call the Duchess but her phone is on voicemail."

"You must be mistaken, no one's portfolio falls by that much, ever. Let me take a look. Henry, the coffee they serve at the clinic is about as strong as a gnat's piss, please be a sweetie and make me a double strength cappuccino."

Henry's mind whirled. He'd been preparing to either comfort her or have an all-out fight to discover whom her mysterious lover was, but this immediate normalcy undermined his planned intentions. "With or without sugar?"

"With, but just one."

As he depressed the button to activate the steamer on their coffee machine, he heard Cristina shout, "It's started. Oh my God, it's started."

As soon as the machine finished its impression of an old man trying to summon a globule of spit into his mouth, Henry called back to her before grabbing the two cappuccinos. "What's started?"

"I don't know; the end of civilization as we know it?"

Henry sipped his coffee and looked at the screen. The first column listed the names of companies, while the second showed their current share value. The numbers in the second column alternated from red to green, with about half red and half green. "Does the red mean the prices are falling?"

"Yes, all the reds are falling, but most are dropping at a massive rate. Hang on a second, I'm going to apply the filter to show which companies Dromedary has large investments in. Oh my God, all of them are crashing in value. Henry, have you transferred our money today?"

"No, not yet."

Cristina typed frantically on the keyboard and said, "Why not?"

"I had something on my mind. I was worried about something."

As the screen flicked to the login display for their Dromedary accounts, Cristina turned to face him. "Were you worried about me?"

"Sort of, I was worried about us. I'm finding it very hard to accept what's happened and your being so secretive just makes it worse."

Cristina looked directly into his eyes and scrunched up her nose in the way she knew he liked. "I can understand how shocked you were. I was also shocked. Look, the only reason I'm being secretive is for your own protection," she said, taking his hands in hers."If I told you everything you'd screw up later and that could cost you your life and mine as well. You have to trust me."

"It's not that easy," Henry said, pulling back slightly from her.

"I'll never have sex with anyone else as long as we are committed to each other, and I hope that's for a very long time. When you find out what I did, what I've planned, I think you'll understand, but until then you are going to have to take a gamble that I'm right."

"I'll try. Come on then, open up your account first and let's take out some money while there's still some left."

Cristina entered the codes and passwords to access her account and shrieked when the page opened.

Henry turned to her and saw the expression of alarm on her face. "What's wrong?" he asked.

"It says 'This account is now closed'."

"What about my account?"

Cristina clacked on the keyboard and sat back on the rest of the stool. "The same."

"What do you think has happened?"

"I don't know for sure. Give me about twenty minutes so I can check out something."

"What shall I do?"

"Well having sat so close next to you, I suggest you have a shower and put on some clean clothes. After I've checked this out we're going to make a call on the Duchess."

When Henry walked back into the kitchen, Cristina was hurriedly scribbling notes in a pad and flicking from screen to screen. "Did you find what you were looking for?"

"Actually not quite, but I discovered something very odd. Almost without exception, every company that is spiralling into financial oblivion is owned by individuals or consortiums that are, how should I put this, not the nicest of people."

"Why am I not surprised?"

"I've checked through all the main stock markets in the world and they appear to be reasonably stable. What is even odder is that the transaction rate is nearly ten times higher than normal. While some shares are plummeting, others are reaping gains that balance out the total. The main beneficiaries seem to be companies that are owned by organisations representing the general population or have employee stake holder rights," she said, leaning back on the stool and laughing.

Henry twisted his mouth slightly as he prepared his reply. "Are you saying that in effect, this is a bit like Robin Hood? That someone is robbing the rich to pay the poor?"

"You could put it like that, but I can't see how that could be done and what could be gained by it."

"Maybe someone wants to even things out a bit."

"Or, this is part of a grand plan to make an absolute fortune. I don't have enough understanding to see where this is going yet. It could even be a terrorist plot to destroy the world's economy so they can pick up the pieces after the collapse."

"Shall we go and visit the Duchess? Maybe she knows the answer."

"Wait by the front door. I'll be ready in a second; I just need to make one quick call."

A feeling of nausea returned to Henry, when he saw she dived into their bedroom to make the call behind a closed door.

It took them half an hour, by taxi, to reach the prestigious terrace in Mayfair. Cristina paid the driver, while Henry bounced up the six black and white latticed steps and pressed the bell button set in the centre of the door. By the time Cristina joined him, the door had still not be answered. Henry pressed the button again, this time holding it in for several seconds. From behind the door, they heard the muffled calls of someone shouting, "Hold your bloody horses, I'm coming."

The door was opened by a short and stout man wearing a set of white overalls that were covered with splotches of paint of every colour. Henry placed a foot in the doorway and said, "We're here to see the Duchess."

"There's no bloody Duchess here mate, just me and I ain't a Duke or can't you tell?"

Cristina edged forward to Henry's side. "These are the offices of Madam Gremory and I'm a close relative who has come to see her."

"If you're talking about the last lot here, from what I gather they sold the lease to this place last week. I'm here to clean it out and make it ready for the contractors to fit it out. It's going to be an *exclusive* clinic for all the posh birds around here so they can have their tits *enhanced*. I've got a bloody job to get on with and time is money as they say. Goodbye."

As they walked down the steps, Henry grabbed Cristina's hand, pulling it slightly so she would turn to look at him. "What's going on? Do you know what's happening?"

"I wish I did. He never said anything about the Duchess disappearing."

"Who?"

"You'll find out soon enough, he's planning to meet with you in the near future, but I can't tell you anymore at the moment. Sorry."

"What shall we do now?"

Cristina clutched his hand tighter and swung his arm

slightly. "What we do now is buy as much land as we can with what we have left in our off-shore accounts. We'll need to hold back a reserve. For the moment we must wait for the forthcoming Armageddon or Nirvana, but I don't know which one it'll be."

They decided to walk along the edge of Hyde Park and cut through Grosvenor Street, before heading for Oxford Street, Cristina's favourite shopping haunt. As they crossed Park Street, the monotonous strumming of the passing traffic was interrupted by a series of wailing sirens. "Sounds like something's going on," Henry said distractedly.

"It could be a major fire. I'm sure those are fire engine sirens."

"Sound more like police cars to me," Henry replied.

Cristina stopped walking for a moment and turned to face him. Smiling at him, she said, "Do they have different sounding sirens? Do you really know or are you just trying to pick a fight?"

Henry was about to reply when a white flash to his side distracted him. Before he could speak, the ground under his feet quaked alarmingly.

They turned together to face the burst of light that surprised them, but before they could take in the image of a rising black cloud, a rush of air knocked them to the ground as the deep boom of an explosion ripped into their ears.

* * *

Yasuf slowed the rattling Toyota and killed the engine by turning off the ignition. He then turned the key one notch, so that all the little lights came on and the needles on the instruments moved back to show what it was they showed.

The one bothering him was the one with a picture of a petrol pump. He looked despairingly at the fuel gauge, tapping it with his knuckle in a vain hope the needle would rise from the red zone. Earlier, he'd checked the jerry cans, but they were all empty, including the one that held water. He squeezed the last drops of warm water from the last plastic bottle of water he'd found and opened the creaking door of the battered pickup.

Grabbing the field-glasses from a shelf under the dashboard, he climbed up onto the roof of the cab and scanned the horizon. He'd completed about quarter of the arc when he spotted something in the distance. Excitedly, he fumbled with the knurled controls set in the centre of the binoculars, zooming and focusing until he made out the silhouette of a camp and some vehicles.

From his current distance, it was impossible to tell if he was looking at friends or foes, but if he didn't find water in the next few hours, he was already as good as dead. He jumped down and climbed into the cab, started the engine and prayed to any God that might be listening that he was doing the right thing.

Yasuf slowed down as he neared the camp. He could see about twenty tents and six vehicles. There was a flagpole with a black flag hanging down from it, but because there was little wind, he couldn't make out what the flag represented. In the centre of the camp he could see some shapes that looked like the letter 'Y', but because of the heat shimmer he couldn't see what these strange objects were.

As he coasted to within 100 metres of the camp's edge, two men covered by dark robes began walking out to meet him. He instantly recognised the familiar outline of the silhouetted AK 47 each man carried. For a moment, his foot hovered over the gas pedal as he considered making an escape, but the realisation of how terrible it would be to die of thirst, drove him to switch off the engine and step out of the cab with his arms raised. Rather than wait, he walked towards the men.

When he was about twenty paces from the men, one of them shouted something he couldn't make out, but he did understand that the guns, now aimed at him and being thrust aggressively in jerking movements was a sign for him to stop. The men began shouting at him in a language he didn't understand. "I'm Yasuf. I come in peace," he shouted back, hoping they might understand.

The man on the left shouted to him. "Nigerian?"

"Yes," Yasuf shouted back.

The man on the right shouted back to the camp. "Omuya,tueal 'iilaa huna."

Yasuf watched as another man ran out from the camp and joined the other two pointing Kalashnikov assault rifles at him. The men exchanged conversation in a series of guttural outbursts, before the third man advanced a few steps and shouted to him. "I am Omuya. What are you doing here?"

Yasuf took a step forward, but stopped when he saw the pair of guns raised slightly by the other two men. "The people I lived with were all killed in an attack. I managed to escape but now I'm lost. What did they shout to you?"

"They just called out for me to come to them. Who attacked your people?"

Yasuf looked to check the flag, but it was still hanging limply from the pole. He would have to take a chance he'd picked the right side. "We were attacked by Americans. I'm a member of Boko Haram."

Omuya turned and shouted back at the other two men in a language Yasuf did not know.

The two men holding guns on Yasuf started to walk nearer, but they didn't lower their weapons.

Omuya rubbed his chin with his hand and stepped to one side before speaking. "Tell me the name of your leader?"

"He was Akubar, but now he's dead, they're all dead."

"Tell me something special that Akubar did; something for the cause of Allah."

Yasuf didn't understand what Omuya meant at first, but then

he thought of something that would be known by many. "He made films. I am the cameraman."

"You? You're only a boy."

"No, I'm a man and I've killed many. I want to kill as many Americans as I can, so if you're on their side shoot me now."

Omuya spoke back to the men with the guns and this time they laughed as they lowered their weapons.

"Where did you get your truck from?" Omuya asked.

"I stole it from two Christians. I shot them dead."

"Come into our camp, there may be a place for you here."

"Shall I drive or walk. If I'm walking there's something I need to get from the pickup."

"You can drive and give us a lift at the same time."

Only as he entered the camp, did Yasuf see what the letter 'Ys' were. In the centre of the camp, six men were suspended upside down by their ankles from an overhead rope supported by two thick timber struts.

He turned to Omuya who was sitting beside him in the passenger seat and made a quizzical expression. Omuya grinned before speaking. "They are a group of Christian militia sent here by American Special Forces to spy on us. They should have been executed this morning, but Bendouli broke the chainsaw while he was cutting notches in the poles to hold up the ropes they're hung from. As soon as he fixes it we will finish them off."

"What are you going to do them?" Yasuf asked, as he stopped and shut down the noisy engine of the pickup truck.

"You'll see later. I'm going to take you to our leader, Hassan. He'll want to meet you before assigning you to a suitable post."

Yasuf reached under his seat and pulled out a canvas bag, which he slung over his shoulder as he got out of the vehicle.

Hassan's tent was one of the larger and grander erections among the randomly scattered and varied fabric dwellings of this isolated group. The main entrance was open, with its flap tied back by a multi-coloured silk rope. Omuya gestured at Yasuf to enter first, by extending his arm into the heavily shaded opening. Hassam sat, cross-legged, on a deep pile of brightly coloured cushions, their exotic hues tamed by the low light levels.

Omuya stepped forward and spoke softly in an Arabic dialect, before turning to Yasuf. "I have told him as much as you have told me. I will act as your interpreter."

Over the next few minutes, Yasuf answered Hassan's questions as truthfully as he could. When Omuya asked him, "What do you want to do aid Allah?" Yasuf replied, "I want to kill as many American's as possible. Can you send me to America?"

Hassan laughed when Omuya relayed his answer, but then spoke back energetically.

"He says it is not possible for you to go to America, but at the moment some of our members are entering Europe. It is very expensive to send someone to Europe and if he had enough money he would willingly send you there."

"Ask him if this is enough?" Yasuf replied, as he took the bag off his shoulder and placed it on the floor in front of Hassan.

Hassan carefully opened the bag and began to remove the wads of money and gold items that were Yasuf's treasure. He spoke briefly to Omuya.

Omuya turned to face Yasuf and said, "He says there is enough here to send ten men to Europe. You can be one of them, but first you must prove you are a man and not a boy."

Yasuf looked up into Omuya's face; he then turned to directly face Hassan. "Tell him I will do whatever he wants me to do. I will prove that I am a man."

Hassan rose to his feet and walked to the opening of his tent. He shouted out loudly, but Yasuf had to wait to understand what he said, as Omuya did not offer a translation. Two men ran over, with one of them carrying something long that seemed to wobble as he ran.

Hassan spoke with the men first, then he spoke to Omuya, who looked darkly at Yasuf. "This is what you have to do to prove you're a man. Take the saw and execute the six prisoners. Hassan wants you to saw each man in half, starting between their legs and continuing to cut down through their body until you have cut their heads in half. He wants you to cut each man a bit at a time, so they won't die quickly. He says this is a fit death for these Christians, as that is how they used to execute Muslim prisoners hundreds of years ago."

Yasuf reached out to take the long and rusty saw held out to him. He walked over the hard, barren and dry ground until he reached the 'Ys', flexing the wobbly saw in his right hand as he stopped at the first man. With the start of his first saw strokes, he blanked out the screaming by picturing Susan's exploded abdomen in his hate filled head.

EIGHTEEN

Through the long warm days of a glorious summer, Kunrat established his grip on Castle Boese. Rather than follow his previous tactic of torturing and executing the inhabitants as quickly as possible, he offered all those he thought might be of use to him a chance to save their souls and mortal life by agreeing to make a full confession to him in person.

By day, he listened to the accounts of two or three of the men by pulling faces as they told him their innermost darkest secrets and yearnings. He concluded by asking each man how he could atone for his sins, dropping hints that promises of servitude to God's Master may be considered favourably when he reached his final decision for sentencing.

On approximately every fifth evening, one of the girl servants he'd selected earlier was brought to his room. After a brief discussion, he began his ritualistic interrogation of the woman by discovering how depraved and perverted she was willing to be, through the mechanism of offering her body for his carnal pleasures. He limited the number of nights with anyone one woman to five, as he had so many to work through.

Once he was satisfied the woman was indeed a Devil's whore, he would have her taken down to a basement room that housed his pet bear. He found the sensation of watching Sophie consume the living flesh and blood that had yielded to his demands for pleasure, a refreshing alternative to the thoughtful process of guiding that flesh to stimulate his wicked desires.

As summer relinquished its barmy breezes to autumn's cool winds, a messenger arrived with a letter for Kunrat. In the privacy of his room, he broke the Pope's seal on the rolled parchment and read the short, but unwanted message.

My Dearest Kunrat,

I have heard great tidings of your successes and fruitful gains for our beloved Church. After much consideration, I am sending you west to continue your mission in France. It is rumoured that there are many witches and demons inhabiting these lands and as you know, God has recently punished these wretched people by unleashing the Black Death among their corrupt souls. Please await the arrival of Cardinals Accardi and Baglio. They will replace your current position and assist with setting up a force to accompany you on your new quest. Expect the arrival of these Cardinals in about four days from receipt of this letter.

Yours humbly,

Niccolo Cesarini.

Kunrat threw the scroll down on his desk and rose to his feet. He paced back-and-forth, biting his knuckle as he thought. All his plans of wintering here and warming his body against the yielding flesh of willing whores were over. Instead he would travel by day on horseback, fighting against the encroaching winter storms, and freeze at night in a flimsy tent with no body to press against his. He would have no time to segregate the spoils he destined for his own coffers, and his pet, Sophie, what was to become of her? Through the creeping black anger growing inside him, he made a decision. He would entertain one last whore and feed her to Sophie as a final treat, before killing and removing all evidence of the bear.

He threw open the door and strutted forcibly down to the

rooms holding the women, his women. As he approached the locked door, he gestured to the guards to open it and accompany him in his quest for his final victim. He walked through the rooms, pausing when he thought he saw a potential harlot and eventually stopped to face a girl with dark auburn curls hanging over her shoulders. He turned to one of the guards at his side and said. "Who is this girl? What do you know of her?"

The guard consulted with his peers and after prolonged whispering, spoke in Kunrat's ear. "Her name is Amalie. It is said she was the King's favourite lover and seduced many of his soldiers to gain a better position for herself. Some have said she uses the arts of the Devil to seduce men so she can hold them under her power."

"That is very interesting. It seems this one is truly a powerful witch. I must interrogate her at once. Have her bathed and then bring her up to my interrogation chamber. I will go there now and prepare for what I must do."

"Yes Master," the guard replied, as he signalled for the other guards to remove the woman from her shackles.

The girl sitting to Amalie's left nudged her, and looking at her with sad eyes she said, "Be brave. Maybe the stories aren't true."

Amalie smiled back to her and replied, "Don't worry about me. I have no intention of ending my time as a meal for his beast."

Kunrat made his preparations. He plumped up the cushions on the large bed and removed his cloak. As he hung the cloak on a hook near the door, he heard something thump lightly against the wall. He slipped his hand into the deep pocket and withdrew the pocket watch he'd found in the hand of one of the villains in the forest. *That's odd, I'm sure I put this watch in the chest under my bed,* he thought as he opened the case. *Even if you are the work of the Devil, you are still a beautiful trinket. I will carry you always from now on.* He jumped when he heard a loud rap on the door. *Surely they cannot have bathed her properly in such a short time.* "Enter," he shouted without thinking.

He stepped back a pace when he saw his visitor was not his new whore, but a very tall and neatly bearded stranger he'd never seen before. "Who are you to enter my private chambers?"

"I followed your command to enter. Please, let me introduce myself. I am Duke Gomory. I meant to meet with you earlier, but I had to go away for a while."

"You can't stay, I am expecting a guest. You must leave now," Kunrat said, taking a step towards Gomory.

"Your guest will not be coming. I must speak with you about something of mine that's in your possession."

"I have nothing of yours in my possession. I'm going to call the guards and have you locked up in a cell. I will deal with you later for the impertinence you have shown me."

"There are no guards within earshot. Now, the object I'm referring to is a small pocket watch. It is mine, but I don't want it back. You are its keeper and I must advise you that you should keep this timepiece for as long as you live. Do not pass on this object to any other soul, it will find its next keeper once you are finished with its use," Gomory said, stroking his beard with his hand as he finished speaking.

"How did you find your way into this castle? Every room was searched and you couldn't have been here before."

"I entered the castle the same way I left. I have nearly finished speaking with you, but I would suggest that you leave this castle now. There are visitors coming and they will discover everything about you. I see that if you do not leave at once, my watch will soon pass to another keeper."

"Are you telling me you can see into the future?" Kunrat asked, sensing this stranger might be useful to him.

"To me, all time is one. You may observe the passing of time by watching water flow in a river, but my essence comprises not the flow, but all of the water. Remember my words."

Gomory withdrew from the room, pulling the door shut behind him. Kunrat immediately lunged at the door, threw it open and looked in both directions along the landing, but no one was to be seen.

He was just about to return to his room, when he heard the sounds of hurried footsteps and heavy panting coming from the far end of the long and gloomy corridor. He shouted, "Who is there?"

As the man approached, Kunrat saw in the dim light it was one of his messengers. The man came up to him and bent over for a moment to catch his breath. "Master, we have visitors. Two Cardinals have arrived with a large escort of soldiers. They are emissaries from the Pope and wish to speak with you at once."

"They are here now?"

"Yes, Master."

"Why was I not warned of their arrival earlier?"

"You were busy with the witches and you commanded that you are not to be disturbed when you are with them. The Cardinals are in the old throne room and wish to speak with you at once."

Kunrat rubbed his head with his hands and paced in a tight circle. "Tell them I am coming now, but before you give them that message, find the head guard and tell him to send archers to the basement and kill the beast that lurks there."

"Do you mean the bear you feed the witches to?"

"Yes. How did you know that?"

"Master, everybody knows about that. It's all anyone has talked about these last few weeks."

Kunrat hesitated, wondering if he should tell the messenger to relay a message warning everyone they would be killed if they mentioned his pet again, but decided he could not afford to provoke his potential enemies. "Do as I have commanded;

kill the beast."

"Yes, Master."

Kunrat returned to his room and pulled on his cloak. His hope was that outwardly, everything would appear to be in order. He was only at risk of being exposed if someone told the Cardinals directly what he'd been up to. Even then, he could bluff his way through by telling them this place was crawling with witches. Why, he'd only have to show them the horde of Goblin-like spawn he'd locked in the dungeons for future mass incineration when sufficient firewood was collected to complete the task.

Kunrat entered the throne room, throwing his arms wide as he greeted the two Cardinals. "Your Eminence, Accardi, your Eminence, Baglio, I am delighted you have graced my soul with your presence. I trust you had a safe journey and have been made comfortable?"

Cardinal Baglio heaved his considerably overweight frame from the throne he sat in and waddled forward a few steps. He extended his short, but thick set arms and urged Kunrat to come to him by twitching his fat white finger back-and forth. "Come here my son, let me embrace you."

Kunrat stepped into the space between the Cardinal's outstretched arms, steadying his balance as heavy limbs enclosed him and nearly made him fall to his knees. He turned his right cheek to receive a kiss from the thick wet lips of Cardinal Baglio, before turning his left cheek for similar treatment. "My Eminence, I trust you will find everything is in order," he whispered.

"I'm certain we'll discover all of your achievements, my son. His Eminence, Niccolo, Cardinal, Cesarini, is most concerned with reported activities of witchcraft in France and, having heard word concerning your expertise at disposing of witches, requires you to travel there at once to bring an end to this threat on our great church."

Kunrat swallowed hard in an attempt to hide the nausea rising from the pit of his stomach.

"Already an army is assembling and is at your disposal. You are to leave at first light tomorrow morning. You will be escorted by twelve soldiers that are the most ruthless fighters in my personal army. I know this is very sudden, but it's a matter that must be dealt with urgently."

"It's an honour to be chosen for this venture, but surely there are others more suited to this task then me?"

"Your name is spoken by everyone of importance in Rome, and your conquests have become legendary. Do not think badly of me, but I'm very tired after such a long journey and I must retire for the night. You have a significant journey ahead of you and should also make the most of your last night in a comfortable bed. Have no fear, Cardinal Accardi and I will ensure your work here is brought to a suitable conclusion. Goodnight, my son, and I pray that God will be with you always," he said, making the sign of the cross as he yawned.

Kunrat crawled into his bed and curled up into an embryonic ball. Dark thoughts cascaded through his mind and he was certain he would not sleep tonight. As he played through the words spoken by Cardinal Baglio, he opened his eyes to see a twilight sky.

The horse he rode, along a mountain road, ambled at a sedate pace and seemed at ease with the burden of carrying him. He turned to look behind and caught sight of twelve mounted horsemen several horse lengths back, each rider bearing a shield and spear.

As he turned his gaze back, he caught sight of something dark slinking to his side. It darted from behind boulders and bushes, stopping briefly to gather up something in its mouth. He looked to the other side, drawn by an instinctual sense that another creature stalked him.

Suddenly, as the moon broke from the clouds, he saw a large white wolf carrying a mouthful of twigs and small branches in its mouth. For a moment the wolf stopped and stared at him with fiery red eyes, before it disappeared into the undergrowth.

He awoke, realising someone was shaking him. "Master, it's time for you to leave. Your horse and escorts are ready."

Kunrat crawled out of his bed and, still half asleep, reached for his cloak. "Is it already morning?" he asked drowsily.

"It is half an hour before sunrise and the sky lightens with the approaching break of day. Come, they are waiting for you."

The dark dream continued to play in Kunrat's head as he descended down the flights of stairs leading to the ground floor. Before he realised it, he was mounting a horse and grimacing at the austere faces of his assigned escort. Baglio's soldiers were the ugliest and fiercest men he'd ever seen and the thought of spending the next few weeks in their company appalled him. "Wait, I've not packed my things yet," he cried as his horse surged forward.

"We have everything you will need," one of the soldiers shouted, as he rode to the side of Kunrat's horse and flayed it with his whip.

The horse bolted through the castle's gates, causing Kunrat to clamp his legs tightly to the horse's flanks and grip his reins harder. They rode in silence throughout the day without rest. As darkness crept overhead, Kunrat found the confidence to finally callout. "How much longer are we to ride?"

"We are nearly there, look ahead of you," one of the soldiers shouted back.

Kunrat lifted his head and peered into the distance. At first he saw nothing to indicate there was anything significant ahead, but then he picked out orange pinpricks of light flickering through a small copse to his right. Is that the army we are meeting? Are they this close?"

"It is a small party waiting to greet you. Once we are there you can dismount your horse," someone shouted back from behind him.

Kunrat became aware that several of the soldiers had overtaken him and rode on ahead. To his left and right, riders pulled up alongside him and reached to take the reins of his horse. "We will guide you to the place you'll rest," one of the men said.

As they passed through the clump of trees, Kunrat noticed there was a dark mound set in the middle of a clearing. At first he thought the conical shape was a tent, but as he drew nearer, he realised it was comprised of thousands of intertwined branches. There was a single pole poking out from the top of the mound and something large and dark appeared to be bound to it. Whatever it was, it moved.

More soldiers emerged from the trees at the edge of the clearing, several holding flaming torches. As Kunrat's horse was pulled up by the soldiers to his sides, a cloaked figure stepped into the light cast from the torches held by the assembled men. The soldier to the right of Kunrat tapped his shoulder and said, "Dismount from your horse now, we have reached our destination."

Kunrat pulled his aching leg over the back of the horse and stepped down. He felt two of the soldiers tightly grip his upper arms before leading him to face the cloaked figure. Kunrat felt his legs shaking as he addressed the shrouded figure in front of him. "Who are you?" he asked assertively.

"I am your judge, juror, executioner and replacement."

Kunrat looked around him, at the eyes locked on him by the soldiers and other men standing in the clearing. "I don't understand. What's this all about?"

"I have recently returned from visiting Pope Eugenius the fourth. He has been informed of all your actions over the past months and has given me authority to bring you to trial and justice. Kunrat, you are charged with the despoiling, rape and murder of forty-two innocent virgins. In addition you are charged with breaking your vows of celibacy, ordering the torture and execution of over a hundred innocent souls, using the symbol of Christ's crucifixion as an instrument of death and conspiring to steal from the Holy Catholic Church."

Kunrat fell to his knees and making the sign of the cross said, "All the deeds I have done were in good faith. I was seduced by witches of great power, but kept my resolve and destroyed them. I am God's most faithful servant."

The hooded figure stepped forward and issued his orders. "Bind his wrists and search through his pockets."

One of the soldiers handed something to Kunrat's accuser. "I have found this."

Kunrat watched the robed outline of his unknown executioner as he pressed on the snake's eyes of his trinket. "This indeed is an artefact of the Devil. Gag his mouth as I do not want to suffer hearing his final screams. Kunrat, not only have you destroyed innocent lives, but you saw fit to have many of your victims devoured alive by a wild beast. I find you guilty and sentence you to be burnt alive at the stake alongside your vile creature. Turn and look now, she is set atop the pyre," he said, pointing at the shadowy mound.

Kunrat knew his end was near as he looked up and saw the shifting silhouette of Sophie. Before panic overtook him, the commanding voice of his nemesis froze his thoughts.

"You are to be tied to the same pole as her and die as one. Her muzzle is bound so she will not end your suffering by biting into your head. Take him up to the platform and fasten him with iron chains beside his beast. We will then set the fires to give him, in his mortal life, a taste of the fires that wait to consume him for all eternity."

Before Kunrat could call out, a twisted cloth was pulled tightly across his mouth. Two soldiers brought ladders from the edge of the clearing and set them against the steep slope of the pyre.

He tried to kick as he was dragged up the side of the pyre by a pair of soldiers climbing the ladders, but his efforts were in vain. As the heavy metal chain was wound around his waist, he felt her moving and heard her grunts through her clamped muzzle, but was unable to see her as she was behind him.

He watched as the soldiers climbed down the ladders and removed them. As several men with flaming torches advanced to the base of the pyre, he saw another figure, also hooded, step up alongside the man who ordered his death. He wanted to scream, 'Who are you?' as the torches were thrown onto the base of the dry wood, but the gag held him in stifled silence.

At first he felt a rush of warmth, then accompanying the rising tongues of flame; he felt his skin receive the first taste of the agony it was going to endure. Through the dancing veil of fire across his face, he saw the two robed figures pull back their hoods and his urge to scream reached a pinnacle as he stared into the faces of Duke Gomory and Amalie.

NINETEEN

It sounded as if someone was shouting at him under water. "Henry, are you alright? Henry." He opened his eyes and the face in front of his came into focus. It was Cristina. "I think so, what happened?"

"There's been an explosion, quite a large one by the look of it. Is your head okay?"

Henry eased up onto his elbows and felt something trickling down his face. As he opened his mouth to reply, he caught the distinctive taste and odour of blood. He twisted and raised a hand to his head. "Does it look bad?"

Cristina placed her hands between his shoulder blades to help him to sit up. "It's only a scratch. I think you were hit by a piece of glass. That blast has blown out every window in the street."

Henry climbed to his feet and looked around him. A few feet away, a woman was lying still in a large pool of blood that appeared to be slowing growing larger. There were pieces of glass and broken roof tiles scattered everywhere, several people were pulling themselves upright, but several more remained motionless on the ground. He turned to where he'd seen the flash and saw a thick column of black smoke boiling up towards the sky. "Where is that? What's been blown up?"

Cristina grabbed his arm and guided him nearer to the prostrate woman. "I think it must be near Grosvenor Square. Listen, have you ever heard so many sirens? Henry, I think this woman is still alive, I can see her chest moving, but she looks like she's losing too much blood. We must try to help her."

As Henry stepped in the direction Cristina led him, he tried to recall what the large building they sometimes passed was. "Is that where the American Embassy is located?"

"Yes, I think we've been caught on the edge of terrorist attack. Stay where you are, I'm going to have a look at this woman."

Henry looked on as Cristina knelt next to the woman who was in her early twenties. He inwardly winced as he saw a long shard of glass protruding her neck. "Is she okay?" he mumbled.

"I don't think so. I can't find any sign of a pulse and the blood's stopped pumping from her neck."

"Cristina, the police are coming. I'll call for help."

Henry shouted and waved at the uniformed officers running into the street from every direction. "Here, help us. There's someone who's seriously hurt. We need your help."

Two of the policemen ran towards him and knelt next to Cristina as he pointed to the woman lying on the ground. One of the policemen checked her pulse and opened her mouth, before inserting his finger to check her tongue had not fallen back to obstruct her airway. "I think she's lost too much blood. I'll try and get an ambulance here, but there are so many casualties at the Embassy, I'm not sure how long it'll take."

"Is it the Embassy that's been attacked?" Henry asked.

"Yes, they've near enough blown it to pieces. I shouldn't tell you this, but we had an alert that a lorry full of construction materials for the contractors working on the Embassy was hijacked earlier today. We tried to stop it, but it detonated the second it arrived at the front of the building. If you're not hurt badly, I suggest you go home as this whole area is about to be cordoned off."

They detoured by walking up Park Lane to the western end

of Oxford Street and cutting through the back streets to their flat. Five minutes before they were due to reach home, Henry's phone started to chime. "I expect it's my mum checking to see if I'm alright," he said to Cristina, as he removed his phone from his pocket. "That's odd, it's a private number."

Cristina saw Henry's face turn pale as he answered the phone. He didn't speak, but twitched aggressively when he cut off the call. "Is everything okay?" she asked.

"If you call a death threat from, Saddam, or, Frank, to use one of his aliases okay, then yes. He says I will be dead within twenty four hours unless I recover all his losses."

"I think we need to think about disappearing. Henry, is that your phone pinging?" Cristina asked, as she heard the sound of faint chimes repeating.

Henry's fingers contacted the cool surface of the watch as he reached into his pocket. Through the metal casing, he felt minute vibrations as the watch chimed for the sixth time. He pulled it out and depressed the eyes to open the case. "It's this watch. It's been doing this for a while now. It's weird, but all the little holes on the rings are starting to line up into a pattern. Here take a look."

Cristina looked at the face of the watch and saw that the inner seven rings were in a position that aligned their small circular openings in a symmetrical pattern. Only the two outer rings were misaligned, but as they moved faster than the others, denoting the hours and days, she could see that they would soon line up with the other rings. "I wonder if there's any significance about this," she said, trying to work out what the final pattern might be.

"Well maybe soon we'll find out," Henry said as they neared their flat. "Oh shit. Stop and turn around without making it obvious," Henry hissed when they turned the corner.

"What's the matter?" Cristina hissed back.

There's a man outside the building our flat's in. I've seen him before and it's not good."

"Who is he?"

"I think his name is Pablo, he's a henchman of Garcia, my first client, and I doubt he's here for a casual conversation."

"He won't know who I am. I'm going to the flat to collect my laptop and a couple of other things. You go to our favourite coffee shop and wait there for me. We'll book into one of the small hotels near Euston Station. We'll pay with cash and use fake names. We'll plan from there, but I think it's time for us to move on. Is there anything of yours you need me to pick up from the flat?"

"I don't think so. How did he find out where I live?"

"If he's got your phone number then it's easy to hack into it and use your location finder. Ditch your phone. Take a short bus ride and leave it on the bus. We'll get knew phones later. I'll need to change mine as well, but I have to make a couple of important calls first."

Henry travelled one stop on a bus down Oxford Street and tried not to attract attention as he forced his phone down a gap between the seats after turning it off. Ten minutes after he sat at a table, sipping the chocolate sprinkled froth from the top of his cappuccino, Cristina arrived, carrying two large shopping bags. "Did it go okay?" he asked quietly.

"Yes, but that man, Pablo, he gave me a description of you and asked if I'd seen you. I told him you normally come home around midnight, so I think he'll wait there for a while."

"So what's the plan?"

"When we leave here, we'll go to a cash machine and draw out as much cash as we can. Then we'll go to a phone shop and buy two cheap phones that will be harder to trace. We'll find a hotel and book in as Mr and Mrs Saunders."

"Why Saunders?"

"Because I don't know anyone by that name, do you?"

"No."

"That's perfect then. At the hotel I'll use a discrete browser to see if I can find out what's happening. In the next five or six days, I think I can sort out new passports for us. We'll have to decide where we're going."

"You seem to have everything planned. It's almost as if you knew something was going to happen."

"Henry, I have a couple of very useful contacts and one in particular is going to help us out of this mess. I may have to go away for a couple of days, but I promise you I will return."

"Why all the secrecy?"

"Because I can't let you know what will happen, it would ruin everything."

They found a suitable hotel a few minutes walking distance from Euston Station. The first thing they did on entering the room was to switch on the television to discover more about the explosion.

The emerging story, told of how a lorry full of explosives had detonated right outside the front of the building, but ironically, the hijacked vehicle belonged to contractors that were installing extra defences against such an attack.

The death toll stood at nineteen, with over three hundred wounded, mainly passersby caught by flying glass and debris from the explosion. A recently formed militant group comprising of the remnants of ISIS and Boko Haram were claiming responsibility. Initial investigations suggested the suicide bombers driving the lorry had entered the country using false American passports. They were believed to have originated from somewhere in North Africa.

"I suppose it could have been worse," Henry sighed, touching the raised wound on his hairline.

"I'm just glad you didn't get hit by a larger piece of glass like that poor woman," Cristina replied, as she plugged her laptop into one of the two available sockets in their cramped bedroom.

"Do you want me to go out for basic supplies, like toothbrushes and toothpaste?" Henry said, rising from the bed to his feet.

"No I'll go. You'd only forget half the stuff we need and there are people looking for you," Cristina replied, as she picked up her handbag and opened it to check something.

Later that night, in a pokey hotel room, Cristina exclaimed, "This can't really be happening."

Henry turned to look at her face, which was garishly illuminated by her laptop screen. "What can't be happening?"

"I've been expecting the whole financial scene to collapse into a heap of worthless rubbish, but it's booming."

"Is that all?"

"No, it's not all. There has been a massive shift of assets and whoever or whatever is behind this has carefully manipulated how funds have moved from one place to another. It seems every corrupt nation, organisation and individual has been wiped out financially. This is an incredibly sophisticated operation and I don't know how it could have been done."

"Where has all the money been transferred to?"

"I've only just started looking, but it seems to have gone to organisations and companies that operate in ethical ways. There are a lot of formerly very wealthy individuals who are going to be really pissed at what's happening," Cristina chirruped, with a huge smile breaking out on her garishly lit face.

The following morning they shopped for clothes and decided around midday, to eat lunch in one of the many pubs adorned with seductive blackboards that offered identical menus at the same price. "Do you think they're part of a cartel?" Henry said, as he hovered between picking the lasagne or beef and ale pie.

"It seems to me most of this planet is composed of *cartels,* have you noticed how few independent retailers are left? I can see a time when everything is owned by just one single organisation, well at least I could, but what's currently happening will put a stop to that," Cristina said, as her finger stopped at the scampi dish on the plastic coated menu.

"How will it put a stop to that?"

"Already some of the largest corporations are breaking up their assets into smaller independent groups to hedge their bets on where this will go. I think in a few weeks from now, we'll be living in a very different world."

"Will it be better?"

"I hope so."

Cristina's new phone buzzed into life and started to track across the table as if it had a life of its own. She picked it up and checked the screen. "Excuse me for a minute, Henry. I've been expecting this call and it's really important I answer it now."

As Henry sipped his lager, he wondered who she was talking with. Was it her mysterious lover or was she still in contact with the Duchess? She returned quickly, sat down and smiled at him. "Is everything alright?"

Cristina reached over the table and took his hand before replying. "I think everything is perfect. I have to go away tomorrow for a couple of days. Henry, after this we can be together for as long as you want. I promise you I'll never leave you again unless you want me to."

"Are you seeing *him*?"

"Who do you mean by *him*?"

"You know who I mean, the man who made you pregnant."

"I will be honest with you. Yes I'm seeing him but not in that way. There is one last part to be completed so we can live our lives in peace together. I'm doing this for you as well as me and before you ask, I won't be sleeping with him."

The two days Henry spent cocooned in the tiny double bedroom of the hotel, were two of the most miserable days of his life. All he could think of was Cristina opening her legs for another man. The pain seemed unendurable, and on the second night he couldn't face watching television or reading one of the yellowed books provided by the hotel for guests to relieve their boredom.

He opened the pocket watch and studied the lined up apertures of the seven inner rings. As he watched the outer rings imperceptibly move, he attempted to predict what the final pattern formed on the face would look like. Already, he thought he saw the hint of a star-like shape with other shapes inside it. He jumped when the watch chimed without warning. This time the watch chimed seven times, but on the seventh chime, the third and fifth ring from the centre rotated into new positions. Before Henry could recognise any new pattern, his phone began to bleep.

"Hi, Henry, it's me, Cristina. I'm on my way back to London on an overnight train. Everything is going to plan. I have to meet with someone outside St Paul's Cathedral at ten tomorrow morning and then I'll come back to the hotel to meet you. I should be there by..."

The phone cut out. Henry knew that signals from trains were notoriously bad because of deep cuttings and tunnels. He tried to call back, but was transferred straight to Cristina's voicemail. Her call gave him some comfort, enough for him to roll over and fall asleep for the first time in two days.

Henry woke up early the next morning, and after showering, brushing his teeth and putting on his new clothes, he selected a dark hoodie and ventured out. It was only 7 o'clock in the morning, but the streets were full of people rushing to wherever they needed to arrive in a hurry.

He ambled slowly, making his way east and then southwards with no idea where he was going. Just after nine, he realised he was close to the vicinity of St Paul's Cathedral, but had no conscious thought of how he'd ended up where Cristina was having her mysterious meeting.

As he approached the west side of the Cathedral, he pulled up his hood and looked out for Cristina. He saw a small group of protestors on the steps holding up boards condemning Islamic Fascists. He could hear the chants of "Death to Allah and all who follow him," echoing around the tall buildings.

A sense of depression fell over him as he contemplated why the world had to suffer the prejudice of ignorant bigots like these protestors, but then he spotted Cristina sitting alone on a bench. He wanted to call out, but held back and watched. She was rummaging through her bag and checking to see that no one was watching her. She didn't see him as he turned and walked a short distance, looking away from her as he strolled.

As he resumed looking in her direction, he saw her dropping something small under the bench. She then removed a loosely wrapped parcel from her bag and placed it on the bench before standing up and walking nearer to the protestors. He waited for a moment and then ran down to greet her.

"Cristina, sorry I didn't mean to intrude. I just went for a walk and found myself here. It's so good to see you."

"For God's sake, Henry, you'll ruin everything. Get away from here as fast as you can. I've never been so serious about anything in my life. Run as fast as you can in that direction and don't stop for anyone," she squealed, pointing west.

Something in her voice panicked him. He turned and ran, kept running until, for the second time in three days, he was blown off his feet. If he had remained for a minute longer, he would have seen a young man named Yasuf walk up to the protestors.

No one took notice of the boy with a large rucksack on his back as he strolled by, looking up at the magnificent edifice of the Cathedral. Yasuf knew his instructions, he was to meet with a fellow conspirator near the Cathedral and pass on the rucksack of explosives for a future mission.

As he passed by the chanting protestors, he was ignorant of their cause as he neither spoke nor read English. He never heard the single ring tone of the hidden phone, buried and wired to a detonator in the pack he carried, and didn't feel the force of the blast that ripped his young body into pieces small enough to be mistaken as scattered pigeon food.

Henry climbed onto his hands and knees first, then took a deep breath and internally checked for any sign of pain or injury. Everything felt normal, so he slowly rose to his feet.

He turned back to see a pall of smoke rising into the air. Overtaken with fear, he ran back to the place he'd last seen Cristina. Choking on the smell of burnt flesh and acrid chemicals, he looked on in disbelief at the carnage of the scene. With rising nausea, he saw that the body parts scattered around him were embedded with shards of metal and large bent nails. He could see by looking around him that anyone exposed to the force of the blast had been cut into unrecognisable chunks of meat and splintered bone. He vomited and fell to the ground.

His first thought, when he came to in the accident and emergency unit of Bart's Hospital concerned Cristina. He was lying on a trolley in a corridor, and all around him, uniformed staff walked urgently as calls for named doctors, defibrillators, and plasma, ping-ponged from every direction.

A sense of dread that Cristina must have died in the explosion passed through him. Another dark thought crossed his mind immediately after. Surely, she'd not planted the bomb? What was in that loosely wrapped parcel she left on the bench? He wanted to call for someone to tell him what he should do next, but he could see the urgency of the situation as a team of doctors and nurses guided a trolley holding a blood-soaked victim past him. He attempted to dismount the trolley, when someone held him by the shoulders.

"Please don't try to move, someone will see to you shortly. It's the triage system, you've been assessed and have no life threatening wounds," a young nurse said, attempting to smile at him through the surrounding horror.

"I'm not hurt. I ran back to find my girlfriend and I think I passed out when I saw what had happened."

"I'm so sorry. What's her name? I'll see if I can find out anything about her."

"It's Cristina, Cristina Smith."

He waited for an hour, but no one came back, so he climbed off the trolley and made his way to the reception desk. He left forty minutes later with a card that gave him an emergency number to call, but was told not to call until later in the afternoon as it would take a few hours to coordinate the details of the known dead and injured.

From the claustrophobic confines of his hotel room, Henry nervously dialled the number on the card. He calmly gave all the details asked for by the friendly female voice on the other end of the line. When asked if he would be available between nine and ten the following morning, he said, "Yes."

Henry tried to sleep, but haunting images of Cristina's face, her smile, her laughter and her unique devilment plagued him throughout the night. He tried watching the news on the television, but the figures showing a death toll rising to eighty-four scrolling across the bottom of the screen added to his sickness of what had occurred. In desperation, he rang Cristina's phone several times, leaving two messages on her voice mailbox. As he lay back on the bed, resting his head into the lumpy pillow, the bedside phone chirped alarmingly, causing him to pull a muscle in his back as he quickly sat up.

"Good morning Mr Saunders. I have two police officers down here asking for a Mr King. I don't suppose you know anything about this, but they're asking for your room number."

He'd forgotten they used the name Saunders when they registered at the hotel and had given his real name to the woman on the phone yesterday evening. "Please can you send them up, it's me they want to see. Sorry about the confusion."

He was already gripping the door handle when they knocked, but paused a moment before opening the door to them. The uniformed policeman on the left removed his flat cap, while the one on the right, dressed in an immaculate black suit held out his hand and spoke gently. "Mr King?"

"Yes."

"I'm Inspector Deaken from the Metropolitan Police. My colleague is Sergeant Carruthers. He's here to take notes and call the incident centre we've set up, if it proves necessary. We're here to help you discover what has become of your missing girlfriend. May I come in?"

"Yes, please do. Sorry, the room's a bit small."

"Are you on holiday?"

"Err no; we're just staying here for a few days while our flat is being sorted out."

"I understand you saw your girlfriend in the vicinity of the explosion shortly before it happened."

"Yes, she was meeting someone and I just happened to see her."

"We'll come to the other details later. How are you feeling?"

"Not good, I'm worried sick about her," Henry said, feeling a tear rolling down his cheek as he spoke.

"I understand. We can come back later if you want."

"No, I want to know what's happened. Are there any – wounded people that match her description?"

"Not on my latest check. I have to tell you something. The type of explosive device used in this attack was deadly at a range of up to fifteen metres, nearly all the fatalities were within that distance from the explosion. There were only ten victims who suffered serious injuries and none of those match your description of Cristina."

Henry didn't want to ask the next question, but knew he had to. "What about those who were killed? Do any of them match her description?"

"I'm going to be brutally blunt with you Mr King. The explosive used in this attack was Semtex laced with large nails, pieces of sheet steel and ball-bearings. The people directly hit by the full force were cut to pieces and partially vaporised by the intense heat of the blast.

We're estimating the death toll is between ninety to one hundred people, but nearly all the dead are unrecognisable. In fact, all we have are fragments of body parts. At this moment a DNA sample is being taken from every recovered part. If you can provide us with a DNA sample of your girlfriend, it would help us to confirm if she was caught in this terrible incident. If you have a hairbrush or toothbrush of hers, we can most probably obtain what we need from that."

Henry walked into the tiny ensuite bathroom and looked in the usual place for Cristina's toiletries, but there were none. He realised she must have taken everything with her went she went away three days earlier. He came out and rubbed his chin with his hand before speaking to the Inspector. "There's nothing there, she went on a brief trip before this happened and took everything with her." *Why didn't she have her overnight bag with her when I saw her outside St Paul's?* he thought.

"That's okay. My next question might seem odd, but do you have any of her worn clothes you can give us? It's just they usually hold a good supply of cast off cells or hair we could use."

Henry looked around the room and saw Cristina's laptop was still sitting on the small desk. Something triggered in Henry's mind. "Wait a minute. We recently sent DNA samples to one of those companies that check for genetic disorders. I can find out where she sent them, it'll be on her laptop."

"If you can that would be very helpful. If they've already produced a DNA profile we can match it against our result as they come in."

Henry lifted the lid, and as soon as Cristina's laptop loaded, he typed in her password, turning slightly so Sergeant Carruthers couldn't see him type in 'Cameltoe69'. "Here it is," he said excitedly.

The Sergeant dabbed at the screen of his tablet and after a couple of minutes, broke into a broad grin. "Amazing how this technology makes our job easier. They're sending her DNA profile over now."

"Do you have Cristina's phone details, Mr King? We've recovered a few phones from the scene and one of them might be hers. Could I also confirm your phone number? I will contact you directly if I have any news."

Henry gave them all the details, and as they left, he fell onto the bed and wept in utter despair.

Just after two that afternoon, Inspector Deaken called Henry. "Mr King, I'm sorry to say we have a positive match for Cristina's DNA from one of the body parts. Could you meet me at the station in an hour so I can tell you what we've found?"

So this was it, she was dead. He dropped his phone onto the bed and walked to the window, which looked out onto the back of another building.

Gazing out of the window, he followed the line of a grey extraction flue that led up to an equally grey sky. He picked up his phone and thought about calling his mother, but she wouldn't understand how he felt. He couldn't face hearing her change the conversation to the mundane occurrences happening in her street. Checking the time on his phone, he reckoned he would make it to the police station on time if he set off now and walked without dawdling. As he put his phone in his pocket, he heard the old pocket watch start a series of eight pinging chimes.

He listened abstractly as Inspector Deaken relayed to him information about Cristina's phone, how it had been found almost undamaged at the base of a building. He heard, but did not listen, as he was told they had matched two body parts to Cristina's DNA profile, but he suddenly jerked into a hideous reality when the Inspector said his next words. "I don't know if we'll find anymore of her. At present we have part of her right foot, but I'm afraid her little toe is missing. We also found a section of her lower jaw, complete with five teeth."

Henry thought he was about to pass out as he spoke. "That means she's dead. You're telling me she is dead."

The Inspector paused and waited until he saw Henry had absorbed what he'd said. "I envisage you will want to organise funeral arrangements and would anticipate we can release these remains in no more than three weeks from now. You said earlier you don't know anything about her family members. If you do find out more, do not hesitate to contact me and I will arrange for them to be informed of the tragic circumstances of her untimely death."

An incessant drizzle permeated through the cool dank air as Henry stepped out of the undertaker's limousine that gracefully pulled up a short distance from the church door. Despite trawling through Cristina's laptop, he'd been unsuccessful in finding any link to her living relatives. In the end, he decided to organise a short church service before her burial, but after much pondering, he did not invite any of his family to her final service. He brushed the accumulated frosty looking coating of water droplets from the lapels of his new black suit while walking down the echoing central aisle of the empty church. At the same time, he absently gazed at the cavernous coffin adorned with a single red rose, but containing within its confines no more than part of her jaw bone and right foot.

He crushed his feelings of hypocrisy as the priest said a short prayer to bless the life of Cristina Smith. He did not believe in the afterlife promised by the unknown frocked man, who had reluctantly agreed to hold this short service in his church. But a sense of other- worldliness overtook him as he sat alone on the austere wooden pew, used for prayer by unknown persons from past generations.

The signal the service was over came when the priest made the sign of the cross, before walking away and disappearing through a set of maroon coloured curtains. Henry turned, expecting to see the head undertaker and six coffin bearers, but was surprised to see that two other people were seated in one of the back pews. That corner of the church was poorly lit, so all Henry could see was the outline of a man wearing a top hat sitting next to a woman covered by a hooded, dark shawl. The two mysterious guests rose quickly and headed out of main doors before he could see who they were.

The drizzle seemed to be heavier when Henry walked out from church, but he felt relieved to breath in fresh air, rather than inhaling the remnants of stale incense that hung like invisible dust coated cobwebs in the gloom of the chapel.

He waited for an usher to open his limousine door and slipped coldly onto the polished, black leather seat. It was a twenty minute drive to the nearest cemetery, the only one he could find that would accept Cristina's body parts for a fifty-year leased resting place. He wanted something permanent for her, but at least he could visit where she rested until his seventy-second year of life, if he lived that long.

Already the world was changing, governments had toppled, half the world's politicians had resigned in disgrace and many terrorist groups were folding up as they were starved of funds. There was optimism in the air, a sense that something was going to change, but all this fell from him like the conglomerated raindrops rolling down his new black silk suit.

His car pulled up behind the hearse at the cemetery. He sat and waited until the coffin was unloaded and hoisted up by six pallbearers, then he stepped from the car and followed discretely a few paces behind.

The sense of loneliness and isolation seemed unbearable to him. Withdrawing from reality, he abstractly watched on as the coffin slipped silently into the freshly dug grave, lined on three sides with ridges of orangey coloured soil that were hungrily soaking up the minuscule dancing droplets of moisture falling onto their textured surface. As his view of the coffin diminished with its descent into the dark hole, he noticed two people standing a little way off near a gravestone, the same couple he saw in the church.

As someone dressed in a white and black gown spoke their final words to Cristina's remains, the task of replacing the waterlogged earth began. Henry walked over to the obscure couple.

Through the thinning haze of minute water droplets, he recognised who the man was. His immaculate beard was immune to the effects of the penetrating spray, his clothes appeared dry and when he smiled at Henry, no creases of joy formed in his face.

"What are you doing here?" Henry asked anxiously.

"I have come to aid you at this time of conjunction. A past cycle is about to restart."

"I can't deal with your nonsense now. I've just buried Cristina."

"I know what you have done, but I also know what you have not done. There are numerous cycles and you are party to many. There comes a time when a cycle needs to be broken, you and Cristina recently played a part in breaking one."

"Do you mean the changes in the economic situation?"

"It is more than just that, it is a realignment of power and dominance."

"Did you know Cristina?"

"I knew her well. I have recently met with her on a few occasions to put into place the last pieces of something that is preordained."

Henry felt his anger suddenly rise. "Are you the man she slept with? Are you the father of the baby she conceived – then aborted?"

"That child was not for this world."

"Why did you sleep with her? Who is this with you?" Henry shouted, pointing at the shrouded woman standing next to Gomory.

"I will answer your first question for now. I did not sleep with her, but I did open her to the wonders of making love in ways she never knew existed. I never force myself on any woman, but I accept those who offer their essence to me. Henry, it is time."

"Time for what?"

"Listen."

The forcefulness with which Gomory spoke made him pause momentarily. From his inside jacket pocket, he heard the first chime. He reached to pull out the watch and felt a faint vibration as the second chime was emitted.

"Open the casing," Gomory said firmly.

He pressed on the snake's eyes as the third chime rang out. The case flipped up and Henry became transfixed as he saw all nine rings were now turning in different directions at different rates. The fourth, fifth, sixth, seventh and eighth chimes rang out, sounding like a distant church bell. He felt a hard click as the watch issued the ninth chime. He saw the rings come to rest, recognising at once the small holes had aligned to make up a perfect five-pointed star with a pentagram set in its middle.

"Place the watch to your ear and tell me what you hear," Gomory said in a soft voice.

Henry listened, but heard nothing. "It's stopped ticking."

"That is because it has completed the task it was made for. Soon, I will have to make a new watch as this one has completed its cycle and will never keep the passing of time again."

Henry lowered the watch, his head filling with questions he wanted answering from the man standing in front of him, but before he could paraphrase his first query, the deathly silence that had grown around him was broken by a familiar tune.

Coming from Gomory, the opening bars of Tubular Bells, his old phone ringtone, seeped across the space between them and made his spine shudder. Gomory reached inside his cloak pocket and pulled out a phone. He glanced at the screen and smiled. "She's on time. It's for you," he said to Henry, handing him the phone.

Henry lifted the phone to his ear and nervously said, "Hello."

"Henry, it's me. Are you okay?"

He whipped the phone from his ear and stared darkly at Gomory. "What are you trying to do to me? She sounds just like Cristina."

"Talk to her, she's missed you these last few weeks."

Shaking, Henry slowly lifted the phone to his ear again. "Cristina, is that you?"

"Yes, Henry. I'm alive and well despite what you think. Listen, we're going to live in Italy. I want you to meet me at Heathrow airport at six this evening. I'll explain everything later, but in the meantime ask him, he'll answer your questions, but you may not understand all of his answers."

"Do you mean Gomory? Are you really alive? What do you mean Italy? I don't have a passport; it's still in our old flat and..."

"Henry, stop. I'm definitely alive and don't worry about your passport. We are going to have new identities and I've already sorted out your passport and air tickets. I hope you like your new name. I'll explain everything when I see you, promise. Call me back from the phone you're speaking to me on now. You'll find there're only two contact numbers on it so far, me and your mother. I'd like to meet her soon, despite what you say about her. I've got to go as I have a couple of last-minute errands to sort out. Bye."

Henry stood with the phone to his ear and looked at Gomory. "Is she really alive? I don't see how that..."

"Henry, I'll explain some of what happened."

"But those were her body parts in the coffin. They were DNA matched."

"True, but they were not Cristina's *body parts*; they were the remains of a girl killed in a tragic road accident. I passed on those parts to Cristina the day before the explosion so she could leave them at the scene."

"What about her DNA sample, how could that have matched?"

"The sample Cristina sent to the medical company came from the same girl. I provided Cristina with a sample when I met her earlier. The girl died many weeks ago but the two body parts have been kept preserved."

Henry scratched his head and shuffled from one foot to another. "You're telling me all this was prepared weeks before the explosion. How could you know that was going to happen unless you had a part in it? I saw what that explosion did to people; they were cut to pieces in that blast. If you knew it was going to happen you should have warned them."

"I played no part in that attack, but it was preordained. Since humankind evolved, religion has been used by those obsessed with power as a vehicle to increase their dominion over their fellow man. In the past, so called men of religion created legions of demons and other myths to scare the populace into submitting to their laws, to ensure they surrendered their property, will and lives to these *men of God*."

Henry looked into the unlined face of Gomory. "Are you one of these demons from the past?"

"I told you once before that I exist in all time. The past, present and future are as one to me. I will try to explain it to you. Imagine a waterfall. The water cascades down breaking into separate drops. Each drop forms as a separate entity to journey down the fall, but at the end of its journey it blends back into the flowing water. You are like a water drop, but I am the water. As time flows, so water flows, but the water is always there, always has been and always will be."

"I really don't know if I understand you. Who is this woman standing by you hiding under her cloak?"

Gomory tuned to the woman, "Show him who you are."

As soon as she pulled down her heavy hood, Henry recognised her. "Duchess, I wondered if it was you."

"The Duchess no longer exists. I am Amalie, the other half of Duke Gomory."

Henry felt like he wanted to run, but he needed to ask one last question of Gomory. "Will you tell me who you really are?"

"That is straightforward. I am a creation of humanity's belief, but belief is an illusion."

THE END

A brief note from the author.

I hope you enjoyed reading The Duke of Hell's Pocket Watch. Originally, I was intending to write a novella that compared events across two different periods of time.

Because of my scientific background, I struggle with conceptualizing the idea of time travel as a convincing entity, but can see how many of today's current issues are a reflection of past events. I wanted to focus on present day religious extremism in comparison to the dark period of the Inquisition.

On discovering through my research that the pocket watch was developed around the time of the German Inquisition, an idea formed. The only way forward was to do further research, but the deeper I delved, the more horrific the material I unearthed became. As my notes became longer and I accidently came across further material, and an idea formed for this novel. It is common for nearly all fanatics to embellish their beliefs by creating mythical characters to scare those who waver into becoming devout believers. The Demons of Hell are just one example, and when I saw the powers attributed to Duke Gomory, something connected in my thoughts.

There are sections in this novel that some readers may find distasteful, but it is a harsh reality that what I've depicted fictionally, is a watered down version of events that really transpired. I say this after carrying out extensive research through historical archives and some exploration of the dark web. (Not a good place to go.)

Throughout history, corrupt and evil individuals have manipulated the masses, in the name of *God,* for their own gain. I intend no attack on any faith or belief, only contempt for the members of the human race who brought shame onto *humanity.* As to whether *belief is an illusion,* I'll leave that for you to decide.

If this novel entertained, interested or provoked you, please consider writing a brief review. Every writer wants to hear what their readers thought of their work.

OTHER WORKS BY THIS AUTHOR:

FLAWED: FIRST GENESIS
FLAWED: SECOND GENESIS
FLAWED: REVELATIONS
THE RISE OF THE PAWNS
DOMINANT SPECIES: A DUO OF ALIEN INVASION
BEYOND THE OPENED DOORS
https://www.amazon.com/D-H-ROSENBERG/e/B087PCXCSS/ref=ntt_dp_epwbk_0

Printed in Great Britain
by Amazon